As she attempted to secure a grip on a wet rock, four or five of those onshore – two of them women – made for her. One man lunged at her with a weapon that might have been a pike, or perhaps a pitchfork.

She felt a sudden pain as it struck one of her ribs and slid away again. It caused her to lose her grip on the rock and she fell backwards.

Caught by another wave, she was carried back towards the sea by the swirling water. She heard a sound that might have been water rushing through a narrow gap between the rocks, or it could have been the cries of the mob.

Then, as she struggled in vain against the pull of the sea, her head came into hard contact with a rock . . . and she knew no more.

Winds of Fortune

E. V. Thompson

WARNER BOOKS

A *Warner* Book

First published in Great Britain in 2000
by Little, Brown and Company
This edition published by Warner Books in 2001

A CIP catalogue record for this book
is available from the British Library.

ISBN 0 7515 2528 6

Typeset by Palimpsest Book Production Limited,
Polmont, Stirlingshire
Printed and bound in Great Britain by
Clays Ltd, St Ives PLC

Warner Books
A Division of
Little, Brown and Company (UK)
Brettenham House
Lancaster Place
London WC2E 7EN

www.littlebrown.co.uk

To John St Aubyn, DSC, DL, 4th Baron St Levan, for allowing artistic licence in my depiction of his ancestors. Susan, Lady St Levan, for her warm hospitality on my visits to St Michael's Mount.
The Hon Piers St Aubyn, MC, for his encouragement and enthusiasm.

Prologue

Summer 1812

John Humphrey St Aubyn was standing on the stone-flagged terrace of the fortified house which occupied the summit of St Michael's Mount, talking to his father, Sir John, when the sound was first heard.

It came from the direction of the English Channel, somewhere beyond the extent of the bay which took its name from the Mount. It sounded like a peal of distant thunder but, although a slight haze hid the horizon, there was not a cloud to be seen in the late evening sky.

'What do you think that was?' Known as Humphrey, to avoid any confusion with his father, the speaker was an intense young man of twenty-two, and he put the question anxiously to Sir John.

'I know *what* it was. It was a broadside, fired from a man-o'-war, but I'm damned if I know who is responsible. There have been no answering shots, so there can't be a battle taking place.'

Not very tall, but elegant and still handsome, Sir John looked much younger than his fifty-four years, despite his well-groomed grey hair.

While the two men were still pondering the source of the sound, it was repeated.

Humphrey gave his father a quizzical glance and the older man shook his head. 'That was from the same ship. At a guess, I'd say it's most likely a French privateer, harassing the fishing fleet – but he's a bold man to risk coming so close to our coast, although he's no doubt depending on using the cover of darkness to escape from any pursuit.'

Both men looked out across the bay, frustrated by the haze that prevented them from seeing the farthest point of the Lizard, the thick thumb of Cornwall, which protruded out into the Channel.

On a clear day the occupants of the castle on St Michael's Mount had an unequalled view of the Lizard coast. The Mount itself was unique. A high, rocky island for much of the time, it became linked to the mainland by a glistening stone causeway at low tide.

The castle, perched on the summit of this part-time island, had been in turn a church, priory, fortress and private house during its centuries-old history. Today, it was an architectural blend of all four and, when not simply called 'the Mount', was referred to as 'the castle'.

When the sound of a cannonade was heard yet again, Sir John strode to the battlement, looking out over one of the gun emplacements sited there as defence against the threat of a French invasion.

Since Admiral Lord Nelson's great victory over the French and Spanish navies, more than six years before, such a risk had become virtually non-existent. However, history had taught the inhabitants of this part of England not to underestimate the determination of the French to carry the war to their traditional enemy.

'That was closer, Humphrey. The ship would appear to be heading this way. Run and fetch my telescope. You'll find it on the windowsill in my study.'

About to carry out his father's instructions, Humphrey hesitated. 'What of Juliana? Will she mind . . . ?'

'Mind? You're my son, dammit! Why should she *mind*, eh?'

Humphrey inclined his head and hurried away without replying. Hopefully he would not meet up with Juliana, the mistress who had taken the place of his own mother in his father's affections.

He could think of many reasons why she would object to his presence on the Mount. One in particular was that she was pregnant, yet again. Another was that he was Sir John's son by his *first* mistress, Martha Nicholls. Juliana had never fully accepted that one of Humphrey's brothers, and not her own eldest son, would one day inherit the Mount and much of the St Aubyns' extensive land-holdings.

In truth, the situation was difficult for everyone. Sir John was a genial and generous man, attracted to women. The attraction was invariably reciprocated, but he seemed to have an aversion to matrimony.

Humphrey's mother had been Sir John's mistress

for many years, bearing him three sons and two daughters. Then his fancy had been taken by Juliana Vinicombe, daughter of a local farmer.

Not that Sir John had abandoned Humphrey's mother entirely. Given a generous allowance of three hundred pounds a year, she had been settled in a village, inland from the Mount, when Juliana moved in with the baronet.

That had been some years ago. Since then, Juliana had presented Sir John with a further five sons and three daughters – and was now expecting her ninth child.

The amorous Sir John was also believed to have a daughter, born to him by an Italian woman he had met in France. It was rumoured, there were also a number of unacknowledged children born to tenants on the island, and some on the mainland, too . . .

Clattering down the stone staircase that led from the terrace to the living quarters, Humphrey put all such thoughts to one side. His father had been good to him. Indeed, he had been generous to *all* the children of his long-term mistresses.

Humphrey and his brothers had attended university. Humphrey himself was a student at Jesus College, in Oxford, and both their sisters had made good marriages.

The children had also been encouraged to adopt their natural father's name and he had most generously settled ten thousand pounds on each of them – money he could ill-afford.

Humphrey was in a long corridor inside the castle

when, turning a corner, he came face-to-face with Juliana.

Normally a vivacious, attractive woman, she was not at her best during pregnancy. She tended to put on weight and her skin became somewhat blotchy. Her state also tended to make her short-tempered.

'What are you doing here, in this part of the castle? You have your own quarters.'

'I was under the impression the *whole* castle belongs to my father.' Humphrey showed considerable restraint. He resented this woman who had taken the place of his mother in Sir John's affections, but knew it was wise not to offend her. She wielded considerable influence over his father.

Although she was careful to conceal her feelings from the baronet, Juliana was jealous of the money and affection lavished upon the children who Sir John had fathered by Humphrey's mother.

'I'm in this part of the house because my father sent me to fetch a telescope from his study. It's likely a French warship is offshore, firing at something or another.'

Juliana's resentment was immediately forgotten. 'A French warship? Is it coming this way? Catherine and Richard have been spending the day riding at my father's farm. They will be coming back from the mainland at any time now. What if the French ship sees them and fires upon them?'

Catherine and Richard were Juliana's two youngest children. Despite the bitterness Humphrey felt towards Juliana, he was genuinely fond of both of them.

'The course of the French boat – if indeed it *is* a French vessel – is not certain. But after I've taken the telescope to my father, I'll run and tell one of the boatmen to go to the mainland. He can make certain Catherine and Richard remain there until it's clear what is happening. The causeway will be passable before night falls. They can be brought back to the Mount then.'

'Thank you . . . Thank you, Humphrey.' Juliana was a highly emotional woman and tears suddenly filled her eyes. For a moment it seemed she would say more to him. Instead, she turned and hurried away, heading in the direction of her own room.

As Humphrey emerged on the terrace carrying the leather-bound, brass telescope, he heard the sound of yet another broadside. It was still some distance away, yet he realised it was closer than before.

Sir John greeted him impatiently. 'The damned French ship could have been upon us and away again by now!' Unabashed by such a gross exaggeration, he demanded, 'What kept you so long?'

When Humphrey repeated his conversation with Juliana, Sir John's attitude underwent an immediate change and he became thoroughly alarmed.

'Go and tell Abel to take a boat to Marazion right away. He's to find somewhere safe for the children until any danger has passed. Tell him I shall hold him personally responsible for their well-being . . . And Humphrey!' As Humphrey turned to hurry away, Sir John brought him to a halt, '. . . I'm very pleased indeed to see you showing such concern for the two children.'

Clearing his throat noisily, he added, 'I know it can't be easy for you, but Juliana's children really do think the world of you, you know. Young Richard in particular . . .' He mentioned his youngest son, one of his favourites. 'He's a lot like you. A thoroughly good lad.'

As though embarrassed by such a declaration of affection, Sir John turned away, at the same time putting the telescope to his eye. 'Now, let's see if I can get a sight of the Frenchman – if that's what it is.'

With his back to Humphrey, he added, 'Once you've given Abel his instructions, go to the inn. You'll no doubt find most of the Mount's gunners there. Order them to muster here. Tell them I am waiting and will give them the key to the powder room when they arrive. I only want *sober* men, but God help any man who is too drunk to carry out his duty to his King – and to me.'

Humphrey located Abel Carter in the St Aubyn Arms with a number of other St Aubyn men. He was tall, taller than Humphrey, and there was something about his eyes that always uncomfortably reminded Humphrey of his father.

Ten years older than Humphrey, Abel had been destined for a promising career in the Royal Marines Artillery. Unfortunately, he had received a serious leg wound fighting against Napoleon's army, some years before, and had been discharged.

When he recovered he spent some time at sea

before returning to the Mount as the St Aubyns' senior boatman.

Abel was the son of a Mount woman who, as a young girl, had been employed at the great house as a housemaid. She had fallen pregnant when just sixteen.

It was strongly rumoured that she had been the first of Sir John's fruitful mistresses. However, no one had dared voice such thoughts aloud at the time and she was married off to Isaac Carter, a rather simple woodsman who worked on one of the St Aubyn estates.

She never lived to reveal the secret of her son's parentage, dying while giving birth to a still-born child when Abel was three years old.

Abel had been brought up by his grandparents on the Mount until he joined the Regiment of Marines at the age of sixteen. Now he lived in the village situated at the foot of the Mount, with his widowed grandmother.

It was probable that she knew the identity of his true father, but both grandparents came from generations of loyal St Aubyn retainers. They told him nothing.

Nevertheless, there were others whose love of gossip was stronger than the loyalty they owed to the family they served. Abel was left in no doubt that he had as much of a claim to the St Aubyn bounty as Humphrey and the children of Sir John's two acknowledged mistresses.

The inn frequented by the St Aubyn employees was the end building of a terrace of cottages facing the harbour, at the foot of the Mount. It was crowded and noisy, but the men inside fell silent when Humphrey ducked through the low doorway.

Abel had been drinking, but he seemed comparatively sober. The other St Aubyn employees appeared to be in a similar 'in-between' state.

They broke their silence and set up a rousing cheer when Humphrey told them they were to man the guns on the Mount, with the possibility of action against a French warship before darkness fell.

Abel would have led them from the inn, had Humphrey not put out a hand to detain him. 'Wait. Sir John has a special task for you.'

As the others rushed past him from the inn, Abel protested. 'But . . . I'm a trained gunner. The only one of them with any real experience!'

'Nevertheless, Sir John has said you are to take a boat to the mainland. Catherine and Richard are due back from the Vinicombe Farm at any time now. They'll be looking for a boat to bring them off to the Mount.'

As Humphrey was speaking, he and Abel had followed the other men from the inn. Once outside the sound of cannon-fire reached them. It was more of a ragged volley than a broadside on this occasion, but it was certainly closer than when Humphrey had heard it before.

'You hear that? It's the French ship. I'd lay a bet it's cruising close inshore, shooting at anything that presents itself. If it comes this far the Mount will be an obvious target, together with any boat in the vicinity. You're to make quite certain that isn't one carrying the children. Keep them onshore and out of range of the French guns. If all is clear, bring them over the causeway after dark, when the tide has fallen. Remember, Abel, you're to take no chances with them.'

Abel gave Humphrey what his grandmother would have referred to as 'one of his looks'.

Humphrey shrugged. 'Those are Sir John's orders, not mine.'

'You know as well as I do that I'd be far more usefully employed up at the house, aiming the cannon.'

Humphrey's lips tightened. 'Sir John named _you_ as the one to fetch the boys. Should you not be on your way?'

Abel remained looking at Humphrey for some moments. Then, shrugging his shoulders, he turned away without another word and strode off, heading in the direction of the harbour.

On his way up the steep hill leading to the fortified house, Humphrey looked back and saw Abel making for the harbour entrance, rowing in a small boat. When he reached the mainland there would be men to pull the boat up on to the beach and secure it until it was needed again.

As Humphrey watched, the boat cleared the harbour and began to plunge and rise with the motion of the open waters of the bay. It would pose no problem for Abel. He was a very capable man and thoroughly reliable. But Humphrey always wondered whether Abel had resentment bottled up inside him that would one day come out into the open.

All the same, he could not help feeling sorry for

the man. Aware of Abel's story, Humphrey was sufficiently observant to see the St Aubyn likeness for himself. He wondered how *he* might have felt had his father chosen to acknowledge only Juliana's children and not Humphrey and his brothers and sisters . . . ?

Another ragged cannonade broke into his thoughts. He hurried through the house and made his way to the open gun platform.

'There she is, Humphrey. It's a French ship right enough, not a privateer, but a man-o'-war – and heading this way.' Pointing out across the battlements, an excited Sir John handed the telescope to his son, but it was hardly necessary to use it.

The French ship had emerged from the haze and was now no more than two or three miles distant. An outsize tricolour, almost as large as a top-sail, billowed from a masthead.

All around, on the terrace, men were hurrying to-and-fro, carrying cannonballs, cartridges of gunpowder, rammers and wads for the thirty-two-pounder guns positioned at embrasures around the gun platform.

This was only one of a number of such platforms sited on and around the Mount, but the baronet considered it to be the most effective site if the French ship continued on its present course.

'Load the guns – but keep them back out of sight until it's time to use them,' ordered Sir John. 'We don't want to frighten the Frenchmen away. You! Isaac! Throw that pipe away. Are you mad, man? There's gunpowder all around and you're smoking a pipe! No! Don't knock it out against the wall. That's even more dangerous. Throw it away, over the wall. I'll deal with you later.'

Turning to Humphrey, Sir John demanded angrily, 'Has he been drinking?'

'Most of the men were at the inn when I called them out,' replied his son.

'Heaven help us! They are poor enough gunners at the best of times. I should have kept Abel on the Mount. He's the only man capable of sending a cannonball where it's intended to go – but I've sent him to fetch the children.'

'He said as much himself,' agreed Humphrey, 'but it's too late now. I saw him heading out of the harbour as I entered the house.'

'Then we'll just have to do the best we can without him.'

The French ship opened fire once more and Humphrey counted at least eight shots.

'What are they firing at?' Sir John demanded.

'The cottages beyond Perranuthnoe.' Humphrey named a small fishing community less than two miles from the Mount. 'They don't appear to have hit anything – but one thing is certain. They *are* heading this way.'

'Then we must make quite certain we're fully prepared for them.' Turning to the men loading the guns, he shouted, 'Hurry and have those guns ready – and bring up more powder and shot. The French will be within range before we've a single gun loaded if you don't move yourselves.'

The Mount men redoubled their efforts and Humphrey watched as the French ship drew nearer.

It was not a huge man-o'-war, no more than a thirty-two-gun frigate, and its shooting did not appear to be particularly accurate. But the castle on the Mount was a large target. Not all the French shots would miss.

Humphrey was not alone in such thoughts. Sir John was watching the approaching vessel anxiously. Suddenly he said, 'Humphrey, go down and tell Juliana to remove the children and servants to the north side of the house. We don't want to run the risk of anyone in the household being injured.'

At that moment, much to the surprise of both men, Abel ran up the steps to the terrace, showing little trace of the leg wound which had ended his career as a Royal Marine gunner. He was breathing heavily as a result of the speed at which he had hurried up the steep approach to the gun platform.

'What are you doing here?' demanded the baronet. 'Where are Catherine and Richard?'

'Inside the house. The boat bringing them home was already two-thirds of the way here. It was quicker to bring them to the house than turn around and return to the mainland.'

For a moment or two it seemed Sir John would dispute Abel's assessment of the situation he had encountered. Another salvo from the French ship, this time clearly aimed in the general direction of the Mount, changed his mind.

'Humphrey, hurry down and clear the seaward side of the house . . . Abel, you're the best gun captain we have. See if you can sight the guns so that some shots, at least, are not lost in the sea.'

Relieved that he had escaped the wrath of Sir John,

Abel hurried away to lay the guns on the rapidly closing target.

Humphrey found Juliana and the remainder of her children excitedly watching the approaching French ship from a window in the blue drawing-room, probably one of the most dangerously exposed positions in the castle.

Her initial response was resentment at being obliged to obey an order given to her by Humphrey. However, when he pointed out that the Mount was already the target of the enemy ship, she hurried from the room, ushering the protesting children before her.

By the time he returned to the south-facing gun platform, the sun was already dipping into the ribbon of haze that hid the horizon. The duel between ship and shore would be short-lived. If the French ship was to clear the dangerous Cornish coast before darkness closed in, it would have time to fire no more than a couple of salvoes before turning into the onshore wind and tacking away into the Channel.

There could be little doubt the captain had scanned the Mount through his own telescope, but he could not have seen the guns. As a result he was coming recklessly close to his intended target.

It seemed that his intention was to turn at the last moment and fire a broadside or two at the imposing granite castle.

'Run out the guns . . . now!'

Abel's shouted command startled Humphrey, who had been watching the sailors busying themselves about the guns on board the French ship.

Anticipating the French ship's imminent manoeuvre, Abel hurriedly inspected the elevation of the cannons. He had made chalk marks on the stones of the terrace, indicating the tracks that the wheels of the gun carriages should follow. There were further marks where they were to stop.

As the heavy guns were trundled into position, Abel exhorted the men to even greater efforts. The French warship had almost reached the position upon which he had laid his guns. He was anxious to hit the French vessel before its gunners fired upon the Mount. An unexpected salvo should effectively throw the French aim off balance.

Abel's plan was more successful than anyone could have dared to hope, his timing perfect. An officer on board the French warship saw white smoke belch from the embrasures on the south-facing terrace and shouted a warning, but it came too late.

A number of the heavy cannonballs splashed harmlessly into the sea around the vessel, but as many more succeeded in striking their target – and with considerable effect.

One carved a path through the packed ranks of a gun crew on the open deck. Two more tore away sails and rigging. The most telling shot of all was one of which any gunner would have been proud. It struck the mainmast at one-third of its height from the deck, bringing it crashing down, tearing sails and severing rigging as it fell.

The French gunnery officer made a call upon his men to return the fire. They did so, but, as Abel had intended, the volley from the Mount had thrown the ship off course. Not one of the French cannonballs struck its large, immobile target.

Meanwhile, on the Mount, Abel was exhorting his jubilant gunners to swab out the barrels of their cannons and reload, in order to open fire once more.

While they carried out his orders, he hurried among them, depressing the elevation of the guns slightly.

It was unnecessary to change the direction in which they would fire. A stiff onshore wind was bringing the French vessel ever closer to the shore. Still broadside on to the Mount, the vessel pursued an almost straight line from the spot where she had been hit by the Mount's salvo.

The men on the Mount could clearly see the panic on board the French ship, as officers and crew sought to hack away the broken mast and rigging in a desperate attempt to regain at least some control of the vessel.

But the French captain's arrogant recklessness had already sealed the fate of his ship.

'*Fire!*'

Another volley thundered from the guns on the terrace of the Mount. Once again many of the cannonballs struck home on their target. The skills gained by Abel during his service with the Royal Marines Artillery had not been forgotten. The French ship was doomed.

The only uncertainty now was the exact spot where the French vessel would come ashore.

Sir John ordered the St Michael's Mount cannons to

cease firing when it became apparent that the French crew could do nothing to save their ship.

The gunfire directed by Abel had brought down a second mast and spars. Rigging and tattered sails lay in a tangled mess on the main deck and spilled over the side of the ship, blanketing the gun ports.

By now darkness had closed in on the scene of the one-sided battle. Although it hid the confusion on board the French ship, the excited voices issuing and countermanding orders could clearly be heard.

All thoughts of hostile action were forgotten now. The only aim of those on board was survival. The stiff onshore breeze was accompanied by a heavy swell. Born in the depths of the Atlantic Ocean, the rollers died a noisy death on the rocks around the Mount and they were bringing the ship ever closer to destruction.

'Where do you think the ship will come ashore? It looks almost as though it might be driven past us and on to the mainland.'

Humphrey put the question to his father, but it was Abel who replied. 'It will strike below the old warren.'

The spot he mentioned was at the foot of one of the steepest parts of the Mount. Pointing in the direction of the causeway, he added, 'They know where it's coming aground.'

A great many shadowy figures were hurrying along the barely visible causeway and making their way around the shoreline of the Mount, heading for the spot where Abel had predicted the ship would be driven ashore. Some carried dim lanterns and these cast an eerie yellow light on others about them.

Now, those on the gun platform became aware of excited voices as men and women scrambled over the rocks on the foreshore.

'The causeway is barely open,' exclaimed Sir John. 'But whole families are coming from the mainland, hoping to salvage something from the wreck.'

'They'll be out for blood too,' said Abel. 'The French have taken many Cornish fishermen who'll never be seen again – and this particular ship has just been bombarding villages along the coast. There'll not be many prisoners taken tonight.'

Humphrey possessed a gentle nature that would one day lead him to become a member of the clergy and he was appalled by the statement of the Mount boatman. 'But . . . that's murder! Can't we put someone at this end of the causeway to turn the mainlanders back from the Mount?'

Sir John looked at his son pityingly. 'You've never seen your fellow-men when there are spoils to be taken from a wreck, Humphrey. I have. All the constables in the county couldn't stop them. All we can do is go down there when the ship strikes and try to save as many Frenchmen as we can.'

Calling to the men who had manned the cannons, Sir John said, 'I want you men down there too – saving lives. You can pass the word that if I see any Mount men doing harm to the French sailors, they'll have neither work nor a home tomorrow. Abel, you've got more about you than most. Hurry to the inn. Tell the landlord to prepare to receive French prisoners – and arrange for a guard to be placed on them. They'll be held there until we can hand them over to the Admiralty.' The Admiralty was the authority responsible for prisoners-of-war.

The men who had only a short while before been intent on reducing the French warship to an unmanageable hulk were unhappy at not being allowed to take part in plundering the vessel when it came ashore. There was some subdued grumbling among them, but they knew better than to express their dissatisfaction openly in the presence of the baronet who employed them.

Aware of their feelings, Sir John called after them, 'You did well this evening, men. I'll see you're rewarded for your efforts. You especially, Abel. I was impressed by your gunnery skills. Very impressed indeed.'

If Abel was pleased by Sir John's praise, he did not allow it to show. Following the other men from the terrace, he made no reply.

'Did you hear that there Humphrey when he thought it likely there might be blood-letting when the French ship comes ashore? He wasn't so particular when we was shooting at 'em and couldn't see any blood. I reckon the time he's spent at that university has softened him up.'

One of the Mount men made the comment as the St Aubyn gunners made their way down the steep path from the castle. They were not dawdling and would be on hand to see the vessel come ashore. However, with no chance of acquiring any plunder, there was little sense of urgency among them.

'Shooting at men in battle is one thing. Killing them

when they're beaten and defenceless is something different,' said Abel scathingly.

'Tell that to *them*,' retorted the man who had made the derogatory remark about Humphrey St Aubyn. He pointed to the crowds gathering on the rocks ahead of them. 'I wouldn't try to stop them doing what they've come here for, if I were you. In the darkness they won't be fussy whether they're killing a Frenchman or a St Aubyn man.'

They had rounded a corner of the path which brought the causeway into view. The tide had receded enough to make the rock and shingle path passable between Mount and mainland, but the swell was still occasionally sending water swirling over it. However, by the light of the many lanterns being carried, it was possible to see a great many people – men, women and children – heading towards them.

'Good God! It looks as though the whole of Marazion is heading this way,' said Abel.

'They'll be from all along the coast and the Frenchmen have only themselves to blame,' said one of his companions. 'Their cannonading has stirred up the fishermen and their women. Besides, they have many old scores to settle. It'll be the Devil and not Sir John who'll be calling the tune tonight.'

At the last minute it seemed as if the French warship might cheat those waiting eagerly on the rocky foreshore of the Mount in the hope of plundering something of value from the stricken vessel and wreaking revenge on its crew, and a howl of frustration went up.

Then, just as it seemed that the ship would drift past the rocks of the Mount and into the bay, a capricious wind swung it back towards the waiting Cornish men and women. An obliging swell immediately lifted it and carried it over the outermost rocks.

The listening mob heard the screech of tortured timbers as the stricken ship was battered mercilessly by a combination of rocks and a restless sea. Panic-stricken, the unfortunate crew-members began jumping overboard in a bid to save their lives.

This was the signal for the waiting horde to swarm down upon them. Scrambling over rocks and splashing dangerously through the heaving water, they sought to intercept the Frenchmen.

The ensuing scene was one that would never be forgotten by those from the Mount who witnessed it. The mainland Cornish men and women were armed with a wide variety of makeshift weapons. Staves, spades, pitchforks, pieces of timber, axes and more conventional weapons were all used to batter those survivors who made it to the shore – and many who were still in the sea.

When a French seaman was felled, he was immediately surrounded by a swarm of men and women. Robbed of everything of value, even the clothes he was wearing, he could consider himself fortunate if he escaped with his life.

Soon the whole foreshore was a heaving mass of screaming, shouting and fighting humanity and Abel felt unable to stand back from it any longer.

Calling on the Mount men to follow him, he did not wait to see if they were obeying his call. Scrambling down to the rocks, he plunged among the mob, trying to pull his fellow-countrymen from those who were being attacked.

He was aware of others with him. Whether it was Mount men, or mainlanders with a conscience, he did not know – and no longer cared.

Coming upon a seaman crawling painfully from the sea, Abel put his shoulder to a man intent upon bludgeoning the bedraggled and exhausted survivor. As he did so, the distressed man cried out, 'For God's sake save us! There's almost a hundred English prisoners on board – most are Cornish men . . .'

A wave rose from the sea, threatening to drag the man back out with it, but Abel reached forward and held him firmly until he was able to pull him to safety.

Others had heard the man's words and a shout went up – 'There are Cornish men on board . . . save the Cornish men.'

The cry was taken up and the mood of many plunderers changed immediately. It was one thing to kill Frenchmen who had been bombarding homes in the vicinity, quite another to attack their own kind, unfortunate enough to be taken prisoner.

Hands began to drag men from the sea and pass them back to others behind them.

Not all the plunderers were ready to give up a chance to enrich themselves. They showed no mercy to survivors from the ship, whatever their nationality. Others ignored the floundering men altogether, as they pulled from the sea any item that floated free of the doomed vessel.

Not far from Abel, the lantern held up by a woman

from the mainland showed a young lad desperately trying to secure a grip on a smooth, glistening rock in order to pull himself clear of the sea.

As Abel scrambled over the rocks to go to his assistance, one of the mainlanders, armed with a stout, pointed pole, struck at the desperate young man, knocking him backwards. When the sea sucked the helpless survivor back on to rocks, the pole was used in an attempt to pull him closer and rob him.

So angry was Abel that when he reached the rock, he wrenched the pole from the man's grasp. Knocking its owner into the sea, he pulled the young survivor close enough to heave him clear of the swirling water.

The young man was of slight build and much younger than Abel had at first thought. It took little effort to pull him clear of the water.

Ignoring the cries of the man he had knocked off the rock into the sea, Abel carried his unconscious burden to safety, leaping from rock to rock until he reached dry land.

He was pulled up a slope clear of the chaos of the foreshore by Humphrey St Aubyn.

'I saw what you did, Abel. Had I been closer I would have helped you. That man was an animal. He deserves to drown . . . But the boy? Is he badly hurt?'

'I don't know. He's certainly unconscious. Can you find someone with a lantern?'

The young boy was laid on the ground and a lantern brought to the scene. In its pale yellow light, he appeared pathetically young and possessed skin that Abel thought had never yet felt the touch of a razor.

'He's still breathing, at least,' said Humphrey.

'Yes, but he's been hurt. There's blood showing through his shirt.'

The boy was wearing no coat, only a light shirt of finer material than that worn by most seamen. If he was French, Abel thought he was probably a young gentleman, perhaps training to become a ship's officer.

'The wound would have been caused by the sharp stave,' said Abel. 'We'd better check and see how badly he's hurt.' As he spoke, he pulled the shirt clear of the boy's trousers and lifted it.

He frowned. There was a wide band of cloth wrapped about the boy's chest. It looked as though it might have been placed there earlier, perhaps to serve as a bandage. If so, it was possible the blood that could be seen came from an earlier wound. It must have reopened when he was being thrown about in the sea.

The source of the blood appeared to be beneath one of the boy's armpits. Abel called, 'Does anyone have a sharp knife? I'll need to cut this bandage away.'

One of the Mount men handed him a knife. Inserting the blade beneath the wide cloth bandage, he sliced through it before gently peeling it away from the boy's body, hoping that by doing so he was not going to open the wound further.

Suddenly, a gasp went up from the men standing about them. Abel, too, rocked back on his heels. He had found the wound. Slicing through the skin between two ribs, it was not particularly serious.

But it was not the wound that had caused the gasp from the watching men. The cloth bound about the young survivor's chest had not been a bandage to hide any injury. It had been worn to flatten the breasts of the young survivor. It was not a boy whom Abel had pulled from the sea – but a young *woman*!

Book One

1

Summer 1810

'Thomasina! THOMASINA!'

Standing in the doorway of a small cottage on the hill above the fishing village of Mevagissey, Mary Rowe called her niece yet again, her impatience increasing.

Turning, she called into the cottage, 'Dolly, did Thomasina say anything to you about where she might be going?'

Dolly shrugged her indifference. 'Nothing at all, Ma, but you know her as well I do. She's probably somewhere along the cliff, day-dreaming – or off with a boy.'

Mary Rowe expelled her breath in a sound that combined anger and frustration. 'I really don't know what's the matter with that girl. However unhappy she may be about starting work as a live-in maid, you'd think she'd show some gratitude to me for getting it for her. It's a job most girls would give their eye-teeth to have. Yet she goes missing just when she should be getting ready to set off to Trebene. I despair of that girl, I really do.'

Adding a couple of stitches to the hem she was letting down on one of her frocks, Dolly spoke without looking up, 'She really hates the thought of going to work as a servant, Ma.'

'What she thinks of it is neither here nor there,' snapped her mother. 'She has far too many ideas above her station in life, that one. We all have to do things we don't want to do and it's about time she realised it. I didn't want to be widowed, or have a young girl who isn't my own to look after – but it happened, and I've had to get on with it. I don't know what her mother would have said, had she known how Thomasina would turn out. The girl might have been born to my own sister, but she's like no other girl I've ever known. Anyway, she's going to work at Trebene House, whether she likes it or not. They'll be paying her six pounds a year, all found, and half of that is coming to me. It's little enough return for what I've spent on her all these past years – but it's better than the nothing I'm getting from her right now. By now most girls of her age have gone off and found themselves husbands – but not our Thomasina, oh no! She thinks she's too good for any of the village lads. I'm expecting better things from you, my girl, and don't you forget it, but at least your sewing brings a few coppers into the house. Now, put that dress down for a while and go off and find her. When you do, tell her I want her back here – *this instant.*'

*   *   *

Huddled in the shelter of a free-stone field wall, Thomasina Varcoe hugged her legs tightly and rested her chin on her knees. In front of her the field ended in a sheer cliff, beyond which were the grey waters of the English Channel.

Thomasina was not a typical Cornish girl. Her fair hair set her apart from her dark-haired contemporaries. Nor was she 'pretty' in the conventional sense. Her mouth was too large, her nose too proud and her firm jaw set a little too determinedly. Yet most people who glanced at her, whether they were men or women, usually looked again.

She had heard her aunt calling and knew why she was wanted, but she had no intention of returning to the cottage just yet. Trebene House would not fall to the ground because she was not there to begin work when they were expecting her.

She gazed out to sea, to where a formation of eight men-o'-war, in line ahead, ploughed through the choppy water, leaning away from the wind. The ships had put out from the nearby naval port of Plymouth and were bound for the open waters of the Atlantic, doubtless to seek out the ships of Emperor Napoleon's navy.

Resentfully, Thomasina thought that if only she had been a boy, *that* was where she would be. A sailor on a man-o'-war. She probably already had as much experience of the sea as many of those on board. More, certainly, than most who had been impressed into the King's navy.

Thomasina's father had been master of a modest sailing vessel, trading between Bristol and the smaller English Channel ports.

It had not been a grand vessel – indeed, it was scarcely larger than a fishing boat – but Thomasina had thought it the finest boat that had ever sailed from Mevagissey harbour.

After her mother died Thomasina had gone to live with Mary Rowe, her mother's sister, but she was happiest when accompanying her father on his coastal voyages, allowed to help work the boat.

Then, four years ago, when Thomasina was fifteen, her father and his boat had failed to return from what should have been no more than a short voyage between Falmouth and Portsmouth.

The weather had been fair along the coast at the time, but no trace of his vessel was ever found.

It was believed it must have been sunk by a French warship, or perhaps a privateer. Had it been taken as a prize, word would have been received from France long before now. Many such tragedies had been visited upon the families of seafaring men during the long struggle with France for supremacy of the sea.

His loss had devastated Thomasina, but she had received scant sympathy from her aunt, who seemed far more concerned about the loss of income than about the fate of her widowed brother-in-law.

This had done more to turn Thomasina against Mary than anything else she did, or would do, but she would not allow her dislike to show. It was then that Thomasina had learned to control many other emotions, too. She often came to the spot where she was now and for more than an hour cried as though she would never stop. But eventually she *did* stop and, by the time she returned to Mary Rowe's home some hours later, she had succeeded in putting an almost impenetrable shutter between herself and the rest of the world.

Since that time, Thomasina had not settled at anything for very long. For a while she had repaired fishing-nets in Mevagissey, then she tried her hand as a dairy-maid. This had been followed by general work on an inland farm, housework for an elderly widow crippled with arthritis and, more recently, preparing fish in a Mevagissey fish-cellar.

She particularly hated working in the fish-cellar. No matter how many times she bathed, she could never rid herself of the smell of fish.

Now Mary had found work for her at Trebene House, the manor home of the Vincent family, who owned much of the land in the Roseland area, a few miles away, opposite the busy sea port of Falmouth.

No doubt such employment would have delighted many young girls of her acquaintance. It offered security, regular food and the possibility of marriage to a fellow-household employee, who had the added attraction of enjoying a job for life.

However, Thomasina had long been aware that she did not share the aims and ambitions of other girls of her acquaintance. For most, the acquisition of a sweetheart and the prospect of an early marriage dominated their whole outlook on life.

Thomasina *had* a sweetheart, but he was frowned upon by Mary – and by the mothers of most of the girls in the area, too. Considered a ne'er-do-well, Jeffery constituted the only chink in the defences she had put up against the world. He alone had been kind and understanding at the time she had lost her father – and Thomasina loved him for it.

Jeffery scorned the aims and ambitions of his contemporaries, believing there were easier ways for a man to earn a living than by working his way into an early grave. He was fond of pointing out that while men, women and children in the countryside spent their lives in poverty and drudgery, those who lived in the great houses grew rich from their labours. He vowed he was not going to break his back in order to keep such people in idle luxury.

Thomasina fiercely defended Jeffery in the face of his critics, chief among whom was Mary Rowe. But this attitude led to him being shunned by those who were content to accept their lot in life. Because of her loyalty to him, Thomasina too was excluded from their company.

During these past few years Jeffery had spent an increasing amount of time away from his home village. Left behind, Thomasina had become more and more of a 'loner', refusing to conform to the ways of her aunt and the friends whom the older woman had gathered about her.

Not that Thomasina minded. Unlike many of the other girls, she had learned to read, and she read well. She was quite happy to lose herself within the pages of a book – one of an unclaimed consignment acquired by her father, many years before. Engrossed in the pages of a book, she was able to exclude the world about her.

When she was not reading, Thomasina would often come here, close to the cliff, and sit gazing out to sea. At first it had been in the vain hope that one day she would see the ship captained by her father sailing home, its increasingly long absence miraculously explained away.

The hope, although never entirely abandoned, had gradually receded. Sometimes, if Jeffery was home, he would come here with her, unbeknown to the disapproving Mary.

More recently, Thomasina would sit and watch the large ships with envy, wishing she were sailing with them to parts of the world she could otherwise only learn about through the pages of the books she read.

'Our ma's been calling you till she's gone blue in the face.'

Dolly's words broke in upon Thomasina's thoughts. The feet of the younger girl had made no sound on the soft grass as she approached the wall that sheltered her cousin.

'I heard her.'

Thomasina spoke truculently, resentful at Dolly's intrusion on what were probably the last moments she would ever spend here, in the spot she had come to regard as a personal sanctuary from the world about her.

'Then why didn't you come? You'll only make Ma mad by staying out here, pretending you haven't heard her.'

'Well, she's not going to have to put up with me for very much longer, is she? After today there'll only be you to grumble at.'

'Ma isn't that bad, Thomasina,' said Dolly unhappily. 'She'll miss you, really . . . I will, too.'

Thomasina looked up at the young girl who was five years her junior and her expression softened. 'Don't take any notice of me, Dolly. I'm just miserable at the thought of going off somewhere I don't want to be, to live and work. I'll miss you too – and your ma,' she added grudgingly. 'Life can't have been easy for her since my pa . . . since he didn't come back. I don't suppose I've helped very much, have I? I should have looked out for some farmer's son and trapped him into marriage. That way, you and your ma would never have been short of something to eat, at least.'

'You could still do that if you wanted to.' There was a hint of mischief in Dolly's expression as she spoke. She was very fond of Thomasina and wanted desperately to cheer her up. 'Billy Kivell's still single and his pa's got a nice-sized farm.'

Billy Kivell was a middle-aged simpleton who possessed the mind of a six-year-old. Desperate to find someone to care for Billy before he and his wife became too old, the farmer had let it be known that whoever married Billy would one day inherit the farm along with him. So far there had been no takers.

Thomasina smiled. 'That's something *you* can think about when you're a year or two older, young lady. But don't be in too much of a hurry to marry. I won't be able to save much for a wedding gift from the money I'll be earning for working at Trebene.'

Dolly looked at Thomasina sympathetically. 'I know you hate the thought of going there to work, but I'm sure it won't be as bad as you think. You'll eat well, have a nice uniform to wear and be able to come home to see Ma and me for one day a month, at least.'

'Yes, you're right, Dolly, but will you do something for me?'

'That depends on what it is,' replied Dolly guardedly.

'It's nothing much, really. If Jeffery comes looking for me, will you tell him where I am?'

'All right – but I won't be able to do it if Ma's around. She won't let me talk to him.'

'You'll find a way. Tell him I'll be free on Sundays, after the family have been to church – and I'll be back here on the first Sunday of each month, after I've been paid.'

'I don't know whether I'll be able to remember all that.'

'Of course you will,' said Thomasina sharply.

'What if he doesn't come around asking for you?' Dolly asked mischievously.

'He will.'

Thomasina spoke with more confidence than she felt. Jeffery had promised he would return to her, but she believed he had gone to London. There would be a great many temptations for him in the capital city of England.

Putting such thoughts to the back of her mind, she rose to her feet. 'Come on, Dolly. Let's get back to the house and put your ma out of her misery.'

2

Thomasina approached Trebene House carrying a bundle containing the few personal items she was being allowed to take with her to the great house.

She had been told she did not need very much. The Vincents would be providing her with uniform, toiletries and bedding, but she carried a neat outfit to wear on the one day of the week when she would be allowed to leave the house.

She also had a few items of simple jewellery, acquired during her young lifetime. Among these was a bangle given to her as a birthday present from Dolly, a crucifix that had been a gift from her father, and a few ribbons she had bought herself from the pedlars who would occasionally call at the Mevagissey cottage.

There was also a leather-bound Bible which had belonged to her mother, given to her by her own father, on the day she was married.

Thomasina walked alone to Trebene, following a route which took her along many miles of narrow country lanes. There was a quicker route which would have reduced the distance by almost one-third, but it would have taken her across fields and through a muddy, wooded valley.

Mary Rowe had warned her niece against taking this route. It would not do, she said, for Thomasina to arrive at Trebene with mud clinging to her shoes and staining the hem of her dress.

When she eventually turned into the open entrance gate of Trebene House and passed by the Lodge, Thomasina pondered irritably about the merits of the advice she had been given by her aunt. It was a hot day. She wondered whether arriving with a little mud attached to her might not have been preferable to presenting herself as she was now: hot, cross and bathed in perspiration.

The driveway to the house was long and it curved away through well-wooded parkland. Not until she was quite close to her destination did the house itself come into view.

It commanded a view over Carrick Roads, one of England's safest and busiest anchorages, but it was the house that took her attention. Seeing it at close quarters for the first time, Thomasina found it quite awesome.

A very large, square-built building, Trebene was bigger than any house she had ever seen. There seemed to be innumerable windows and Thomasina became uncharacteristically self-conscious as she drew closer. She felt her approach was being observed from every one of them.

As she paused, looking at the house uncertainly, she heard the sound of a horse coming along the driveway behind her at a fast trot.

Moving to one side, she peered up beneath the wide peak of her bonnet to see a horse and rider coming towards the house. They formed a contrast of colours. The horse was white, but its rider was dressed in black from his top boots to his tricorne hat. The only relief in his dark ensemble was a white cravat worn high at his throat.

The rider gave only a brief glance at Thomasina as he passed by – then he glanced again, longer this time.

Pulling his horse to a halt, he asked, 'Who are you, girl? What are you doing here?'

From the manner of his speech, Thomasina realised at once that he had been drinking heavily.

'I've come to work in the house . . . sir.' The respectful word was expected, she knew, but servility did not come easily to her.

'Have you, now?'

Swaying in the saddle, the rider took in Thomasina's body, from head to foot, in a manner that angered her more than she dared show. She bristled with defiance, but avoided meeting his gaze.

The moment was brought to a halt by his mount. Restless at being pulled up only minutes from water and a hay bag, it tried to move on.

Before the horse was brought under control it had made a full turn and moved farther away from Thomasina.

'It's high time Aunt Harriet brought some young blood into the house. What are your duties to be?'

'In the house . . . sir. A maid.'

'Then we shall certainly see more of each other in the future, young lady.'

As the horseman was about to dig his heels into his horse, Thomasina asked hesitantly, 'May I ask who you are, sir?'

The young man raised an eyebrow at her boldness, but he gave her an answer.

'Sir Charles Hearle, nephew of Mrs Vincent, your new employer. You'll find she demands much of you, but don't let her break your spirit. I like women who have a boldness about them.'

'You just keep clear of Sir Charles, he's a wrong 'un, and no mistake.'

The warning came from Lily, a big-boned, ungainly maid in her early fifties. She and Thomasina were working together, making up the bed in the room of Henry Vincent, owner of Trebene House.

Much to her disgust, Thomasina was now known as 'Ethel' within the Vincent household. On her first full day at the house she had been taken before Harriet Vincent, a tall, stern-faced woman whose opening words to her had been, 'Thomasina? *Thomasina?* What sort of a name is that for a servant girl. I'll not have a maid in my household called Thomasina. Do you have a second name, girl?'

When Thomasina admitted she had not, the mistress of the household said, 'Then you shall be called "Ethel". It's a name far more in keeping with your position. Off you go, Ethel. Be sure you put in a full day's work for the money you are being paid.'

Lily had been given the task of familiarising Thomasina with the layout and routine of the big house and acquainting her with the duties she would be required to perform.

'I've known Sir Charles since soon after he was born,' continued the senior housemaid, warming to the subject of the Vincents' titled nephew as she expertly folded and tucked in a corner of the bed-cover. 'There's not been a housemaid in Trebene safe since Sir Charles was old enough to know what it was all about. He's caused more grief here than Napoleon, that one. Master Henry should have had him put in the army, when he was persuading other men from hereabouts to go off and fight for King and country. I doubt if Sir Charles would make much of a fighting-man, but it'd have saved many a young girl a whole lot of sorrow.'

Lily spoke with such bitterness that, somewhat unkindly, Thomasina wondered whether she was genuinely angry about the downfall of the girls of whom she spoke, or aggrieved because Sir Charles Hearle had not included plain and ageing servants among those to whom he made his overtures.

'Do Master Henry and the mistress have any children of their own?' Thomasina had seen no one about the house who seemed to belong, and no one had mentioned any offspring.

'Yes, Master Francis. He's off at university right now, so you won't be seeing much of him for a while. Different as chalk and cheese, him and Master Charles are. They can't abide one another, neither.'

Smoothing out imaginary creases in the silk coverlet with her hand, Lily said, 'There, that's the bedrooms finished in this part of the house. We'll go and see if Mrs Mudge has anything more for us to do before we check out the linen cupboards. When we've done that I'll pass you over to Mr Pengelly. He'll show you what goes on in the dining-room before the family come in for their meals. There's a sight more to it than sitting down with a pasty in your hand, I can tell you that.'

Cyril Pengelly was the family's butler. A tall, somewhat rotund figure with a pompous manner, he was the true ruler of the servants' domain – although it was a claim that would have been hotly contested by Eliza Mudge, the Trebene housekeeper.

The professional feud between the two was exploited to the full by the household servants, although none would dare openly offend either of them.

Thomasina had learned the names of the more important members of the staff, but had not yet been able to ascertain the full extent of their duties. Equally confusing was the routine of the house, as explained to her by Lily.

The only thing that had been made quite clear to her by the other servants was that she was very much an outsider. At Trebene, servants were usually taken on because he, or she, was related to another member of staff.

Thomasina had been employed on the recommendation of the local rector. A man who had been friendly with Thomasina's missing father, the cleric had become concerned about the worsening state of Mary Rowe's finances.

Thomasina was made aware that many of the other servants had relatives waiting for a vacancy to occur in the great house. As a result of her own appointment outside the established procedure, she was resented by the others.

Although she tried to shrug off the unfriendly attitude of the other servants, it did not make settling in easy for her. She felt that even Lily resented having to teach simple household duties to a complete stranger.

Although Thomasina was finding it difficult to fit into the household routine and had made no friends, she did not believe she had actually made any enemies. Then, one day, Mistress Vincent took Thomasina to task for not checking and emptying the wash-basins in each of the bedrooms when the members of the family came downstairs to breakfast.

It was a task she had not realised was hers. When she complained to the middle-aged maid responsible for the omission, the maid shrugged, disinterestedly.

'I've got my own work to do. I can't go around teaching you every little thing you ought to know. If you want to blame anyone, then blame the mistress for taking you on in the first place. It should have been quite obvious to her that you don't know the first thing about working in a big house.'

'No, I don't,' admitted Thomasina, 'but I'm doing my best to learn. I don't suppose *you* knew everything when you first came to work here.'

The maid sniffed her indifference. 'It was different for us. We all have mothers, aunts and grandmothers who've worked in the house. What goes on here comes natural to us. Trebene House has always been part of our lives and we're part of Trebene. We all know it – and the house knows it, too. You'll not see your time out here, young lady, you mark my words.'

Angrily Thomasina retorted, 'If you're an example of what the house does to people, I'm sure I don't want to live my life out here anyway.'

She glared at the other woman until she turned and went on her way without another word.

Thomasina felt she had got the better of the exchange, but it had disturbed her and left her feeling unsettled. It had been an uncomfortable insight into what the other servants felt about her.

Although she had now been working at the house for some weeks, she had come no closer to being accepted by the others. She wondered if she ever would.

Thomasina told herself it did not matter. She had already decided she had no intention of spending the rest of her life pandering to every whim of the Vincent family.

The big problem was what else she could do to ensure that regular money went to her Aunt Mary and to Dolly.

3

Thomasina had hoped that matters at the house would improve with the passing of time. That the other servants would gradually accept her as one of their number.

They did not.

The maid with whom she had argued spread the word that Thomasina regarded her employment at Trebene as purely a temporary expediency. This immediately set her farther apart from the others.

For each of the servants working in and about the house, Trebene was at the very heart of their being. A servant who did not hold such a view, especially a *female* servant, was regarded as a heretic. Soon even Lily, who was comparatively easy-going and simple-minded, began to avoid her.

Another thing that upset Thomasina was the name

given to her by Harriet Vincent. The other servants quickly realised how much she disliked it and made use of the name far more often than they might otherwise have done.

Then, one Saturday evening, an event occurred which temporarily drove all thoughts of domestic quarrels from the minds of the servants. Henry Vincent, travelling in his carriage with two elderly women neighbours, was held up by a highwayman outside the gates of Trebene.

The women, on their way to a dinner party at the house, were wearing a considerable amount of jewellery. By the time the highwayman disappeared into the night, the two near-hysterical ladies had been relieved of all such inessential accoutrements and a feebly protesting Henry Vincent had handed over a heavy purse.

Before dinner at the house could be contemplated, the two swooning ladies had to be plied with an amount of brandy that in any other circumstances would have raised eyebrows.

By now, Henry Vincent had recovered from his fright and was beside himself with blustering fury.

'The sheer impudence of the fellow!' he declared to the assembled family guests. 'Had the ladies not been with me, I'd have tackled the blackguard, pistol or no pistol. As it was, of course, I dared not take the risk of having the ladies involved. A rogue who's bold enough to hold up a gentleman's carriage within sight of his own house would not think twice about shooting at women.'

'Then it was fortuitous you had them with you,

dear,' said his wife placatingly. 'Had you been alone and tried to resist, you might not be here to tell the tale now.'

There were murmurs of agreement from the sympathetic guests. One said, 'Should you not inform the constable, Henry? After all, if there's an armed highwayman at large, he might well strike again.'

'The constable wouldn't risk his own skin by turning out after dark,' declared Henry Vincent derisively. 'No, I armed two of the grooms and sent them off to find Magistrate Williams. He'll organise a search party. Hopefully we'll have our man by morning.'

'I sincerely hope they *do* catch him,' said one of the more timid of the ladies. 'I shall be a bundle of nerves by the time I arrive home tonight. Indeed, I shall be praying that I reach my home safely.'

'There is no need for anyone to be alarmed,' declared Henry Vincent with pompous reassurance. 'Anyone who wishes to stay at Trebene overnight is quite welcome to do so. For those who feel they must return home, I will provide an escort – an *armed* escort. Now, we've done all that can be done. Let us forget about highwaymen for a while and try to enjoy the remainder of our evening together.'

There were servants in the room during the exchanges about the highwayman and the conversation was repeated with the addition of a few imaginative embellishments in the servants' dining-room, later that evening.

'Heaven help any honest stranger who's travelling the lanes of Cornwall tonight,' commented one of the footmen. 'If the gentry are in the same mood as

Master Henry, he'll be shot before he's able to explain his business.'

Thomasina was in the room with the other servants. Although she took no part in the conversation, she was concerned about a highwayman being at large in the countryside. The following day she would be walking along the lanes to pay a visit to her Aunt Mary and Dolly – and in her pocket she would have her month's pay. Half to hand over to her aunt and the other half to be 'put by' on her own behalf.

She comforted herself with the thought that a highwayman who held up carriages, and stole jewellery and the purses of rich men, would hardly be likely to want to rob a young servant girl.

The Sunday church service seemed to go on for an exceptionally long time, the elderly rector being carried away by the message of his sermon.

He preached on the subject of the eighth Commandment, 'Thou shalt not steal'. The text pleased Henry Vincent, but Thomasina grew increasingly impatient, knowing she had a long return journey to make once the service was over.

As soon as the service had finished and the servants had waited respectfully for the Vincent family to end their conversations with the rector, Thomasina set off.

She had been hoping, unrealistically, that she might arrive at her aunt's cottage in time to join them in their Sunday lunch. Taken in mid-afternoon, it was the highlight of the small family's culinary week.

Thomasina knew that she had no hope of making it now. She would be lucky to arrive in time to gulp

down a cup of tea before making her way back to
Trebene.

As she hurried along the church pathway she was
pursued by the voice of Eliza Mudge, the Vincents'
housekeeper, warning her to return to Trebene before
nightfall, in order to ensure she was not waylaid by the
highwayman.

Thomasina had no intention of obeying the housekeeper's instruction. She would pretend she had not
yet grown accustomed to the name of 'Ethel' and so
did not realise the housekeeper was talking to her.

4

Thomasina had only just left the last house of the village behind when she saw a horse and rider standing in the road ahead of her.

Even at this distance, Thomasina could see that his clothes were those of a gentleman. The fact that he was making no attempt to move out of her way vaguely disturbed her, but she cast her eyes down, with the intention of passing by without acknowledging the presence of horse and rider.

The horseman had other ideas.

'Has working at Trebene made you so high-and-mighty that you no longer recognise your friends, Tom?'

Startled, Thomasina looked up at the smiling rider.

'Jeffery!' As the horseman swung from the saddle, Thomasina ran to him with a cry of delight. Still holding the rein of his horse, he hugged her to him with his free arm.

Suddenly, she pulled back. 'But . . . what are you doing dressed like a gentleman – and riding a horse?'

'Is there a law in England which says I can't ride a horse – or give a lift home to my sweetheart – if that's what you still are and are on your way home?'

'The answer is yes – to your last question. I promised Aunt Mary I'd come to see her once a month and give her half my earnings – but you still haven't answered *my* questions.'

Instead of replying, Jeffery climbed back in the saddle. Steadying the restless horse, he extended a hand to Thomasina. 'I'll tell you on the way to Mevagissey. Come on.'

Holding her hand, he paused in the act of pulling her up behind him, 'What is your aunt's share of your month's pay?'

'A half – four shillings and ninepence. It should have been five shillings, but I was clumsy and broke a saucer. Mistress Vincent deducted sixpence from my pay.'

Releasing her hand and feeling inside a waistcoat pocket, he pulled out a number of coins and said, 'Here, share these with her, too.'

Glancing down at the money he had given to her, Thomasina saw that she was holding four dull, golden coins. She looked up at him in astonishment.

'You've given me four guineas!'

'That's right, two for you and two for your aunt.'

'But where did you get them – and your clothes, and the horse?'

'You ask too many questions, Tom – but you always did. For now, just let's say I didn't get it by touching my cap to the sort of people you're working for. Now, do you want a ride home, or not?'

After tucking the coins away safely, Thomasina took his hand again, this time a little uncertainly, and he pulled her up to sit behind him on the horse.

When she was about to resume her questioning, Jeffery put the horse into a canter and she encircled his body with her arms in order to maintain her balance.

He smiled back at her over his shoulder. 'Do you have to go straight home, or shall we stop somewhere along the way? I know a barn with plenty of fresh hay in it. We wouldn't be disturbed. The farmer's a lay preacher. He'll be out praying around the countryside all day today.'

With her face pressed against his back, Thomasina said firmly, 'We'll go straight home to Aunt Mary's, Jeffery Kent. You may have given me four guineas, but you haven't bought *that*.'

After a few moments she added, 'Besides, it's not decent to do it in the daytime. It might be a different story if you were to bring me back to Trebene again tonight, when it's getting dark. That's if you've told me by then where your money's coming from.'

He grinned back at her once more and kneed the horse to greater speed.

The change of gait caused Thomasina to grip him tighter than before. As her arms slid down to his waist, she felt a bulge beneath his coat.

Curious, she slid a hand between two of his coat buttons. What she felt there caused her to pull back from him so suddenly that she almost fell from the horse. He brought the animal to a halt immediately.

'Jeffery! You have a pistol tucked inside your belt!'

Seemingly unconcerned, he put the horse to a walk, 'You're *almost* right. In fact, there are *two* pistols.'

'What for . . . ?'

Suddenly, things dropped into place. His clothes, the horse, the money he had so casually given to her – and the incident involving her employer the previous evening.

With a thrill of excitement that was mixed with a degree of fear, she said, 'You . . . ! You've become a highwayman. It was you who held up Mr Vincent and his guests last night.'

'So *that's* who it was? I wish I'd known at the time. As it was, he was so scared he practically begged me to take his purse. The ladies were a bit more reluctant, but they coughed up in the end and presented me with some very nice baubles. They'll fetch a guinea or two when I go back to London.'

Jeffery spoke in an almost jocular vein, but Thomasina could feel a tenseness in him that had not been there before.

When she said nothing, he said, 'So now you know how I get the money to buy the fine clothes I'm wearing. What are you going to do about it, Thomasina?'

'I . . . Nothing . . . but it's come as a shock.' She had no intention of telling him of the excitement she felt. Of the contrast between the lives they were both leading.

'Will you tell your Mr Vincent who it was who held him up last night?'

'Of course not,' she replied sharply. 'But what will happen to you if they ever catch you?'

'They'll hang me. You know that as well as I do – but they're going to have to catch me first.'

Thomasina made no reply and they rode on in silence for a while. Then Jeffery said, 'It beats working, Thomasina. I've got things now I could never have bought if I'd worked all my life.'

'But . . . it's not honest.'

'Isn't it, Thomasina? Perhaps you can tell me what honesty is? Do you know how that Mr Vincent of yours can afford a fine house, lots of servants and all the other things he has?'

When she said nothing, he continued, 'I'll tell you. He's got shares in half the mines down Camborne way. He takes a huge profit from them, although he won't spend a penny on safety measures. A month or two back there was an accident at one of the mines. Five men were killed. Your Mr Vincent parted with twenty-five pounds for the widows. Five pounds for each man's life. Five men dead, and twenty-five pounds is all it takes to wipe his conscience clear. Afterwards he probably went home and spent more than that on the drink he and his friends enjoyed while he boasted about his generosity in looking after the families of the "poor dead miners". No doubt he added that their deaths were caused by their own carelessness.'

As he spoke, he jerked angrily on the reins and the horse threw up its head uncertainly.

When he had brought it under control once more, Jeffery said, 'I take money from the rich, Thomasina. Vincent and his kind take fathers, husbands and bread-winners from their families. Tell me, which of us is the robber?'

Thomasina said little for the remainder of the ride home, but Jeffery was aware of her side-turned head resting against the expensive cloth of his coat back, and of her arms encircling his body. He knew she was thinking deeply about what he had said to her.

5

'So you still enjoy letting me love you then, Thomasina, even though you know how I earn a living?'

In the darkness of the barn, Jeffery straightened his clothing and brushed unseen wisps of hay from his hat before replacing it on his head.

'Don't flatter yourself that it's love, Jeffery Kent. You don't need to be anything special to do what you've just done. There's not a man or boy over fifteen around here who can't do the same.'

'True, but not with you, Thomasina. I know that.'

'Like I just said, you think too much of yourself for your own good.'

Despite her words, Thomasina reached out and her fingers found his cheek.

'Perhaps I do, Thomasina, but I think even more of you.' Reaching up, he moved her hand from his cheek to his lips. 'Why not come away with me – tonight?

Don't go back to Trebene. You're not happy there. You never will be.'

Thomasina knew she dare not let him know how genuinely tempted she was to take up his offer. How much she wanted to be with him and never see Trebene again.

She *hated* working for the Vincents and living among their spiteful servants. She would dislike it even more now, thinking of Jeffery and the dangerous, yet exciting life he was leading.

Nevertheless, she said, 'There can be no future in going off with you, Jeffery, as well you know. One day you're going to be caught. You'll either hang or be transported. What would I do then?'

'By the time that happened you'd have enough money put by to set yourself up in a little business – or perhaps a grog shop, whatever suited you best.'

'If I went off with you it would be because I wanted *you*, not your money.'

He grinned in the darkness. 'Come away with me and you can have me *and* my money.'

'Only until they catch up with you – and they will, one day.'

'There'd be less chance of being caught if you were working with me, Thomasina. Think about it. If after I'd held someone up, you were hiding nearby with a change of clothes and another horse, we could ride off together and no one would even think of stopping us. They'd be looking for a highwayman, not a respectable couple of travellers.'

'If they ever caught up with us then we'd *both* hang. That doesn't bother you, I suppose?'

'I wouldn't let them catch you, Thomasina, even if it cost me my own life. I promise you that.'

She shuddered. 'I'd rather we didn't talk about it – and I'd better be on my way now. I'll be in trouble as it is from Eliza Mudge. She told me to be back at the house by nightfall. It's been dark for almost an hour now.'

She was aware that Jeffery was disappointed because she would not go off with him, but she thought it a stupid idea – albeit an exciting one.

As they approached Trebene House, Thomasina said she would walk the remainder of the way, just in case they met up with one of the family. She would need to make some awkward explanations if she was seen sharing a horse with an apparent 'gentleman'.

Jeffery did not dismount. Standing beside his horse, she looked up and said, 'Will I see you again soon?'

'Do you want to?'

'Of course I do! Will you still be in Cornwall next Sunday?'

'I might be.'

She realised he was sulking because she had not seriously considered the suggestion that she should go away with him. She dared not let him know just how tempted she was by the idea.

'If you are, I'll be free for the remainder of the day after the morning church service. I could walk along the Tregony road and you could be waiting for me somewhere along the way.'

'If I'm around I might be there.'

'You will,' she said confidently, laying her head against his leg. 'You want to see me as much as I want to see you. Take care, Jeffery – and don't do anything foolish.'

Turning to walk away, she suddenly stopped. Calling back softly, she asked, 'If I want you for any reason before then, where can I find you?'

'If I'm still in Cornwall you'll find me at the Heron Inn at Malpas, close to Truro. It's a comfortable, out-of-the-way inn where a man can come and go without any questions being asked of him. Do you think you're likely to come looking for me, Thomasina?'

'Who knows? It wouldn't be difficult to fall out with the Vincents. There's no telling what I might do then.'

6

Asking Jeffery where he was staying had been prompted by no more than curiosity on Thomasina's part, but the events of the next few days would make her thankful she had asked the question of him.

On the Wednesday after Thomasina's visit to her former home, the servants at Trebene were called together by the housekeeper before they sat down to their breakfast. This was to be a very special day in the Vincent household. One for which plans had been laid for many months. It was the ruby wedding of Henry and Harriet Vincent and to celebrate it there was to be a grand ball at Trebene.

It was an exciting occasion for the family – and also for the servants, especially the young, unmarried girls. The carriages of the gentry would be arriving all day, bringing friends and acquaintances of the Vincents.

With them would be coachmen, grooms and perhaps

one or two footmen. There was speculation, too, among the men-servants about the numbers of ladies' maids who would accompany their mistresses, to ensure they looked their best for the evening ball.

Such occasions served as 'marriage markets' for all strata of rural society. It also provided an opportunity for those who did not have marriage in mind to flirt with members of the opposite sex.

At the gathering of household staff, called by Eliza Mudge, the servants were warned about the possible consequences of forming hasty liaisons with the servants of guests. It was one thing to fall pregnant by one of the Trebene men-servants. Many marriages had begun in such a fashion. It was quite another to bring a man to the altar when he lived many miles away and would probably deny responsibility for the condition of a girl he had met only once.

The Trebene servants were also reminded that the esteem in which the Vincent family was held in Cornwwall would suffer if they – each and every one of them – did not work hard to ensure that the ball was hailed by the country's gentry as a great success.

When Eliza Mudge was certain each servant had been made aware of the pitfalls of the day, she allocated them their duties.

Thomasina was given the lowly task of ensuring the fires in the bedrooms along each side of a long corridor were kept alight, coal-scuttles replenished and hearths kept clean. She was also to ensure that wash-basins were emptied and cleaned and water jugs kept filled at all times.

Such heavy carrying was usually delegated to a footman but, as Eliza Mudge explained, all the footmen would be employed on ground-floor duties beyond the capabilities of an inexperienced housemaid.

Thomasina's duties meant she would see little of the splendour of the ball. Nor would she meet any of the men-servants from the other country houses.

Neither omission bothered her too much, but the smirks on the faces of the other servants when her duties were given to her showed that they, at least, thought it would.

The evening was particularly busy for Thomasina. She hurried hither and thither fetching hot and cold water for guests as they prepared themselves for the evening's celebrations.

Most would be returning to their own homes when the ball ended, but some would remain at the house until the following day.

Although large, Trebene did not possess unlimited resources and many of the unmarried young guests were required to share a room with others. This put an additional burden on Thomasina and the other housemaids.

Two of the men sharing a room along Thomasina's corridor were Sir Charles Hearle and Francis Vincent, who was home from university for his parents' wedding anniversary.

Despite their reputed dislike for each other, both had given up their own, larger rooms in order that more guests might be accommodated on this special occasion.

When Thomasina went into their room to make up

the fire, only Sir Charles was there. He said nothing to her, but she was aware he was watching her movements closely. It gave her an uncomfortable feeling. She was glad that other guests were constantly passing along the corridor outside.

Once the ball began and the guests had left their rooms, her duties became far less onerous. There were still fires to be made up, water jugs to be filled and rooms to be tidied, but she could take her time now. The ball would not end until the early hours of the next morning.

She even had time to snatch something to eat from the kitchen, despite the frenzy of activity there.

By midnight Thomasina was feeling the effects of the long working day. There was little to do now except occasionally check the rooms and clean up any cinders from the grate.

Making one of her routine checks, she entered the room occupied by Francis Vincent and his titled cousin. She was startled to find Sir Charles Hearle there. He was standing in front of the fire wearing a dressing-gown. A pair of pantaloons lay crumpled on the floor close by the fire.

Backing away towards the door, Thomasina said, 'I'm sorry, sir. I didn't realise you were in here. I'll come back later.'

'No, you won't, I need you.'

His speech was slurred, as it had been on their first meeting, and Thomasina realised he had been drinking heavily during the evening.

Bending down, he picked up his crumpled pantaloons. As he straightened up he temporarily lost his balance and took a shaky half-pace forward. Recovering, he said, 'Some damned fool of a young woman spilled half a jug of cold water over my pantaloons. Look . . . they're soaked!'

Although she tried to appear suitably sympathetic, Thomasina wondered whether it might have been a deliberate act, but Sir Charles was still speaking. 'This isn't my usual room and I have no other pantaloons here. It's inconvenient, to say the least.'

Thrusting the offending item of clothing at her, he said, 'Iron these for me, then bring them back here – and be damned quick about it, you hear?'

Taking the pantaloons, Thomasina backed away from him. 'I'll be as quick as I can, sir, but it'll take a little while to find an iron and heat it. Everyone's busy and there's too much going on in the kitchen to have an iron anywhere near the fire there.'

'I don't want to hear any stupid excuses, girl.' Suddenly lunging across the room, he took back the pantaloons from her. 'Go off and find an iron and bring it back here. You can use this fire to heat the iron. While you're gone I'll stir some life into it.'

As Thomasina had anticipated, she could find no one in the kitchen with time to tell her what she should do. It was left to the Vincents' cook, the busiest servant there, to say, 'You'll find what you want in the ironing-room, girl. Next to the laundry – it's back there.'

She pointed to a door which led to the many utility rooms at the back of the house.

Thomasina had not known there was a separate

ironing-room at Trebene, but she did have an idea where the laundry was situated.

The ironing-room had shelves on one wall, on which was a confusing array of flat-irons. There was a special fireplace here too, with hobs to hold the irons while they were being heated, but it seemed that this was the one room in the whole of the house where a fire was *not* burning.

Choosing a middle-weight iron, Thomasina hurried back upstairs. She found Sir Charles Hearle pacing the bedroom impatiently.

'You've taken your time,' he grumbled, unreasonably. 'Get the iron heated and press these pantaloons dry – and quickly.'

Thomasina placed the iron on the small hob fitted to the fire. While it was heating, she put the damp pantaloons over the back of a chair, moving it close to the fire. She then laid a towel on the marble top of the wash-table. She would iron the pantaloons here.

As she hurried back and forth between fire and wash-table, she was aware that Sir Charles was watching her every movement. It made her increasingly uneasy.

The iron did not take long to heat and she set about the unexpected task. She was quite used to ironing, but never anything as fine as Sir Charles Hearle's pantaloons.

At last she put the iron to one side and handed the garment to him. She was greatly relieved she had not scorched them.

'What's your name, girl?' Charles Hearle put the question to Thomasina as she prepared to leave the room.

'Ethel, sir.'

'Ethel, eh? I don't care for the name. It's not the name for a pretty girl – and you are a damned pretty girl, Ethel, but I'm sure you've been told that many times before, eh?'

Thomasina had reached the door and was about to open it when Sir Charles hurried across the room and leaned against it. 'Don't go just yet, girl. Stay and talk to me a while. No, better still, have a drink with me. It's the least I can do. I appreciate a servant girl who's prepared to go beyond the call of duty to please those for whom she works.'

Sir Charles Hearle's drunken leer left Thomasina in no doubt about what he meant by going 'beyond the call of duty'. She had other ideas. She had already seen the half-empty bottle of brandy on a bedside table. Harriet Vincent's nephew was amorously drunk.

'I must get back to work, sir. Mrs Mudge will be here soon to make certain I'm working.'

'Nonsense, girl! She's far too busy downstairs to worry herself about anything that's happening anywhere else in the house. Besides, everyone is enjoying themselves, so why shouldn't you have a little fun too, eh? You and me.'

Putting an arm about her shoulders, he began leading her across the room towards the bottle – and the bed. 'Come along, Ethel, you'll feel more relaxed when you've had a drink.'

'All right, thank you, sir.' Thomasina knew she could not match his strength, so she decided to resort to subterfuge.

'Good girl! I knew I hadn't misjudged you. Shall we now . . . ? Or would you like a drink first?'

'Yes, please. A large one.'

'That's my girl!' Releasing his hold on her, Sir Charles picked up the bottle. Clumsily he began to remove the cork.

This was the opportunity Thomasina had anticipated. She ran for the door. Yet again, Sir Charles Hearle foiled her. Moving surprisingly swiftly, he forced the door shut once more, before she could escape from the room.

'I thought you changed your tune a little too quickly. It was a good try, girl, and I do like a woman with some spirit. We're going to get on well, you and I. Come on, over to the bed.'

He had an arm about her again, while his other hand gripped her forearm. She began to struggle now, but he gripped her even harder.

Wriggling in his grasp, Thomasina suddenly found the side of his face against hers. Turning her head sharply, she gripped his ear between her teeth and bit him – hard.

She tasted blood on her tongue as he shrieked in pain. Releasing her, he reached up to her face to push her away, at the same time crying, 'You little bitch! You'll pay for this . . .'

Thomasina turned to run for the door, but Sir Charles recovered far more quickly than she had anticipated. He hit her on the back of her head with his clenched fist, causing her to stumble and fall to her knees.

Before she could rise, he dropped on her and twisted

one of her arms, forcing her down to the floor, on her back.

He continued twisting and she cried out in pain. Then, as he lay on top of her, she tried to bite him once more, but in the struggle his head came down sharply, striking her on the forehead with considerable force.

Afterwards, Thomasina was not certain whether or not she had been knocked unconscious for a while. She was certainly dazed and it was long enough for the drunken baronet to achieve his aim.

She felt him force his way inside her and opened her mouth to scream, but the sound was cut off by his free hand. She tried to throw him off her, but, quickly realising that the movement of her body only excited him further, she attempted to prevent her body from responding to what he was doing to her – and hated Sir Charles Hearle all the more because of it.

The ordeal lasted no more than a few minutes, although it seemed much longer.

It ended almost as violently as it had begun. Then he sagged, a dead weight on top of her, and now she was able to push him from her without any resistence on his part.

This time she made it to the door and fled along the long corridor, heading for the servants' quarter.

She returned to work later that night, but did not go near Sir Charles Hearle's room again and had no idea if he ever returned to the ball.

A fierce hatred for the baronet burned inside her with an all-consuming intensity, but, as with the loss of her father, she succeeded in pulling down a shutter that set it apart from reality.

She would never forget what he had done – and certainly never, ever forgive him. But life would go on.

7

It was a decidedly jaded Charles Hearle who tackled his aunt the morning after the grand ball. It did not help that Harriet Vincent, who could not have had more than a couple of hours' sleep, appeared to be her usual immaculate self.

Looking at him critically as he entered the breakfast-room, she said, 'Well! If I thought all my guests were going to look like you this morning, I would cancel breakfast. You look absolutely *awful*!' Leaning forward to peer at him more closely, she asked, 'What have you done to your ear? You have a very nasty wound there.'

Sir Charles put a hand up to his ear, guiltily. 'I went out in the garden in the dark last night and became entangled in one of those climbing roses of yours.'

'It looks painful. You should have Mrs Mudge put something on it for you.'

'I'll think about that later. I have come down early to speak to you about something of rather more importance than a scratched ear, Aunt Harriet. I very much fear that one of the maids is a thief.'

Harriet Vincent looked at her nephew sharply. 'That is a very serious accusation to make, Charles. I think you had better tell me about it. Who is the girl in question?'

'I can't remember her name – to be quite honest I can't even recall her face, but she was working in my room last night.'

Frowning, Harriet Vincent tried to remember the arrangements that had been made for the ball.

'I think it might have been Ethel. A new girl – and not local. She was recommended to me by Parson Trist, and had some ridiculous name when she came to me. Quite unsuitable for a servant. I said that she was to be called Ethel. She has not proved entirely satisfactory, but are you saying she's dishonest? What do you think she has stolen?'

'Two guineas, Aunt. I had an accident at the ball last night. Water was spilled over my pantaloons. I went up to my room, found this maid there and asked her to iron the pantaloons dry. She did so, but when she'd gone and I went to return the items I had taken from my pockets, two guineas were missing.'

'Are you absolutely certain, Charles? This is an extremely serious matter for such a young girl.'

'I am quite certain, Aunt Harriet. I took the two guineas from my pocket, but when I went to return them, they had gone.'

Walking to the bell-pull in a corner of the room,

Harriet Vincent gave it a tug. 'I think we should speak to Mrs Mudge about this.'

When the housekeeper came into the room, Harriet Vincent had her nephew repeat his accusation.

Eliza Mudge looked sceptical. 'The girl doesn't really fit in with the other servants, ma'am, but I've never had cause to call her honesty into question. Shall I send for her now and see what she has to say?'

'Not yet. Take one of the senior maids with you and search her room. If you find nothing, you will search the girl's person. If you still find nothing, we will discuss the matter again and decide what to do next.'

The search was brief. Less than five minutes after leaving the morning-room, Eliza Mudge returned, grim-faced, holding something clenched in her hand. When she opened it out to show her employer, two guinea coins were nestling in her palm.

'I found these in a drawer in her room, ma'am. No attempt had been made to hide them. Shall I have one of the footmen go and fetch the constable?'

'No!'

Sir Charles spoke more loudly than he had intended. When both women turned towards him he said, pale-faced, 'What will happen to this girl if she is taken before a court and found guilty? What will they do to her?'

'That need concern none of us. She's a thief and the law will deal with her as she deserves.'

'If she is found guilty the court will sentence her to hang, Aunt Harriet. You know the girl, she's been working here, in your house. Would you have her put to death for a mere two guineas?'

'Her fate is of her own making,' said his aunt unfeelingly. 'The girl is dishonest. I have no doubt she is fully aware of the consequences of her act.'

Eliza Mudge was looking at Sir Charles Hearle with a quizzical expression on her face. It was out of character for him to have any regard for others. Fully aware of his reputation with the female staff, she felt there was more to his concern than the fate of a dishonest housemaid.

'I'm damned if I'll see a young girl hanged for two guineas. I have my money back, I'll lodge no complaint with a magistrate.'

Harriet Vincent looked at him contemptuously. 'You disappoint me, Charles. I had thought you favoured my side of the family, but it seems you have inherited the feebleness of your father. Well, whatever action *you* take, the girl will not remain in my house for another hour. Mrs Mudge, bring her here, if you please.'

'Yes, ma'am. Right away.' With a final speculative glance at Sir Charles, Eliza Mudge hurried from the room.

The housekeeper was badly shaken. She did not particularly like Thomasina and felt that Harriet Vincent should have consulted her before taking on a new housemaid. Nevertheless, knowing how close Thomasina had come to a hangman's rope horrified her. It was too dreadful to contemplate. She felt more strongly than ever that Sir Charles had not told the full story of all that had happened in his room the previous evening.

*   *   *

Thomasina was that morning cleaning and tidying the rooms for which she was responsible in the normal household routine. She was making up the bed just vacated by two house guests who had left the room to go in search of breakfast.

She was still in a state of considerable shock as a result of what had happened to her the previous night. She felt sickened and dirty, and doubted whether she would ever feel clean again. Nevertheless, she automatically speeded up her work when Eliza Mudge entered the room.

'You can stop that and come with me.'

The tone of the housekeeper's voice made it clear to Thomasina that this was more than a temporary change of duties.

'What is it, Mrs Mudge? Is there something I've forgotten to do?'

'Yes. To keep your hands off other folk's property, it would seem.'

The housekeeper adopted an expression of thin-lipped disapproval. 'Come with me. Mrs Vincent wants a word with you – although why she should want to waste her breath on the likes of you, I don't know.'

As they hurried along the passageway from the room, Eliza Mudge went on, 'You're lucky you're not being taken straight before the magistrate, young girl – but perhaps there's something you'd like to tell me about what's been happening? Something that might have happened last evening?'

Thomasina's stomach contracted in sudden fear, but she said nothing and the housekeeper continued,

'We've never had a thief in this house, not in all the thirty-odd years I've lived and worked here.'

Hurrying to keep up with the older woman, a bewildered and frightened Thomasina asked, 'But . . . what am I supposed to have stolen?'

'There's nothing "supposed" about it,' snapped the housekeeper grimly. 'I found the proof myself. Proof enough to have you hanged, had Sir Charles decided to press charges against you.'

While she was speaking, Eliza was looking at Thomasina to gauge her reaction. What she saw confirmed her earlier suspicions even before Thomasina spoke again.

'The only thing I took from Sir Charles was a little blood from his ear when he attacked me last night, in his room.' Bitterly she added, 'Had there been a knife to hand, it would have been more than his ear.'

It was as Eliza had thought. However, there was still the matter of the money she had found in Thomasina's room and she had a word of caution for her.

'You'd do well to be careful what you say about Sir Charles – especially to the mistress. If she was to persuade him to change his mind and have you arrested, you'd hang, for certain.'

Thomasina looked aghast at the housekeeper. She did not doubt that this whole incident had to do with what had occurred in Sir Charles Hearle's room the previous evening. But she had stolen nothing. This must be his way of getting rid of her. She should, perhaps, be grateful that he had stopped short of having her hanged – but gratitude was not an emotion that immediately sprang to mind.

By now they had reached the morning-room. When they entered, Harriet Vincent was alone, Sir Charles having refused to remain in the room until Thomasina arrived.

The mistress of Trebene came straight to the point. 'My nephew tells me you stole money from his room last night . . .' She held out the two dull-gold sovereigns. 'These were found in your room. Can you tell me where you obtained them?'

'They're mine . . .' Even as she spoke, Thomasina was remembering who had given them to her and how he had come by them. '. . . they were given to me.'

Harriet Vincent raised an eyebrow. 'Can you tell me the name of the person who gave them to you?'

When Thomasina remained silent, the mistress of Trebene said scornfully, 'Of course you can't. You are not only a thief, Ethel, you are a liar too. If I had my way, you would be taken before a magistrate and suffer the fate you deserve. However, my nephew feels he cannot have your execution upon his conscience. Needless to say, I do not agree with him. I feel that you should be punished as you deserve. Be that as it may, I want you out of this house immediately. You will gather your belongings and be gone by the time breakfast is over. Do you understand?'

'Yes, but . . .' Thomasina was trying to put on a brave front for this woman, but was finding it difficult, '. . . the two guineas – they're mine.'

'Such impertinence! You will leave this house immediately, or I will ignore my nephew's wishes and have you charged. Mrs Mudge, take her away –

and do not leave her side until she is out of this house. We do not want anything else to be stolen.'

Breakfast for the Vincent family and their guests was a somewhat subdued affair until Francis Vincent entered the breakfast-room.

Unaware of the atmosphere that prevailed, he made for the end of the table where Sir Charles was picking at his food next to his stern-faced aunt.

Taking a seat, he said cheerfully, 'You must have had a very good night at the ball, Charles.'

'Why do you say that?' Sir Charles reacted guiltily.

'Well, you'd obviously been throwing your money around. I knew you'd had more than enough to drink when you had to return to the room to change your pantaloons. Then, when I went to bed, I found two sovereigns beside my slippers. You must have dropped them when you changed, but you were nowhere to be found, so I kept them for you until this morning . . .'

Suddenly aware of the looks that both his aunt and Sir Charles were giving him, he said, 'What's the matter? Have I said something . . . ?'

8

The small bundle that Thomasina carried away with her from Trebene House contained all her worldly possessions and was no larger than the one she had taken to the house only a few weeks before.

The only extra thing she now possessed was a smouldering resentment against the Vincent family in general – and a burning hatred for Sir Charles Hearle.

There was no doubt in her mind that he had deliberately engineered her dismissal, either because he felt guilty or, more probably, because he wanted her out of the way in case she said anything about what had occurred.

She was also angry with Harriet Vincent for taking her two guineas. Then she managed a wry smile as she realised just how unreasonable her anger was over this particular aspect of her dismissal. The money given to her by Jeffery had been stolen from Henry Vincent and the two guests travelling with him.

Thomasina was forced to admit to herself that there was a certain wry justice in the whole affair. However, it did not lessen the very deep bitterness she felt towards Sir Charles Hearle for what he had done to her.

Then she began to wonder what life held in store for her now. She could not return to her old home. The revelation that she had been dismissed for dishonesty would shock Aunt Mary beyond belief. She would take the shame of it upon herself, but would never allow her niece to forget that she was the cause of it.

There was a moment of conscience when Thomasina thought that her aunt would already mentally have spent the money she should have earned at Trebene House. Then she consoled herself with the knowledge that the half of Jeffery's gift she had already given to Aunt Mary represented eight months of the wages she would have received from Harriet Vincent.

Thomasina was now heading for Truro, in the hope that Jeffery was still at the Heron Inn at Malpas. He might be able to help her. If he was not there, she did not know what she would do. She had only two shillings in her possession – all that was left over from her previous month's wages.

She had been owed more than a week's wages by Harriet Vincent, but in the circumstances she had felt it would not have been prudent to ask for it!

It was a long walk to Truro, but not unpleasant. The day was fine and time passed more quickly when she fell in with an itinerant fiddle-player. He called himself Ulysses Smith, although he admitted to her along the way that Ulysses was not his true name, adding, 'My real name is Joe, but tavern keepers wouldn't give work to a fiddle-player named Joe Smith. It sounds too much like a gipsy name. I've had much more work since I began calling myself Ulysses.'

In answer to Thomasina's question, 'Ulysses' replied that he had taken the name from a play put on by a troupe of actors he had once travelled with. He also informed her that he was now on his way to earn some money in the Truro taverns.

He was not much older than Thomasina, but she doubted whether he would enjoy his new-found success for very long. Slightly built and bowed over as he walked, Ulysses had a cough that suggested he was suffering from a serious lung complaint.

However, the fiddler was an amusing companion and the long walk to Truro passed more quickly than it might otherwise have done. When they arrived at Truro town and parted company, Thomasina felt she had said goodbye to a friend.

The lane to Malpas ran alongside the Truro river. It was normally a very busy waterway, but the tide was low. Only a narrow channel remained, winding its tortuous way through a wide expanse of glistening, evil-smelling black mud.

A number of ships were settled in the mud on both sides of the river and cargoes were being unloaded, or carried on board. A number of seamen were taking advantage of the low tide to paint the sides of their vessels. Suspended on cradles, they were able to reach parts of the ship normally underwater.

Farther downriver the lane began to rise above the river bank. It was more wooded here too. Then, turning a bend in the lane, Thomasina saw the Heron Inn.

It was an ideal spot for a highwayman. She doubted very much whether any constable from Truro would put himself at risk by coming out here. It seemed too that most of the inn's business took place later in the day.

Thomasina had left Trebene House very early. It was now mid-morning, but there was little sign of life in and around the inn.

Ducking in through a low doorway, she found herself in a public room, the stone floor of which was being swabbed by an elderly pot-man who saw no urgency in the task he was performing, spending a great deal of time leaning upon the mop. Through a nearby open doorway Thomasina could hear the clatter of pots in what she took to be a kitchen.

When she asked about Jeffery, the pot-man said that he knew the names of none of the guests staying at the inn, preferring to mind his own business. The landlord was in the cellar, but would be up in a few minutes. She would need to speak to him.

The 'few minutes' stretched to twenty and when the heavily bearded landlord eventually entered the public room, he smelled very strongly of ale, much of it on his breath.

When she asked after Jeffery, the landlord shook his head. 'There's no one of that name staying here, Missie.

As far as I can recall, we've *never* had anyone of that name at the Heron Inn.'

Belatedly, Thomasina realised she had probably committed a serious error of judgement. Jeffery would not want his real name known here. She immediately tried to put things right.

'I must have got the story wrong. It's probably his friend who is staying here. I can't remember his name, but . . . She proceeded to give the landlord a full description of Jeffery and his dress, as she had last seen him.

Stroking his beard thoughtfully, the landlord said, 'That sounds like young Mr King. He's waiting here for his father's ship to come in from the West Indies, or somewhere out that way. But I haven't seen any friend with him – at least, not a *man*-friend.'

Choosing to ignore the implications of the landlord's statement, Thomasina said, 'No doubt he'll know where Jeffery can be found. Is Mr King in right now? Can I go up to his room?'

The landlord cast an eye over Thomasina. She looked highly respectable, dressed as might a maidservant on her day off. Not at all the type of young woman who usually frequented the Heron Inn.

'I expect he's in, but he hasn't been down yet. I'll send Albert upstairs to see if he's decent and tell him you're here. Who shall I say is wanting to see him?'

'Tell him it's Thomasina – I think he'll remember me,' she added, as an afterthought.

It transpired that Albert was the lethargic pot-man. After grumbling about not being left in peace to get on with his work, he could be heard stomping heavily up the wooden stairs which led to the first floor from the passageway outside.

'Can I get you something to drink while you're waiting?' asked the landlord.

Thomasina hesitated. She was hot and thirsty after her long walk from Trebene, but she was also remembering the state of her purse.

'I'll wait until Mr King comes down. If he has a drink, I'll have one with him – but for now I would be grateful for some water.'

The landlord grunted disapprovingly. 'It's a good job everyone else who comes to the inn drinks more than water. If they didn't, I'd soon go out of business.'

Pointing to an alcove, he said, 'Take a seat in there while you're waiting. I'll have water sent in to you.'

Gratefully Thomasina sank down into a wooden-armed chair in the alcove. Some minutes later she heard Albert coming heavily down the stairs and could follow the progress of his metal-studded boots on the flagstones of the passageway.

Entering the room, he looked about him, frowning, before he saw her. When he did, he said irritably, 'He'll be down in a few minutes – that's if he's got the strength left in him to climb out of bed.'

Making no attempt to explain his remark, Albert retrieved his mop and bucket and resumed his task.

Shortly afterwards a serving girl came from the kitchen carrying a jug of water and a mug. As she reached the alcove, Thomasina heard someone running down the stairs to the passageway outside.

Thinking it might be Jeffery, she rose to her feet, only

to sit down again, almost immediately. The footsteps were too light to be Jeffery's.

As the serving maid put the water down upon the table in front of Thomasina, a young girl hurried into the room. She too was dressed like a serving girl and was probably quite pretty.

However, at this moment she looked as though she had just woken up and dressed in a great hurry. Not all her buttons were fastened and her hair was dishevelled, her eyes bloodshot and the lids puffy.

The girl who had brought water for Thomasina rounded on the new arrival sharply. 'Where have you been? You should have started work an hour ago, helping me get the dining-room ready.'

'I overslept,' said the girl briefly. Belatedly she pulled the drawstring at the neck of her dress, tying it in a bid to hide at least some of her bosom.

The girl who had brought water to Thomasina made a sound that indicated disbelief. 'If you had more sleep and less of the other, you'd probably be able to get out of bed – whosoever's bed it might be – and get to work on time. I suggest you put a brush through your hair before you go and say you're here, but don't be long about it. There's already talk of taking someone else on in your place.'

The tardy serving girl disappeared through the kitchen door, making a futile attempt to smooth her hair with a hand. A few minutes later Thomasina heard heavier footsteps clattering down the stairs outside.

When Jeffery entered the room it was apparent to Thomasina that he had taken more care with his toilet than the girl who had no doubt been sharing a bed with him.

'Tom! What are you doing here?'

Aware that Albert was within hearing, she replied, 'I came here to see if you had any news of Jeffery. I'm sorry, I don't remember your first name from when we last met.'

For a moment, Jeffery was taken aback, but when her glance shifted meaningfully to Albert, he recovered quickly and followed the lead she had given him.

'My name is Jeremy, Jeremy King – but you're enquiring after Jeffery, you say? I've heard nothing from him for a while. But where are my manners? Would you care to have a drink with me?'

'Thank you, but I've just had a drink of water. As it's a fine day, why don't we take a walk along the river bank. You can tell me about the last time you saw Jeffery, and what you think his plans might be . . .'

9

As Thomasina and Jeffery walked together by the river bank, she told of her meeting with the landlord of the Heron Inn and the realisation that Jeffery had taken on a new identity.

'That was very astute of you,' said Jeffery approvingly. 'But then you were always brighter than most of the other Mevagissey girls.'

'Bright enough to realise that my coming here is likely to cause you some embarrassment, certainly,' commented Thomasina acidly. 'Perhaps you'd like to tell me about the girl who was in your bed when Albert came to tell you I was at the inn asking for you?'

Jeffery's immediate instinct was to disclaim all knowledge of the girl Thomasina had seen. He had actually opened his mouth to voice a protest when he saw the expression on her face. He realised that denial would be a waste of time.

'She doesn't mean anything to me, Tom, I promise you.'

'I didn't ask what she means to you. I want to know who she is.'

'Her name is Hebe. She's one of the serving girls at the inn. Yesterday was her birthday. The customers gave her a birthday celebration.'

'It seems that some gave her more than others,' retorted Thomasina. 'Or are you saying she slept with all the customers?'

'I'm saying only that it was her birthday and we all had more to drink than was good for us. She means nothing to me, Tom. You do – but you still haven't told me what you're doing here. Why aren't you at Trebene?'

Jeffery had not fully explained his involvement with Hebe to Thomasina's satisfaction, but she let the subject drop – for now. She had decided she would not tell him what Sir Charles had actually done to her, only that he had tried and that he had trumped up theft charges against her in revenge for the bite she had given him.

Jeffery was incensed. 'The money he took – was it what I had given to you?'

'Yes. I was very cross about it at first, but then I saw the funny side of it. I wonder what Mrs Vincent would have said, had she known it was stolen from her husband in the first place!'

'But she didn't know, although her nephew must have known it wasn't *his* money. He could very easily have had you hanged for something you hadn't done.'

'Doesn't it worry you that *you'll* probably end up

on the end of a hangman's rope?' Thomasina asked, grateful for an opportunity to move the conversation away from the reason for her dismissal from Trebene House.

Jeffery gave a nonchalant shrug. 'My pa spent his short life slaving his guts out catching fish. That's what he was doing when he died. During his working life, if the weather was kind for a week or two, he'd earn just about enough money for us to have food in our bellies, but there was nothing left for luxuries. If the weather was bad for more than a few days, we'd go hungry. Then there was my grandpa. He'd worked in the fields all his life, going out in all weathers. By the time he was forty he was crippled with rheumatism and couldn't work any more. He was in constant pain all the time I knew him, and what hurt him even more was knowing he was a liability to his family.'

It was an emotive subject for Jeffery. When he stopped talking he came to a halt, looking out over the river, away from her.

For a few minutes they stood together in silence, watching a mist-grey, stoop-backed heron, standing long-legged and motionless at the river's edge.

Aware that it was being watched, the bird eventually became unnerved and took off on long wings in ungainly flight, legs trailing as it flew downriver to find a more secluded spot in which to fish.

'The sort of life my pa led isn't for me, Tom,' Jeffery spoke again, more quietly now. 'One day I may have to dance the Tyburn jig for what I'm doing now, but before I do, I'll have enjoyed life as I never could if I'd stayed in Mevagissey.'

'I've no doubt there are plenty of girls like Hebe who are happy to help you spend your money and enjoy life,' commented Thomasina.

Jeffery looked only mildly embarrassed. 'Hebe's fun – but no more than that. I know it, and so does she.' Turning to her, he continued, 'You're the only one I've ever really cared about, Tom. I think you know that.'

'I thought I did. That's why I came here when I lost my job. Now I'm not so certain.'

'You *can* rely on me, Tom, I promise you, but now you're here we need to decide what we're going to do with you. Do you have anything in mind?'

'That depends.'

When she did not attempt to clarify her brief statement, he asked hesitantly, 'Depends on what, Thomasina?'

'On you and this . . . Hebe.'

'I've already told you, she means absolutely nothing to me. Nothing at all.'

'So you say – but does she know this?' Thomasina was not ready to offer him absolution just yet.

'It's never been more than a bit of fun. She knows that . . .' Jeffery was now suffering agonies of remorse. 'I really am sorry, Tom, but I thought – I thought you had given yourself up to a career as housemaid in the Vincent household. That you wouldn't want to be mixed up with someone like me.'

'You, of all people, should know me better than that, Jeffery. I couldn't spend the rest of my life curtseying and saying "Yes, sir" and "No, madam" every time they spoke to me. You and I have talked often enough about that sort of thing.'

'True, but lots of people say one thing yet do something different when it's time to act.'

'Do they? Is that why I've come here, when I know how it is you get your money?'

'I'm sorry, Tom,' said Jeffery dejectedly. 'But now you're here, what can I do to help you?'

'More to the point, what can I do to help *you*?'

Thomasina's question took Jeffery aback. 'What do you mean? You know what I am. There's no permanent place for a woman in the sort of life I'm leading.'

'Why not? I've been thinking about it while I was on my way here. When you rob someone you need to be far away before they report it to a constable or a magistrate – and that isn't always easy. You said so yourself, the last time we met.'

'Yes . . . but there's nothing that can be done about that. A highwayman needs to be miles away, before a "hue and cry" is raised. Anything else would be too risky – whatever I said to you before.'

'Not necessarily. In fact, it means you can usually rob only those who are miles away from their homes. For that very reason they'll not be carrying anything of real value. What if we were to hold up those who are in towns, or so close to their homes that they don't even consider the possibility that they might be robbed?'

'It wouldn't work, Thomasina. They'd be able to set up an immediate hue and cry. I'd most likely be arrested before I could get clear of the area.'

'Not if I was helping you. Waiting somewhere nearby? You could rob someone, then come to where I was hiding. We'd swap horses, then ride off together as though we were a gent and a lady. You've said yourself it would work – and it *would*. They'd be looking for a *man* on a particular type of horse. They wouldn't think of looking at the horse *I* was riding. I could even help you in a hold-up, sometimes. Dressed as a man. My pa taught me to shoot when we were out on the boat. I'm better than most men with a gun. We could leave the horses hidden somewhere, carry out the robbery on foot, then go back to the horses. I'd change clothes and suddenly we'd be a respectable couple. While we rode off they'd be looking for two men.'

Jeffery was doubtful. 'I don't know, Thomasina. I know I suggested it, but I can't think of anything like it having been done before.'

'Exactly! That's why it would work. Nobody's done it before, so they wouldn't be expecting it.'

Jeffery was still uncertain. 'I'll need to think about it . . .'

'Oh? And what will I do while you're making up your mind?'

'Why, stay at the Heron, of course. Alf, the landlord, will be only too glad to find you a room. He provides clean linen, good food and stands for no nonsense. Mind you, it gets a bit rowdy when a smugglers' boat comes in – and that seems to have been most nights, just lately.'

'I can think of two snags with that idea. One, I've no money to pay for a room. Two, I have no intention of having a dispute with a certain Hebe about who's sleeping where.'

Jeffery looked embarrassed. 'I keep telling you, Thomasina, Hebe means nothing to me.'

'As I said before, are you quite certain *she* knows that?'

'Of course. You'll see, she's as friendly with every-one who comes to the Heron.'

'You mean . . . she's a whore?' said Thomasina scathingly. 'Perhaps I've made a mistake in suggest-ing we should work together. A highwayman who spends his time with whores isn't going to last very long. Whores talk to whoever they go to bed with, be they highwaymen, smugglers, revenue men – or constables. I'm not prepared to risk my neck with such a man. I was probably wrong to come here in the first place. Perhaps I should go back to Aunt Mary, say I'm sorry and find work in Mevagissey. Yes, that's what I'll do.'

'Now, don't be hasty, Thomasina. I've told you that Hebe means nothing to me – what more do you want? Besides, if you're staying at the Heron, I'll have no need to look at anyone else, will I now?'

'No,' agreed Thomasina, 'but will that stop you? It never has in the past.'

'Thomasina, you're worth more than all the girls I've ever known put together. Stay here with me and I promise I'll never, ever look at another girl.'

'And you'll put my idea to the test?' Thomasina asked. 'We'll work together?'

Jeffery hesitated, but when he saw her expression harden, he said hastily, 'All right. We'll give it a try – after I've thought about it – but if it doesn't work we'll talk about it again. Is that a deal?'

Thomasina nodded, 'All right, it's a deal.'

'That's wonderful!' Jeffery could hardly hide his

relief. 'Now, let's go back to the Heron. We'll book you into a room, then I'll buy you a lunch that will be like nothing you've ever had before. You'll not regret coming to Malpas to find me, Tom. I promise you . . .'

10

The first robbery carried out by Thomasina and Jeffery together took place on a road just outside Truro. While she waited in a nearby copse, her heart beating at an alarming rate, Jeffery held up a light carriage belonging to Rector Wheeler, whose church was at nearby Ladock.

The reverend gentleman protested indignantly about a man of the cloth being held up in such a fashion, promising eternal damnation for Jeffery's soul. There was a markedly more secular tone to his protest when Jeffery forced him to hand over his heavy purse.

The rector was returning from market, where he had that day sold a number of milking cows, grown fat on the pasture acquired from a local farmer who had defaulted on his tithe payments.

Chiding the rector for his unclerical language, Jeffery gave the victim's horse a resounding whack on the rump and stood back as horse, carriage and angry rector disappeared into the night.

The amount taken that evening was the largest purse Jeffery had ever stolen. It remained so even when he had passed on half the takings to Thomasina.

Declaring that Thomasina had brought him renewed luck, Jeffery forecast a happy and profitable partnership for their illegal venture.

The next purse was also a heavy one. This time it was taken from a drunken farmer, also returning from market. However, on this occasion Jeffery had to discharge a pistol before his victim was persuaded to part with his money.

The shot attracted the attention of a party of militiamen returning from a duty parade. Had Thomasina not been waiting in a nearby copse and able to join Jeffery before the arrival of the part-time soldiers, he would most likely have been taken.

As it was, they were clear of the shouting farmer before the militiamen arrived on the scene. Not suspected of any involvement in the robbery, they were able to take a leisurely ride to the Heron Inn and, once there, were safe from any pursuit.

Thomasina's first impression of the Heron Inn had been that of a tranquil rural tavern, tucked away at the end of a quiet country lane. The reality was very different.

When darkness fell men flocked to the Heron Inn, for all the world like bats emerging from caves at sunset and congregating at a feeding ground. The inn was then a busy, lively place until well into the early hours of the morning.

Thomasina had taken a room next to that occupied by Jeffery, paid for by him. It was an open secret among the inn staff that she rarely used it, choosing instead to share the bed of 'Jeremy King'. It mattered little to anyone at the inn – except, perhaps, Hebe, the serving girl.

Despite Jeffery's assertion that she had never meant anything to him, Thomasina was aware of the other girl's smouldering resentment towards her whenever the two girls met. Nevertheless, Thomasina was a paying guest and Hebe a servant girl whose own conduct made her employment at the inn less than secure, so she caused no serious trouble. Besides, Hebe did not lack suitors among the inn's late-night customers.

Many of the men who came to the Heron Inn after dark were smugglers; others were their customers. Evading the Customs men downriver at Falmouth, the smugglers' boats would ride the tide to Malpas. If there was insufficient tide left for them to arrive at the inn before daylight, or if the Customs men were active on the river, they would hide their boats. There were a great many remote creeks to provide hiding places or, if the boat was not too large, it could be safely tucked beneath the overhanging branches of one of the many trees bordering the river.

Much money changed hands at the inn, but such traders and smugglers remained safe from the night-time activities of Jeffery and Thomasina. The Heron Inn was an invaluable refuge. They would not put it at risk when there were rich pickings to be had elsewhere.

*   *   *

After their close brush with the militia, Jeffery and Thomasina lay low for some days. Then they both felt the time was ripe for Thomasina's first active involvement in highway robbery.

Although they had been lucky with their victims, so far, Jeffery felt it might be safer – and more profitable – if they could select their intended victim *before* the event.

With this in mind, when another market day came around Jeffery took Thomasina to dine at one of the most popular hostelries in Truro.

At first, she was anxious lest she meet up with friends of her late employers, but Jeffery persuaded her that she had no cause for concern. Even if she *were* to be seen by anyone who had met her at Trebene House, it was doubtful whether they would recognise her now.

The proceeds of Jeffery's two most recent robberies had provided Thomasina with sufficient money to purchase clothes that would not have disgraced a young woman of considerable means.

Jeffery had chosen this particular hostelry because it was frequented by gentlemen farmers and others who had been to the market that day. He and Thomasina intended enjoying a meal surrounded by such men, listening to their conversations and choosing a prospective victim.

The choice was made surprisingly easy for them. Seated at a table not too far away was a red-faced, heavily perspiring farmer whose voice became progressively louder as more and more drink was consumed by him and his friends.

Careful to give no sign that they were listening with great interest, Jeffery and Thomasina learned that the farmer intended retiring and was in the process of selling up his farm. With this in mind, his men had brought a herd of milking cows to market. Their sale had fetched more than two hundred guineas for him.

'That's a handsome sum indeed,' said one of his companions, suitably impressed. 'Your banker will have been pleased to see you today.'

'Bankers!' The farmer spat out the word, disdainfully. 'I've got no time for such men.' Patting a bulging pocket in the waistcoat distended across his ample belly, he added, 'I like to know where my money is. I'll not put it in the hands of them as takes other men's money, only to spread their hands wide one day and say it's all gone – claiming they don't for the life of 'em know where to.'

A local bank had recently gone into bankruptcy and the men about the farmer's table nodded their agreement with his sentiments.

'All the same, you be careful on your way home, Howard,' warned another of them. 'There's word that a highwayman's been at work around Truro in recent weeks.'

'That don't bother me none,' said the farmer, boastfully. 'Truro men have always been parted from their money a sight easier than us folks from Probus. A highwayman wouldn't find me such easy pickings. Besides, one of my men is coming to pick me up in my chaise soon. Come on, gentlemen, let's have another drink. Now my cows have gone, I don't have to get up early tomorrow to make certain the milking's being done properly . . .'

'I think we've found our man,' said Jeffery, the softness of his voice hiding the excitement he was feeling.

'What about the man who's coming to fetch him?' Thomasina voiced her misgivings equally quietly.

'It evens things up, but we'll be more than a match for them. You finish off your meal while I settle the bill. We know which way they'll be heading – but you'll need to be a man by the time they take to the road.'

There was a full set of men's clothing in the saddle bag of Thomasina's horse, which had been left saddled in the stables behind the hostelry. There were also four loaded pistols in the same bag. Two for Jeffery and two for herself.

The saddle itself was Jeffery's own brainchild. Made by a saddler who worked in a village ten miles from the Cornish capital, it was ostensibly a normal saddle for a male rider. However, by detaching the right stirrup and screwing in a specially adapted, padded leather attachment – the work of no more than a minute – it was converted to a temporary, albeit somewhat uncomfortable and insecure, side-saddle.

When the bill was settled, the two made their way to the rear of the building. On the way Jeffery outlined a decidedly sketchy 'plan' of action. They would retrieve the horses and make their way to the edge of town. There, in the darkness, Thomasina would change into the clothing of a man. They would then return to town once more and wait in the shadows within sight of the hotel for the money-laden farmer to leave.

Thanks to the farmer's indiscreet boasting, they knew where he lived. Once he came out of the hotel they would hurry off and waylay him on the Probus road.

When the robbery had taken place, Thomasina would once more change into women's clothing and they would ride back into Truro together and make their way to the sanctuary of the Heron Inn.

The farmer was in no hurry to break off his celebrations and make his way home. A light chaise with a farm labourer holding the reins was standing outside the hostelry door when Thomasina and Jeffery returned to the town, but it was a full hour before the farmer left, supported by two of his friends.

Helped upon the vehicle, the farmer sat slumped in his seat while the farmhand climbed up beside him and flicked the reins to set the horse in motion.

Thomasina and Jeffery were waiting beneath a wide-spreading oak tree on the edge of town when the chaise left the houses behind and trundled along the Probus road. It was not travelling fast, the farmworker fearing that his employer might fall from the vehicle if they dropped into a pothole at any speed.

Frustratingly for the two would-be robbers, a farmer mounted on a cart-horse left town at the same time as the chaise and kept pace with it for almost a mile. Not until the unknown farmer had turned off along a farm track did Jeffery and Thomasina canter past the chaise.

The road led downhill to a narrow bridge. Here it levelled off – and this was where they decided they would waylay the farmer.

With Thomasina a shadowy figure in the background, Jeffery kneed his horse to the centre of the bridge and called upon the driver to bring the chaise to a halt. The farmworker obeyed the command immediately, the suddenness of the stop causing his drunken employer to fall forward.

Saved only by a light rail from tumbling to the ground, the farmer began cursing his worker. Then he saw Jeffery.

'What d'you think you're doing, stopping us like that? You might have caused an accident. Get out of the way.' He spoke belligerently, unaware that Jeffery had deliberately brought the chaise to a halt.

'My friend and I will be on our way when you've handed over your purse, sir. Be kind enough to oblige without causing us any trouble.'

Struggling to gather his wits about him, the farmer said, 'I'm damned if I will! That's money for my retirement. I'll not give it to any thieving rogue.'

Raising his pistol, Jeffery said, 'Then I'll have to take it, sir, and I fear your retirement will be short-lived.'

Thomasina sucked in her breath, but the chaise driver said, 'Give him your purse, Mr Dainty. It's not worth dying for, no matter how much is in it.'

'It's not your money, so you can shut up . . .'

While the farmer was remonstrating drunkenly and foolishly with his employee, Jeffery brought his horse in close. Leaning forward now, he raised his heavy pistol and brought it down hard on the side of the farmer's head.

The farmer slipped off the seat and lay half-hanging out of the chaise.

'There were no need for that,' said the farmworker. 'I'd have got him to give it to you, without you needing to hit him.'

'Shut up and find his purse for me – and hurry, I'm getting angry and that causes my finger to twitch on the trigger of my pistol.'

The farmworker was concerned for his employer – but even more concerned for his own life. He knew where the farmer kept his purse and less than a minute later had found it and thrown it to Jeffery.

Unfortunately, the man was nervous. The purse fell short and dropped to the road with a heavy thud. Cursing the clumsy farmworker, Jeffery swung down from the saddle and felt around on the ground for the purse.

He did not find it immediately and, while he was searching, Thomasina saw the farmworker lean over his employer once more. At first she thought he was merely checking on his well-being. Then, with a shock of horror, she saw him straighten up – and he had a pistol in his hand.

Afterwards, she realised the pistol would not have been cocked and it was doubtful whether the farmworker knew how to fire it, but her first thought was for her companion.

'Look out! He's got a pistol.'

Jeffery's pistol was cocked and ready for use. Before the other man had even pointed the pistol in his direction, he had fired.

She could not see where the farmworker had been shot, but he was knocked backwards off the chaise, the pistol falling from his hand.

Thomasina was not certain whether or not she screamed. Jeffery neither noticed nor cared. He continued groping on the ground until he said triumphantly, 'Got it! Come on, let's get far away from here as quickly as we can.'

'But the driver . . . He might be badly hurt!'

'What do you suggest we do, bind his wound and take him to a doctor? Come on. We've got what we were after. Now let's get out of here in case someone heard the shot and comes to see what it was all about.'

11

The farmworker shot by Jeffery survived. His employer did not. News circulated the following day that he had died from a fracture of the skull, the injury having been inflicted by a highwayman.

Local residents were incensed by this latest incident of highway robbery. A reward of a hundred pounds was posted for the arrest of the two men responsible for the farmer's death.

Thomasina was contrite about the death of their victim, but Jeffery professed indifference.

'The risk of hurting, or even killing, someone has to be accepted when you take up this life, Tom. It's certainly not a one-sided affair. If you hadn't called out when you did, I too might be lying dead somewhere today.'

Thomasina shuddered at the thought of it. 'Is it worth such a risk, Jeffery?'

'What sort of a question is that? Think about it. You've already made more money than you'd have earned in a lifetime of working for Mrs Vincent. We only need to make a little more and you'll be able to go somewhere you're not known and open a little shop – if that's what you want from life.'

'I don't think I'd find it any easier to settle down to that sort of life than you would,' replied Thomasina, adding, 'well . . . not yet, anyway.'

'Good. Then we'll carry on with what we're doing – but not around here. There will be far too many people out looking for us now, all eager to earn the reward.'

'Won't it seem suspicious if we move on and the robberies cease right away?'

Jeffery laughed. 'You're assuming we're important enough to be noticed, Tom. We're not. People come and go all the time from inns and taverns without it being commented upon – especially from the Heron. Even if we *were* suspected, there's nobody from here would tell on us. Anyway, the magistrates are looking for two men, not a man and a woman.'

'Where will we go?' Thomasina asked the question uncertainly, not sure whether Jeffery intended that they should go off somewhere *together*.

He shrugged, 'We could go to London, I suppose, but the constables and Bow Street Runners are making things pretty hot there for strangers these days. I know, why don't we give Bristol a try?'

Happy that Jeffery intended taking her with him, Thomasina nodded. She had been to Bristol on two occasions with her father. It was a sprawling, bustling city, with a very busy docks area and many impressive houses. 'Yes . . . I wouldn't mind going to Bristol – but you need to know a place well in order to succeed in what we're going there for.'

'I know it as well as any other city,' replied Jeffery, surprisingly. 'In fact, that's where I started doing what we're doing now. I met up with another Cornish man there. Yes, Jack and I did quite well . . . for a while.'

When Jeffery fell silent, Thomasina prompted, 'Why didn't you carry on working with him? What went wrong?'

'He fell out with his woman and she turned him in for a reward. He was hanged.'

Thomasina shuddered, 'Are you sure you want to go back there? What if this woman sees you? She could tell on you too.'

Jeffery shook his head. 'Jack had many friends. She was warned that if she stayed in Bristol she'd be found floating in the docks one morning. She left in a hurry. We'll be all right there. Anyway, I think it's time we left the Heron Inn.'

Something in the way he spoke made Thomasina ask, 'Why are you so positive about that?'

Looking mildly embarrassed, he replied, 'I don't entirely trust Hebe any more. She always used to ask me too many questions about myself. I've been told she's started asking others about me now.'

Alarmed, Thomasina said, 'Then we ought to have left before this. What if she finds out the truth about you?'

'She won't – but she might pass on any suspicions she has. The way things are at the moment that could be enough to have me arrested.'

'Then we must leave right away.'

'We'll go first thing tomorrow morning. I'll tell the landlord I feel I've waited long enough for my father to return. That I'm returning home, just in case he's put in to another port. I'll leave a false address for him to send on any information he might get.'

'What excuse will we give for me leaving at the same time?'

'You'll say you don't want to stay on here on your own and that you believe the man you're waiting for is probably on the same ship as my father.'

The stories sounded convincing enough for Thomasina and she nodded her agreement.

Thomasina and Jeffery left the Heron Inn the following day. They would be leaving their horses at a stable in Truro, having sold them to Alf, the Heron innkeeper, but Thomasina's 'special' saddle would be travelling with them.

'Did the landlord believe your story?' asked Thomasina as the inn passed from view.

'I think so, although he did say that you hadn't seemed too unhappy that the man you were waiting for hadn't showed up.'

'I don't believe he missed very much that was going on,' commented Thomasina. 'We're not leaving the inn before time.'

In Truro the couple caught a coach to Penzance, uncomfortably aware that a constable was closely scrutinising the passengers boarding the vehicle. But he took little notice of the young couple and soon the coach was bouncing along the potholed road from Truro, heading westwards.

From Penzance they would board a boat that would take them around Land's End and on to Bristol.

Thomasina enjoyed the sea voyage immensely. It reminded her of better days when she would go to sea with her father. Jeffery did not share her pleasure. A bad sailor, he was very sick for much of the time they were on board.

He did not improve until they arrived at the upper reaches of the Bristol Channel. They were on deck together for the final part of the journey, which took them between the high cliffs on either side of the River Avon.

When they stepped from the boat to the quay at Welsh Back, in the busy port of Bristol, Thomasina was immediately caught up in the bustle, noise and pace of life in the great West Country port.

On the quayside a gang of young lads, some with two-wheeled handcarts, others with nothing, jostled each other in a bid to take charge of the luggage of the disembarking passengers.

Brushing them aside as best he could, Jeffery hailed a waiting hire-carriage. Well used to dealing with the persistent young boys, the coachman dispersed them by the simple expediency of vigorously cuffing a few ears.

Observing Thomasina's expression of concern, he said gruffly, 'You need to watch those young lads, Miss. Eight or nine of them will be clamouring around, then they'll suddenly disappear – along with your luggage. I don't doubt that half of 'em will end up dangling on the end of a hangman's rope one day. If it's sooner, rather than later, then the property of honest folks like yourselves will be a whole lot safer.'

Neither Thomasina nor Jeffery dared look at each other until they were both safely inside the vehicle, out of the coachman's view.

In Bristol, they stayed at an inn near Temple church. It was close enough to the busy city centre for their comings and goings at odd times not to excite comment, and it was within easy reach of the cattle market. It was a similar situation to that which they had found to be profitable in Truro.

Their luck held here, too. Farmers from outlying districts who attended the market would make for the nearest inn at the end of a successful day. Here, as in Truro, they were inclined to boast to each other about how much money they had made.

Another factor in Thomasina's and Jeffery's favour was the almost universal mistrust that farmers had of banking institutions. They believed it safer to take their money home with them – until Jeffery and Thomasina came on the scene.

Thomasina took a more active part in the robberies in Bristol. She possessed a naturally deep voice and it took little effort on her behalf to sound like a young man, once she had learned to control the excitement she felt each time she drew a pistol and spurred her horse forward.

She perfected a speedy means of changing her clothing. Within minutes of a successful robbery, the two highwaymen had disappeared. In their place was a pleasant young couple riding together on the King's highway, shocked at having passed so close to the scene of a robbery.

The couple remained in Bristol for a full two months. During this time they made more money than Thomasina had ever dreamed of possessing.

However, although the thrill of a successful hold-up did not wane, she was always aware that the day would come when their activities would need to be brought to an end. Nevertheless, as the weeks of successful highway robbery slipped by, thoughts of arrest and its inevitable consequences became more remote to both of them.

As a result, it came as a shock to Thomasina when, as she and Jeffery sat together at a table in the dining-room of their inn, Jeffery suddenly lowered his voice and spoke urgently to her.

'Say nothing, Thomasina. Just smile at me as though all is well – but get up, go to our room and stay there until I join you.'

Startled, Thomasina asked, 'Why . . . do you have something planned? Have you seen someone interesting?'

It was market day and the room contained a number of farmers making their way home after selling stock and produce.

'Just do as I say. Go . . . *now!*'

Thomasina had come to know Jeffery very well during the weeks they had spent together. He was not a man to overreact to any situation. Her heart beating rapidly, and wondering what was happening, she succeeded in smiling sweetly at Jeffery before rising to her feet and making her way from the dining-room.

Most of the men in the room followed her progress with admiring glances. She had always been an eye-catching young woman and the clothes she was now able to afford had transformed her into a fetching beauty.

Once in the room she shared with Jeffery, she awaited his arrival with increasing apprehension until she heard his hurried footsteps in the passage-way outside.

When he entered the room, she demanded, 'What's happened? Why did you send me up here so hur-riedly? Has someone recognised us?'

She knew this was highly unlikely. The wide, black felt masks they wore when carrying out a robbery hid too much of their faces for recognition to be possible.

'I think someone has realised that all the men we've robbed these past few weeks dined here shortly beforehand.'

Thomasina breathed a sigh of relief. The authorities were not close to them yet. Jeffery did not share her relief.

'One of the local constables seems to be smarter than most. He's brought two of the farmers we've robbed to the dining-room to see if they could identify anyone who was in the room on the night they were robbed. If both men identified us, we'd become prime suspects.'

Her relief gone, Thomasina asked anxiously, 'Do you think they recognised us?'

Giving her a wry smile, Jeffery replied, 'They were

all far too interested in watching you leaving the room
– as a woman, that is, not as a suspected highwayman. But now the constable has his suspicions about
this place, I think we'd better leave Bristol – and
right away.'

'You don't think he'll check on who's been staying
here and try to trace us?'

'He might, but we'll be long gone by then. On the
other hand, if we stayed and they became suspicious,
they'd search this room and find the money and other
things we've taken. We've got no alternative, Tom. We
have to go.'

'Where to this time?'

'To London first of all, to lay a false scent. Even if
they got on to us, they could search there for years
and never find where we were and we'd have moved
on again long before they got on our trail.'

When she made no reply, wrapped up in her own
thoughts, Jeffery said, 'I think perhaps it's time to go
home, Tom. Back to Cornwall.'

It was a matter they had discussed on a number
of occasions. Cornwall had become something it had
never been for either of them in reality . . . an idyllic
place where they would both be happy.

'We've made a lot of money, Tom,' Jeffery continued
enthusiastically. 'Enough to buy a small farm.'

Thomasina made no comment, but Jeffery was
warming to the subject. 'It would be a nice little
place, Tom. We'd have sheep, cows and a pig or two.
There could even be a couple of dogs – and a cat.'

'I thought you didn't like farm work? That's what
you always told me when we were in Cornwall.'

'I don't like working for someone else. This would be different.'

'Am I included in these plans of yours? The farm . . . and all that?'

Jeffery looked at her in surprise, 'Of course! We'll get married and be just as respectable as any other married couple.'

'I'm glad you want me to be your wife, Jeffery.' Thomasina meant it. 'But won't people want to know where our money's come from?'

'No one who knows us will find out where we are. At least, not for a long time, because we wouldn't go back to Mevagissey right away. We'll find a farm somewhere in the far west, where we'll be strangers. If anyone becomes curious, I'll think up a story – tell them that an aunt died and left me the money, perhaps. Something like that. Well, what do you say?'

'I say it's a wonderful idea, Jeffery. Not least because you've said you want us to be married. You've never said so before.'

She was close to tears and Jeffery held out his arms to her. Standing pressed close to him, Thomasina tried hard not to give way to a fit of trembling.

She had an incredible feeling of relief. Until today she had not realised how much of a strain the life they were leading had become.

Now it was all over. Now they could go home. Together.

12

Jeffery and Thomasina spent a week in London, during which time they visited a great many of the capital city's attractions and Thomasina was left awestruck by the sheer size and beauty of London's buildings.

Jeffery took the opportunity to dispose of the jewellery, watches and other valuables they had acquired during their nefarious activities in Cornwall and Bristol.

When he returned to the hotel where they were staying he complained that the pawnbroker to whom he had sold the items was a more accomplished robber than he or Thomasina had ever been. Nevertheless, they now had a great deal of money to share between them.

Only one incident happened to mar their stay. One day, when riding in a hired carriage through the streets close to Newgate, they were brought to a halt by a great crowd. When Jeffery asked the reason for the delay, the carriage driver said that there was to be a public hanging outside the prison, a short distance ahead.

He added that he had friends living nearby, with rooms overlooking the scaffold. For a few pounds he could guarantee them an unimpeded view of the proceedings.

Thomasina shook her head, but Jeffery asked who was being hanged. He was told it was Will Cullen, a notorious highwayman. For many months he had terrorised every man and woman of wealth who had occasion to venture across Hampstead Heath, by day or by night.

Thomasina insisted that the carriage be turned about and a new route taken. She would not even allow Jeffery to mention the execution at Newgate.

It was this incident, as much as anything else, that hastened their decision to leave London. Thomasina declared she had tired of city life. She wanted to return to the fields and shores of Cornwall, where the air was sweet and untainted.

Jeffery raised no objection. However, remembering their voyage from Cornwall to Bristol, he insisted they travel by road and not sea.

They journeyed in a leisurely fashion, travelling only by day. Their nights were spent at coaching inns along the way – and Jeffery did not stint on the food and wine they bought there.

This was the most relaxed time they had ever spent together. It was with almost a sense of regret that Thomasina acknowledged the coachman's call that they were crossing the bridge spanning the River Tamar, near Launceston.

Moments later they were in Cornwall.

That night was spent at the Jamaica Inn, on Bodmin Moor, where the landlady, Widow Elizabeth Broad, impressed by their apparent wealth, suggested that they might like to aid the digestion of their food with fine wines and brandy, brought in from France.

When Jeffery expressed his surprise that such luxuries were available, when Britain and France had been at war for many years, the innkeeper retorted that war was fought by soldiers, on behalf of politicians. The Cornish had never allowed such considerations to stand in the way of trade with those who had been their friends for generations.

Widow Broad's words were brought home to Thomasina later that same night. Awakened by sounds in the early hours of the morning, she peered from behind the bedroom curtain and saw a number of pack-laden donkeys being hurriedly unloaded in the cobbled yard outside the inn. She knew immediately what was happening, having spent much of her life in a coastal community.

The men unloading the donkeys were smugglers. The Jamaica Inn was about as far from the sea as it was possible to be in Cornwall, but it was ideally situated as a well-established outlet for smuggled merchandise.

She released the curtain and went back to bed when one of the men turned his face up to her window.

The following morning, when Thomasina and Jeffery went down to breakfast, she found a delicate silk scarf folded beside her plate. When she questioned the serving maid, she was told that the scarf was by way of being an apology from one of the gentlemen who had disturbed her during the night.

It was a warm welcome back to the Cornwall she had always known.

Jeffery and Thomasina had decided that their destination in Cornwall would be somewhere beyond Falmouth. This should prove far enough away from both Mevagissey and Truro to serve as a suitable base while they sought a farm somewhere to the west of the region.

They had thought of returning to the Heron Inn for a while, but decided against it. In view of the stories they had told during their previous stay, suspicion would inevitably be aroused. It was highly unlikely the landlord would comment upon their new and open relationship, but there were others on his staff who were less discreet.

An additional reason was that Jeffery intended purchasing a farm in his real name. That would pose problems if they were staying at the Malpas riverside inn.

They eventually chose to stay at an establishment known as the Norway Inn, close to the river on the Falmouth road and some few miles from Truro. From here Jeffery set about the task of finding a suitable farm for sale.

It did not take long. Within a week he had located a delightful property some twelve miles farther west of where they were staying.

When he took Thomasina to see it, she fell in love with the farm immediately. Small enough not to require an excessive number of farmhands to work the land, it was sufficiently large to ensure they could enjoy a comfortable lifestyle.

However, they encountered a problem immediately. The asking price was higher than they had anticipated. Although Jeffery possessed enough money to purchase the farm, there would not be enough left over to buy livestock and keep the farm running until it began to pay its way.

Talking about it during the evening, after they had both looked at the farm, it was apparent to Thomasina that Jeffery was bitterly disappointed. She did her best to console him.

'Never mind. We'll find another farm that's just as nice – but perhaps a little bit smaller.'

'I doubt if I'll ever find one that appeals to me quite as much as this one, Tom. It's *exactly* what I want. You feel the same way about it, too. I know you do.'

It was true, but she shrugged, 'We haven't been looking for very long. There must be dozens of others out there that I'll like just as much. Besides, if we haven't got enough money to stock and run it, then we'll just have to look for somewhere else.'

Giving her a calculating look, Jeffery said, 'There's nothing to stop us going out to get more money, is there?'

'*No*, Jeffery!' Thomasina looked at him aghast. 'You promised we'd finished with that sort of thing, once and for all.'

'I thought we had – I *hoped* we had, but if it's going to

make the difference between getting the farm we want and settling for second best, then I'm ready to go out once more. On my own, if need be.'

Although his words made her desperately unhappy, Thomasina shook her head. 'If that's what needs to be done, we'll do it together – but I'd much rather we kept to our decision to lead an honest life now we're back in Cornwall. We stirred up the magistrates here once before. We got away with it then. We might not be so lucky the next time.'

'It will be all right, Tom, I promise you.'

Reaching across, he took her hand and gripped it tightly. 'I'll tell the agent that we'll have the farm, but he'll need to give me a few weeks to raise the money. We'll try to get it all at once.'

He smiled at her, 'We'll do it, Tom. We're a great team, you and I.'

'I'm not happy with the idea, but if you're deter-mined to go ahead . . .' She shrugged. 'How are we going to go about it? I don't fancy going back to looking over farmers on market day. I believe our luck has run out using that ploy.'

'We won't need to do anything like that again – and the one job should be all we'll need do.' Suddenly enthusiastic, he continued, 'It's the Duchy Ball this weekend. It's attended by all the richest men and women in the county. They go there wearing their finest clothes and most expensive jewellery. There'll be riches for the taking. Enough to purchase the throne of England, if we wanted it.'

While Thomasina was digesting his words, he leaned towards her and added, 'We'll only need to hold up one coach as it's on the way home, then we'll have all the money we need. I know a pawnbroker in Plymouth who pays top money for good jewellery. I've never used him before because it's a bit too close to home, but as it's going to be just this once . . .'

'I still wish we weren't going to do another robbery, Jeffery.' Thomasina spoke unhappily. 'I have a bad feeling about it. Very bad . . .'

13

It was not the best of nights on which to wait to waylay a coach. Autumn was being rapidly superseded by winter, there was a heavy drizzle and the wind was steadily increasing in strength.

Jeffery had decided on the eastern outskirts of Truro as a suitable spot to hold up a coach that was homeward bound from the Duchy Ball.

He chose a spot where the road narrowed before climbing uphill from the town. They could shelter from the rain beneath leafy trees lining the road.

They had been waiting for almost an hour, and as Thomasina grew colder, Jeffery became increasingly impatient.

'The ball should have come to an end at least half an hour ago,' he complained. 'There should have been some movement along the road by now.'

'Shh! Listen.' Thomasina silenced him in a low voice.

Jeffery stopped talking immediately. After a few moments they both heard the sound of a coach and horses coming from the town. Then the lights of a carriage came into view.

'This is it, Tom. I'll stop the coach. You stay here ready to back me up, if I need you.'

It took a while for the labouring horses to reach them, but suddenly Jeffery was kneeing his horse into motion. Riding out in front of the carriage brandishing one of the two pistols he carried, he shouted, 'Halt! Stop there, coachman – or I'll shoot you dead.'

The driver of the carriage was not a man given to heroics. Hauling back on the reins, he brought the horses and vehicle to an immediate stop.

There was a small lantern suspended from the roof of the carriage illuminating the interior. It was this that alerted Thomasina to the fact that the occupants of the carriage were not as craven as their coachman.

As Jeffery approached the offside of the coach, she saw the sudden glint of glass from the *nearside* door, as it swung open silently.

'Look out! The other side of the coach.'

She remembered only just in time to adopt the gruff voice of a man, at the same time jabbing her heels into the flanks of her horse and driving it forward.

Her warning came too late. Jeffery swung his pistol to aim at the far side of the coach and pulled the trigger – but nothing happened. Rain had seeped inside the pan of the pistol, causing it to misfire.

At the same moment came the flash and report from a pistol on the nearside of the carriage. Thomasina heard a grunt of pain or surprise – or both – from Jeffery.

Pointing her own pistol in the direction of the unseen marksman, she pulled the trigger.

The pistol leaped in her hand and there was a cry of pain from the man who had shot Jeffery. A pistol dropped from his hand and bounced off the carriage step.

'Are you all right?' She brought her horse alongside that of Jeffery and put the question to him anxiously.

'No, I'm not,' Jeffery spoke to her through clenched teeth. 'Get me out of here, Tom.'

In the faint light from the interior of the carriage Thomasina could see him slumped in the saddle. Alarmed, she reached out to take hold of his reins.

The coachman, suddenly rediscovering his courage, seized the opportunity to slap the reins across the back of his horses and startle them into motion.

As the coach moved away, Thomasina caught a glimpse of its occupants. Incredulously, she saw that Harriet Vincent was one of the passengers. She was in the act of pulling back the coat sleeve from Sir Charles Hearle, revealing a bloody shirt sleeve. Then the coach passed on into the night and was gone, leaving Thomasina alone with the wounded Jeffery.

'I'm sorry, Tom . . . but I won't be able to make it as far as the Norway Inn.'

Jeffery's words were in response to Thomasina's attempt to urge the horses to a trot in order to take them clear of the scene of the abortive hold-up as quickly as possible.

Slowing the horses once more, a distraught

Thomasina said, 'There's nowhere else to go? We've got to get away from here – and quickly. The Vincents will waste no time in sending a search party out to look for us.'

'Take me to the Heron, Tom. That's close by. I'll be safe there.'

'Are you sure . . . ?' Thomasina was uncertain. She remembered they had felt it advisable to leave the waterside inn on the previous occasion they had both been staying there, and that Jeffery had not wanted to stay there more recently.

'Yes . . .' The pain he was in was causing him to speak through clenched teeth. 'Hurry! If I fall from my horse before we get there, I'll be found and be as good as dead. You know that.'

Twenty minutes later they were approaching the Heron Inn. By now Thomasina was riding alongside Jeffery, supporting him in the saddle. But he was conscious enough to realise where they were.

'Leave me here, Tom. Go on back to the Norway Inn and make up some story to account for my absence. You'll think of something.'

'I can't just leave you. You can hardly stay in the saddle without me holding you.'

'Do as I say,' he spoke angrily and painfully. 'I'll make it as far as the inn door. The landlord will get me inside and send for a doctor. One who can be trusted.'

Thomasina began to argue that she wanted to remain with him, but he cut her short. 'You've *got* to go back to the Norway. All our money is hidden in the room. If the landlord gets concerned that we might have run off without paying him, he'll search the room and find it. Then all this will have been wasted. Go . . . but change your clothes before you ride through Truro. The constables might already be out.'

Thomasina had no time to put forward any further arguments. Jeffery urged his horse into motion and headed for the inn.

She waited in the shadows as he halted outside the door and called out to those inside. A few minutes later he was being helped through the door by the landlord and his cellarman, leaving Thomasina to ride off alone, desperately worried about Jeffery and filled with renewed hatred for the man who had twice changed the course of her life.

It was as well that Thomasina heeded Jeffery's warning and changed her clothes before riding through Truro. The Vincents had already managed to get word back to Truro of the attempted robbery. Constables, accompanied by a great many sworn men, were out on the streets in force.

One of the latter stopped her to warn her of the dangers of riding unaccompanied at such a late hour. He informed her that 'desperate villains' were at large. He also passed on the information that one of them had shot a young gentleman 'well nigh to death'.

Thomasina told the sworn man that the reason she was out so late was that she had been to visit a sick relative and had left much later than she had intended. In spite of her protests, the man insisted upon accompanying her to the Norway Inn – and it was a most uncomfortable ride for Thomasina. The improvised side-saddle was never intended to be used over any distance.

Fortunately, he was flattered by her apparent interest in him and neither noticed her constant changing of position, nor questioned her too closely. Instead, he was content to do much of the talking himself, before turning his horse about and returning to Truro when they were only a short distance from the Norway Inn.

A grumbling inn servant, awakened from slumber to perform the duties for which he was employed, opened the door to her. She told him the same story she had given to the sworn man who had ridden with her to the inn. She added that Jeffery had stayed with the sick relative and intended accompanying him to a renowned doctor in London, so he would undoubtedly be away for some time. In a day or two she would be settling the bill and travelling to join him.

Thomasina had already decided that if she had received no word from Jeffery in a couple of days, she would go to the Heron Inn and join him there whatever the consequences.

Despite her intentions, Thomasina remained at the Norway Inn for a week, fully expecting that the following day would be the one when she would receive a message from Jeffery. Then, desperately worried by the total absence of news from him, Thomasina made the decision to leave the Norway Inn and go to Malpas to find out what was happening.

The landlord was sorry to see her depart. Business was decidedly slack at the moment. He was also concerned that she would be travelling alone. However, as she was about to depart, he commented, 'Mind, you'll be a lot safer now that the desperate highwayman who has caused so much trouble in the past has been taken.'

Thomasina swung around so quickly that she startled the landlord. 'What highwayman? Where did they find him?'

'I don't suppose you know anything about it. A coach was held up on the outskirts of Truro the other night. One of the passengers was shot and has been left with a crippled arm. The men who did it are believed to be responsible for a number of robberies around the town a while back. Their luck certainly ran out this time. One of the highwaymen got himself shot too. Hopefully he'll die of his wounds. He'll only hang if he lives, so it would save everyone a lot of time and money.'

Trying desperately hard not to show the distress she was feeling, Thomasina asked, 'You say there is more than one . . . ?'

'There *was* a second highwayman, but if he has any sense, he'll have put a great many miles between himself and Truro by now.'

This, at least, provided Thomasina with a grain of comfort. They suspected Jeffrey's accomplice was another *man*. Nevertheless, news of his arrest came as a great shock. He had been convinced that he would find safety at the Heron Inn. It was a place usually avoided by the magistrates' men. What could have gone wrong?

She decided someone must have told the constables of his whereabouts. She went cold when she realised that she had come within a hair's-breadth of sharing the same fate as Jeffery.

Had she gone to the Heron Inn with him – or even called there to check on his well-being – she too would probably have been arrested.

The problem now was what she should do? Truro would be too dangerous a place in which to make enquiries about where Jeffery was being held. There was even a remote possibility that she might be recognised as having been associated with him.

A similar problem arose about visiting the Heron Inn. If someone there had betrayed Jeffery, they would probably know of her association with him.

The landlord of the Norway Inn unwittingly provided the answer to her dilemma.

'The trial will be held in Bodmin – that's where the highwayman is being held. I know one of the court ushers there. If you're going to be around that way, just mention my name and he'll see that you have a place in court for the trial. You might like to stay there for the hanging, too. A fair comes to town and people come from miles around to enjoy the festivities and have a grand time.'

His words sickened Thomasina. She tried not to think of the part Jeffery would play in the 'festivities'. But at least she now knew where he was being held.

She would travel to Bodmin and find some way of visiting him in prison.

14

Arriving in Bodmin town on a coach, Thomasina put up at the Royal Hotel, just out of sight of the grim, grey-walled prison where Jeffery was being held prisoner.

The coach had passed close by the prison on its way into Bodmin. It was a forbidding place, and she was greatly distressed at the thought of the wounded Jeffery being held within its high walls.

He would be enjoying scant comfort in such a place, and it was this thought that made her decide to throw caution to the wind and visit him as soon as possible.

She found it surprisingly easy to obtain information about the prison and the occupant she had come to Bodmin to see. The young servant girl who arrived to tidy her room the following morning actually volunteered information about the 'desperate highwayman' locked up inside the gaol, without Thomasina finding it necessary to broach the subject.

The servant girl informed her that he was known to be wounded, but would be well enough to stand trial when the judge arrived in town to conduct the Assizes in a couple of weeks' time.

The garrulous servant also volunteered information that the gaoler was a certain Herbert Carminow who, according to town gossip, enjoyed his comfort and drink a little too much. Because of this, it was said that he made little real effort to provide any unnecessary comforts for those prisoners placed in his care – especially if it was going to cost him money.

Armed with this information and wearing some of her finest clothes, Thomasina called upon the gaoler that evening.

Her looks and appearance gained her immediate entry to the gaoler's office. However, when she expressed a wish to see 'Jeremy King', the name by which Jeffery had been known at the Heron Inn, the gaoler was taken aback.

'The highwayman? I'm amazed that anyone would want to see *him*. Besides, he told me he knows no one in these parts.'

'He probably doesn't,' agreed Thomasina easily, 'but news travels fast and far in Cornwall, as you must know. I once knew someone named Jeremy King. When I heard that a highwayman of that name had been arrested, I thought I must come at once and see if it was the same man.'

Smiling sadly at the gaoler, she explained, 'If it *is* him, then his poor mother would have been deeply distresed, were she still alive. She was once very kind to me. This would be an opportunity to repay that kindness in a manner of which she would have approved.'

'Such thoughtfulness!' said the gaoler ingratiatingly, sensing that a profitable transaction might be in the offing. 'I doubt if the young rogue will appreciate it, but then, even the worst of men is some poor mother's son. Besides, he only has a few weeks left in this world. Come the Assizes, he'll be tried, convicted and hanged.'

Doing her very best to blot out the picture that his words conjured up, Thomasina asked, 'May I be permitted to see him right away?'

The gaoler shook his head doubtfully. 'It would be extremely dangerous, Miss. He's being held with men who have no respect for decent young ladies like yourself. I don't think I dare take such a risk.'

'Wouldn't it be possible for him to be moved to a cell on his own? I could visit him safely then.'

The gaoler appeared to be thinking, 'Well . . . it's not out of the question, Miss, but such a move would cost money. You see, there's extra work involved in guarding a prisoner who's on his own. Then there's the business of cleaning out his cell, taking his food in separately . . .'

'How much would this involve?' Thomasina interrupted him, well aware that the gaoler was out to get as much money as he could from her.

'At least two pounds a week, Miss. At the very least.'

Thomasina thought of the work she had carried out

at Trebene for the Vincent family for a grand total of less than two shillings and sixpence a week.

'I'll give you five guineas for accommodation and special food for the remainder of the time he's in your care. If he's here for longer than a month, I'll make it more – but only if he's moved immediately and I'm permitted to see him right away.'

The gaoler's wife would be cooking the 'special' meals for the prisoner and the cell cleaning would be carried out by one of the older prisoners, in return for the promise of a more relaxed routine. Consequently, the gaoler knew he was assured of a handsome profit, but he agreed with apparent reluctance.

'You strike a hard bargain, young lady, but as you're doing this as an act of charity, why then, I can't refuse. You wait here and I'll have this young rogue moved to a cell that's as comfortable as any in the prison. Once he's there, you can go in and speak to him.'

Just before the gaoler left the office, he added, 'It might take me a little while. The prisoner was shot by one of the men he tried to rob and still needs help to get around. It's fortunate he's a fit young man, or no doubt he'd have died. As it is, he'll be fit enough to be put on trial when the time comes – and I've no doubt he'll stand straight enough for the hangman to place a noose about his neck.'

Once again Thomasina needed to shake off the horror she felt at the gaoler's callous words.

It was twenty minutes before the gaoler returned to his office. Beaming obsequiously at her, he announced,

'The young man who is benefiting from your generosity has been moved to a single cell. It's as comfortable a room as you'll find in any prison. It could almost be an inn room. Indeed, if you add another guinea to what you are going to give me, I'll see that he has all the ale or spirits he wants while he's here.'

'Can I see him now?' Thomasina asked eagerly.

'Of course . . . You have the money with you?'

Thomasina took six guineas and a half-guinea from her purse and handed the coins to the avaricious gaoler. 'That's half-a-guinea more than we've agreed. Make absolutely certain that he lacks for nothing and you'll be thanked generously when he . . . When he passes out of your care.'

In the gaoler's experience, when a prisoner had suffered the fate meted out to him by a judge, the generosity of his friends died with him. However, this young woman had already given him more than the agreed sum. It was just possible she might keep her promise.

'As I said to you before, Miss, he doesn't deserve to have such a friend. Come, I'll take you to him.'

Inside the prison, following in the wake of the gaoler and a turnkey, Thomasina found the stench overpowering. She did her best to ignore the lewd shouts and general clamour of the prisoners who sat or lay upon the straw strewn upon the floors of the communal cells.

Eventually the small party arrived at a single cell that was by no means palatial. However, it did have a wooden bunk upon which Jeffery was lying beneath an old blanket, his eyes closed.

His face looked gaunt and he had an unhealthy pallor. Thomasina had to resist the urge to drop to her knees beside him and hold him close.

'There, you see, he even has a window in here.' The gaoler pointed to a tiny barred aperture, high up in one of the walls, through which a shaft of feeble, dusty sunlight lit up a small square on the opposite, whitewashed wall.

Jeffery had opened his eyes at the sound of the gaoler's voice and was now looking up at Thomasina in disbelief.

'Thank you, sir. Can you leave us alone for a while now?'

'Well . . . I shouldn't, but seeing as how *you're* performing an act of kindness, I'll do the same. But I can give you no more than ten or fifteen minutes – and I'll need to lock you in.'

As the footsteps of the gaoler and turnkey receded along the corridor outside the cell, Jeffery pushed back the blanket and held his arms out to her. At last, she was able to cuddle him to her.

When she released him, he said, 'What are you doing here, Tom? You shouldn't have come, it's far too dangerous for you.'

'Nonsense. I told them your mother had once been kind to me and I owed her a debt. They suspect nothing. More to the point, what are *you* doing in here? How were you caught? I thought you would be safe at the Heron Inn.'

'I should have been, but the Truro magistrates put out a reward for me – a very large one. More than they've ever offered for anyone before, I believe.' He spoke of it with something very like pride in his voice. 'The temptation was too great.'

'Too great for whom? Who actually led the magistrates' men to you?'

'Hebe.'

'That bitch!' Thomasina spoke angrily. 'I knew she wasn't to be trusted. I ought to lie in wait and shoot her.'

Jeffery managed a weak, tired smile. 'I'm glad to know you still care for me, Tom, but don't even think of doing anything like that. You shouldn't come to see me again, either. It's far too risky. You might be recognised by someone. You've done more than enough by having me taken out of that stinking hole I shared with the others. I'm beholden to you. If you can arrange for me to be brought some decent food, I'll be even more grateful. For the rest . . . I knew the risk I was taking when I set out to do what I did. I'll pay the price. It's been a good and exciting life. It was even better when you joined me.'

Thomasina would have liked to be able to give him some words of comfort and hope, but the lies would not come. Instead, she said defiantly, 'I'll come as often as I like, Jeffery. I've already given the gaoler enough money to make sure you're well looked after in here, but here's another twenty guineas. Use it to buy any extras you need. If you find a turnkey who'll help you to escape, then offer him all the money we've made – your share and mine – and get word to me. If we need even more, than I'll get it for you, you can be quite certain of that.'

He smiled at her once more, a watery smile this

time. 'Thanks, Tom. I couldn't have wished for a better partner – in anything that we've done together, but it's the parting of the ways. You know that, and so do I. Use the money we've made wisely. Make certain you'll never need to rely on anyone else for the rest of your life. If you promise me that, I'll die happy and know that all I've done has been worthwhile.'

15

A few days after Jeffery had been transferred to the single cell, Thomasina called on him again and found him in an agitated state.

No sooner had the turnkey left them, locking the cell door behind him, than Jeffery said, 'You've got to go, Tom – and you mustn't come back here again to see me.'

Taken aback by his words, Thomasina demanded, 'Why? What's happened to change things?'

'Half a dozen smugglers were taken and brought here during the night. They're from Mevagissey!'

This was alarming news for both of them. Mevagissey was a small, close-knit community. Any man from the fishing village would be likely to recognise both Jeffery and Thomasina.

Yet, desperate to find a way to continue to visit Jeffery, Thomasina said, 'But you're in a cell by yourself – and wounded. There's no need for them ever to see you. To see either of us.'

Jeffery shook his head. 'I'm able to go out to the exercise yard now, Tom. To get there I'm taken past the cell where they're being held. No one's recognised me yet, probably because of this . . .' he stroked the stubbly beard that had grown during his imprisonment, '. . . but if they were to catch a glimpse of you, it wouldn't be long before we'd both be identified. The magistrates' men would realise what's been going on and you'd be arrested, too. We can't take a chance on that happening.'

Jeffery managed to communicate to Thomasina the fear he felt. She had passed a number of communal cells on the way to visit him and it was not inconceivable that some of the men who had called out to her were Mevagissey men and had already recognised her.

'What should I do, Jeffery?' Thomasina was more scared than she could ever remember.

'Leave Bodmin right away. Go to Falmouth, to the inn close to the ferry, where we once thought of staying when we were looking for a farm, remember? I think it's called the Ship Inn. Don't try to get in touch with me again until after the trial. The newspapers will publish details of when the Assizes are due to begin. The Mevagissey men assaulted the Customs men who arrested them, so they'll probably be sentenced to transportation and sent off to a hulk right away. I'll get a message to you when it's safe to come and see me again. I have money enough to get it brought to you by a horseman.'

'I don't like to think of you here, with no one to care about you and with your trial coming up soon . . .' Thomasina found herself close to tears.

'I'll be happier knowing you're somewhere safe, Tom. You've done all you can for me, and I'm more grateful than I can say. Take care now and remember: don't come back to Bodmin until it's safe to do so.'

'I wish there was some way to get you out of here, Jeffery.' The tears were uncontrollable now.

Giving her the wry semblance of a smile, he said, 'So do I, Tom – but there isn't.'

He wiped away her tears with the heel of his hand and then he was holding her. He held her for perhaps five minutes before saying gently, 'You must go now, Tom. Remember to turn your head away when you're passing the men in the main cells on the way out. Fortunately, the light isn't very good along there, and the gaoler is too careful with his money to have candles burning at this time of day.'

As she pulled away from him, he said, 'I meant what I've already said to you, Tom. I couldn't have wished for a better partner, but it's the parting of the ways now. It has to be. You know it and so do I.'

When Thomasina made no reply, he went on, 'Make good use of the money we've made, Tom – for my sake. Do that and nothing that happens will have been in vain.'

As Thomasina walked away from the prison, she thought of all he had said to her. She realised that Jeffery had not only accepted that he would be found 'guilty' by the judge, but had spoken as though he did not expect to see her again.

* * *

Thomasina conceded that it would be unsafe for her to remain at the Royal Hotel until the trial. Many relatives of the Mevagissey smugglers would be visiting their menfolk in the prison. Some would no doubt find their way to the town's inns and taverns. It was always possible that she would meet up with some of them. The unnecessary complications so caused would help neither herself nor Jeffery.

She decided she would do as Jeffery had suggested and go to Falmouth, to the Ship Inn – but she intended returning to Bodmin as soon as was prudent.

16

Thomasina returned to the Royal Hotel in Bodmin on the first day of the trial, but remained in her room for the whole of the first couple of days.

To have attended Jeffery's trial would have proved far too dangerous. The families of the Mevagissey fishermen would have been there in support of their men.

Not only would Thomasina have been recognised, but her presence would have aroused considerable speculation, and suspicion might have fallen on her.

Jeffery's arrest and forthcoming trial had already excited much interest in the newspapers. All the reports had mentioned *two* highwaymen being involved in the robberies and had declared that Jeffery's accomplice was still actively being sought.

No one had suggested that the accomplice might be a woman, but it was not beyond the intelligence of an astute constable or magistrate to arrive at an accurate conclusion. It would be even more likely if the apparently wealthy woman taking an interest in the highwayman was recognised as one Thomasina Varcoe, a poor, orphaned servant girl from Mevagissey who had been dismissed from Trebene House for dishonesty.

It was also possible that Hebe, the servant girl from the Heron Inn, would be called to give evidence. Quite apart from the danger that posed to her, Thomasina did not feel she could trust herself if she came face-to-face with the woman who had betrayed Jeffery to the authorities.

At the hotel, the trials being held at the Assize Court were the main subject of conversation, both among servants and customers.

From the maid who brought food to her room, Thomasina learned that, of the six Mevagissey fishermen, three had opted to be pressed into service with the Royal Navy rather than take their chances in a trial. The others had been found 'guilty' by the judge. As expected, they had been sentenced to transportation, two for fourteen years, the other for seven.

The outcome of their trial meant that seeing Jeffery again would now be less dangerous than before. Nevertheless, Thomasina decided it would be better to wait until his trial had been over for a day or two before attempting to visit him again.

Sir Charles Hearle and the Vincents would no doubt be called upon to give evidence against him. A confrontation with them would be even more dangerous than meeting the families of the Mevagissey fishermen.

However, Thomasina's plans were thrown into confusion late on the very day of Jeffery's trial.

Feeling it still unsafe to eat in the hotel's dining-room, she once more arranged for a meal to be brought to her room. When the servant girl entered bearing a tray, Thomasina's first question to her was whether or not the trial of the highwayman had been concluded.

'Yes, indeed,' affirmed the girl, evidently eager to share her knowledge. 'He pleaded "guilty" and was tried, convicted and sentenced in less than half an hour.' She sounded disappointed.

As Thomasina composed herself to ask a question about the inevitable sentence, the servant girl asked cheerfully, 'Will you be going to the hanging?'

'Hanging?' Thomasina repeated, stupidly. 'When?'

'They're going to hang the highwayman in the morning. The judge said there was no sense in prolonging the life of such a rogue for a single minute more than was absolutely necessary. He's to be hanged at eight o'clock. There'll be a great crowd to see it, I can tell you. I don't know how news gets around so quick, but folk'll be coming overnight from miles around to watch him get his just desserts. If you'd like to watch, there's a young stable lad who'll be happy to keep a good place for you . . .'

Thomasina did not know how she managed to keep control of her voice when she informed the girl that she had no intention of watching a man die . . . watching *Jeffery* die.

Not until the girl had left the room did Thomasina discover she was shaking. There was no question of attempting to eat the meal that had been brought to the room. It would have choked her.

It took her many minutes to pull herself together. Even when she had succeeded in calming herself, she was incapable of logical reasoning. The one thought dominating all others was that she must go and see Jeffery right away.

Leaving the untouched meal on the table where the servant girl had placed it, Thomasina put on her outside clothes and hurried from the hotel.

At the prison, the turnkey answered her insistent knocking and called the gaoler when she insisted she wanted to see Jeffery.

The gaoler shook his head. 'I'm afraid that's not allowed, Miss. Not when a prisoner is due to die the next morning. Besides, the vicar of Bodmin is due to come and spend time with him. Even a villain the likes of him must be given an opportunity to make his peace with God.'

'I'll go as soon as the vicar arrives,' promised Thomasina. 'But I *must* see him.'

When it became evident to her that the gaoler was about to refuse once more, Thomasina said, in desperation, 'I'll give you ten guineas if you'll allow me in.'

The offer brought an immediate change in the gaoler's attitude, but greed and long experience in such matters caused him to hold out for a little longer.

'Well . . . I'd be willing to oblige, of course, but it's not just me as is involved. There's the turnkey . . .'

'I'll give you fifteen guineas to share with the turn-key as you see fit. It's all the money I have on me.'

'Then I've no doubt we can come to some satis-factory arrangement, Miss. Do you have the money to hand?'

Ten minutes later Thomasina was let into Jeffery's cell.

He was seated on the edge of the wooden bunk. Both hands had been pressed to his head when he heard the footsteps of Thomasina and the gaoler.

Now, pale-faced, he looked up at her, but made no move to rise to his feet as the gaoler left the cell and closed and locked the door behind him.

Hurrying to the prison from the inn, Thomasina had mentally rehearsed a dozen different versions of the words she would say to Jeffery. Now that she was here, all were forgotten.

Dropping to a seat beside him on the hard wooden bench, Thomasina threw her arms about him and cried, 'Jeffery! My poor darling. What have we done?'

For a few moments he said nothing, but she could feel him trembling in her arms. Then, pulling himself together, he said gruffly, 'I knew what I was doing, Tom – and was carrying out robberies before you joined me. There was always the risk of being caught. We both knew that.'

'But it's so unfair,' declared Thomasina fiercely. 'To have this happen after we'd given up that life.'

'Do you think we'd ever have given it up altogether?' Jeffery asked philosophically. 'We went back to high-way robbery this time because we needed some extra money. Don't you think we'd have turned to it again and again when times were bad, or when we needed money for stock, or feed – or a hundred and one other things?'

'No! We wouldn't have, Jeffery. We'd have married, had a family and settled down to make a success of our own farm.'

'It's a wonderful picture, Thomasina. One I shall take with me to the scaffold tomorrow. I'd have gone through with it, too – for your sake. But I don't really think I would have made a successful farmer. The only thing I've ever *really* enjoyed is carrying out highway robbery. The excitement . . . the sense of power when someone trembles before you because you're pointing a pistol at him. I've enjoyed the money I've got from it, too. So have you. We've made more money than either of us ever dreamed we'd have when we were kids together in Mevagissey. That reminds me . . .'

Feeling inside his sock, he pulled out the small bag of coins she had given him on her earlier visit. 'Here's the money you gave me when you had the gaoler move me to this cell. I won't have need of it now.'

Thomasina hesitated – taking the money from him seemed somehow disloyal. An acceptance of his fate. 'Is there nothing we can do to save you, Jeffery? Perhaps have the sentence commuted to transportation?'

Pushing the small bag of money into her hand, he shook his head. 'I couldn't spend the rest of my life as a convict. I've had a full and exciting life, Tom. Having you share it with me for these past months has been best of all. Leaving you alone is the only thing I'll regret, but I'll die happy in the knowledge that I've made you a rich woman.'

For some time Thomasina clung to him, too choked with unhappiness to talk. Then they both heard the jangling of keys and the sound of voices approaching along the corridor outside.

'That'll be the parson,' said Jeffery. 'Goodbye, Tom. Will you . . . will you be outside tomorrow?'

She shook her head, seeing him only dimly through her tears. 'I couldn't bear it. But I'll be thinking of you. Praying for you.'

As a key turned in the lock, Jeffery said huskily, 'There'll be a whole lot of praying for me between now and the morning. Goodbye, Tom. Think of me sometimes – but think of the happy times . . .'

His voice broke as the door swung open.

The vicar's expression indicated deep disapproval, but Thomasina pushed past him without a word. The door was closed behind her, then the gaoler was leading her along the dark, evil-smelling corridors towards the prison entrance.

17

The cheer that rose from the thousands who witnessed Jeffery's plunge through the wooden trapdoor to eternity reached Thomasina as she rode out of Bodmin town.

Fully aware of the event they were applauding, she urged her horse on. She should have been crying, but yet again she had brought down the shutter on reality and emotion and felt only a dull numbness.

She had purchased a horse and tack the night before from the stableman at the inn. She wanted to travel to Falmouth on her own, unwilling to face anyone just yet.

She was returning to Falmouth only because she had left her belongings at the Ship Inn. She had no real plans for the future. She would not pursue the purchase of a farm, as she and Jeffery had planned.

She could not manage such a venture on her own and did not know enough about farming to make a success of it using hired help.

Besides, an idea she had always kept at the back of her mind had come to the fore, even before Jeffery met his fate. It was the germ of a dream she had always entertained, although it was not one she could ever have shared with him.

The Falmouth inn would prove ideal for what she had in mind, and when another week had passed she put her newly formed plans into action.

The inn was frequented by masters, owners and brokers of merchant vessels based in Falmouth. Thomasina listened in to their conversations as they ate at the tables around her and was able to decide that the most honest of the town's solicitors was a company called Bennett and Pengelly.

It was to their offices that she made her way one morning, ten days after Jeffery's execution.

Seated across the desk from one of the firm's partners, Zachariah Bennett, she exaggerated the status of her late father as a ship-owner and master.

She informed the solicitor that she had recently inherited some money, as a result of his death. While it was not sufficient to enable her to buy a deep-sea vessel outright, she believed it would be sufficient to purchase a half-share in a vessel where a co-owner had the qualifications, like her late father, to take the vessel to sea as its master.

The solicitor declared that he knew of a number of such men who were seeking a partner to invest in their vessels. He promised to submit details of their ships to her, together with the amount of investment required, accounts of their recent voyages and plans for future ventures.

When these had been passed to her, Thomasina said she would interview those owners she felt most likely to suit her and decide whether to invest her money in one of them.

It was perhaps not the most usual means of carrying out such a business, as Thomasina was aware, but the continuing war with France was making life extremely difficult for many ship-owners. Some were desperate to attract additional capital. The solicitor felt that few owners would refuse to cooperate.

Forty-eight hours later details of no fewer than twenty-three desperate ship-owning masters were delivered to Thomasina.

By the following morning she had whittled down the number in which she was particularly interested to four. Wasting no time, she began interviewing them that same afternoon.

By early evening she had ruled out three of the men and was feeling increasingly despondent. Then Captain Malachi Wesley Ellis arrived at the Ship Inn.

Captain Malachi was a Scillonian whose family had been island fishermen for countless generations. Malachi had been the first of the Ellis men to break with family tradition. At the age of thirteen, he had persuaded his reluctant father to allow him to enter the Royal Navy as a midshipman, serving on a ship commanded by a naval officer who had married Malachi's aunt.

With his uncle, the young Scillonian had sailed

E. V. Thompson

the world. Before long, his intuitive skills of seamanship had earned him grudging promotion in a service dominated by patronage, titles and family connections.

Eventually, given command of a frigate in the West Indies, Malachi set a record for the amount of prize money won by a ship of such size. Then came the fateful day when Malachi's ship encountered a French fleet in the Caribbean.

Under normal circumstances, the unwritten rules of naval warfare said that the French would fire a warning shot or two and allow the smaller vessel to go on its way, without further molestation. However, such was the reputation of this particular British frigate and its captain that the enemy made a determined attempt to send them both to the bottom of the ocean.

Malachi's superb seamanship enabled him to escape from the French fleet under the cover of darkness, but not before the frigate had received a number of hits. Malachi himself suffered a severe wound. When the ship reached Kingston, in Jamaica, it was necessary for a surgeon to amputate his right leg, below the knee.

It marked the end of Malachi's naval career, but not the cessation of his seagoing days. With his prize money he purchased a merchantman, the *Melanie Jane*.

Sailing this ship, Malachi traded to and from the Mediterranean, making a satisfactory living. He even purchased a second vessel – and this was his undoing. It was taken by a French privateer off the coast of Africa and Malachi learned that the master had failed to insure the latest cargo.

Now Malachi had secured a valuable cargo, with

profit virtually assured, but all the money he had was tied up in property and investments. He needed ready cash to purchase the cargo – and he needed it quickly. This was why he was seeking a partner to purchase a half-share in the *Melanie Jane*.

As he spoke with modesty to Thomasina of his past achievements and of the ambitions he had for the future, she observed him with increasing interest.

A man of perhaps sixty years of age, Malachi was tall, broad-shouldered and bearded. Despite his age and disability, his blue eyes twinkled in a manner that proved he had lost none of his zest for living – which for him meant sailing.

When he had ended his narrative, Thomasina asked, 'Have you never married, Captain Ellis?'

The eyes twinkled once more as he replied, 'I never have, Miss Varcoe – 'though I've come almighty close to it once or twice. But I reckon my way of life put 'em off, when it came down to it. The sea is a demanding mistress.'

'An orphan-maker too,' said Thomasina, with a trace of bitterness in her voice. 'That's how I lost my father.'

'It happens,' commented the sea captain philosophically.

Thomasina had already decided she liked this man, but now she wondered how he would react to the proposition she intended putting to him. There was only one way to find out.

'I like the ideas you have for your ship, Captain Ellis, and I'm very impressed by your own record. I'm prepared to buy a half-share in the *Melanie Jane*, but I have a condition which you may not feel able to accept.'

Malachi shrugged. He liked this young woman, too. He felt she knew what she wanted, but would not prove to be too difficult as a partner. 'Try me, Miss Varcoe. I'm not an unreasonable man. If I can remain master of the *Melanie Jane* and continue to make decisions about where we trade, I'll go along with most things. The ship will be safer in my hands than under the command of anyone else. What's more, I'll return a handsome profit for both of us.'

'I don't doubt it, Captain Ellis. That's why I'd like to have you as my partner, after interviewing three other masters and rejecting a score more.' Looking straight into the blue, bright eyes, she continued, 'I'm prepared to go into partnership with you, Captain Ellis, but only on condition that you take me with you on your voyages.'

Malachi's eyebrows rose in unison and he stared at her for a few incredulous moments before shaking his head reluctantly. 'I'm very sorry, Miss Varcoe, but the *Melanie Jane* has no facilities for women passengers. Besides, seamen are a superstitious bunch. Many consider it unlucky to carry women on a working ship.'

'I'm not talking of travelling as a passenger, Captain, and if we do it my way they won't even know there's a woman on board the *Melanie Jane*.'

Frowning, the sea captain said, 'I think you'd better explain what it is that you're suggesting, Miss Varcoe.'

'I'm suggesting that I join your ship as a boy and learn to become a seaman.'

Malachi looked at her as though she had just suggested she could fly. 'It would never work. They'd realise in no time that you were a girl. Even if they didn't, you couldn't keep up the pretence for long, not

living in such close proximity. No, it wouldn't work.'
He shook his head emphatically.

'I needn't live in close proximity with them,'
Thomasina persisted, 'I could go on board as a
relative of yours. You could fix up a place for me
to sleep, close to your own cabin.'

She nodded in the direction of the wooden stump
that served as the lower part of his right leg. 'You
could say the leg is beginning to trouble you and
you need someone to help you out – as a servant,
perhaps. I could help with a seaman's duties when I
wasn't working for you.'

'It still wouldn't work,' declared Malachi, shaking
his head emphatically. 'Someone would see through
your disguise the moment you stepped on board.'

Thomasina stared at him and for a while it seemed
she would argue further. Then, abruptly, she said,
'Perhaps you're right – but I've been interviewing
all afternoon and have a few things I must do right
now. Look, return to the taproom here at nine o'clock
tonight and send word to me that you've arrived. I'll
come down as soon as I can and we'll go to a private
room and talk about this some more. See if we can
work something out. But, remember, I *do* want to go
into partnership with you.'

Before Malachi could either agree or disagree, she
had risen to her feet and swept from the room, leaving
him shaking his head in disappointment.

He would keep the appointment, but he felt they
would never find a way to enter into a partnership.
Not on Thomasina's terms.

*   *   *

The taproom of the Ship Inn was not a place where Captain Malachi Ellis would have chosen to meet a lady. It was a drinking room favoured by seamen of various nations and was both noisy and boisterous.

One of the rowdiest groups was in a corner of the room. Choosing a table farthest away from the noisy drinkers, Malachi ordered an ale and asked the serving girl to send someone to the room occupied by Thomasina to inform her that he had arrived.

He had consumed half of his ale and was becoming impatient at being kept waiting when a figure detached itself from the group he was avoiding.

A young man walked with a swagger across the room towards him. Malachi was aware that he was heading in his direction, but took little notice. He did not know the lad and his thoughts were of Thomasina.

He wondered whether she knew the type of clientele that a taproom attracted in a busy port such as Falmouth. She might even have looked in and decided not to enter. He would finish his drink and see whether she was waiting for him outside.

'Are you deliberately avoiding me, Captain Ellis? We agreed to meet here, remember?' The speaker was the figure who had crossed the room towards him.

The voice was that of a young lad, not fully a man, but with childhood left behind. It was hardly deeper than the voice he had heard earlier in the day, yet the subtle change made all the difference. The 'lad' was Thomasina.

As he leaned back against the wall behind him, Malachi's disbelief changed to delight and he bellowed with laughter. Looking up at her, he shook his head in amused acknowledgement of her deception. 'Had I not seen this with my own eyes I would never have believed it possible – and if you can fool me, you can fool anyone!'

'So, what are you going to do . . . *Uncle* Malachi?'

'First of all, you'd better tell me what I should call you . . . Nephew.'

'Tom. My name is Tom.'

Malachi reached up to brush away a laughter tear before reaching out his hand. 'Put it there, Tom. I think I'm going to enjoy sailing with a partner. Especially one as lively as you.'

Book Two

1

'Come on in, Tom. You'll never have swum in water like this around Cornwall. You could almost boil an egg in it!'

The Cornish accent sounded strangely out of place in the small, palm-fringed bay, warmed by a breeze from the inland desert.

The *Melanie Jane* was anchored close inshore, off a seemingly deserted stretch of the North African coastline. The vessel had taken a cargo of salted pilchards from Cornwall to Sicily. Here Malachi had loaded a cargo of wine and a quantity of polished marble, for delivery to the West Indies. On the third leg of its voyage the *Melanie Jane* would return to England with a highly profitable cargo of sugar and, possibly, rum.

'I can't swim.' Thomasina's reply to the man who had called her was a lie. She was an excellent swimmer, her father having taught her by the time she was three. However, in view of her subterfuge, it would have been impossible to join the other crew members, especially as they were all swimming in a state of utter nudity.

Patting the long-barrelled musket lying across her knees, she added, 'Besides, someone's got to stand guard.'

This, at least, was the truth. The North coast of Africa was home to the infamous Barbary corsairs. All appeared peaceful about them now, but a single pirate ship could change the picture immediately.

Posing as Captain Malachi Ellis's young nephew, Thomasina had settled in to seaboard life and been fully accepted by the men. In spite of the confined conditions of life on board ship, none of the seamen appeared to entertain the slightest suspicion that 'Tom' was, in fact, a young woman. The deception was made possible by the fact that she had her own tiny cabin and did not share their cramped quarters.

Scarcely more than bunk's width, the 'cabin' was adjacent to Malachi's own cabin and had been converted from a small store room where the captain had previously kept a number of old trunks and chests.

The crew had also accepted that such accommodation had been made available not solely due to the fact that 'Tom' was supposed to be Malachi's nephew, but because the main reason he was on board was to help take care of the ageing, one-legged captain.

However, Thomasina had never intended to be merely a passenger on board the *Melanie Jane*. In addition to learning navigation and sailing skills from Malachi, she enjoyed taking on many of the crew's duties when the opportunity arose.

She particularly enjoyed working in the rigging, helping to furl and shake out the sails, whatever the state of the weather.

They had recently been hit by a storm that Malachi declared was the worst he had ever encountered in the Mediterranean, a sea not normally given to such excesses. The suddenness and sheer violence of it had taken Malachi by surprise. Before all the sails could be furled, some of them had been torn asunder. Malachi had anchored in the North African bay to repair or replace them.

The storm had long since passed and the repairs having been effected satisfactorily, Malachi was allowing his hard-working crew to enjoy the rare pleasure of a swim, before they resumed their voyage.

'Can you really not swim, Tom?'

Seated in the shade of a spare sail, stretched above a section of the deck, at the stern of the *Melanie Jane*, Malachi sat enjoying a pipe of tobacco.

The hot weather did not suit him. He found it difficult to ignore the perspiration which stood out on his forehead and irritated his neck, beneath the bushy grey beard.

'I can swim like a pilchard,' replied Thomasina, 'but can you imagine the sensation it would cause if I were to strip off and go swimming with the men?'

Malachi chuckled. 'They'd be too busy trying to hide their own embarrassment at having you see *them* naked, I reckon.'

Puffing on his pipe, Malachi looked at Thomasina

admiringly. He had gained an increasing affection and respect for her during the months she had been accompanying him on his voyages. 'You're quite a remarkable young woman, Tom. One day I'll sit you down and have you tell me the story of your life. I've learned little enough about you in the time we've been together.'

Thomasina shrugged. 'You wouldn't want to hear it, Malachi . . . and I have no intention of telling. We enjoy a very satisfactory arrangement right now. One that's making a handsome profit for both of us. Let's keep things that way.'

'It suits me, girl. Having you on board has added a bit of sparkle to life. At times it's had me wishing I was a younger man with two good legs.'

'Had you been any different from the way you are now, we wouldn't be sailing together,' retorted Thomasina. Suddenly relaxing and smiling at him, she added, 'But I do enjoy sailing with you. The *Melanie Jane* is a very happy ship.'

It was true and the two got on very well. She had in many ways become the 'son' he had never had. In turn, Malachi reminded Thomasina of the father she had lost.

Malachi had never questioned the story of how she had come by the money with which she had purchased a partnership with him, but he was shrewd enough to realise there was a great deal more to her background than being orphaned. However, he never tried to probe too deeply into her past. She was a cheerful presence on board his ship and the remainder of the crew all liked the young cabin 'boy'.

Suddenly, Thomasina stood up, only just succeeding in grabbing the musket before it slipped to the deck.

'What's that, Malachi?'

She pointed to where a ship was rounding the finger of land to the east of the bay. Carrying a sail that was quite unlike their own, it had been hidden until this moment by the scimitar of palms around the shoreline.

'It's a corsair ship! Get the men out the water – quick, Tom. I'll prime the guns. We're going to need them.'

As Thomasina shouted to the men to clear the water and get back on board, Malachi stomped off as fast as he could to the gun mounted on the bow of the *Melanie Jane*.

2

The bay was not very large. By the time the last member of the *Melanie Jane*'s crew cleared the water and was clambering up the rope ladder hanging over the ship's side, the corsairs' ship was within cannon range – and they opened fire.

Fortunately, only the bow gun could be brought to bear and the corsairs' aim was woefully poor. The shot fell far short of its target and well to one side of the *Melanie Jane*. Nevertheless, it added urgency to the already feverish activity on board.

Even as the last of the crew scrambled back on the ship, the *Melanie Jane* was under way.

Such was the danger they were in that few of the crew wasted precious seconds pulling on their clothes. They carried out their duties in the state in which they had emerged from the sea. Naked.

Thomasina hardly noticed. The merchantman did

not carry a large crew, and therefore she, the ship's cook and a sick seaman were busily loading the ship's two cannons, which had been manhandled to the starboard side of the ship.

This was the side from which the Barbary vessel would need to try to board, if it could get close enough in time.

The sails of the *Melanie Jane* were raised and set for all possible speed, but the corsairs were now frighteningly close. Their excited shouts sent shockwaves of horror through Thomasina.

They were hurling unmistakeable, though unintelligible threats across the water, confident that the *Melanie Jane* and its crew would soon be theirs.

English ships fetched a good price on the Barbary coast. English sailors were equally prized – and not only for their seamanship, or their endurance when chained to the oars of corsair ships. When castrated, they were much sought-after as guards in the harems of wealthy men.

But on this occasion the corsairs had reckoned without the determination and skill of Malachi.

'Crowd on every bit of canvas we've got,' he bellowed at the men hoisting the sails. 'We've got the wind in our favour. They expected to surprise us at anchor and will need to turn in order to chase us.'

'Will we be able to outsail them?' Thomasina asked anxiously.

'We'll soon find out,' said Malachi grimly. Then, recognising her concern, he added, 'The *Melanie Jane* is Fowey-built for the smuggling trade. There's many a time she's outstripped a Customs cutter.

We'll not be caught by a Barbary ship.'

At first, it seemed that Malachi's faith in his ship would be justified. The Cornish vessel was heading out of the bay before the corsair ship had completed its turn.

Malachi ordered the coxwain to steer out to sea, away from the coast. They would head for the Straits of Gibraltar. There they would be certain of finding a British man-o'-war to deal effectively with the pursuing Barbary-coast vessel – if it was still with them by then.

It was soon apparent that they were not, however, going to lose the other vessel as easily as Malachi had hoped. Indeed, the corsairs were actually gaining on them. For the first time Malachi showed some concern.

'What's happening?' Thomasina asked him. 'I thought we would have left the corsairs behind by now.'

'We should have.' Malachi frowned. 'The trouble is, there's quite a strong current close inshore – and it's running in their favour. The ship that's closest to the shore has an advantage.'

'Then why don't *we* move closer inshore?' Thomasina asked.

'I don't know this coast, but the corsairs do. It's their hunting ground. The best thing we can do is stay out here and try to keep out of range of their guns. They seem to be poor gunners, but that ship is carrying almost as many cannon as a British man-o'-war. If we allow them to come close enough to give us a broadside, not all their shots will miss. But there's one more thing we can try.'

'What's that?' Thomasina asked eagerly.

'We can pray. Pray as we've never done before.'

It had been mid-morning when the chase began and Malachi had hoped to shake off the pursuers within a couple of hours. Instead, four hours later, the Barbary-coast ship was about two miles away, on a parallel course with the *Melanie Jane* – and beginning to pull ahead. The crew of the British ship were watching the other vessel anxiously.

'What do you think they're doing, Malachi? Why don't they attack us?' Thomasina was finding the puzzling tactics of the corsairs unnerving.

'They want to make certain we don't escape again. I'll wager they'll begin edging towards us before too long. When they come within range, they'll open fire. But they can see we're fully laden, so they won't want to risk sinking us. They'll need to come close enough to use chain shot, or something similar, to try to bring down the rigging.'

Malachi was talking half to himself now, thinking things out as he went along. 'Yes, they'll need to come *really* close.'

Appearing to reach a decision, he turned to the man at the ship's wheel. 'Stay on this course, Harry – but let me know if the corsairs do anything new . . . You come with me, Tom.'

Thomasina followed the one-legged captain to the rear hatch and down the ladder to where their cabins were situated. Entering his own cabin, Malachi took a bunch of keys from his belt and inserted one of them into a stout cabinet, bolted to a bulkhead.

When the cupboard door swung open, Thomasina saw half a dozen long-barrelled muskets, together with powder and shot.

Lifting some of the muskets out, Malachi said, 'Help me carry these on deck. If the corsairs try to board us, we'll give them something to think about.'

As they carried the muskets to the upper deck, the coxwain called, 'You're just in time, Malachi, the corsairs are edging in this direction. I think they're about to try for us again.'

'What will you do?' An anxious Thomasina put the question to Malachi.

'We'll let them come as close to us as I dare, then I'll need all hands to help with the sails so we can fall astern of the corsair – but still remain close. They've got tiller steering. If we can shoot the men manning the tiller, they'll turn and lose way. Before they are able to bring her under control again we'll be so far ahead they'll never catch us, not now we're both on equal terms away from the shore.'

'Do you have any men who are expert shots?'

'They'll manage as well as any other seamen, I reckon.'

'We don't have to manage,' Thomasina said excitedly. 'Let me do the shooting.'

'*You?* Have you fired a gun before?' Malachi expressed incredulity.

'My pa taught me to shoot – and shoot well,' Thomasina said. 'Besides, you're going to need every man in the crew to work the sails and make sure we get well away from the corsairs.'

'Firing a gun is one thing,' Malachi said doubtfully.

'Do you think you can shoot a man?'

Thomasina recalled the last time she had fired a gun, but it was not an example she could give to Malachi.

'With what's at stake for all of us, I have no doubts at all. I'll load the muskets and carry them up to the bows now.'

While she loaded the guns, Thomasina heard some of the crewmen talking in low tones to Malachi. They were unhappy about a young man taking on such a responsibility, pointing out that all their lives depended upon its success.

'You heard what Tom said,' was Malachi's reply. 'I'd say he's done more shooting than the rest of us put together.'

'Aye, but it's one thing to shoot at rabbits, or gulls, but quite another when you're looking to kill a man.'

'Right,' Malachi said to the man who seemed to be the most concerned. 'As it *is* of such vital importance, I'll tell you what I'll do. You can go up on the fo'c'sle with Tom and reload for him as he shoots. If he hits no one with the first three shots, you can have the next three. If he downs any of the men on the tiller, you'll load twice as fast so that he can shoot some more. Is that a fair enough compromise?'

The seaman agreed with Malachi that it was, although a few minutes later Thomasina heard him telling one of his fellow-crewmen that it should have been *he* who fired the first shots.

The tactics of the Barbary-coast corsairs were exactly what Malachi had predicted they would be.

Maintaining their course, they gradually edged

their vessel towards the *Melanie Jane*, until the two ships were sailing side-by-side.

When they were so close that the English sailors could see the eager grins of anticipation on the faces of the North African seamen, a cannon was fired at the merchantman.

Again, Malachi had guessed correctly. The shot consisted of two balls linked by a chain. Fortunately for the sailors on the British merchantman, it was woefully off target and dropped in the sea behind the *Melanie Jane*.

But Malachi was taking no chances of future shots being equally ineffective. '*Now!*' he bellowed and the seamen standing by immediately began taking in two of the largest sails.

It seemed to Thomasina that it was hardly more than a minute before Malachi was ordering the men to let the sails out once more – but it proved to be long enough.

The *Melanie Jane* was now tucked in behind the Barbary-coast ship, safe from the corsairs' guns – and it was time for Thomasina to carry out her part of Malachi's plan.

The distance between the two ships was much less than she had thought it would be. Nevertheless, her first shot went wide and there were anxious mutterings from those of the crew able to see what was happening.

Picking up another musket, she took careful aim and fired again. This time one of the corsairs steadying the tiller abandoned his duties and staggered away across the deck, one hand desperately clawing at his back.

When Thomasina fired a third time a corsair dropped to the deck of the other vessel. The fourth shot produced a loud scream, although she could not see where she had hit the man at whom she had aimed. But it was enough for the other corsairs about him. With four men out of action, it was already proving difficult – and dangerous – to hold their vessel on course. The remaining men abandoned their now exposed post.

Out of control and with sails flapping unmanageably, their boat veered off course and the *Melanie Jane* surged past.

Thomasina managed to get off one further shot, aiming for a man she thought might have been the corsairs' captain. She could not tell whether or not she hit him, but it no longer mattered. The pursuit was over. The crew of the other vessel ran around the deck in apparent panic, seeming not to know what they should do to bring their boat back under control.

On the *Melanie Jane* the crew cheered Thomasina until they were hoarse. The loudest of them was the man who had questioned her ability to carry out the task for which she had volunteered.

She valued Malachi's praise most of all. When she helped him to carry the muskets back to his cabin, he said, 'Well done, Tom. Your actions today saved my ship – *our* ship – and you were as cool in action as any seaman I've ever sailed with.'

3

The voyages of the *Melanie Jane* under the co-ownership of Malachi and Thomasina continued to be highly profitable. The sea captain told Thomasina she had brought him luck and gave her advice on banking the money she was making as his partner.

He also convinced her that the purchase of houses in and around Falmouth was a sound investment and she followed his advice. The purchase and subsequent renting particulars were negotiated through an agent – again recommended by Malachi.

In addition, when he ascertained that Thomasina had no one with whom she wished to spend time during the brief periods spent ashore between voyages, he insisted that she should stay with him, in his home.

It was a large house, which he had shared with his sister until her death, a few years before. He gave Thomasina the whole of the top storey, declaring dishonestly that his infirmity prevented him from using it, even had he wanted to.

The top floor of the house contained far too many rooms for Thomasina's needs, but the arrangement suited her very well. She was able to enter the house as a young man and leave it as a young woman, if she wished, although she found she felt increasingly vulnerable when she faced the world as a woman.

She and Malachi had agreed that should any of the *Melanie Jane*'s crew suspect anything, they would say that 'Tom' had a twin sister who bore a remarkable resemblance to 'him'.

As it happened, it was unnecessary to put the lie to the test. Malachi's house was situated high on a steep hill beyond the harbour. None of the crew found their way there.

Besides, Thomasina did not venture out very often and the *Melanie Jane* spent little time in harbour. When it did, Thomasina was quite content to remain at Malachi's house, cooking for him and enjoying his company during the evenings.

He was very much a father figure for her by now. She saw in him many of the fine qualities she remembered – or thought she did – being possessed by her father.

For his part, Malachi told Thomasina that he saw in her the qualities of the son – or daughter – he had never been fortunate enough to have for himself.

Yet, although he never tried to pry, Malachi could not help feeling curious about her past. All he really knew was that her father, like himself, had been master of a vessel, but she had never given him any details.

One evening, when the *Melanie Jane* was laden and

ready to sail on the night tide, Malachi taxed her with this in his own quiet way. They were seated in the kitchen of his house, the remains of one of Thomasina's meals on the table between them.

'I enjoy your company as much as I do your cooking, Tom, but, unlike me, you're still young. Are there no relatives you'd like to visit on your last evening ashore – or a young man, perhaps?'

During the meal Thomasina had shared a quantity of wine with Malachi. It made her relaxed, but caution had become instinctive to her.

'I have an aunt and a cousin in Cornwall, Malachi. I send them money regularly, but I have no wish to see them again. We – my aunt and I, at any rate – were never very close. I'll probably go back and see my cousin one day, but not just yet.'

'What about young men? You're an attractive young woman, Tom.' He smiled. 'At least, when you're not being an important part of *Melanie Jane*'s crew.'

'There was someone – but I lost him. If you don't mind, it's something I'd rather not talk about.'

Thomasina had thought less about Jeffery recently, but when she did it still hurt just as much. She gained a degree of comfort from the certain knowledge that he would have been proud of the use to which she had put the money they had made together.

'You can't mourn for ever, Tom, or you'll end up like me, bemoaning all the things that have passed you by.'

'I doubt I'll do that, Malachi, any more than you do. You're happy in the knowledge that you're one of the most respected captains sailing out of Falmouth. I'm doing what *I've* always wanted to do. Now, isn't it time we shut up the house and went to the ship? We need to make a move if we're to set sail on the tide.' Smiling at him, she added, 'I'm getting just like you, Malachi. I get restless when I've been ashore for too long.'

'Heaven help me, Tom, you're becoming something of a slave driver. I never thought when I took on a partner that I'd be taking on a master as well. *I'm* the one to decide when the *Melanie Jane* is going to sail, and don't you forget it.'

Despite Malachi's grumbling, Thomasina knew it was all good-natured and that she had distracted him from his gentle prying. While he went about the house ensuring it was safely locked and secured, she cleared the table and washed up the dishes they had used.

Thomasina was aware that Malachi was even more restless than herself when he was on dry land. Here, he was an ageing, one-legged man with very few friends. On the *Melanie Jane* he was the ship's captain – a highly respected seafarer, in command of all those who crewed the ship and thoroughly at ease with his chosen environment.

They had already taken their goods to the ship for what should prove to be a very interesting voyage. They had loaded salted pilchards for the West Indies, for sale to the sugar planters as food for their slaves.

From the West Indies there was a variety of cargoes they could take on board. Their destination would depend very much on what they had to sell and they would take it wherever it was wanted.

This was one of the great advantages of being an owner/master. They were free to take on board any cargo they wished and deliver it to wherever it would command the best price.

4

The problems of the Cornish people, brought about by a dire countrywide shortage of wheat, were brought forcibly home to Malachi and Thomasina that very same evening.

They were walking to the ship, Malachi having refused Thomasina's offer to arrange for a carriage to take them there. She had not argued with him. Malachi made a habit of proving he could do anything that could be done by a man with two legs.

The *Melanie Jane*'s captain succeeded in covering the distance between house and dock, but by the time they arrived he was perspiring with the effort of walking a distance that might well have taxed the stamina of a man his age in possession of two good legs.

As a result, he was not in the best of moods when they reached the quayside and found it occupied by a mob of noisy, angry men and boys. Many were wearing the hard hats favoured by Cornish tin miners and with them were a number of equally vociferous women.

'What's going on?' Thomasina put the question to a young man, one of many bystanders observing the angry tinners and their followers.

'It's miners from up Camborne and Redruth way,' the young man replied. 'They say their families are starving for want of wheat and barley and they've heard a rumour that one of the ships here is loading barley for an up-country port where it'll fetch more money. One of the miners I've just spoken to said they'll stop the ship sailing, even if it means sending it to the bottom of the harbour. A magistrate was here a few minutes ago, reading out the Riot Act, but the miners booed him down.'

'They're fools,' Malachi declared. 'All they'll succeed in doing is having the army called out against them and getting themselves arrested. A man brought before a magistrate for rioting will either be hanged or transported. That'll not help his family buy food. But it's none of our problem, Tom, we've got a ship to get ready. Let me take the lead. There's nothing like a peg-leg brought down hard on a man's toes to persuade him to move out of the way.'

Using a combination of stamping and pushing, Malachi forced a way through the noisy, but largely well-behaved crowd. Soon, he and Thomasina reached a line of uniformed and nervous militiamen, keeping the crowd back from the water's edge.

It seemed that the ship suspected of carrying grain was moored alongside the quay, immediately astern of the *Melanie Jane*. The militiamen were reluctant to allow Malachi and Thomasina to pass through their extended line.

'I'm sorry, sir,' said one of the harassed militiamen, 'Captain Hearle's orders are that *no one* should be allowed close to the ships.'

At the mention of his name Thomasina went cold. Then she told herself she was being foolish. The man who had twice been responsible for changing the course of her life was not the only man in Cornwall to possess the surname 'Hearle'.

'You can tell Captain Hearle to go off and play his foolish soldiers' games somewhere else. I've a ship to take to sea. Come along, Tom.'

Brushing aside the protesting militiaman, Malachi stomped towards the *Melanie Jane*, closely followed by a somewhat nervous Thomasina, who expected them to be fired upon at any moment.

The miners who had heard the exchange between the sea captain and the militiamen set up a cheer. It was taken up by others, even though they had no idea *why* they were cheering.

The sound only served to heighten the nervousness of the militiamen. Moments later a uniformed officer came running along the quayside towards Malachi and Thomasina, calling out to them, 'Halt!'

The officer's right arm swung uselessly at his side and, to Thomasina's utter dismay, she saw that the officer *was* the same Sir Charles Hearle who had been responsible for Jeffery's death and for her own ordeal at his hands in Trebene House.

She was wearing a colourful stocking-cap she had

purchased in the Mediterranean some months before. It had a long, tasselled end, which she now swung around to fall in front of her body, covering part of her face.

There was little chance that he could possibly remember her, but she felt her heart rate increase, either from fear, her hatred of the man or a combination of the two.

Sir Charles Hearle reached them, angry and out of breath. Placing himself squarely in front of Malachi, he demanded, 'Were you not told you must not pass through my line of militiamen?'

In command of a company of the Second Roseland Militia, Hearle and his men had been carrying out drill in the area when called upon by the magistrate to contain the miners. It was a situation with which he had never before been faced and he was both nervous and uncertain.

'I was told something of the sort by a damned fool with a musket who should have had something better to do,' Malachi growled.

'He was acting upon my orders,' Sir Charles said. 'You had no right to disobey him.'

He hardly glanced at Thomasina, who was trying to keep Malachi between them.

'I had every right,' Malachi declared. 'I'm the owner and captain of the *Melanie Jane*. We're putting to sea on tonight's tide. You're supposed to be here to ensure law-abiding folk can go about their business, not stopping them from doing so.'

Falmouth was a wealthy port. Ship-owners here were often influential men. Sir Charles Hearle had a number of minor business interests in the town and was not a man knowingly to upset anyone with influence.

'That's very true, Captain. Once I had ascertained your business, you would have been allowed to board your ship. Unfortunately, I have few men I can trust to use their discretion, so I need to give them hard-and-fast orders. Please accept my apologies for inconveniencing you.' He shrugged. 'As you can see, I have an ugly mob to control.'

'It's a pity someone can't control the prices charged by farmers and land-owners for their corn,' retorted Malachi. 'If they did, there would be none of this trouble.'

As they talked they had begun walking towards the *Melanie Jane*, passing a number of lanterns hung upon poles at the water's edge. As though noticing Sir Charles Hearle's useless arm for the first time, Malachi said, 'I can see that, like me, you perform your duties with a disability. Is it a war wound?'

'One serves one's country as best one can,' Sir Charles Hearle replied, ambiguously, '. . . and yours?'

Malachi nodded, saying nothing.

'Then I salute you, sir, and wish you a safe voyage. Now I must return to my duties.'

When Sir Charles Hearle hurried away, Thomasina needed to fight an irrational urge to tell Malachi about the militiaman's 'war-wounded' arm. She restricted herself to saying, 'Pompous little man. I can't see him as a wounded hero.'

To her surprise, Malachi chuckled. 'You're a good judge of character, Tom. I've come across Sir Charles

Hearle on more than once occasion, although I very much doubt if he remembers me. He's a young ne'er-do-well. Since he inherited a title and nothing else, he's devoted his life to spending the money of those rich relatives who'll have anything to do with him. The closest he's come to action is shooting a highwaymen from the cover of darkness. He wasn't even bright enough to realise there were *two* highwaymen. The second one shattered his arm.'

Her heart beating faster as memories of that tragic night came back to her, Thomasina said, 'Why did you ask him if it was a battle wound if you already knew it wasn't?'

'I was being sarcastic, only Sir Charles is too stupid to realise it. You'll have noticed he wasn't anxious to give me the true story.'

'You're a crafty and devious old man, Malachi,' Thomasina smiled at him affectionately, but the un-expected meeting with Sir Charles Hearle had disturbed her greatly.

5

A single lantern hanging from a pole illuminated the gangway that linked the *Melanie Jane* with the quayside. By its light Thomasina could see a number of the ship's crew on deck, watching what was going on ashore.

From somewhere in the darkness farther along the dockside, she heard the sound of iron-shod hooves clattering on cobblestones. There was an immediate upsurge of noise from the miners, who began shouting angrily.

Suddenly there was the sound of a shot. It was immediately followed by two more.

Until this moment the mob had been contained opposite the ship astern of the *Melanie Jane*. Now the crowd began to move, spreading out in all directions.

Only the faint-hearted were fleeing. Others, roused

to anger, began prising up cobblestones to use as missiles. Their target was a troop of mounted regular soldiers, summoned from the nearby fortress of Pendennis.

It was these soldiers who had fired the shots. By so doing they stirred the noisy, but previously peaceful, demonstrators into action.

'Quick! Get on board while I douse this lamp.' The order came from Malachi.

Thomasina obeyed him without question. Moments later, after extinguishing the lamp on the shore end of the gangway, he joined her and the remainder of the crew on the deck of the *Melanie Jane*.

Spasmodic firing from the shore continued, accompanied now by shrieks of pain, clearly discernible above the shouting of those in the crowd.

Men, and women too, were running past the ship, fleeing from soldiers who now seemed to be firing upon them indiscriminately.

During a brief lull in the firing those on board the *Melanie Jane* could just make out two figures pursuing an erratic course along the dockside, heading in their direction. The larger of them seemed to be leaning heavily upon the smaller and every so often they both appeared to stumble.

When they reached the foot of the gangway, the groans of one of the two became increasingly audible, while a young voice could be heard imploring his companion, 'Hold on for just a while longer, Pa.'

'Who's that out there?' Malachi called out the question when the taller of the two stumbled and fell to the ground.

The young voice came back in reply, 'It's my pa. He's been shot by the militiamen.'

There was despair in the voice and Thomasina said immediately, 'I'm going ashore. Some of you come and help me get them on board.'

'We can't afford to get involved, Tom. The *Melanie Jane*'s sailing in little more than an hour's time. Leave well alone and let things sort themselves out.'

The words of advice came from Malachi, but they were already being ignored. Thomasina was on the gangway. Calling back, she declared, 'I'm not going to leave a boy and his father to the mercy of Sir Charles Hearle and his militiamen, Malachi. But I'll need help to get them on board.'

The crewmen were less reluctant than Malachi to take a part in what was happening. After a brief glance in the direction of their captain, some of them ran down the gangway to assist Thomasina.

Hurriedly they helped the wounded man and his thoroughly frightened young son on board. Abandoning his stance of non-involvement, Malachi said, 'Get them below to my cabin – quickly. There are soldiers coming along the quayside.'

The seamen hurried the man and boy below, leaving Thomasina uncertain whether to follow them or remain on deck.

She decided upon the latter course for the moment and was at the head of the gangway when the militiamen arrived alongside the ship. One was carrying a lantern.

Thomasina recognised the man who had unsuccessfully attempted to keep them from the ship. Then

Sir Charles Hearle pushed his way to the front of his men. Calling up to those on the ship, he said, 'We're searching for rioters. Some of them were seen heading this way.'

'A lot of people have been running past,' Malachi replied. 'I've no way of knowing whether they were miners or militiamen.'

'Some might have slipped on board without you noticing?' suggested Sir Charles. 'Do you mind if we come on board and carry out a search?'

'Yes, we do mind!' Thomasina stated angrily, before Malachi could reply. Stepping on to the darkened gangway, she glared down at the militia officer.

'I was talking to the captain, not to his cabin boy.'

Sir Charles started up the gangway, but now Malachi pushed past Thomasina to confront him.

'It doesn't matter who you're talking to, the answer is the same. I'm not having clumsy, heavy-booted militiamen tramping over my ship when I'm getting ready to put to sea. Our lives depend upon everything being exactly the way it should be when we leave harbour. I've already told you, there's no one on board this ship who shouldn't be. There have been at least two men guarding the gangway since this trouble began. We intend removing the gangway now, so I'll be obliged if you and your men will stand clear.'

The light from the lantern held aloft by the militiaman just touched upon Thomasina and it was to her that Sir Charles now spoke.

'Your face seems familiar, lad. Don't I know you from somewhere?'

'You're likely to get to know me well if you step on

board this ship. You'll be sailing with us – and we're bound for the West Indies.'

'That's right, Captain,' confirmed Malachi. 'Either you go on your way, or you sail with us. I don't mind. I could do with another hand or two – but you'll do a full day's work, the same as everyone else. What's it to be?'

There were sounds of amusement from the seamen standing on the deck of the ship. Mustering as much dignity as was possible, Sir Charles Hearle said haughtily, 'I'll not waste your time, or mine, by arguing with you, Captain, but the attitude of you and your crew is less than helpful to a man who is only carrying out his duty.' Turning away, he said, 'Come along, men. Spread out and search as you go along the dockside.'

When the militiamen had resumed their search along the quayside, Thomasina breathed a sigh of relief. Despite her disguise, had Sir Charles come on board and taken a good look at her, he might have recognised her as his aunt's one-time maidservant.

She expected Malachi to say something about her confrontation with the militiaman. Instead, he said, 'You'd better go down and see what's happening to the boy and his father. We'll need to get them off the ship before we sail. Hopefully, Hearle and the army will go about their business once they've searched the dockside. Off you go. I'll stay up here and make certain we're ready for the tide.'

Below, in Malachi's cabin, Thomasina found the boy in tears. He crouched beside his father, who was lying on Malachi's bunk, his pale face screwed up in pain.

One of the crew members who had helped him to

the cabin was still with him and it was to him that
Thomasina spoke.

'How is he?'

Looking up at her, the seaman said, 'He's lost a fair
amount of blood and is in quite a bit of pain, but
he'll live. A musket ball hit him in the fleshy part of
his thigh. Fortunately, it seems to have passed right
through without breaking any bones along the way.
The worst thing was the bleeding, but I think I've
stopped most of that – for a while, at least.'

When Thomasina expressed surprise at the crewman's
apparent knowledge of medicine, the sailor replied,
'Many years ago I served with the King's navy and
served as a "loblolly boy" – a surgeon's assistant –
during the war in America. I learned enough to know
whether or not a man was going to live or die. This
one will live, but he'll need someone to help him get
around for a day or two.'

The relief of the young boy was so transparent that
Thomasina had to resist an unmasculine urge to hug
him. Instead, she asked, 'Is there anyone in Falmouth
who can help you with your pa? We're sailing within
the hour. He'll need to be off the ship by then.'

The boy's relieved expression was obvious. 'One of
my uncles lives here, in Falmouth . . . But what about
the militia? If they take Pa, he'll go to prison.'

Thomasina knew that what the boy said was true. If
he was arrested and found to have a wound caused by
a musket ball, it would be sufficient proof that he had
been in the forefront of the rioters. The boy's father
would face the same fate as Jeffery.

She kept such thoughts to herself. 'The militia have

probably left the docks by now. Go and find this uncle. Tell him to get help and come here quickly to fetch your pa. Hurry now. We'll look after him.'

The boy was gone for almost a full hour, during which time Malachi became increasingly concerned that they would be forced to sail with the wounded man still on board.

Much to everyone's relief, the boy returned with two men, his uncle and a friend. Wasting no time in unnecessary introductions and brushing aside the thanks of the boy's uncle, Malachi hustled the injured man and his helpers ashore. Then he gave orders for the *Melanie Jane* to cast off and put to sea.

In the early hours of the following morning, with all sails set and the comforting beam of the Lizard Point lighthouse falling away on the starboard quarter, Malachi sent all non-essential crewmen below.

Taking the wheel himself, he ordered his coxwain to go to the galley and make hot drinks for Thomasina and himself. He delighted in taking the wheel whenever it was possible, especially during the night hours.

At such times as this Thomasina enjoyed being on deck with him, especially when they had just left port. This was when Malachi was most content with his chosen life – but tonight he had other matters on his mind.

In the darkness he spoke softly to Thomasina. 'Back there in Falmouth . . . Sir Charles Hearle thought he'd seen you somewhere before. Had he?'

'It's possible,' Thomasina gave him a guarded reply. 'I've been to a lot of places and met many people.'

'Is it likely to cause any problems to you if he *does* remember?'

Thomasina looked at her companion sharply, but it was impossible to see Malachi's expression in the darkness. 'Why should it?'

'No reason I can think of offhand, Tom – but I like to think we've become more than just business partners. If there *is* any way Hearle could cause trouble for you, I'd like to know. I'm on your side, Tom, come what may, but I have a very strong feeling that your distaste for the man goes far beyond anything that happened last night. I dislike him too. I'm not a man for prying, so please don't think that's what I'm doing now, but if there's anything I can do to help, whatever it might be, I'm always here.'

'Thanks, Malachi, I appreciate your support, but there's really nothing to worry about.'

Thomasina was moved by Malachi's words. However, she had no intention of putting his loyalty to the test by telling him the true story of her life.

Nevertheless, she had an uneasy feeling that Captain Malachi Ellis was not convinced she had told him all he should know about his partner. Thomasina hoped he would never learn the truth.

6

Lush green slopes of long-extinct volcanic mountains hove into view above the horizon long before the crew of the *Melanie Jane* sighted the frond-topped canopies of palm trees that fringed the sun-bleached beaches of Jamaica.

'Have you thought any more of the cargo we'll be taking back to England with us?' Thomasina put the question to Malachi as they stood on the deck together, watching the island ahead of them show up in more detail as they drew closer.

'No, but I'm not particularly concerned. We'll have plenty to choose from.'

'I don't doubt it, but I have a suggestion. I'd like to know what you think about it . . .'

Thomasina hesitated. Since leaving Falmouth she and Malachi had not discussed the events of their last evening there. She was not sure she was wise to risk broaching the subject again now.

'If you don't tell me what's in your head, I can't say whether or not I think it's a good idea.'

Malachi's words broke into Thomasina's thoughtful silence and she made up her mind.

'I was thinking about the miners and their families, starving because they can't afford the price asked for corn. What if we took on a cargo of, say, sugar or rum, in Jamaica, but instead of carrying it back to England, took it to America, sold it there and loaded corn, or flour, for Falmouth?'

Malachi looked at Thomasina in silence for a while. When he eventually spoke he said, 'Would you be looking to sell it again at corn merchants' prices – or at the price the miners were demanding?'

Back in Cornwall there had been much discussion about the fact that, at the height of their unrest, the miners had forced a number of farmers to sign an undertaking to sell wheat and barley at pre-shortage prices.

'Would it mean taking a loss if we sold it direct to the miners?'

'We'd make a small profit, but it would be a mere fraction of what such a cargo would fetch if we landed it up-country.'

'Does that mean you don't agree with the idea?'

Their partnership agreement was that Malachi should have overriding control of all matters appertaining to the type and destination of the cargoes carried by the *Melanie Jane.*

'Not necessarily. In fact this is one decision I'll let you make, Tom. I'm an old man. I already have more than enough money to keep me comfortable for the remainder of my life. You're the one with a future to consider.'

'So you'll do it? You'll take American corn back to Falmouth?' Thomasina could not hide her delight.

Malachi smiled. 'The idea has crossed my own mind, once or twice, but I felt it would be unfair to put it to you. I'm glad you thought of it for yourself. I'm proud of you, Tom.' To hide such unaccustomed feelings, Malachi suddenly became brusque. 'Now, let's prepare the ship for entering harbour.'

Kingston's deep-water harbour was the scene of much activity. In addition to merchantmen and local Caribbean vessels, there was a fleet of British men-o'-war anchored in the harbour.

More excited than Thomasina had ever seen him, Malachi pointed out that the flag flying from one of the impressive seventy-four-gun warships was that of Admiral Lord Cochrane, adding, 'He's one of the few naval officers to have earned more prize money than me!'

In among the tall-masted seagoing vessels, small boats of every description plied between ship-and-ship and ship-and-shore, in a seemingly haphazard fashion on the teeming waters.

The overcrowded harbour presented far too many hazards for a ship to berth without help. The *Melanie Jane* was taken in tow by a multi-oared boat manned by slaves, their black skin glistening with perspiration as they obeyed the orders of the English harbour official in charge of the boat.

The berth allotted to the *Melanie Jane* obliged the merchantman to pass by all the men-o'-war. Thomasina was impressed by the general air of neatness and cleanliness of each ship.

The *Melanie Jane* had two men on the wheel following the course of the towing boat. By the time they reached their allotted berth both men were perspiring as freely as the slaves.

The heat was quite oppressive here and Thomasina was feeling it too, but as the crewmen were throwing mooring ropes ashore to the waiting men, it was not the heat that bothered her.

Sniffing the air, she puckered her nose in an expression of disgust. 'Ugh! What's that horrible stench, Malachi?'

'If you haven't come across it before you can consider yourself lucky.' Taking the pipe he was smoking from his mouth and using it as a pointer, Malachi said, 'There's your answer. It's a slaver, direct from Africa. I swear the smell from some of 'em is so bad you know you're getting close to one at sea even before they come over the horizon. The trade was officially banned a couple of years back, but no one's tried to enforce the law here yet.'

The ship Malachi had pointed out was moored at a jetty protruding at right angles towards their berth from the other side of the dock.

It was not berthed tight against the wall of the dock, as was the *Melanie Jane*, but was being held off by a number of timbers, leaving an expanse of water between ship and shore. A number of men stood on the shore side, many armed with long-handled brushes.

There was a great deal of activity about the boat and, as Thomasina watched, she was horrified to see a number of naked African men, all linked together by heavy chains, pushed into the water from the ship.

As the unfortunate slaves struggled to reach the shore, they were pushed back into the water by those on land, who then used the brushes on them with considerable vigour.

Suddenly, Thomasina realised that not all the slaves were men. A number were in fact young women – and one was desperately clutching a baby to her, despite the fact that by doing so she ran a very real risk of drowning!

'What are they doing?' Thomasina asked in alarm.

'They're bathing the slaves. No one will be over-keen to buy them until the stench of the slave ship's been scrubbed away.'

'But . . . some will drown!'

Malachi shook his head. 'They're worth too much money for the master of the slaver to allow that to happen. They'll be well scrubbed, then pulled ashore . . . see.'

He pointed to where a group of shackled slaves huddled on the jetty, their numbers growing as newly clean slaves were hauled roughly from the waters of the harbour.

'It's barbaric!' Thomasina found it difficult to express the disgust she felt at what was happening on the other side of the dock.

She also experienced a growing sense of disbelief at the astonishing number of slaves being unloaded from a ship that was no larger than the *Melanie Jane*.

'There would have been many more when they left Africa.' Malachi's matter-of-fact tone of voice did not quite hide his own feelings. 'A quarter will have died on the voyage here and been heaved over the side. You can always tell a slaver when you're at sea, even if you're upwind of her. She'll have sharks around her like hounds around a fox.'

Thomasina shuddered as she watched yet another batch of newly scrubbed slaves being dragged ashore to join their terrified and confused countrymen.

'What will happen to them now?'

'They'll be taken to the market and auctioned off. You can go along and see it for yourself, if you like.'

Thomasina shook her head vigorously. 'I can't think of anything I'd like less. People shouldn't be bought and sold like sheep, or pigs, or cattle.'

Even as she spoke the words, Thomasina was thinking back to the days when she worked at Trebene. Although the terms of their employment stopped short of slavery, there had been a feeling among the servants in the great house that they were *owned* by the Vincent family.

She dreaded to think what her fate might have been had she actually been owned by the Vincents. She would certainly never have dared to fight back against Sir Charles Hearle.

'I don't want to see the auction, Malachi, but I would like to go ashore to stretch my legs. It feels as though we've been at sea for months. I'll come with you when you go off to find a buyer for our cargo.'

7

As well as being a seaport, Kingston was also the capital of Jamaica, yet Thomasina found its buildings less than impressive.

'There's two reasons for that,' Malachi explained as he and Thomasina walked together through the town. 'A serious earthquake only a few years ago destroyed most of the older buildings. When they set about rebuilding it, the money wasn't forthcoming from the planters. They prefer to spend their earnings on their own homes and estates. Some of those are truly magnificent.'

Their destination was the office of a merchant with whom Malachi had traded for many years. Having spent so long on board the *Melanie Jane*, Thomasina's legs were aching by the time they arrived.

Malachi introduced her to the merchant as his young nephew. After shaking hands, she was grateful to sit down in a chair while the two men got down to some hard bargaining. Whilst this was going on a bottle of rum was placed upon the table between them, the level of its contents dropping steadily as they talked.

When they began haggling over a matter of mere pence per hogshead of fish, Thomasina lost interest. Rising from her chair, she walked to the window of the office, which overlooked a square where a crowd was gathering.

Then, from the direction of the docks, a large number of the slaves she had seen earlier were led to the centre of the square. Men, women and children, they were indiscriminately linked together by chains. Now Thomasina remembered what Malachi had said to her earlier. This was where the slaves were to be auctioned.

She turned away from the window so abruptly that both men looked up at her in surprise.

'What's the matter, Tom?' Malachi put the question to her.

'It's the slaves we saw at the docks. They're bringing them into the square to be sold.'

'Are they, by God?' exclaimed the merchant, rising to his feet abruptly. 'Either they're early, or you've kept me here for longer than I intended. Get your ship unloaded, Malachi. We'll talk more of this tomorrow. I need to be out there when they start bidding if I'm to buy prime stock.'

It took a moment for his meaning to sink in. Then Thomasina asked, 'You mean . . . you're going out there to buy slaves? To buy men and women?'

'And a few children, if I can get them for the right

price,' the merchant replied cheerfully. 'They sell particularly well because they're quick to train and have a good working life ahead of them. But I buy adults, too. A good buck will make a fine profit once he's got over the voyage and put a bit of meat on his bones.'

Winking at Malachi, he added, 'You ought to make a trip or two from Africa carrying slaves, Malachi, while it's still possible. Bring a few young African girls back with you. This young man will have learned all he needs to know about life by the time you reach Jamaica.'

The merchant hurried from the office chuckling, mistaking the red anger shining in Thomasina's cheeks for embarrassment.

Turning to Malachi, Thomasina asked fiercely, 'Do we need to do business with *him*?'

Malachi nodded, 'You won't find anyone more honest in the whole of Jamaica – and no one here will look at things any differently. Come on, Tom, let's get back to the *Melanie Jane*. I need to work on the figures I've been given.'

Thomasina walked silently beside Malachi as they crossed the square, skirting the huge and excited crowd gathered around the newly arrived slaves.

Looking across to where the raised platform was sited in the centre of the square, she saw two young African women standing there shackled together. Naked from the waist up, each was dressed in a 'garment' consisting of a strip of sacking. Tied about the waist, it extended to just below the knee. Both girls stood silently looking down at the boards beneath their feet.

As she watched, the auctioneer placed his hand beneath the chin of one of the girls and lifted her head, in order that prospective buyers might see her face more clearly.

It could have hardly been more degrading for the girl. Thomasina managed to keep a tight hold on her feelings, but she did not fool Malachi.

'It won't be too long before slavery is abolished altogether,' he said. 'At least, as far as England is concerned. I doubt if it will ever end here – or in the Americas.'

'The whole thing is an absolute disgrace,' fumed Thomasina, with a depth of feeling she would have found difficult to explain. 'First they scrubbed them raw with brooms and now they're selling them off like pigs in a market.'

'They're worth considerably more than animals,' said Malachi. 'For that reason alone a good owner will look after his slaves. Unfortunately, all owners aren't reasonable men – and some have too much money to concern themselves with the welfare of their slaves. Try not to think about it too much, Tom. You can't change the ways of the world, much as you might like to. Let's get back to the ship and see about having the cargo unloaded. Then we'll give the crew some of their pay and let them have a night ashore. It's been a good trip, but a long one. They deserve a break.' He shook his head and grimaced. 'Not that any of their wives or sweethearts would agree. Kingston offers more temptations to a sailor than any other town on this earth.'

8

Thomasina felt a great sense of relief when the *Melanie Jane* had been towed clear of Kingston harbour and she could turn her back on the dockland area and the slave ship. It had given her a glimpse of suffering and degradation which would remain with her for a very long time.

When the ship turned into the open sea and the sails bellied out, filled by a following wind, she felt she had returned to a cleaner, more wholesome world.

'Still thinking of the slaves you saw back there, Tom?'

Malachi had been watching her before he put the question.

Thomasina nodded. 'I doubt if I'll ever be able to forget them.'

'You'll need to hold your feelings in check for a while longer,' Malachi said. 'There are more slaves in the port where we'll be taking on wheat. Upset anyone there and we'll find the price of wheat will rise very suddenly.'

'Can't we buy it somewhere else?'

Malachi shook his head. 'Norfolk is the place suggested by the merchant we've been dealing with here. He's given me a letter of introduction and the cargo we're taking there is his idea. He says coffee always fetches good money. We're in business, Tom. Whatever our thoughts, we mustn't lose sight of that.'

'I'll do my best to keep my feelings to myself, Malachi – but I'm not promising anything.'

'You start talking like that and I'll begin to wish we were heading straight back to Falmouth with a cargo from Jamaica,' Malachi admonished her. 'After what we saw back there, half the crew would gladly take up a crusade against slavery if I gave them time to think about it.'

Before Thomasina could reply, Malachi continued, 'Don't think I'm disagreeing with you, Tom. It's high time slavery came to an end, but we're already heading off on one crusade, right now. Buying wheat for hungry Cornish men, women and children. As I've said, upset the Americans in Norfolk – *really* upset them – and we'll be forced to leave with an empty ship.'

Waiting a few minutes for his words to sink in, he said thoughtfully, 'I remember a tapestry I used to see on the wall of a preacher's house, back home. It was a prayer of some sort. It read, "God grant me the serenity to accept the things I cannot change, courage to change the things that should be changed, and the wisdom to know the difference." They're the words of a wise man, Tom. Think about them. They've saved me a whole lot of grief during my lifetime. They might do the same for you.'

Thomasina could not entirely agree with Malachi's advice, but she knew he was right. There was nothing she could do about what she had seen.

Malachi had never before sailed into Norfolk's deep-water harbour and he took on board a pilot to guide him to a suitable berth. The pilot, a man born and raised in Virginia, was able to tell Malachi that wheat was readily available in the port, brought downriver from established wheat fields away from the coast.

He also confirmed that coffee was a commodity in great demand. He proved it by making an offer to a surprised Malachi to purchase half the *Melanie Jane*'s cargo on his own behalf.

There was a far more relaxed atmosphere in the harbour here than there had been in Kingston. The houses too, those that could be seen from the water, had an air of tranquillity and solidity that had been lacking in Jamaica.

One thing that was distressingly similar for Thomasina was the employment on the dockside of a great many slaves. There was little to distinguish those who came on board to unload the *Melanie Jane* from the slaves she had observed at Kingston.

They were working under the supervision of an American overseer who walked among them wielding a heavy riding crop. He was not slow to use it on any slave who, in his opinion, was not working hard enough.

One slave in particular appeared to be the target of the overseer's whip. Yet, as far as Thomasina could judge, he was as hard-working as any of his companions.

Malachi was about to go ashore to negotiate the purchase of a cargo of wheat and flour when he saw Thomasina watching the slaves.

Placing a cautionary hand on her shoulder, he said, 'Remember our little chat, Tom. Go below – or look over the other side of the ship and see what's going on in the harbour. Better still, come ashore with me.'

Thomasina shook her head. The *Melanie Jane* had encountered a couple of days' bad weather on the voyage from Jamaica. During this time one of the yards had cracked, requiring temporary repairs to be carried out. It had been an exhausting and dangerous task. Malachi hoped to be able to renew the yard here, in Norfolk. Before that, when the day's work was over, the men would want to go ashore and find relaxation in one of the many waterfront taverns.

It was what the sailors usually did when they reached harbour, but Thomasina rarely joined them. She preferred to remain on board, enjoying the peace of a near-deserted ship.

An opportunity to be alone was one of the few things she missed on board the *Melanie Jane*. This apart, she thoroughly enjoyed life at sea.

Malachi had left the ship only a matter of minutes when Thomasina heard shouting on the dockside. She ran to the side of the ship and immediately saw the cause of the commotion.

At the foot of the gangway a split sack of coffee beans lay on the ground. Crouching beside it was the slave who had earlier been singled out for the overseer's attention – and he was receiving it once more.

The overseer was raining blows on the slave's bare back with the riding crop and appeared almost beside himself with rage.

'Stop that! What do you think you're doing?' Malachi's cautionary warning forgotten, Thomasina hurried down the gangway to where the slave was being beaten.

'Keep out of this, son. It's none of your business.'

Whilst talking to Thomasina, the overseer ceased his assault on the defenceless man long enough to enable the slave to scramble out of reach of the riding crop.

'It's my business when you're causing him to bleed all over the cargo we've just brought in – unless you're ready to pay for it out of your own pocket?'

The slave had sustained a bad gash upon his right upper arm. He had probably struck it on the iron corner-piece of the gangway when he slipped and fell with a heavy sack of coffee on his bent back.

The overseer was taken aback by the suggestion that he should pay restitution for the split sack and its contents. Thomasina took advantage of his uncertainty.

'I'll take him on board and bind something around that cut to stop him bleeding over everything in sight, then you can have him back.'

Giving the overseer no time to argue, she took the slave by the shoulder. As he rose to his feet she propelled him up the gangway.

'Make sure you don't let him out of sight for as much as a second,' the overseer called after her. 'If he runs off, *I'll* be the one looking for cash from *you* – and slaves don't come cheap.'

Ignoring the man, Thomasina led the slave to the stern of the ship and sat him down beside the ship's wheel. The *Melanie Jane* was riding on a high tide and the overseer could not see them from his place on the quayside.

Some of the crew who remained on board had seen the incident between the slave and the overseer. They stood around now, murmuring sympathetically.

'It was him and his whip who caused what happened,' explained one of the crewmen, jerking his head shorewards. 'He made this one slip and fall. Had it been his head, and not his arm that struck the gangway, he'd have had a dead slave on his hands.'

'Better he kill me,' said the slave bitterly. 'They don't hand out no beatings in heaven.'

'That's quite enough of such talk,' said Thomasina sharply. Looking up at the watching crewmen, she continued, 'One of you go down to Malachi's cabin and fetch the medicine box. Another go to the galley and find a drink and something to eat – but be quick about it. If we take too long, we'll have the overseer up here ordering him back to work.'

Thomasina was the youngest member of the crew, but in addition to her special relationship with Malachi, she had gained the respect of the other crew members by her presence of mind in an emergency. They hurried to do her bidding without question.

Inspecting the slave's wound, Thomasina asked, 'What's your name?'

'Shadrack.'

He seemed disinclined to talk. Thomasina thought he was probably uncertain why she and the other members of the crew should want to help him.

'My name's Tom. We'll only have a few minutes, but in that time I'll bandage your arm and you'll have something to eat and drink.'

Giving her a puzzled, searching look, Shadrack asked, 'Why?'

'What sort of a question is that? Because you've hurt yourself and need help, that's why. We all need help at some time or another.'

The crew member returned carrying the medicine box. Shortly afterwards a tankard of beer and some bread and cheese arrived.

Shadrack ate and drank hurriedly, using one hand, while Thomasina cleaned and bandaged his arm. As she did so, she asked, 'Why does the overseer pick on you in particular, Shadrack? You seemed to be working just as hard as any of the others – probably harder, knowing he's watching you all the time.'

When he made no reply, she looked up and was startled to see that tears had filled his eyes.

'What's the matter?'

At that moment one of the crewmen called urgently, 'The overseer's coming up the gangway . . .'

In a matter of seconds the food and drink had been whisked away and Thomasina concentrated on securing the bandage she had wound around Shadrack's arm.

'You're taking your time!' The overseer glared at Thomasina.

'Perhaps things appear by themselves in America,' retorted Thomasina. 'They don't on board the *Melanie Jane* – they have to be fetched. I've done it as quickly as I could.'

'Well, you've finished now,' said the overseer ungraciously. 'He can get back to work, and quick.' Shaking his riding crop at Shadrack, who had climbed to his feet, he went on, 'I expect to see you working twice as hard as everyone else to make up for the time you've lost. Now, get back to it, if you don't want to feel this across your lazy back again.'

As the overseer went off, driving Shadrack ahead of him, the slave cast a swift glance over his shoulder towards Thomasina, but she was unable to read his expression.

'That bully boy will make full use of his riding crop, no matter how hard the poor soul works,' said one of the crew sympathetically. 'There's not a single one of the slaves who hasn't got the scars of a whipping on his back.'

'True,' agreed Thomasina, 'but he seems to have it in for Shadrack in particular, for some reason. I wish I knew what it is all about.'

9

The *Melanie Jane* remained in Norfolk, Virginia, for nine days. It was longer than Malachi had anticipated. The cargo had been unloaded and the hold packed with a mixed cargo of corn and flour, but Malachi was unable to find a yard to satisfactorily replace the broken one.

Eventually, he settled for what he complained was a second-rate one, but was far from satisfied with his purchase.

'It will hold as long as the weather does,' he grumbled to Thomasina, 'but I wouldn't trust it in a storm like the one we ran into on the way here.'

'What's wrong with it?' Thomasina asked. 'They make ships here, don't they? They should know what they're doing.'

'Oh, they know all right,' Malachi moaned. 'But they think I don't. The wood they used to make this yard was too green. It needs a whole lot more sea-soning. Unfortunately, right now Englishmen aren't too popular among American shipping men. It seems our navy's been stopping their ships – from this port in particular – and impressing a great many of their seamen, claiming they're British, whether they are or not. Talk is that, if it doesn't stop, we'll not only be fighting the French, but at war with America again, too – and soon. I'm not sorry to be leaving.'

'Do the Americans have a navy?' Thomasina asked, in some surprise.

'Not a very large one,' Malachi explained, 'but they're building ships – good ships – in a hurry. I'm convinced that's where all the decent wood is going.'

'I won't be sorry to leave here, either,' Thomasina said, 'war or no war. The sight of *them* upsets me.'

She pointed to where a line of slaves was being escorted from the dockside. Almost dusk now, it was the end of their long working day.

Thomasina was unable to see whether Shadrack was one of their number, but he had been working on the dockside during the time that the *Melanie Jane* had been in harbour. On the first occasion she recognised him she had waved. She believed he had seen her, but he did not acknowledge her greeting.

Unfortunately, the overseer had also seen her gesture. It brought Shadrack immediate unwelcome attention from the omnipresent riding crop.

Malachi planned to sail shortly before midnight, strik-ing out immediately across the vast breadth of the

Atlantic Ocean, bound for Falmouth – and home.

Less than an hour before their departure time, Thomasina and the crew working on deck heard the sound of iron-shod hooves on the stone-paved dockside. A party of about twenty horsemen cantered into view. Upon reaching the ship, they brought their mounts to a halt at the foot of the gangway which provided the link between ship and shore.

The lanterns on the quayside cast their yellow light upon the grim faces of the horsemen – and upon the guns carried by them.

As they milled around the foot of the gangway, Malachi called out, 'What's going on? Are you wanting something?'

'Yes, sir, we're after a runaway slave.'

'What makes you think he might be down this way?'

'There's nowhere else for him to go. Runaways get short shrift inland, so most try to get on a ship. Besides, this slave's been working here. He knows the docks.'

'There's nowhere for him to hide on my ship,' Malachi said. 'And all my hands have been on deck getting ready for sea. No one could have slipped on board unnoticed.'

'Thank you, Captain. We'll find him down here somewhere, I'm sure of that. The murdering son-of-a-bitch will dance at the end of a rope before the night's out.'

'He's murdered someone?'

'Didn't I say? He stabbed Mick Kellerman to death. You might have known Mick, he was in charge of a labour-gang here, on the dock, and he knew how to treat 'em. They wouldn't dare try anything when he was around.'

Thomasina had listened with growing apprehension to the conversation between Malachi and the horsemen. She had never heard mention of the name of the overseer who had supervised the unloading of the *Melanie Jane*, but it would not have surprised her to hear that *he* had been killed by one of the slaves – and there was probably no one with greater justification for turning on the bully than Shadrack.

'You thinking the same as me, Tom?' Malachi came to stand beside her as the armed men rode along the dockside to the next ship.

'I expect so, but we're probably both wrong. There must be a lot of overseers working on the docks. Even more slaves. We don't even know the name of the overseer we had on board the *Melanie Jane*.'

'I do,' said Malachi quietly. 'He introduced himself to me when he first came on board. It was Kellerman. Mick Kellerman. I think the sooner we leave Norfolk and its problems, the better.'

The *Melanie Jane* slipped quietly out of the American harbour half an hour later, but Malachi's hopes that they were leaving the problems of Norfolk behind would receive a severe blow.

When Thomasina woke and went on deck the following morning for some fresh air, she found three of the crew there, talking together in low voices.

When they saw her they reacted in a manner that made Thomasina immediately curious, especially when she realised that none had duties on deck at this time of the day.

'What's the matter with you, can't you sleep? Or are you excited because we're heading for home?'

The three men did not smile or come back with a jocular response, as she had expected. They put her in mind of three young boys who shared a guilty secret.

Frowning, Thomasina asked, 'What's the matter? Is something wrong?'

The men exchanged glances, as though each was hoping one of the others would be the first to speak.

Impatiently, Thomasina said, 'Is no one going to say anything? You, Ned. What's troubling you?'

Ned shuffled his feet nervously before saying, 'There's something Captain Malachi should know about, Tom, but it would be better coming from you than from us.'

'What you mean is that it's something you're too scared to tell him about, so you want me to do your dirty work for you. All right, tell me about it.'

'It's that slave, Tom. The one the Americans were after last night. He's here.'

'On board the *Melanie Jane*? When did you find him? Where is he now?'

The men appeared even more ill-at-ease. 'We didn't find him, Tom. He came on board last night, about an hour before the men came looking for him. We took him down to the mess-room. He's there now.'

Thomasina was aghast. 'Do you know what would have happened, had they found him on board? There'd have been hell to pay! I'm certainly not on their side, but he's wanted for murder, for Christ's sake!'

Then, feeling sorry for the three downcast men, she said, more normally, 'It *is* Shadrack we're talking about, I presume?'

The three men all nodded. One who had said nothing so far now spoke, 'That's right, it's Shadrack – but before you tell Malachi, I reckon you should come below decks and hear his story.'

'There's no need for that. We all saw how the overseer treated him.'

'There's more to it than that, Tom. Far more. You ought to hear it for yourself before you speak to Malachi.'

In the low-beamed mess-deck where the crew lived, ate and slept, Shadrack was seated hunched on a stool in a corner. When he saw Thomasina, he greeted her eagerly. 'Master Tom . . . ! You've spoken to the captain? He won't take me back to Norfolk?'

'I don't think there's any fear of that, Shadrack, but he'll need to decide exactly what we are to do with you. The first thing he'll want to know is whether or not it's true that you killed Kellerman.'

Shadrack's chin came up in a momentary expression of defiance, then he bowed his head, before replying. 'Yes, Master Tom, I killed him.'

Thomasina remained silent for a few moments, then said, 'I'm not saying the way he treated you was right, Shadrack. It certainly *wasn't* – but neither is murder.'

'That isn't why he murdered the bastard.' One of

the crew standing nearby spoke with great feeling. 'Tell him, Shadrack. Tell Tom about this Kellerman – and your wife. Tell him what he did to both of you.'

Thomasina looked from Shadrack to the seaman who had spoken, then back again to the slave. 'I think you'd better tell me, Shadrack. Tell me everything.'

Hesitantly at first, but with increasing emotion, Shadrack told the story of the events that had led to the murder of the bullying overseer.

He spoke softly in the dimly lit mess-room, surrounded by grim-faced and silent seamen. The only other sounds were the creaks and groans of the wooden ship and the regular slap of the sea against the bow, as the *Melanie Jane* dipped into the waves.

It was a story that Thomasina listened to in growing horror.

Shadrack had been born on a cotton plantation far to the south of Norfolk – in Georgia. He had been happy there, working for an easy-going planter and his wife.

When he was twenty years old, Shadrack had married an attractive young girl named Millie. She was a slave, like himself, although it was generally accepted that her grandfather had been a white plantation owner.

Millie was, according to Shadrack, 'the prettiest girl on any of the plantations for miles around'.

For a year they led a very happy life, occupying a small, one-roomed cabin on the plantation. Then an epidemic swept through their region of Georgia, laying low slave and owner alike.

Millie and Shadrack survived, but many others

fell victim. Among their number were the elderly
plantation owner and his wife.

As a result of their deaths the plantation was broken
up and the land divided among local land-owners. The
slaves too went to new owners.

To the great relief of Shadrack and Millie, they were
shipped off together to a relative of their late employer,
who lived in Norfolk, Virginia. Here their good luck
came to an abrupt and brutal end.

Shadrack was sent to work on the docks, in a gang
supervised by Mick Kellerman. Millie was put to work
as a servant in the house occupied by the bachelor
overseer.

It was not long before she caught his eye. One
night he ordered her from the slaves' quarters to his
bedroom, where he violently raped her. From that
night on she became his unwilling mistress.

Despite this, Shadrack still contrived to meet her
occasionally, but when Kellerman caught them talking, he had Shadrack publicly whipped. It was this
that had caused the extensive scarring Thomasina had
witnessed on his back during the time he was working
on board the *Melanie Jane*.

When the beating was over, Kellerman had warned
Shadrack that if he tried to see Millie again, his pun-
ishment would be even more severe. But Shadrack
had no intention of obeying the unreasonable order.
He continued to meet his wife whenever he could steal
a few moments.

Inevitably, Kellerman caught them together again.

It was now, for the first time, that Shadrack faltered
in his narrative.

'Go on, Shadrack. Did he whip you again?' Thomasina prompted gently.

'No, Master Tom.' The fugitive slave turned his face up to her and there were tears streaming down his face. 'He had Millie whipped and forced me to watch. Then . . .'

Shadrack needed to compose himself before continuing. 'Some of Boss Kellerman's friends held me down on the ground while Kellerman stamped on me, saying that by the time he'd finished I'd never want to so much as look at any other woman. I don't know which hurt worse, Master Tom, what Boss Kellerman did to me, or hearing Millie crying when they let go of me. I ain't a man no more, Master Tom. No good for my Millie, or for any other woman.'

Feeling physically sick, Thomasina said fiercely, 'He deserved to die, Shadrack. A man like that didn't deserve to be given life in the first place.'

There were angry murmurs of agreement from the listening crew, but Shadrack said, 'I wished him dead for that, Master Tom. Many nights I would go down on my knees and pray he would die, but I wouldn't have killed him. Then one day I met my Millie again. She told me that Boss Kellerman was hitting her and doing bad things. She said she didn't want to live no more. She begged me to kill her and put her out of her misery. I wouldn't do that, Master Tom, I couldn't have done anything to hurt her.'

The tears were streaming down Shadrack's cheeks now, but he had not ended his tragic story.

'Yesterday, after I finished working, I was told that Millie was dead. She'd hanged herself from a tree in

Boss Kellerman's garden. That's when I went to his house and killed him, Master Tom. I didn't do it for me, but for Millie. For my wife.'

10

In Malachi's cabin an emotional Thomasina repeated the story related to her by Shadrack. When it came to an end, Malachi reached out and took her hand, squeezing it comfortingly before releasing it.

'It's not a story you should have had to listen to, Tom, but the men weren't to know that.'

'I'll get over it soon enough – but I doubt if Shadrack ever will. What are we going to do with him, Malachi?'

'What do you suggest?' Malachi countered her question with one of his own. 'Do you have any ideas?'

'None, beyond taking him to England with us – and hoping he'll learn something of seamanship along the way,' Thomasina admitted.

Malachi shrugged. 'I can't think of any other course of action, so that's what we'll do.'

'You're not angry with the men for hiding him on board?'

'I'd be happier had they felt able to tell me what they were doing – but no, I'm not angry.' Malachi shrugged once more. 'I probably wouldn't have behaved any differently, had I been one of them.'

'You're a good man, Malachi,' Thomasina gave him a watery smile. 'I'll go and tell the men. They'll be greatly relieved.'

Shadrack settled down to shipboard life well. Impeccably clean and willing to tackle any task, he quickly won the respect of the Cornish seamen.

He was also quick to learn. By the time they had been at sea for five days he could be relied upon to tackle most of the routine duties of shipboard life.

On the sixth day out from Norfolk the weather deteriorated alarmingly and Malachi's fears about the suspect yard on the mainmast were realised. As the wind touched gale force, it suddenly snapped.

Cursing the integrity of the Norfolk boat-builders, Malachi supervised the crew as they fought to remove the broken yard, hampered by the severe weather. When this was done, they needed to clear and unravel a mess of tangled rigging.

The task completed to his satisfaction, Malachi said, 'I'm not happy with things as they are, Tom. I'm not going to risk pressing on without a new yard.'

'Will we need to return to Norfolk?' Thomasina expressed the apprehension already showing on the face of Shadrack. Helping the coxwain on the wheel, he had been listening to the conversation with increasing alarm.

'No, Bermuda's little more than a day's sailing to

the south. There are boat-builders there. They are also gathering stores, with a view to opening a naval-supply depot. Hopefully we'll find what we need there.'

Malachi had seen Shadrack's concern. For his benefit, he added, 'Bermuda belongs to Britain, Shadrack. You'll be safe enough there as one of the *Melanie Jane*'s crew.'

The fugitive slave had come to have great respect for Malachi. He accepted what the captain said without question.

Unlike Jamaica, the island of Bermuda, although hilly, had no tall mountains to guide a mariner to its shores. At first sight it seemed to Thomasina that it might have been floating upon the surface of the ocean.

As they approached, Malachi issued a string of orders, gradually reducing sail and speed until the *Melanie Jane* was hardly moving through the water.

They were close to land now. Without shifting his gaze from the sea ahead of them, Malachi spoke to Thomasina. 'I've only ever been here once before. That was many years ago. I seem to remember it's a difficult approach to the harbour and the town of St George. We'll anchor and hope another ship comes in. Then we'll follow it through the channel. I don't want to lose my ship for the sake of a broken yard.'

Malachi had to wait for twenty-four hours before he was able to put his plan into operation. Then it was not a single ship that guided him into the St George harbour, but six. They were British men-o'-war, the largest a seventy-four-gun warship, flying a commodore's flag.

By the time the last of the warships had passed through the narrow channel to the harbour, the *Melanie Jane* was under way. Inside the harbour she anchored clear of the Royal Navy vessels and Malachi ordered the ship's boat to be lowered.

Thomasina had already told Malachi she would like to go ashore, and Shadrack was delighted when he was chosen to be one of the boat's crew, having informed Malachi that he had occasionally crewed a boat in Norfolk.

'Thank you, boss,' he said to Malachi. 'It will be the first time I've been anywhere as a free man.' Suddenly his expression clouded and he asked, hesitantly, 'I *am* a free man now?'

'I don't have slaves crewing on my boat, Shadrack. You're as free as any other man on board, as far as I'm concerned.'

'You've made him a very happy man,' Thomasina commented, as the ex-slave hurried away to help the men lower the boat.

'It wasn't a hard thing to do,' Malachi replied. 'I only wish everyone else on board was as easily satisfied.'

A few members of the *Melanie Jane*'s crew, anxious to be home, had grumbled that they could have sailed on without repairing the broken yard. In their opinion it had not been necessary to sail so many miles off course to Bermuda.

'Before we go ashore let's go down below and make sure we have enough English money left to buy a new yard. It won't come cheap this far from home.'

11

The boat from the *Melanie Jane* set off for the Bermu-
dan capital, St George, less than half an hour after
the ship had anchored, yet already boats from the
British men-o'-war were busily plying back and forth
between their ships and the shore.

'It's as well we've not called in for provisions,'
Malachi commented. 'It looks to me as though the
navy intends buying up everything they can lay their
hands on.'

Shadrack and three seamen were at the oars of
the *Melanie Jane*'s boat, with Malachi and Thomasina
sitting in the stern. Malachi called out an occasional
order when he thought the boat was straying off
course, and soon it bumped gently against a dock
where stores for the British squadron were piled up
ready to be loaded.

Significantly Thomasina observed that the bulk of

the stores consisted of gunpowder and cannonballs. It seemed the British squadron had either been recently involved in a sea battle or expected to meet with an enemy very soon.

Once ashore the seamen, Shadrack with them, headed for the nearest tavern. Malachi said he would visit the boat-builders along the waterfront but warned the crewmen to be back on the quay in an hour's time.

Thomasina decided to have a walk around the town by herself.

It was quite small, as was the island on which it stood. Indeed, the sea on the other side of the island was within easy walking distance of the harbourside. The buildings of the little town were a mixture of impressive, stone-built buildings belonging to the island administrators, shanties and waterfront taverns. The last had no pretence of permanency about them. They had been thrown up to meet the increase in business brought about by the war with France and the ever-increasing possibility of further conflict with America.

Not wishing to visit any of the taverns, Thomasina slowly made her way back to the quay. The hour given to the crew by Malachi was almost up, yet there was no sign of them. Malachi was not to be seen, either. Thomasina knew the crew would remain in the tavern drinking for as long as they were able, periodically sending a member of the party outside to check whether the captain was in sight.

She hoped they were taking care of Shadrack. He would not be used to strong drink.

Contrary to her expectations, she had seen many slaves on Bermuda, but they appeared to enjoy far greater freedom of movement than their fellows in either Jamaica or Virginia. The reason was undoubtedly because this was a very small island. There would be nowhere for them to hide if they absconded.

While she stood on the quayside Thomasina observed a boat coming in from the direction of the British naval squadron, but she took little notice of it. Boats from the men-o'-war were flitting across the waters of the harbour like so many water beetles.

There was a midshipman seated in the stern of this particular boat. Another man, whom she took to be a petty officer, was seated beside him. Thomasina also noticed in passing that the crew seemed small for the size of the boat. She assumed, with very little real interest, that they were leaving as much room as possible for the stores they would be taking back to their ship.

As the boat bumped alongside the stone wall of the quay, Thomasina turned away, impatient that the crew members from the *Melanie Jane* had not yet put in an appearance.

To her relief, she saw Malachi making his way towards her. Something in the way he was walking told her immediately that his quest for a new yard had not been successful.

She was about to set off to meet him when a voice from behind her called, 'We'll make this our first . . . Take him.'

She turned to see what was happening and was

shocked to see the midshipman from the newly arrived boat pointing at her.

The midshipman led a Royal Navy press-gang!

It was too late to escape. Before she could make a move, a sailor had taken hold of one of her arms, then the other was seized by a second.

Trying in vain to shake them off, Thomasina demanded, 'What do you think you're doing? Let go of me.'

'Now, don't go causing any trouble, lad. You're needed to serve on board HMS *Victorious*. She's a good ship. Agree to join us as a volunteer, and you'll be given a very generous bounty. Refuse, and you'll get nothing – but still be impressed into His Majesty's service. Be sensible about it now, lad. What would you rather do? Serve His Majesty and have money in your pocket, or serve him just the same and have nothing?'

'I'll do neither. Let me go.' Once again Thomasina tried desperately to break free, but to no avail. The grip of the two sailors was too strong for her. 'Let me go, do you hear? I'm needed on my own ship.'

Ignoring her plea, the midshipman said, 'All right, put him in the boat. We'll go off and see how many more we can find.'

Thomasina continued to struggle, but she was not very heavy. It took little effort on the part of her captors to propel her towards the waiting boat.

'WAIT! What the devil do you think you're doing?' Malachi bellowed for all the world like an angry bull as he hurried awkwardly towards them, his peg-leg tapping out an erratic rhythm on the stone-paved quayside.

His authoritative voice was sufficient to bring the seamen holding Thomasina to a halt, but before Malachi reached them, the midshipman stepped into his path.

'This young man is being impressed into the Royal Navy. I advise you not to interfere.'

For a few moments Thomasina thought Malachi would knock the junior naval rating from his path. Instead, the *Melanie Jane*'s captain seemed to swell to twice his normal size.

Fixing the other man with a shrivelling glare, he said, 'Don't you tell me what to do, you young whipper-snapper. I was having midshipmen "kiss the gunner's daughter" when you were still on your hands and knees in the nursery – even though you're older than any midshipman worth his salt ought to be.'

Through his reference to 'kissing the gunner's daugh-ter' – a naval term used to describe being stretched over the barrel of a cannon and flogged – the midshipman was aware that Malachi had once been a naval man. Probably one who had held a senior rank. Nevertheless, he stood his ground.

'I don't doubt you were . . . sir, but as an ex-naval officer, you will appreciate that I have a duty to perform . . .'

'I don't give a damn for your "duty", mister. I've served my country in a manner you will never achieve. By the time I was your age I had command of my own ship and had lost a leg proving my patriotism. I'm on my way to England now with food for my starving countrymen – your countrymen, too. I have a broken yard that I can't replace and need every one of my crew if I'm to get there safely. Tom here, especially. He's the one who helps me do all the things I can't do for myself since I lost my leg. You'll let him go and find someone else to press into service.'

'I'm sorry, sir,' declared the midshipman doggedly. 'I have my orders . . .'

'Orders be damned!' snapped Malachi. 'If Admiral Nelson – yes, and me too – if we'd stuck blindly to orders, the French would have swept us from the sea years ago. Have you never wondered why you're still a midshipman when most men of your age are commanding their own ships? I'll tell you, mister. It's because you follow orders so blindly that you've lost the ability to think for yourself. Do you want to become another Billy Culmer?'

The man to whom Malachi referred had gained notoriety in the Royal Navy by serving as a midshipman for thirty-five years before being promoted to lieutenant at the age of fifty-seven.

Malachi knew he would need to bully the unimaginative officer in charge of the press-gang if he was to persuade him to release Thomasina – and he *had* to succeed. Her sex would be discovered very quickly in the between-decks confines of a man-o'-war.

'I carry out my duties as I see them, sir.' The midshipman was aware that the members of his press-gang were enjoying this one-sided exchange. He wished now they had never chanced upon this lad. But they had. He could not back down now.

To the men holding Thomasina, he snapped, 'I told you to take him to the boat. What are you waiting for?'

As the seamen turned to do his bidding, Malachi suddenly called, 'Not so fast.'

When they turned to look at him, Malachi was pointing a double-barrelled pistol at the midshipman. He was not in the habit of carrying a pistol, but he had brought a lot of money ashore with him in the hope of purchasing a new yard. Knowing very little about crime on the island of Bermuda, he had thought it wise to go armed.

'I suggest you order the release of my lad now. If they try to take him, I'll shoot you dead. I doubt if the navy will consider a ship's boy fair exchange for the life of a midshipman.'

'Don't do anything stupid, Malachi.' Although dismayed at being taken by the press-gang, Thomasina was thoroughly alarmed at this turn of events. 'They won't keep me on a man-o'-war. You know that.'

Thomasina hoped the captain of the *Melanie Jane* would take the hidden meaning in her words. Once on board the warship, she had only to disclose her sex and they would send her back to her own ship. It would mean she would never again be able to sail on the *Melanie Jane* as a crew member, but it was preferable to seeing Malachi die for murdering the midshipman.

'He's right.' The midshipman was trying unsuccessfully not to appear frightened. He did not doubt Malachi would do as he said. 'You might murder me – and possibly another of my men, but you'd be taken and hanged.'

Malachi shook his head. 'I've already said you were lacking in imagination. I wouldn't shoot you. My shot would go there . . .' He waved the pistol in the direction of a stack of small barrels only a few paces away. Each was stencilled with a single word. GUNPOWDER. 'A single shot should be sufficient to blow us all to eternity, but I have a second, if it's needed.'

The midshipman looked at him in disbelief and Malachi said evenly, 'I've lived a full life and done all the things I've ever wanted to do. As for Tom . . . I know him too well to think he'd settle to life on board a man-o'-war. He'd be better off dead – but if he dies, he'll travel to heaven with an escort of good, honest sailors – and you too.'

For the first time, Thomasina became aware that the boat's crew from the *Melanie Jane* had left the tavern. They realised immediately what the duties of the sailors from the man-o'-war were. They were prepared to run if they were targeted, but they remained within hearing and their expressions revealed their horror at Malachi's words. They were in no doubt that he meant every word.

Neither was the midshipman. He was caught between death and humiliation.

Succour came from a welcome but unexpected quarter. All those involved in the drama had been so engrossed in what was going on that they had not noticed the arrival of a boat bringing the commodore of the squadron ashore.

Commodore Sir Benjamin Andrews was a fine commander, well used to rapidly assessing difficult situations. It did not take him long to grasp this one.

'What's going on here?' With apparent casualness, Commodore Andrews walked between Malachi and the naval party.

Malachi was the first to speak. 'Your midshipman wants to impress my cabin boy. I consider my need is the greater. I must have a full crew if I'm to get a ship with a broken mainmast yard back to England.'

Looking at Thomasina, the commodore said disparagingly, 'He's not much of a lad for such a big fuss to be made about him.'

'That's as may be,' replied Malachi, 'but I've lost a leg in the service of the King – and the war has cost this lad his father. Let the midshipman find his men elsewhere.'

The commodore had been looking thoughtfully at Malachi as he had been speaking. Now he said, 'Haven't we met before? What's your name, sir?'

'Ellis. Captain Malachi Ellis.' Malachi eyed the commodore warily, in case he was trying to put him off guard.

'I knew it! We met many years ago, when every man in the service knew of Commander Ellis of the *Pickle*.' Turning his attention to the midshipman, he said, 'Mister, you have the privilege of having met one of the most famous frigate commanders ever to have served in the Royal Navy. A frigate commander who made as much prize-money as my Lord Cochrane. You'd never have found him press-ganging men. Seamen would fall over themselves to serve on board his ship.'

Holding out a hand to Malachi, he said, 'It's a great pleasure to meet you again, Captain Ellis. Will you do me the honour of dining with me on board my flagship tonight? The governor will be there, together with many of the island officials.'

'Thank you for the invitation, Commodore, but I have my ship to repair as best I can – and a load of flour and corn to get back to Cornwall.'

'You say you've lost a yard from your mainmast?'

'That's right.'

'We've got a number of spares among the various ships of my squadron. Midshipman! Take the details from Captain Ellis of what's required. If we have nothing of the exact size, have one adapted.'

Returning his attention to Malachi, the commodore said, 'The yard will be a gift from a grateful navy, Captain Ellis – but it is conditional upon you accepting my invitation to dinner. You're a legend among senior officers. An inspiration to young, would-be frigate commanders. Your presence would be a social coup for me.'

'What of young Tom? Do I get him back?'

'Of course. He should never have been taken. The place to find new recruits is from the ships we stop at sea. Taking men here will only antagonise the local residents. We can ill afford to do that at a time when it looks as though we're likely to go to war with America before the month is out. If that happens, Bermuda will be a most important naval base. We'll try to recruit men here, of course, but they will need to be volunteers, not pressed men.'

'In that case I shall consider it an honour to be your guest tonight, Commodore – and I'm most grateful to you for your offer of a yard. I thought I would need to sail without one, and it's the wrong time of year to take such a chance. Come on, Tom. Let's take the crew back to the ship. We've had quite enough excitement for one day.'

It was not quite the end of the day's events. Shadrack was very quiet for much of the remainder of that day, before speaking privately with Malachi that evening.

When Malachi went to dine with Commodore Andrews, Shadrack went to the flagship with him. He had been highly interested in what the commodore had said about war between Britain and America being in the offing. If it happened, he wanted to be part of it – fighting against the Americans.

With Malachi's recommendation, Shadrack went aboard the flagship as a recruit for the British navy. A free man.

12

In the summer of 1812 the *Melanie Jane* slipped her moorings at Plymouth, setting off on a voyage that was like many others the vessel had made.

Loaded with a general cargo, the ship was bound for Gibraltar, the British-occupied stronghold that guarded the entrance to the Mediterranean Sea. Malachi hoped to return with a cargo of fruit, port wine and lace goods, taken on board at Lisbon.

It was a fine, warm day with nothing to indicate that this would be the last voyage which the ship, master and crew would make together.

Yet, no more than three hours out from Plymouth, events were set in motion that would take the lives of all but one of the crew and change the future of the sole survivor for ever.

A French frigate, daringly disregarding the fact that it was almost within sight of one of the busiest naval ports in the country, intercepted the Cornish merchantman.

Malachi had seen the vessel approaching them from an oblique angle and was fully aware it was a man-o'-war. However, being so close to a major naval port, he thought it must be a British warship.

Not until it closed to within range and opened fire with a powerful salvo did the *Melanie Jane*'s captain realise his mistake.

Malachi immediately ordered the man on the wheel to put the helm hard over and steer towards the Cornish coast, still clearly visible on the horizon. But his attempt to evade the French man-o'-war was already too late. The French vessel was under full sail and steering a steady course, parallel with the *Melanie Jane*.

Drawing level with their intended victim, the French gunners let loose a second devastating broadside that brought down the *Melanie Jane*'s foremast and swept two seamen into the sea.

It might have been better had Malachi surrendered his ship now. However, during his illustrious naval career he had never once struck his colours to an enemy. It was a habit he found hard to break.

Maintaining course as best he could, Malachi shouted, 'Hack the rigging clear. Hurry, or they'll be upon us . . . !'

The French captain was hoping for prizes, but if it was not possible to take this laden English merchantman, then he was determined it would not escape him. He would sink it first.

The French seamen were experienced gunners. The

next salvo struck the *Melanie Jane* along the water-line, the merchantman shuddering under its impact.

At the same time, French sharpshooters began firing at the men on deck as they struggled to free the mast and rigging and heave them over the ship's side.

Two more members of the *Melanie Jane*'s crew fell dead as a result of this volley. The helmsman was wounded and momentarily knocked clear of the wheel.

He had been hard put to maintain the course of the damaged ship for some minutes. Now, free from his restraint, the wheel spun madly and the ship veered off course, sails flapping wildly in the breeze. Splintered timbers were now below the water-line and the *Melanie Jane* began settling in the water as the sea flooded its hold.

Malachi knew his beloved ship was doomed. Had it been possible, he would have had the ship's boat lowered and struck for the shore with the surviving crew members, leaving the *Melanie Jane* to its fate.

Unfortunately, the boat had been an early casualty of the French cannonade, its splintered woodwork strewn across the deck.

'Leave what you're doing, gather up as many personal belongings as you can carry and muster on deck,' Malachi shouted the order to the crew. 'The Frenchmen will probably come alongside and take us off. If they don't, we'll clear the rest of the rigging and try to run the *Melanie Jane* ashore.'

The men ran to do as he ordered, but Thomasina remained on deck with Malachi. 'Is there anything you want, Malachi? I'll go and fetch it for you.'

'There are many things, Tom.' Malachi spoke carefully and deliberately, trying to hide his deep emotion. 'Possessions collected over a lifetime spent travelling the world, but the Frenchmen will steal anything of real value that we take on board their ship. I'd rather it went down with the *Melanie Jane*. To be honest with you, I'd prefer to go down with her, too. She's been a great ship, Tom, one of the best. A part of me. It'll be a sight more painful than losing a leg. But you go below for anything you might want to rescue. If it's not of too much value, then the French will likely let you keep it.'

'I've a bag of gold sovereigns in my cabin. I'll fetch them and hand them out among the crew. Between us we might be able to hold on to a few. They'll no doubt come in handy.'

'You'd better hurry. The French ship is coming alongside now. When they take us on board, stay close to me. Keeping your secret will be more important than ever when we're taken prisoner and you'll need all the help you can get.'

The French frigate swiftly drew alongside the sinking *Melanie Jane* and it was a very dejected crew who transferred to the enemy warship.

Thomasina helped Malachi from one ship to the other as they rose and fell unevenly alongside each other. Other men helped two wounded seamen board the French warship. One had a serious leg injury which would need immediate attention.

With the other survivors, Malachi and Tom were herded down a ladder to a lower deck. Here they found a couple of dozen more British seamen, many of them Cornish men who had been taken prisoner during the course of the previous twenty-four hours.

The prisoners were sharing their accommodation with a number of live pigs, which they had managed to pen in a corner, making use of a number of wooden stools lashed together.

From the conversations which were immediately struck up, it was learned that the French frigate had been cruising back and forth along the coastline of Devon and Cornwall for the past twenty-four hours, preying on English shipping.

Many of the captives were fishermen. There were also the crews of two coastal trading vessels. Both ships had been captured intact and sent to France, crewed by French sailors.

The *Melanie Jane* was the French captain's largest prize, to date. However, although the French sailors made a hasty attempt to loot their latest prize, they would not be able to sail her to France. The *Melanie Jane* was sinking and would never leave Cornish waters.

From the conversation of the French sailors, one of the captured English seamen who understood their language gathered that the *Melanie Jane* was expected to be the final victim of the daring French captain. The man-o'-war now intended cruising westwards, staying close to the Cornish coast and bombarding a number of coastal villages before returning across the Channel to France.

Shut in below decks, with very little fresh air entering the crowded accommodation, the odour of the pigs was almost unbearable. It was so bad that one of the *Melanie Jane*'s sailors suggested they should slaughter the animals, dismember them and drop them, joint-by-joint, through the tiny single porthole that was all the compartment possessed.

However, as no one had yet been able to open the tiny, brass-ringed aperture, the suggestion was not acted upon.

Not long after the *Melanie Jane* had been abandoned, the French ship got under way once more and commenced firing at targets onshore as they presented themselves. Speculation among the imprisoned men immediately switched to which of the Cornish coastal communities was coming under attack from the French raider.

All the prisoners were in agreement that, although the French captain was a naval man, his reckless behaviour was that of a privateer. He seemed contemptuous of the fact that the gunfire might be heard by any of the English men-o'-war en route to, or from, Plymouth.

For many hours the Englishmen incarcerated with the pigs were forced to listen to the bombardment of the fishing villages where many of them had their homes.

Then, suddenly and unexpectedly, came the sound of splintering wood and the unmistakeable thud of cannonballs bouncing across the deck above them. The sounds were accompanied by excited shouting from the French sailors.

'What's happening?' Alarmed, Thomasina put the question to Malachi.

'I'd say someone's decided to shoot back!'

Malachi's elation was tinged with anxiety. They were locked in, with no means of escape. If the ship were to be holed and sunk . . .

'Do you think we've met up with a British man-o'-war?' Thomasina asked.

'I doubt it. If we had, there would have been a great many changes of course to put the ship in the most advantageous position. It's probably one of the fortresses along the Cornish coast. St Mawes, or Pendennis, perhaps. It might even be St Michael's Mount.'

'I didn't know the Mount had any guns.' This from one of the *Melanie Jane*'s crew.

'The Mount has a great many guns,' confirmed Malachi. 'They've used them in the past when other guns in Cornwall have remained silent . . .'

He was interrupted by another volley from the unknown battery, and the French ship shuddered under the weight of the cannonade.

'Whoever is firing on us, their gunners have got the range of this ship. They've caused damage too, by the sound of things. Listen to that . . .'

From the deck above the imprisoned men, they could hear the frantic shouts of the crew. Something serious must have happened to cause such consternation among the Frenchmen.

Suddenly, the hatch above their heads was thrown open. A heavily accented voice called down, 'Up on deck, all of you. The ship is running on to rocks. Save your lives – if you can.'

In the ensuing dash for the ladders, Malachi hung back, not wishing to slow down the others. After initial uncertainty, Thomasina and the surviving crew members of the *Melanie Jane* stayed with him.

When the ladder was clear, Malachi was helped from the small hold. As he climbed awkwardly to the upper deck, he glanced shorewards. It was dusk now, but there was no mistaking the triangular shape of the island that rose from the sea between ship and shore.

'It's the Mount right enough,' he said. 'But those waiting there are not *all* from the Mount.'

They were clear of the hatch now and he pointed to where a vast number of men and women could be made out crowding the foreshore beneath the castle that occupied the summit of the small island.

'They're wreckers. The French are going to find them even more dangerous than the rocks.'

'How will they know who are French and who are Cornish men?' Thomasina asked.

'They won't,' Malachi replied grimly. 'Even if they did, there'll be those among them who wouldn't care. We're in trouble, Tom. Very real trouble.'

The French man-o'-war was so close to the rocky foreshore that the sailors had given up all attempts to save the ship. Their one thought now was how best to save themselves. It would not be easy.

Waves were breaking against the menacing, water-blackened rocks, hurling spray over the mob, which was noisily anticipating the spoils that the sea was about to bring them.

Suddenly the stricken ship rose on a swell that accelerated its progress towards the shore. It seemed to Thomasina they were travelling at breakneck speed.

Onshore, the mob thought so too and howled in primitive approval.

Sailors began leaping from the French vessel now, hoping to save themselves before it struck. Many more remained, reluctant to leave the ship which had carried them safely to all parts of the world and had been the only home they had known for many years.

Just short of the shore, the ship struck a number of underwater rocks and came to a violent and unexpected halt. The force of the impact knocked those on deck off balance and many were catapulted into the sea. They immediately struck out in a desperate attempt to reach the shore.

The howling of the mob was now blood-curdlingly close and Thomasina asked, 'What shall we do, Malachi?'

'There's nothing I can do for you, Tom – or you for me. We're on our own in this. Good luck to you. I couldn't have wished for a finer nephew . . .'

As he spoke, another wave lifted and turned the ship, spilling more of its occupants into the sea, Thomasina among them.

She tried to see what was happening to Malachi, but the cold salt water closed about her, sucking her down, and all else was forgotten as she fought her way back to the surface.

When her head emerged above water, she gulped in air gratefully, then instinctively she struck out for the shore, only to be lifted and thrown against a rock that stood proud of the water. She attempted to cling to it, but the sea prised her free, pulling her back down.

Another swell lifted her, threw her over the rock

and carried her on, battering her against other rocks closer to the shore. Suddenly she found herself floundering in a pool of comparatively calm and shallow water.

As she attempted to secure a grip on a wet rock, four or five of those onshore – two of them women – made for her. One man lunged at her with a weapon that might have been a pike, or perhaps a pitchfork.

She felt a sudden pain as it struck one of her ribs and slid away again. It caused her to lose her grip on the rock and she fell backwards.

Caught by another wave, she was carried back towards the sea by the swirling water. She heard a sound that might have been water rushing through a narrow gap between the rocks, or it could have been the cries of the mob.

Then, as she struggled in vain against the pull of the sea, her head came into hard contact with a rock . . . and she knew no more.

Book Three

1

Thomasina regained consciousness painfully slowly. With her eyes still closed, she tried to recall what had happened to her. Her mind was in a state of utter confusion. Feeling cautiously about her, she made the discovery that she was lying in a bed. A large bed with a luxuriantly soft mattress.

Opening her eyes slowly and apprehensively, she thought it must be night. Then, gradually, she made out a window at which there were closed curtains. There was light showing around the curtain edges and she realised it must be daylight outside.

In the faint gloom she could see that the walls of her room were of unplastered stone. It reminded her of the cell in which she had last seen Jeffery. For a moment she thought she too must be in a prison. Then fragmented memories began to return.

When she moved her head she suffered blinding

pain. She recalled feeling a similar pain when her head had struck against a rock after the French warship had been driven ashore.

Recalling more details of the shipwreck, she started up in sudden anguish. This time the pain in her head proved so acute that she cried out. Dropping her head back on the pillow once more, she lay still and allowed the pieces of the jigsaw to fall into place.

She relived the moment when she was washed from the deck of the French ship and attacked by a Cornish mob . . . Here the recollection came to an abrupt end.

How had she escaped – and where was Malachi? Had he been responsible for bringing her here – and where was *here*? If it had been him, where was he now?

Suddenly she realised she was wearing a nightdress: women's clothing! Whoever was responsible for her rescue must have realised she was a woman. How had they found out?

When she tried to change her position in the bed, the answer to this question dropped another piece of the confusing jigsaw into place. A sharp pain at the side of her ribcage reminded her that she had been attacked with a pike, or something similar. Whoever had treated the wound must have discovered her secret.

That would surely not have been Malachi? But if not him, then whom?

As she thought about the events of that dramatic evening, the unanswered questions multiplied in her mind.

Thomasina must have been pondering the situation for about twenty minutes before the door opened and she heard someone enter the room.

Any movement of her head still pained her, but Thomasina turned it slowly and saw that a woman of about forty had entered the room. Dark-haired and attractive, she was also heavily pregnant.

'So you have returned to the land of the living? We were becoming anxious for you.'

Thomasina could detect neither pleasure nor regret in the woman's voice.

'Can you understand me? What's your name? Are you English, or French?'

As she spoke, the woman drew back the curtains. The light was like a hammer striking at Thomasina's brain. Closing her eyes, she turned her head away, although this too caused her pain.

The question was repeated, this time in French.

'I'm English, my name is Thomasina.' She found speech difficult and slurred her words alarmingly. 'Where am I? Where are the others from the *Melanie Jane*?'

'You are in the castle on St Michael's Mount. I am Juliana, but I am afraid I know nothing of the *Melanie Jane* . . . I presume you are talking of a ship? You were rescued from the wreck of a French man-o'-war, dressed in a man's clothing. No doubt there were good reasons. I can think of some myself. However, because you are a woman, it meant you could not be treated in the same way as the others who were rescued. We brought you here and sent for a physician. He said you have suffered concussion and possibly a cracked skull. He also looked at the wound in your side. You have a fractured rib, but he says the injury should heal well. No doubt you will wish to inform your family of your well-being and return to them as soon as you are able.'

Juliana was brusque and matter-of-fact. As soon as she heard Thomasina talk, she realised she was Cornish and from a working background. When the doctor said she was fit to be moved, Juliana would have her transferred to the house of one of the tenants. She could remain there until she was fit enough to return to her own home.

This was neither callousness nor snobbishness on her part, but self-preservation. She was the mistress of Sir John St Aubyn. The baronet was devoted to her, of this she was certain – for most of the time – but she was heavily pregnant and feeling particularly insecure. Sir John's head was easily turned by a young girl – and this one had a strangely attractive quality about her.

Juliana's was also a far from regular situation. She could be excused for being neurotic about having Thomasina in the house, particularly in view of the unusual and rather romantic manner in which she had arrived on St Michael's Mount.

'I have no family – unless Malachi survived the shipwreck?'

It was a forlorn half-question. Conditions on the evening of the wreck had been such that even the fittest of men would have considered himself lucky to escape with his life.

'I know nothing about survivors, my dear, except

that Sir John said there were pitifully few. The sea and the wreckers between them took a heavy toll – but you'll not want to be talking about that right now. I believe Humphrey – Sir John's son – has a list of survivors and the names of . . . others. I'll send him along to see you, if I can have him found. He'll be relieved you've regained consciousness. He's looked in on you at least three or four times a day while you've been here.'

'How long *have* I been here?'

'This is the fourth day, dear, but by the look of you you're not fit to be moved just yet.' Observing Thomasina's squint, she asked, 'Is the light hurting your eyes?'

'Yes.'

'Then I'll draw the curtains again, leaving just a small gap to allow a little light in.'

'What time is it?' Taken aback by the duration of her unconsciousness, Thomasina tried to gain a grip on reality.

'Late afternoon. Do you fancy something to eat?' Without waiting for a reply, Juliana said, 'I'll have a maid bring some broth up to the room. You really should have some food inside you.'

Thomasina did not feel she would be able to eat anything, but she was thirsty and said so.

'I'll have some milk and water sent up for you, too. We'll talk again later, when you are a little stronger. In the meantime I'll send word to the doctor that you've regained consciousness. He'll be relieved, I've no doubt. I don't think he was terribly confident of your survival.'

*   *   *

When Juliana left the room, Thomasina lay in the comfortable bed and tried not to think of Malachi and the others. It was not easy, but she knew that if she were to dwell upon their possible fate in her present weakened state, she would dissolve in tears and thoroughly exhaust herself.

Besides, thinking of what had occurred would achieve nothing. She urgently needed to think of the future, and what she was to do with her life, if she was on her own once more.

If there was no Malachi to lean upon.

Despite her resolution, Thomasina could not stem the tears that sprang to her eyes at the thought of what must have happened to Malachi. She had been sailing with him for two years. During that time he had taken the place of the father she had lost years before.

She tried to exclude such thoughts and concentrate on practicalities, but no matter how hard she tried *not* to think about him, every thought led her back to Malachi.

If he was no longer alive there would be a great many loose ends to tie up in connection with their partnership. She had accumulated a number of possessions at the Falmouth house she had shared with him. She would need to collect them before the house was sold, as she felt certain it would be if Malachi had not survived the wreck.

She wondered whether the *Melanie Jane* and its cargo had been insured. It was not something she and Malachi had ever discussed. As soon as it was possible, she would need to speak to the solicitor who had drawn up the partnership agreement and who had managed Malachi's affairs. He would be able to answer many of her more pressing questions.

Not until then would she be able to make a reasoned appraisal of her future.

All these things were passing through her mind when she heard the door to her room open once more.

Opening her eyes, she saw a man looking at her uncertainly. No more than a year or two older than herself, he appeared hesitant to cross the room to the bed. Curious, Thomasina asked, 'Who are you?'

Approaching the bed, he said eagerly, 'I'm Humphrey. Humphrey St Aubyn. It's John, really. Humphrey's my second name, but they call me that so that I'm not confused with my father. I'm glad to see you with your eyes open. When Abel and I pulled you from the sea I thought at first you were dead.'

Seemingly embarrassed by being alone in the room with her, he gave a short, nervous laugh and with words tumbling over themselves, he added, 'But then I thought you were a young boy – I was wrong about that too.'

'You're the one who pulled me from the sea?'

'Yes . . . well, that's not *strictly* true. It was actually Abel who rescued you from those *creatures*, who would have killed you, but I helped bring you ashore on that dreadful night. It was Mount guns that sank the French ship, you know. There was such a frightful and unnecessary loss of life – and a great many of those who died were our own people. It was *awful*.'

'I owe you my life,' said Thomasina, '. . . you and

E. V. Thompson

the others. Thank you. But I'm very concerned for the members of the *Melanie Jane*'s crew. Especially Malachi . . . Captain Ellis. Juliana said you would know about them.'

'You've already spoken to Juliana?'

'She was in here a short while ago. Why?'

'Well, she knows I've been anxious about you, but she doesn't really approve of me wandering about the house.' Hesitatingly he added, 'It's a long and somewhat complicated story but, although Sir John is my father, Juliana is not my mother. She lives at Ludgvan, across on the mainland. I live there too for most of the time, although I like to spend time on the Mount when I'm not at university. Mind you, Juliana and Sir John don't spend much time here, either. They are usually in London, or at Clowance.'

The story sounded too complicated for Thomasina in her present state. Although she was mildly intrigued, she could not cope with matters of a complex nature just yet. Besides, there were more immediate issues to be settled.

'Do you know anything of the crew of the *Melanie Jane*?' she asked.

'Only what the Frenchmen were able to tell me.'

'I'm sorry . . . I don't understand. Juliana said you have a list of the survivors.'

Humphrey nodded unhappily. 'That's right – but there were none from a ship called *Melanie Jane*, although the French survivors told me they had sunk a ship and taken prisoners on the day they were wrecked on the Mount. Would that ship have been the *Melanie Jane*?'

It took a few moments for Humphrey's words to sink in. 'You mean . . . there were no survivors at all from the *Melanie Jane*?'

'Only you – if that was the name of your ship.'

Thomasina winced, but the expression had nothing to do with the pain in her head, even though that had begun to throb unmercifully. Nevertheless, there was a further question that needed to be asked.

'Among those who died . . . Was there a man who had lost the lower half of a leg, his left leg?'

'Yes. One of the Cornish fishermen said he was the captain of the last ship that the French had sunk, but he could not remember the name of either the captain or his ship.'

Aware that his news had distressed Thomasina, Humphrey asked unhappily, 'Was he someone particularly close to you?'

Not trusting herself to speak, Thomasina gave a slight nod of her throbbing head, saying nothing.

'Was it *his* idea that you should dress as a boy? So the French would not know they had captured a woman?'

Thomasina's grief went deep and the pain in her head made logical thought difficult. Yet she realised that the assumption made by Humphrey St Aubyn would simplify a great many of the problems she would have to face in the future. Especially if there were no survivors from the *Melanie Jane* to contradict such a story.

'Yes . . . Yes, that's why Malachi made me dress as a boy. He thought it would be for the best.'

Thomasina turned her head away from Humphrey

St Aubyn now and allowed the tears to flow freely.

After standing by her bedside in embarrassed silence for a few minutes, Humphrey tiptoed from the room. At the doorway he paused to look back at her, his expression one of sympathy and concern.

Then he left the room, closing the door silently behind him.

2

In spite of Juliana's initial reservations about her
unexpected guest, she found herself increasingly
drawn to Thomasina as the days passed and her
health improved.

There were a number of reasons for this. One was
that Thomasina displayed no hint of disapproval in
respect of Juliana's own unusual situation.

Juliana thought this was because, from what little
Thomasina had chosen to reveal about herself, she
too had enjoyed an unusual and interesting lifestyle.
Travelling around the world with her 'uncle' on his
ship, Thomasina would have experienced more real-
life adventures than most girls – or young men – could
even imagine.

In Thomasina, Juliana thought she recognised a
kindred, non-conformist spirit, albeit one whose non–
conformity had taken a different direction from her
own.

Her more relaxed attitude was also helped by the fact that Sir John, who held a local parliamentary seat, had gone to London, accompanied by James, his eldest son.

Had it not been for her heavily pregnant condition Juliana would have gone too, taking the younger children. In truth, she was not looking forward to this confinement and was pleased to have Thomasina staying at the Mount to keep her company.

In her turn, Thomasina enjoyed Juliana's company and got on well with the children. She also found an unexpected relief in not having to maintain the pretence of being a young man.

The ancient castle on St Michael's Mount had been built many hundreds of years before as a monastery. Extensive modifications had been made in later years to fortify it against attack, with scant regard for comfort. Only in its more recent history had it become a home, but practical considerations had not yet caught up with intent. It would be many years before the castle became a comfortable home.

Juliana was quite old to be carrying a child. This would pose additional dangers during the actual childbirth. Summoning a doctor from the mainland was dependent upon the vagaries of weather and tide.

Fortunately, the baby was not due for more than a month. When the time for her confinement drew closer, Juliana would probably move to Clowance, the St Aubyn home on the mainland, although builders were in the house, carrying out extensive alterations.

A regular visitor to Thomasina's room was Humphrey St Aubyn, Sir John's third son and namesake by his first mistress.

Although Juliana had never attempted to hide her antipathy towards the offspring of the baronet's earlier liaison, she tolerated Humphrey's attendance upon Thomasina. His visits gave Thomasina someone new to talk to and it amused Juliana to see how besotted he was with the young castaway.

Eventually the doctor decided Thomasina was well enough to leave her room to go outside and take advantage of the current spell of fine weather. It was Humphrey who insisted upon helping her to the terrace and fussing over her there.

'Humphrey is terribly smitten with you, Thomasina,' Juliana commented as the young man in question hurried off to find drinks for them all.

'He's a very nice young man,' Thomasina commented, non-committally.

Juliana did her best to hide a smile at Thomasina's description of someone who could be no more than a year or two older than herself. However, she felt that although Humphrey had received a university education and was soon to take up a career in the Church, he lacked the worldly maturity of Thomasina.

'I hope I'm not giving him the wrong idea by letting him do things for me. There's no place for a man in my life just yet,' Thomasina said to her hostess. 'I've got things to do before I think about taking a husband.'

'What sort of things?' Juliana never missed an opportunity to learn more about her guest.

'For a start, I need to visit Falmouth to settle my

uncle's affairs. I'm his only relative and am not even certain his solicitor knows he's dead.'

Even now, Thomasina found it difficult to talk about Malachi without a keen sense of loss. She felt tears well up in her eyes.

Realising that Thomasina was upset and aware of the reason, Juliana said gently, 'If he was master of his own ship and you're his only relative, you could learn you are quite a wealthy young woman.'

Thomasina nodded. 'It's always possible, I suppose, but I'd much rather have Malachi back with me.'

'Life doesn't always take our wishes into account, my dear. As for Humphrey . . . you could do a great deal worse. His father intends to settle ten thousand pounds on him. With that, and your own money, you could be very comfortably off. Very comfortable indeed.'

There was a degree of resentment in Juliana's statement. Sir John was an extremely generous man, especially where his children – all his *acknowledged* children – were concerned. Juliana often thought his generosity stemmed from a need to compensate for the many things his unorthodox domestic circumstances deprived them of. For instance, his eldest son would not be able to inherit his baronetcy, and many of the St Aubyn lands and estates would be lost to his illegitimate offspring.

Nevertheless, Sir John was giving them money he could ill afford. No one was more aware of this than Juliana. Sir John was inclined to juggle with his debts. There had been one occasion when he had been obliged to hide inside a wide, but extremely sooty chimney in order to evade a deputation of determined tradesmen to whom he owed money.

Further talk on the subject was brought to a halt by the return of Humphrey, carrying a tray upon which were drinks for them all.

When the two women fell silent upon his approach, Humphrey asked perceptively, 'Have I interrupted an important conversation, or were you talking about me?'

'You're as conceited as your father!' declared Juliana. 'If you must know, Thomasina was saying she needs to go to Falmouth as soon as possible.'

'To stay?' Humphrey's expression was one of dismay. 'Do you intend leaving the Mount soon, Thomasina?'

'I sincerely hope not.' Juliana had arrived at a surprising decision. 'I would like you to remain here for as long as you possibly can, Thomasina. Preferably until the baby arrives, or until Sir John returns. I know there are many things you must attend to, but you have said you have no relatives to go to. Why not stay while you consider your future? I very much enjoy your company. I know the children do, too.'

Juliana had not mentioned Humphrey, but she knew he was as eager as she was herself that Thomasina should act upon her suggestion.

'That's very kind of you.' Thomasina meant it. She was not yet ready to face an uncertain future on her own. 'I would like that – for a while, at least, but I must go to Falmouth as soon as I'm able. I have a great many things to do there. I'm not sure how long they will take. It could be a day or two.'

'That's splendid!' Juliana was genuinely delighted. 'But when do you think you will feel fit enough to make the journey to Falmouth?'

'It depends very much on how I travel. If I were to go by sea, I'm fit enough to go at any time. By road . . . ?' She shrugged. 'In three or four days' time, I suppose.'

'Shouldn't you check with the doctor first?' Humphrey asked hurriedly. 'He might not agree with you. After all, you were hurt quite badly. You don't want to hurry things.'

His concern was so transparent that Juliana was amused. Before leaving for London, Sir John had said he would be discussing his son's future with the Church authorities there. Humphrey expected to be called to London for an interview any day now. He was concerned lest he should be called away during Thomasina's absence from the Mount.

Unaware of the reason for his concern, Thomasina replied, 'The doctor has already told me I'm fit enough to do anything I feel up to.'

'Then, if you are agreeable, I'll have Abel, our senior boatman, take you to Falmouth tomorrow,' said Juliana. 'It isn't a terribly large boat, so I hope your recent dreadful experience won't make you nervous of sailing in it for such a distance.'

Despite her earlier confident assertion that she was fit enough to travel by sea, Thomasina felt a brief twinge of fear at the thought of setting out on a voyage from the place where so many of her former companions had died.

Putting such thoughts behind her, she asked, 'Isn't Abel the man who pulled me from the sea?'

'Yes,' Juliana replied. 'I was forgetting you have not met him yet. That is very remiss of me. From all I have heard, he put his own life at risk in order to rescue you from the combined efforts of mob and sea. Never mind, that can be put right tomorrow. Now . . . would it be inconvenient for you to remain in Falmouth for three nights, Thomasina?'

Thomasina felt it would suit her very well. She said so, adding that probably she could not complete her business in less time.

'Good! It is high time I got off the Mount for a while, and I will need new clothes to wear once the baby is born. I don't want to leave the children overnight without me, but even the shortest sea journey makes me sick. I'll travel in the coach to Falmouth on Friday and return the same day.' Juliana became suddenly enthusiastic, 'We can meet up at some point during the day, do some shopping together, then return late in the evening. How are the tides on Friday, Humphrey?'

Somewhat sulkily, because Juliana had suggested that Thomasina should stay away for three nights, he replied, 'You'll be fine if you leave early in the morning – but you'll need to return by seven-thirty in the evening, at the latest.'

'That is earlier than I had intended, but it should create no real problem. Splendid! Now, where shall we meet in Falmouth, Thomasina? How well do you know the town?'

3

Juliana had referred to the boat which was to convey Thomasina to Falmouth as being 'not very large'. Much to Thomasina's relief, she found it to be of sufficient size to require a crew of three to sail the vessel comfortably.

Abel Carter was in charge of the boat and Thomasina was introduced to him by Humphrey, who had taken it upon himself to rise early in order to accompany Thomasina to St Michael's Mount's small, sheltered harbour.

'I'm delighted to meet you at last,' Thomasina said to Abel. 'Everyone tells me I owe my life to you and that you rescued me at no small risk to yourself. I am very, very grateful.'

She found the St Michael's Mount boatman disturbingly attractive. Indeed, he was the only man to have seriously caught her attention since Jeffery.

The thought of her one-time lover provoked a stab of conscience within her. It was the first time Jeffery had come to mind for some time.

'You were unconscious for so long that it was rumoured you weren't going to pull through. I'm glad the rumours have proved to be unfounded.'

Listening to the exchange between Thomasina and the boatman, Humphrey felt a need to stamp his authority on the conversation.

'You be sure to carry Miss Thomasina safely to Falmouth, Abel. Take no chances with her. She is still not strong.'

'I am quite sure she's strong enough to tell me if she thinks I'm not handling the boat the way it should be done,' countered Abel. 'From what I've heard, she's sailed more miles than most sailors ever will.'

For a moment Thomasina was startled by his statement. Surely Juliana would not have gossiped about her to this man? Then she remembered she had talked of sailing the world to the maid who cleaned her room. She must have passed the details of the conversation on to Abel.

The maid had been a comely young Cornish girl. Thomasina wondered about the relationship between her and Abel.

'Are you certain you're going to be warm enough, Thomasina?' asked Humphrey anxiously. 'There's a stiff breeze blowing.'

'I'll be fine, Humphrey. The breeze means we'll get there more quickly.'

'How long will the voyage take?' Humphrey put the question to Abel.

'No longer than three hours – once we get under way,' Abel added pointedly.

'Then let's not waste any more of the day,' Thomasina said. 'I have a great deal to do once we arrive.'

Turning from the boatman, she said, 'Thank you for seeing me safely to the boat, Humphrey. It was very kind of you. I hope to see you again when I return on Friday.'

'You will, if I'm not called to London before then,' Humphrey replied unhappily.

'If you are, then I wish you good luck with your interview,' Thomasina spoke firmly, but kindly. 'May we go now, Abel?'

Without replying, Abel nodded to his crewmen. The boat was quickly cast off and the two men used oars to clear the harbour. Once beyond the break-water, sails were raised and the boat began slicing through the choppy water, quickly leaving the small harbour and a still-waving Humphrey behind them.

'The motion of the boat doesn't trouble you?' Abel put the question to Thomasina as the boat left the shelter of the Mount.

'It comes as naturally to me as walking,' Thomasina replied honestly. She found the wind on her face clean and fresh and the movement of the boat exhilarating.

'Then I think we might crowd on a little more sail and gain a knot or two.' Abel said.

'Would Humphrey approve of that?' Thomasina put the question to him with an air of mock concern.

Abel countered the question with one of his own. 'Is his approval important to you?'

It was an impertinent question. One that Abel

would not normally have put to a guest of Sir John St Aubyn and Juliana. However, he was aware that Thomasina did not belong to the aristocracy. Nor did he believe that she had a similar background to Juliana. Indeed, his observations, based upon a very brief acquaintanceship with her, tended to confirm the rumours spread by the servants who worked on the Mount.

Thomasina was a working-class girl.

Had it not been for the dramatic circumstances associated with her arrival on the Mount, she would never have seen the inside of the castle.

'His approval – or disapproval – matters neither way,' Thomasina replied. 'But I'm grateful for the kindness he and Juliana have both shown me.'

As an afterthought, she added, 'I'll always be grateful to you, too. I realise I owe you my life.'

Embarrassed by her words, Abel said, 'Had the tide been higher and the Mount cut off from the mainland, we'd have been able to save a whole lot more lives. I'm convinced the mainlanders killed as many as did the sea.'

Thomasina gave a brief shudder. 'Do you know how Captain Malachi Ellis – the one-legged sea captain – died?'

She asked the question, although she was not certain she wanted to know the answer.

'I'd say it was the sea. I found him the next morning when we went out to look for bodies.' Watching her as he spoke, he asked, 'Was he close to you?'

Thomasina nodded and repeated the story she had

told everyone else. 'He was my uncle – and a wonderful man.'

'Do you have any other relatives in Cornwall?'

'No one close enough for me to care if I ever see them again. I'm on my way to Falmouth now to speak to Malachi's solicitor, in the hope that I can settle his affairs.'

'Then you might need to call on me, to say what I know about finding his body. The solicitor will be able to confirm the details of my story with the coroner. He took a full description of all the victims who couldn't be named. I'll stay in Falmouth for a couple of hours, just in case.'

'Thank you.'

There was a silence between them for some minutes, each of them lost in their own thoughts. Then Thomasina asked, 'Are you related to the St Aubyns? You look a lot like Humphrey.'

One of the two crewmen who heard the question made a strangled sound deep in his throat, which might or might not have been a stifled laugh.

Abel glanced briefly at the man before replying, 'In all honesty, I'm not sure exactly who I'm related to – except for my grandmother. I live in her home, on the Mount. Mind you, some folk think they know more than I do. The truth is, I never knew the name of my father. My ma died without telling me, and if my grandmother knows she's never told me.'

'Oh! I'm sorry.' Thomasina realised her question had been both rude and tactless. Hastily she went on, 'I don't know whether it's best never to have known your father, or to lose him when you know and love him. My father was lost at sea some years ago. He set off in his own boat one day and was never seen again.'

Abel looked duly sympathetic. 'So the sea is pretty much in your blood?'

'Very much so. In fact, the last couple of years spent sailing with Malachi were the happiest of my life . . . but now he's gone.'

'What will you do when you've settled your uncle's affairs?'

'I don't know. Juliana has asked me to stay on at the Mount, at least until the baby is born.'

'You're honoured,' Abel said. 'She doesn't take readily to many people.'

'I can understand that, for she's in a very difficult situation.'

'Why?' asked Abel, unexpectedly sharply. 'She has a fine home – more than one, in fact – and wants for nothing. Although Sir John hasn't married her, she's known as M'Lady and her children have taken the St Aubyn name – as have the children by his earlier mistress, come to that. What's more, every one of the sons has been given a gentleman's education.'

There was an element of bitterness in his voice now. Thomasina thought it surprising that it was not more evident. She had no doubt there was St Aubyn blood in his veins. From the expressions on the faces of the other men in the boat, it seemed others thought so, too. It must have been a bitter pill for Abel to swallow when the other illegitimate children of Sir John were given the recognition of their father and a place in life that had been denied to him.

'Have you always been a boatman?'

She asked the question as a means of changing the subject. Most of the St Aubyn retainers seemed to have been employed on the Mount since childhood. She thought Abel was probably the same.

His reply surprised her.

'No, I served in the Royal Marines as an artilleryman, until I was wounded. Then, after spending some time at sea, I came back to look after my grandmother, and Sir John took me on as his senior boatman.'

Interested now, Thomasina asked, 'I know very little about the Marines, what did you do?'

'I was a gunner – a sergeant gunner – serving both on ships and on land. I was considered an expert gunlayer. I was the one who was in charge of the guns which sank the French ship that was carrying you as a prisoner.'

'Oh!'

Abel was quite obviously proud of the vital part he had played in sinking the French ship, but Thomasina's thoughts dwelled on the fact that it was Abel who was responsible for the death of Malachi.

Her silence lasted until they came within sight of Falmouth town.

4

Malachi's solicitor, Zachariah Bennett, who also represented Thomasina, listened to all that Abel had to tell him, shaking his head sadly when the St Michael's Mount boatman told of the conduct of those who waited to plunder and murder the survivors as they struggled desperately to save themselves from the doomed French ship.

'Sadly, there have always been those around our coasts who seek to benefit by such tragedies. Of course, this *was* a French warship, which had been bombarding the coastal communities in the vicinity. It could be argued there was some justification for taking revenge upon those believed responsible for such an unnecessary act of war.'

Pushing his spectacles higher on his thin nose, the diminutive solicitor added, 'I am very grateful to you for coming to see me and acquainting me with the sad fate of Captain Ellis, Mr Carter. I had already learned of the sinking of the *Melanie Jane*. The incident was witnessed by a number of fishing vessels in the area. However, when nothing was subsequently heard of the crew, it was assumed they had been taken to France, possibly in another French vessel.'

'Miss Varcoe is the only survivor from the ship – and has only very recently recovered from her experiences,' Abel said.

'Thank you again, Mr Carter. Perhaps you will be kind enough to come with me and make a signed declaration to my clerk in the outer office. I will make arrangements to obtain a report from the coroner in order to satisfy the legal requirements in this sad matter. If you will kindly remain here, Miss Varcoe, we have a few business matters to discuss . . .'

With a glance at Thomasina, Abel stood up to follow the solicitor from the room. As he reached the door, she called out, 'If you are finished before I am, will you wait for me, please, Abel? There are a few things I'd like you to take back to the Mount for me.'

A few minutes later Zachariah Bennett returned to the office. Seating himself behind his desk once more, he examined her over the top of his spectacles in a manner which had become familiar to her.

'Reading between the lines of that young man's story, I feel you probably owe your life to him.'

'I do,' Thomasina replied. 'He put his own life at risk to save me.'

'You will soon have the means to reward him, if you so wish, Miss Varcoe.'

'From the insurance money, you mean?'

'That will, of course, be quite substantial, but the investments you so wisely made on Captain Ellis's recommendation have also paid handsomely.'

'I owe Malachi such a lot,' Thomasina spoke emotionally.

'Far more than you know . . .' Zachariah Bennett hesitated for a moment. 'I shouldn't really be telling you this until all the legal requirements have been complied with, Miss Varcoe, but you will soon have rather more money than you anticipate. You see, when Captain Ellis was last in this office he made a will, naming you as his sole beneficiary.'

'What exactly does that mean?' Thomasina looked at him uncertainly.

'It means that you will soon be a wealthy young woman, Miss Varcoe. Indeed, a *very* wealthy young woman. Captain Ellis left everything he owned to you.'

'That's typical of Malachi's kindness,' Thomasina said emotionally, 'but I'd happily forgo all the money to have Malachi and the crew alive and the *Melanie Jane* still afloat.'

'Captain Ellis was a fine man. A *splendid* man. He will be sadly missed. He was also far more organised than most sea captains. There will be a number of claims to be settled with owners of the cargo, but all his affairs have been left in good order. He has also kept the *Melanie Jane*'s insurance at a level commensurate with the increasing value of the vessel.'

Leaning back in his chair, Zachariah Bennett looked at her in silence for some minutes, before adding, 'I have a complete list of Captain Ellis's assets and will give them to you in the fullness of time. Meanwhile, I will keep you informed of my progress. You have no immediate marriage plans, I take it?'

The question took Thomasina by surprise. She shook her head vigorously, 'None whatsoever.'

'Good. A husband tends to complicate things when a young woman inherits such a large sum of money. There are also a number of unscrupulous men of breeding eager to marry wealthy women, whatever their age – tempting them with social status, or perhaps even a minor title. Should such a man appear in your life, Miss Varcoe, I will be happy to have enquiries made into his background, on your behalf.'

Despite the sadness she felt at the reason for being in the solicitor's office, Thomasina smiled. 'Thank you very much for your concern, Mr Bennett. I will remember it, should an offer of marriage come my way.'

'Then it only remains for me to bid you good day, Miss Varcoe. I trust you will allow me to extend to you the service I like to feel we always gave to Captain Ellis. Should you have need of money for an urgent major project, before the estate is settled, I am quite certain we can be of assistance.'

'Thank you again, Mr Bennett. Malachi always spoke well of you and I trusted his judgement implicitly. I am most grateful to you.'

'Will you be staying in Falmouth for a while?' Zachariah Bennett put the question to her as they walked from his office.

'Only for a couple of days, at Captain Malachi's

house, then I'll be returning to the Mount as a companion for Miss Juliana. At least until her next child is born. You can send any letters for me either to the Mount or to Malachi's house . . . I'll have to get used to calling it *my* house now, I suppose. I shall call in there from time to time, until I've decided what I'm going to do. But I'm glad you've reminded me. Do you have a key to the house? I lost mine when the *Melanie Jane* was abandoned.'

'Of course. My clerk will give it to you.'

When she had the key, and while they waited for Abel to complete his statement to the clerk, the solicitor said quietly, 'Sad though this occasion is – and I realise it is a most unhappy time for you – I trust you will think about the opportunity that Captain Ellis has given to you. It is one rarely given to any young woman. The chance to prove you can succeed in commerce, should you so wish. I feel you will, having already proven that you can compete in what is ostensibly a man's world.'

'I will need to give it a great deal of thought,' Thomasina said. 'I no longer have Malachi to advise me.'

Peering over his spectacles, the solicitor said, 'You were indeed fortunate to have the advice and guidance of Captain Ellis, Miss Varcoe, but he considered you a quite exceptional young woman. I have every confidence that you will make the most of the opportunity you have been given – for Captain Ellis's sake, if for no other reason. Now, it would appear that Mr Carter has completed his declaration.'

Holding out his hand, he said, 'I look forward to our

next meeting – and to hearing of any plans you might have made by then.'

5

When Thomasina and Abel left the solicitor's offices, she was still thinking of all that Zachariah Bennett had told her. Abel broke into her thoughts to remind her that she had said there were things she wanted taken back to the Mount.

'Yes, that's right. At the moment I'm wearing clothes that Juliana has found for me. If you have the time to come to Malachi's house and take a few clothes back to the Mount for me, I'd be very grateful.'

If Abel was surprised that Thomasina's clothes should be in Malachi's home, he made no comment on the fact. 'I've got all the time in the world. Miss Juliana has put the boat and its crew at your disposal for the day.'

Soon they were walking together along Falmouth's narrow streets, climbing the hill away from the busy harbour. For a while the steepness of the incline made the conservation of breath more important than communication.

When they turned to follow a street along the side of the hill, Abel asked, 'Were you able to get all your business completed, back there at the solicitor's?'

'Only some of it,' Thomasina replied. 'I'll need to call in to see Mr Bennett again before I leave Falmouth. It's also going to be necessary for me to come back here once or twice in the next month or so. It would probably be more sensible to remain here, but I've promised Juliana I'll stay with her until after the baby's born.'

'You can always travel by sea when you think you need to come back here,' Abel pointed out. 'As long as wind and weather are right, there's no reason why you shouldn't be able to leave the Mount in the early morning, spend six or seven hours in Falmouth and be back in time for dinner.'

'With you in charge of the boat, of course?' said Thomasina, glancing at him.

'Of course! I couldn't guarantee anyone else getting you to Falmouth and back in the same time.'

Thomasina smiled, but for all his apparent boastfulness, she conceded that he was probably right. Abel was a natural seaman. He had handled the boat with considerable skill on the way from the Mount that morning. She felt his talents were wasted as a St Aubyn boatman.

They chatted quite happily as they continued on their way to the house of the late sea captain. Not until they reached it did Thomasina's mood undergo a change.

Hesitating as she was about to insert the key in the lock, she said unhappily, 'It's going to be strange not to have Malachi call out to me as I go upstairs.'

'Does no one else live in the house?' Abel asked.

'No. Malachi employed an elderly woman to come in and clean twice a week while we were at sea and every day when we were here. Her husband looked after the garden. I don't know whether she'll want to carry on, now Malachi's no longer alive. I suppose I'll gradually take over the whole house, instead of using only the first floor. But I'll stay up there for a while, at least.'

Her words answered a question that Abel had been curious about, but would have left unasked. Thomasina lived in a separate part of the house.

He had another question. 'Is the house yours now?'

'Malachi's will hasn't been read yet,' Thomasina's reply was cautious, 'but Mr Bennett says I can stay here.' Squaring her shoulders she said, 'Let's go in.'

Turning the key in the lock, she pushed open the heavy door. Stepping through the doorway, she immediately stopped, her nostrils assailed by the heavy aroma of Malachi's tobacco smoke. It was stale, but unmistakable.

She remained motionless for so long that Abel, standing behind her, asked anxiously, 'Are you all right?'

'I will be. Memories of Malachi came flooding back when I walked through the doorway, that's all. I . . . I half-expected Malachi to call out to me, as he always did when he heard me coming in.'

Turning to look at him apologetically, she managed the semblance of a smile. 'I'm all right now.'

Leading the way to the stairs, which rose from the hallway, she resisted an urge to look in through the doorway to the study where Malachi would sit surrounded by charts and mementoes from his many voyages.

'Apart from the *Melanie Jane*, this is the only home I've known for the last couple of years. I wouldn't have had even this, had it not been for Malachi's kindness.'

Walking up the stairs behind her, Abel said sympathetically, 'You were very fond of him, weren't you?'

'He was a great sailor and a wonderful man.' Thomasina spoke feelingly. 'He's probably had a greater influence on my life than any other person – more, even, than my father.'

Consciously shaking off the melancholy that threatened to overwhelm her, she pointed to a small trunk on the landing. 'If I put some clothes in that, do you think you'd be able to carry it back to the boat?'

'Easily.'

There were a great many questions Abel would have liked to ask Thomasina about the life she had led with Captain Malachi Ellis, but this was not the right moment. If she thought him presumptuous it could destroy any chance he might have of getting to know her better – and he had already decided that was what he wanted to do.

*　　　*　　　*

Thomasina and Abel remained in the house together for almost an hour. When the clothes she wanted to wear at the Mount had been placed in the trunk, she made a pot of tea for them.

As they sat drinking in the kitchen, Abel felt an unaccustomed sense of cosiness. It bordered on a domestic situation that was strange to him and tended to make him somewhat shy. As a result, it was left to Thomasina to ask questions in order to keep the conversation from flagging.

She learned a great deal about Abel and his background. Far more, perhaps, than he realised he was telling her.

He had obviously enjoyed serving with the Marines – the 'Royal' being added to their title in the year 1802, whilst Abel was serving with them.

After service at Aboukir at the turn of the century, he had transferred to the Royal Marines Artillery in 1804, seeing fierce action, first in South America and, later, in the Dardenelles.

Then, when his battery was sent to Spain, Abel received a wound which resulted in his discharge from the Royal Marines. Although he quickly recovered, he would always walk with a slight limp, but this did not prevent him from going to sea for a few years before returning to the Mount.

'Are you fully recovered from the wound now?' Thomasina asked solicitously.

Abel grinned. 'I can forget it for much of the time, but it forecasts bad weather far more accurately than a piece of seaweed.'

Suddenly embarrassed at having chattered about

himself for so long, he said, 'I'd better be getting your things to the boat, before the others fear I've run off somewhere and leave for home without me.'

'Not to mention a certain young maid who will be anxious if you haven't returned by the time you're expected.'

Thomasina was aware that she was being obvious in her attempt to establish the relationship that existed between Abel and the Mount housemaid who often talked to her about him.

Aware of this too, Abel was delighted. 'You must mean Carrie? Yes, she'll start worrying if we don't return on time – but it won't be me she's concerned about, even though she's my cousin. Young Perran is one of my crewmen and she is due to marry him later this year. As we both have the same grandmother, she's often at the house. That's how I hear much of what goes on up at the castle. She's a great one for gossip – so be warned!'

Far more pleased than she ought to have been at the discovery that there was nothing between Abel and the pretty young housemaid, Thomasina said, 'She'll find little enough to gossip about as far as I'm concerned. I've been far too ill to provide anyone with any scandal.'

'Don't you believe it!' Abel declared. 'The very manner of your arrival caused more excitement than the Mount folk have had for many years. Then, of course, there's Master Humphrey. They do say he's taken quite a shine to you.'

'You mean, *Carrie* says so,' Thomasina retorted. 'You've already said she's a gossip.'

'Perhaps, but it's well known that Humphrey is an incurable romantic – and he's a good catch for any girl.'

'You're the second person to describe him to me as "a good catch",' declared Thomasina. 'Well, as far as I'm concerned "good catches" are for fishermen. I'm not on the look-out for a husband!'

Grinning at her, Abel said, 'I've heard that making such a positive statement is tempting fate. However, it's time I set off back to the Mount.'

Reaching down, he lifted the small trunk and swung it up on to a shoulder. Shrugging it to a comfortable position, he said, 'Enjoy your stay in Falmouth. I hope we'll meet up again when you return to the Mount.'

Watching from a window as Abel walked down the hill from the house carrying the trunk on his shoulder, Thomasina decided that if fate was going to tempt her with anyone, it might do worse than put Abel her way.

6

Although Thomasina had told Abel that the elderly cleaner came to the house during the absence at sea of Malachi and herself, in fact she cleaned only the part of the house occupied by Malachi.

She had been told to leave the first floor. Nevertheless, Thomasina had locked her clothes cupboards and hidden the keys, just in case the cleaner decided to be nosey. The discovery of men's and women's clothes in the flat would have been certain to arouse her curiosity.

As a result of this ruling, Thomasina's rooms had gathered a great deal of dust. There were also one or two items that needed washing. She spent the remainder of that day attending to the chores, but went to bed early, aware that she had not yet fully recovered from the wrecking of the French man-o'-war.

The following day was fine, so she spent a couple of hours in the garden, weeding and generally tidying up. Later she went downstairs to Malachi's rooms to sort through his possessions and clothes and decide what should be done with them.

Reminders of Malachi were everywhere. They ranged from the rack containing some of his tobacco pipes to a spare peg-leg propped against the wall in a corner of his study.

Thomasina was able to cope with these items, but then she entered his bedroom. After glancing in his wardrobe, she turned to see Malachi staring down at her, with his familiar quiet smile.

It was an oil-painting for which she had persuaded him to sit and which had been her Christmas present to him, only months before.

The portrait was such a remarkable likeness that it completely unnerved her. Fleeing from the room, she ran back upstairs. When she came to a halt in her own sitting-room, she was trembling.

Thomasina told herself she was behaving in a ridiculous fashion, yet she knew that she would not be able to return to Malachi's rooms again that evening. She did not even feel comfortable remaining in the house alone.

As night descended upon the town, bringing with it a cool, damp mist, she decided she would go to the Falmouth waterfront, dressed once more as a young man. There she would seek the noise and warmth of a harbour-front tavern.

Dressed in male clothing, Thomasina felt somehow more certain of herself. Less vulnerable. Looking in the long, hallway mirror, she was satisfied that she would once more be accepted as a young man.

Letting herself out of the house, Thomasina made her way down the hill, heading for the Ship Inn, the tavern where she had first met Malachi. Although usually busy, it had a reputation for being less rowdy than many other inns and taverns in the town.

Entering the crowded taproom, it seemed to her that the Ship Inn was in danger of losing its reputation. Crowded with men, mainly seamen, there was an inexplicable air of anticipation in the room.

Two serving girls were having to force their way through the crowd to carry out their duties. Perspiring visibly, they warded off the attentions of the seamen, who made the most of the opportunity afforded by the crowded conditions to take liberties with the hard-working women.

Thomasina decided it would be quicker to obtain her own beer. This she did, purchasing a tankard of small beer from the leather-aproned landlord drawing drinks to order from a selection of barrels. He and the barrels were separated from the customers by a fold-down counter, upon which he placed the overflowing tankards.

When she had been served, Thomasina located a space at a table occupied by a number of men whose dress identified them as sea captains, or perhaps senior mates. Carrying her beer with difficulty through the crowd, she made her way to their table.

'Do you mind if I sit here?'

Thomasina put the question to a bearded, pipe-smoking seafarer seated at the end of a long bench

stool, where she thought there was room for one
more.

Without replying, he moved along the bench to
give her a little more space, others on the stool doing
the same.

'I've never known it so busy in here,' she commented as she settled herself.

'Then you'll not be here hoping to find a berth on
Hearle's ship then?'

At the mention of the name Thomasina started
involuntarily, going cold for a moment and spilling
some of her beer on the table. 'Hearle? You're not
talking of Sir Charles Hearle?'

She thought the glances exchanged by some of the
mariners at the sound of his name contained a hint of
contempt.

'That's the man. He's interviewing prospective
crewmen in a private room. You know him?'

'I know *of* him.' Thomasina's reply was cautious,
unsure of her company. 'But I've never thought of him
as a sailing man.'

'Neither has anyone else,' said another of the men
at the table. 'Until now he's contented himself with
playing at soldiering with his militiamen – and he's
made a mess of that, whenever he's been called upon
to carry out more than an hour or two's drilling.'

'He'll be no better as a ship-owner, you mark my
words,' declared another of the seafaring men. 'Why,
a ship's cat knows more about sailing than Sir Charles
Hearle.'

His companions chuckled. Satisfied that the men at
the table regarded Sir Charles no more highly than she

did herself, she asked, 'Then why has he bought a ship
– and where has the money come from? The last I
heard, he'd drunk or gambled all his money away and
was being supported by an aunt.'

'That's about right,' said the man seated beside her.
'The aunt was Harriet Vincent, of Trebene. She died
some months ago, only weeks after her husband. The
house and lands have gone to their son, Francis, but Sir
Charles was left enough money for him to prove just
how foolish he is. Someone has managed to convince
him there's a fortune to be made in the shipping
business. He's bought a ship that's been laid up in
the Fal for nigh on two years. The packet service to
Corunna has just been resumed and, thanks to another
relative in the Postal Service, he's hoping to secure a
contract with 'em.'

'He'll not get it,' said another of the men at the table.
'Even if he did, he wouldn't keep it. He'll not have his
ship for long, either, especially if he takes on some of
the men I've seen in here today. I wouldn't have them
on board a ship of mine if they were kept in chains.'

The others at the table nodded in agreement.
Thomasina frowned. The course taken by Sir Charles
Hearle was something she had considered doing with
some of the money she had at her disposal. 'There's
money to be made carrying cargoes, surely, especially
between here and Spain? Napoleon's had the country
closed to us for so long that they'll be eager to trade
with us.'

'Of course they will,' agreed the bearded seaman.
'But Spain has a merchant fleet as big as our own and
they've spent recent years blockaded by the Royal

Navy. They'll be falling over themselves to carry cargoes once more. As a result their prices will be keener than ours, you can safely wager on that.' He looked at Thomasina with increased interest. 'But what would a young lad like you know about such things?'

'I sailed with Captain Malachi Ellis,' said Thomasina proudly. 'I learned more from him in two years than most seagoing men learn in a lifetime . . .'

Thomasina broke off, aware she suddenly had the full attention of her companions.

'You've sailed with Malachi? Then you'll be worth two of any other seamen to a good captain,' said one of them, removing a pipe from his mouth. 'But we won't be seeing him around for a while. I heard his ship was sunk by a French man-o'-war. He'll be a prisoner in France right now.'

The last thing Thomasina wanted was to talk about Malachi, fearing that she might break down, but she felt she had to put these men right.

'The French ship that took him prisoner was crippled by gunners at St Michael's Mount. It came ashore on the rocks. Malachi was among those who died. The man who took his body from the sea was in Falmouth today making a statement to his solicitor.'

The seafarers about the table looked shocked. 'Are you sure of this, boy? This man – the one who claims to have taken Malachi from the sea – could he have been mistaken?'

Thomasina shook her head. 'I'm afraid not. No one would be happier than me, were it otherwise.'

She hoped they would soon stop talking about

Malachi – and at that moment came an unexpected diversion. The inn door was flung open and someone shouted, 'Quick! The press-gang . . . !'

The cry created pandemonium inside the crowded taproom. All thoughts of being taken on as a crewman for Sir Charles Hearle were forgotten as men sought to evade the very different recruiting techniques of His Majesty's navy.

'Quick, lad – under the table. Get tight up against the wall. We'll bunch up and hide you. The press-gang won't trouble us, and they won't see you in this light . . .'

Thomasina dived beneath the table and scrambled to the wall, crouching as close to it as she could. A moment later her tankard was passed down to her.

All she could see from her hiding-place was a mêlée of feet and legs beyond the table under which she was hiding. The patrons of the Ship Inn seemed to be running this way and that in a bid to escape from the press-gang. However, for all but the boldest and most determined, their attempts to escape were in vain.

The press-gang was unusually large, made up of sailors and marines from a holding ship moored off the town. They were familiar with Falmouth and much of what went on here. They knew that seamen were being recruited at the Ship Inn – and experienced sailors were what they were looking for. They had placed a strong guard on all the inn's exit doors before entering the building.

Some of those inside *did* succeed in making good their escape, but only by showing great resourcefulness. They ran upstairs, through rooms occupied by startled residents, and dropped out of any window they believed to be some distance from the well-guarded doors.

It was some time before things quietened down inside the inn. Just as she felt she might come out from beneath the table, Thomasina found herself staring at the white hose and buckled shoes of a naval officer, visible between the legs of two of the seafaring men who had remained seated at the table throughout the fracas. She froze instantly.

'Good evening, gentlemen. I trust I and my men have not disturbed your drinking too much?'

'It would take more than a press-gang to do that,' came the reply from the man who had been seated beside Thomasina. 'Most of us here have served in the King's navy and we're all too old to be taken now.'

'I have no doubt you served His Majesty well,' said the officer. 'Kindly allow me to buy you all drinks – for past services. Landlord, drinks here, if you please. This coin should take care of it . . .'

Thomasina heard the coin thrown on to the wooden counter in front of the barrels. Then the naval officer said, 'Goodbye, gentlemen. We have taken more than our quota of men for tonight. We won't be troubling you again.'

She listened as the footsteps crossed the flagstone floor to the door. A few seconds later the bearded seafarer who had suggested her hiding place smiled down at her. 'It's all right, lad, you can come out now.'

Crawling clear of the table, Thomasina returned the smile and the seafarer called, 'Landlord, bring another for the lad. He's got something to celebrate. He came within a hair's-breadth of being carried off to serve His Majesty. The lieutenant's money will stand another beer, I don't doubt.'

'It's not going to make up for all the custom I've lost as a result of his press-gang, that's certain,' grumbled the landlord. Nevertheless, he topped up another pewter tankard and the two serving girls carried them to the table.

'The last person to save me from a press-gang was Malachi, in Bermuda . . .' Thomasina said.

She was telling the seafarers of the incident in question when two men entered the taproom from another room.

One was Sir Charles Hearle – and he was angry. For a moment Thomasina froze, but he was not looking in her direction.

'Damn the navy,' he was saying to his companion. 'How am I supposed to know whether or not I have a crew? They might all have been carried off, for all I know.'

'We'll manage,' replied the other man. 'I'll be able to make up the numbers when we're taking cargo on board. There are always seamen hanging about the docks looking for a berth.'

'Aye, and most would cut their best friend's throat for a shilling or two.'

The opinion was voiced by one of the men at the table with Thomasina. He spoke quietly so that only his companions might hear. 'Only a captain like Silas Carberry would even think of taking on such men as crew.'

'He and Hearle deserve each other,' said another of the seafarers, equally quietly. 'I gave Carberry his marching orders when he served with me as a second mate. He's a drunkard and a bully. Those he signed on, who've been taken by the press-gang instead, can consider themselves lucky. They'll enjoy a better life on a man-o'-war than on a ship with Carberry as captain. They'll be a sight safer, too – war or no war.'

The table at which the seafarers and Thomasina were seated was the only one in the room fully occupied. Few had more than two or three men at them, all too old to have run from the press-gang, even had they needed to.

Around the room the two serving girls were picking up overturned stools, benches and chairs and replacing them at empty tables.

When she first saw Sir Charles Hearle, Thomasina experienced the same chill of fear and hatred she had known at all their previous meetings. The fear increased when he stopped talking to his companion and made his way to the table at which she was seated.

He stood for a few moments, looking from one man to another, and Thomasina realised that his flushed face was not due entirely to anger.

'I'm looking for experienced men to crew my ship . . .' he began.

'Then it's no use talking to us.' Sir Charles Hearle was interrupted by one of the seafarers. 'Not unless you want a crew made up of captains, some of whom should have retired years ago.'

The amusement which greeted the words caused Sir

Charles to flush even more deeply than before. 'I'm not suggesting you sign on personally. I ask only that if you know of any young seamen looking for a ship, you tell them I'm paying top wages for the right men.'

'There are some things more important to a man than money,' responded the seagoing man who had just spoken. 'You ask Mr Carberry. I told him what they were many years ago – when I threw him off my ship for ignoring them.'

Sir Charles Hearle's befuddled state became apparent when he looked from the man who had spoken to Silas Carberry. Deciding not to pursue the matter, he now turned his attention to Thomasina.

'You, lad. Have you ever been to sea?'

'Indeed I have, sir – have you?'

Thomasina's confidence had returned when it became evident that in the dim light of the inn room Sir Charles Hearle had not recognised her.

Unable to decide if Thomasina was being impertinent, the new ship-owner said, 'Whether or not I've been to sea doesn't matter. Do you want to be taken on?'

'Would I be paid as a full deckhand, or as a boy?' Thomasina was beginning to enjoy herself.

'You'll be paid what you're worth,' Silas Carberry said, aware – as Sir Charles was not – that Thomasina was being deliberately insolent.

'I doubt it,' said Thomasina. 'When I sailed with Captain Malachi Ellis, he would tell me I was worth my weight in gold.'

The seafarers around the table chuckled and Carberry scowled. To Sir Charles he said, 'Come along. We're wasting our time here. We'll not find a crew among old men who should have been paid off years ago, and a boy with more lip than a wash-jug.'

Silas Carberry turned to go, but Sir Charles was peering drunkenly at Thomasina, a frown on his face. 'We've met before . . . where was it?'

Trying hard to hide her alarm and fearing that she might have gone too far with her insolence, Thomasina said, 'Right here in Falmouth. You were chasing miners who were trying to prevent corn being taken from Cornwall. Your men wanted to stop me and Captain Malachi getting to our ship. You didn't succeed.'

Sir Charles was not convinced of the accuracy of her explanation, but he had been drinking too much to argue with it. Turning away, he followed the captain of his vessel from the Ship Inn.

Later that night, on the way back to the house, Thomasina thought over the incidents of the evening. The confrontation with Sir Charles Hearle worried her. If he ever recognised her as 'Ethel', the house-maid he had raped when she worked for his aunt, a great many awkward questions might be asked about the manner in which she had acquired the money with which she had bought a partnership with Malachi.

She found some small consolation in the knowledge that each of the captains who had been her drinking partners at the Ship Inn had told her there would always be a place on their ships, should she choose to go back to sea once more.

7

Thomasina was waiting outside the Packet Inn when the St Aubyn carriage arrived in Falmouth. Juliana climbed stiffly and heavily from the carriage. She showed no signs of the enthusiasm she had evinced for the shopping expedition when it had first been proposed at the Mount.

Her first words to Thomasina were, 'I wish I had your sea-legs, Thomasina. Travelling here by carriage has left me black and blue. The coachman assures me he followed the roads, but I swear it would have been a more comfortable journey had we travelled in a straight line, across country.'

'Would you like to take some tea before we go shopping?' Thomasina felt concerned for Juliana. Heavily pregnant, she was supporting her bulging stomach as though fearing that the baby was likely to drop into the world at any moment.

'Yes. Yes, I would – perhaps something a little stronger, too. Where shall we go? Inside the inn?'

Thomasina had already peeped inside the building and decided it was perfectly respectable. She said so now.

'Good, then let's go inside. The coachman can find something for the horses and wait for us here. God! I really do need something to revive me – and quickly.'

Juliana linked her arm through Thomasina's and the two women entered the inn. The landlord had seen the carriage arrive and recognised the crest painted on its door. Hurrying to meet them, he escorted them to an alcove at the side of the dining area. Here, fortified by a large brandy, cake and a pot of tea, Juliana gradually regained her balance and composure. It was not long before she declared herself ready to face the shopkeepers of Falmouth.

They had not been shopping for long when Thomasina began to wonder whether the shop-keepers were ready for the mistress of St Michael's Mount. She found Juliana's method of shopping quite amazing.

Although Juliana had already given birth to eight children and must have amassed a mountain of baby clothes, it seemed to Thomasina that she was intent on buying a new outfit for every day of the unborn child's life!

She also purchased a great many items of clothing for herself, in anticipation of the day when her figure would have returned to normal.

She paid cash for very few of her purchases. In

the vast majority of shops Juliana told them to bill Sir John St Aubyn, directing that her purchases be taken to the Packet Inn and placed on the St Aubyn carriage.

Such was the esteem in which the St Aubyn name was held that not once did a shopkeeper question the arrangement.

Eventually Thomasina found Juliana's enthusiasm for shopping contagious. She bought more clothes than at any time in her life. She too delighted in having them delivered to the St Aubyn carriage, although in her case she was required to pay cash for her purchases.

If Juliana was surprised that Thomasina had such sums of money readily available, she made no comment.

After they had both bought what Thomasina considered to be a phenomenal quantity of goods, the two women returned to the Packet Inn for a late lunch. Here Juliana ensured that the St Aubyn's coachman had safely locked away their purchases in the secure box situated beneath his carriage seat.

In the dining-room they occupied the same alcove as before. They were settling themselves when Thomasina was startled to see Sir Charles Hearle and Captain Silas Carberry passing through the dining-room, heading for the door.

She and Juliana were wearing hats, which helped hide their faces to a greater or lesser degree. Juliana's was a wide-brimmed hat of silk and lace, which she had told Thomasina was currently the height of fashion in London.

Thomasina wore a more traditional poke-bonnet, which had lace and ribbon trimmings – and a short veil. It had been purchased only that day. She had found it so appealing that she insisted upon wearing it there and then.

She was grateful for the veil when Sir Charles Hearle looked up from the conversation he was holding with Captain Carberry and caught sight of Juliana. He immediately changed direction. Leaving his companion behind, he headed towards the two women.

Stopping just short of the alcove, he bowed to Juliana. After only a moment's hesitation, he inclined his head briefly to Thomasina, too. Returning his full attention to the mistress of St Michael's Mount, he said, 'Good day to you, ma'am, I am delighted and surprised to find you here, in Falmouth. I trust you are well?'

'Very well, thank you, Sir Charles.'

Thomasina had the impression that Juliana was saying no more than courtesy demanded from her.

'Sir John, and your family – they are well too?'

'All well, thank you.'

Now Thomasina knew for certain that Juliana was merely being polite.

'I trust Sir John will look kindly upon my request, in due course.'

'Sir John was absent from the Mount when your letter was delivered, Sir Charles. He is still away. It will receive his attention when he returns.'

'Of course.' Sir Charles switched his glance to Thomasina, but could see no more than a vague outline of her face beneath the veil of the bonnet.

He returned his attention to Juliana. 'If I may be of any service to you while you are in Falmouth, pray consider me your willing servant, ma'am.'

'Thank you, Sir Charles. Good day to you.'

'Good day to you, ma'am . . . Miss.'

Giving the two women a half-bow, Sir Charles Hearle turned away and made his way across the room to rejoin Captain Carberry. After an exchange of words, the latter glanced across the room to the two women, then both men left the inn together.

'I make no apology for not introducing you to Sir Charles,' said Juliana, when the two men had gone. 'I can't stand the man. He's a notorious roué of the worst possible type. A cousin of mine found herself alone with him some time ago and, had she pursued charges, Sir Charles would have been transported. Fortunately for him, she felt that the shame of having others know what had happened to her would have been a worse experience than letting him get away with what he did – or tried to do.'

'Malachi warned me about him,' said Thomasina, wishing she could tell Juliana of her own ordeal at the hands of Sir Charles. 'He had nothing but contempt for Sir Charles Hearle – and I valued Malachi's opinion more highly than that of any man I've ever known.'

'He seems to have been a good judge of character,' Juliana agreed. 'Sir Charles has applied to Sir John for permission to use the harbour at the Mount to load and discharge cargoes. I've suggested that permission is refused, but he probably won't take any notice of my wishes. Sir John is a very understanding man in many ways, but he believes that personal opinion should have no part in business. He will probably allow Sir Charles to use the harbour at the Mount, although if I have my way he will charge higher dues than he takes from the other ship-owners. However, I have not come to Falmouth to waste time talking of Sir Charles Hearle. We will order lunch, then might have time for a little more shopping before we need to set off to return to the Mount.'

Her words took Thomasina by surprise. 'Shouldn't we leave straight away for the Mount? Abel said . . .'

'Abel is boatman to the St Aubyn family, not its guardian.'

Juliana spoke so sharply that Thomasina looked at her in surprise.

Aware that her reply had been sharper than she had intended, Juliana explained, 'Abel occasionally tends to take too much upon himself. He means well, I have no doubt, but it can be annoying.'

Thomasina said nothing. Juliana's resentment of Abel was quite unreasonable. It was possible that she, too, was aware of the rumours about his parentage.

'Now, what shall we eat? When I arrived in Falmouth this morning I felt quite certain I would not be able to look at food for days, but all our shopping has given me quite an appetite . . .'

8

By the time the two women ended their lunch even Juliana was forced to admit that more shopping was out of the question. It was now almost four o'clock in the afternoon. The St Aubyn coachman had twice looked in through the doorway of the dining-room at the two women, his anxiety plain to see.

'I suppose we should start back,' said Juliana, looking unusually petulant. 'Being an island for much of the day is one of the Mount's major drawbacks. Never mind, Thomasina, once the baby is born and life returns to normal, you and I must go on a *real* shopping spree. Have you ever been to London . . . ?'

When the carriage set off, the coachman drove at breakneck speed, soundly cursing any waggoner who did not move to one side quickly enough to allow the carriage to pass. Inside, the two women were bounced about alarmingly until, risking injury by putting her head outside the window, Juliana ordered the coachman not to drive the horses so hard.

'We need to make up time, if you don't want to take a boat across to the Mount in the dark, ma'am. We're running late.'

'The child that I'm expecting will be running early if you don't do as you're told and slow down.'

Thomasina remembered what Humphrey had said about the need to be back on the Mount before seven-thirty, but she remained quiet. Although she felt sympathy for Juliana's state of extreme discomfort, she was concerned about the crossing from Marazion to what would probably be an island by the time they arrived.

It was dusk when they reached Marazion and the carriage came to a halt at the water's edge. The castle atop the Mount was a dark, irregular shape, silhouetted against a cloud-patterned sky, tinged by the embers of the sun that had sunk beneath the horizon.

The colours of the sky were reflected in the water that stretched between land and island.

'There we are, ma'am,' said the coachman, trying not to sound smug. 'I knew we wouldn't make it in time. Shall I go off and find a boat?'

'No!' replied Juliana. Her reply was made firmer by the knowledge that it was her fault they had arrived at Marazion later than had been intended. 'The causeway can only have been covered for a short while. Surely you can get to the Mount? It will take only a few minutes.'

Thoroughly alarmed, Thomasina protested. 'Surely that would be very dangerous – especially now, in this light.'

'Sir John would dismiss me on the spot if he knew I had taken such a chance, ma'am. I might risk it in daylight, but now . . . ! I'll go and look for a boat, if you like, but if you don't want to make use of it I suggest it would be better for you to remain in Marazion for the night.'

'I'm not asking for your suggestions,' Juliana retorted angrily. 'Only your expertise – such as it is. I feel ill enough as it is after enduring the abominable ride here. I have no intention of making things worse by crossing to the Mount in a boat. As for remaining here . . . I have children in the castle who will be waiting for me. If you won't drive me, then I will take the reins myself and *you* can spend the night here. If I have to take such measures you needn't bother coming to work in the morning.'

She had placed the coachman in an impossible situation. He turned to Thomasina in near-despair. 'I've tried my best, you'll bear witness to that, Miss.'

'He's right, Juliana, it *is* far too dangerous.'

'Then you can stay in Marazion, too. *I'll* take the carriage myself . . .'

'That won't be necessary,' said the coachman unhappily. 'I'll attempt the crossing – but only to prevent you from trying to do it yourself.'

'Are you coming?' The question was put very stiffly to Thomasina and she remembered Humphrey telling her that Juliana could be impossibly stubborn on occasions. Even more so if opposed.

'Of course I am – but I still believe the coachman is right.'

Juliana ignored her. Instead, she snapped at the coachman, 'Well, what are you waiting for? The longer you wait, the deeper the water will be.'

Making no reply, the coachman shook the reins and the coach swayed from the road, down the slope that led to the sea-covered causeway.

The horses were as reluctant as the coachman to attempt the crossing. He needed to bring his whip into play before they could be coaxed to step into the featureless sea.

The coachman had crossed the causeway by day and night on many occasions. He knew the route, guided by the lights of certain cottages situated around the harbour. He also knew there was a particularly dangerous spot where the causeway narrowed, just short of the harbour wall. It was this that was to prove the undoing of the coach and those it carried.

Juliana had been right about one thing. The water was not particularly deep, although the causeway dipped slightly as they neared its narrowest point. Here the water was axle-deep. There was also a slight swell running. This, coupled with the meeting of two currents at the spot, meant that the actual depth of the water was unpredictable.

The two horses were actually on the narrow section of causeway when the two currents came together, accompanied by a swell. Suddenly the horses were chest-deep and the coach was lifted by the water and swung to one side.

The coachman tried desperately to keep the horses on a safe course, but the floating carriage pulled them askew. Then one of the horses slipped from the causeway.

Frantically attempting to regain its footing, the horse pulled the carriage farther off course. When the swell subsided once more, only two wheels on one side of the vehicle were still on the causeway. Suddenly the carriage tipped over, causing the two passengers to slide helplessly along the bench seats inside – and throwing the coachman into the water.

Juliana screamed and the coachman shouted in terror before he disappeared beneath the waves. At that moment both horses regained their footing on the causeway and began pulling in the right direction once more. The whole of the carriage was off the causeway now and, as water poured inside, it tilted over even farther.

It was impossible to open either of the doors. Fortunately, the windows were open. As the water rose inside the carriage, it righted itself temporarily and Thomasina was able to climb out through the window, pulling Juliana after her.

'Can you swim?'

Thomasina put the question to Juliana as they both clung to the carriage, which was now almost totally submerged. It seemed to be resting on the sea-bed at the moment. The horses, unable to shift the water-filled vehicle, struggled to keep their footing. By so doing they prevented the carriage from drifting into deeper water.

Of the coachman there was no sign.

'Not very well,' gasped Juliana in answer to Thomasina's question, the sudden coldness of the water robbing her of breath.

'Then hold on tight to the rail on the carriage roof. I'll try to keep the horses on the causeway.'

Making her way hand-over-hand along the edge of the carriage roof, Thomasina took advantage of another rising swell to swim to where the horses were struggling to retain their footing on the causeway.

When she reached the horses' heads, she found she could just maintain her own footing. The horses were also holding their ground for the moment, but pulling the water-filled carriage back to the causeway was an impossibility.

With the tide rising steadily, women and animals were in a particularly precarious situation. Then Thomasina heard a shout. Turning her head, she saw a boat heading towards the stricken carriage from the direction of the harbour, the blades of oars churning up white foam as the oarsmen strained to their task.

'We're here . . . hurry!' Thomasina called out to the boat's crew, before shouting the good news to Juliana. 'Hold on, Juliana, a boat's almost here.'

The St Aubyn boat reached them in a couple of minutes, although it seemed an age as Thomasina fought to keep the horses steady.

The oarsmen stopped rowing and, as the boat glided towards her, Thomasina called, 'Get Juliana. She's clinging to the carriage. Hurry!'

A voice she recognised as belonging to Abel called an order and the boat passed her by and collided heavily with the almost submerged vehicle. Then she heard the men shouting to each other as Juliana was unceremoniously hauled on board the boat from the Mount.

Moments later the boat was alongside her. As Thomasina was pulled on board to join Juliana, Abel gave orders to the men to cut the horses free in order that they might make their own way to the Mount.

As this was being done, Abel asked, 'Where's Harry . . . the coachman?'

'I don't know. He was thrown from the coach. I heard him shout before he went under. I haven't seen him since then.'

'I doubt if you will,' said one of the oarsmen. 'He can't swim.'

'We'll stay out and search for him,' said Abel. 'Not that Sir John will thank us for saving him. He must have been mad to attempt crossing after dark, with the causeway covered – and on a rising tide, too.'

Thomasina said nothing, waiting for Juliana to accept the blame for what had happened. But Sir John St Aubyn's mistress had other matters on her mind.

'Get me back to the Mount and send other boats out looking for the coachman,' she said in some distress.

'We'll call them out if we can't find him ourselves,' said Abel, 'but as we're here . . .'

'Get me back,' a hard-breathing Juliana demanded. 'Once we're ashore you can send out as many boats as you like – but if you don't hurry . . .' She paused in obvious pain. 'Quickly . . . the baby's on its way.'

9

By the time the boat bumped alongside the jetty at the foot of the Mount, Juliana was writhing in agony. Deeply concerned, Abel tried to comfort her by saying, 'It'll be all right, we'll have you up at the castle in no time.'

'Don't be a fool, Abel,' she snapped at him. 'The baby would arrive before we were halfway there. What's more, if we don't get me somewhere quickly, it's likely to be born right here in this boat.'

Alarmed, the boatmen who were preparing to help Juliana from the boat turned to Abel for guidance.

He looked at the sodden, bedraggled mistress of Sir John St Aubyn. Oblivious to his uncertainty, she doubled over with a cry of pain, clutching her stomach as yet another spasm took control of her body.

Her time was very close. It was now apparent to

him that she would not be able to contain the child within her body until they reached the castle atop the Mount.

Making a hasty decision, he said, 'Take her to the house of my grandmother.'

The anxious boatmen had been waiting for him to take the initiative and give them a clear directive. They obeyed with alacrity.

Helped ashore, Juliana was supported to the house of Verity Trannack by a couple of the boat's crew. Every minute or so they were obliged to call a halt when labour pains forced Juliana to double over in agony.

By the time the party reached the small, terraced cottage occupied by Abel's grandmother, Juliana was in very real distress and hardly able to walk.

One of the boat's crew had hurried ahead of the slow-moving party, but when Thomasina and Juliana arrived, Verity Trannack had still not recovered from the shock of being told that the mistress of St Michael's Mount was on her way to her home to give birth to Sir John St Aubyn's child.

After settling Juliana on her own bed, Verity said querulously, 'I don't know who we can get to help bring the child into the world. Mother Sennett is the one who takes charge of births on the Mount, but she's over to Marazion, helping to deliver the first of her great-grandchildren. I doubt if we can have her back here much before dawn.'

'By then I'll have either presented Sir John with another child or he'll need to go into mourning for me,' gasped the distressed Juliana. 'Thomasina, you'll have to take care of me – and of Sir John's child. There's no one else I can trust.'

'Don't worry, you'll be all right, I'll look after you.' Reaching out, Thomasina grasped Juliana's hand as yet another spasm racked her body.

'I know you will,' said the other woman, between gritted teeth. As the spasm passed she added, 'I've known you only a short time, Thomasina, yet I already trust you more than anyone else I know.'

'I'll do what I can,' Thomasina promised, 'but I've never helped at a birth before.'

'I've gone through it enough times to know what to expect,' said Juliana. 'I wish I could say it's going to come easier because of that, but it never does. Each time I say it will be the last – but this time it's going to be, Thomasina, I swear it . . .'

Her head went back on the feather-filled pillow and her body arched as yet another pain knifed through her. As it subsided, Abel entered the room carrying a bowl of steaming-hot water. His grandmother walked behind him bearing a number of towels, most borrowed from neighbours.

The sight of Abel aroused Juliana to fury. 'What are you doing here? Have you no sense of decency? Get out, do you hear me? GET OUT! All of you get out . . . No, not you Thomasina. You stay with me – but *only* you.'

As the others hurried from the room to escape Juliana's wrath, Thomasina said, 'They were only trying to help, Juliana. I'm sure Abel's grandmother knows far more about childbirth than I do.'

'We don't need her. I don't want strangers fussing

about me at a time like this. I'll tell you what has to be done. Now they've gone, you can pull my clothes up – right up around my body . . . that's right. Now, I'm going to raise my knees and spread my legs apart. When I do, you'll realise why I didn't want anyone else around. Giving birth is the most inelegant situation any woman can ever find herself in . . .'

Despite all the pain that occurred before Juliana's child entered the world, the birth itself was surprisingly easy – much to Thomasina's relief.

No more than forty minutes after entering the Trannack home, Juliana held her latest son in her arms. Meanwhile, Thomasina bundled up the bloody towels. When things were tidy she would call in the rightful occupiers of the tiny cottage.

'Isn't he a delight, Thomasina?'

Now the birth was over, Juliana was as relaxed as though she had never been close to drowning and had suffered the pains of childbirth immediately afterwards.

Satisfied she had done all she could with the room, Thomasina looked to where Juliana held the baby. Wrapped in a towel, only a shock of black hair and his blotchy-skinned face were visible, although he had a strong voice. She felt vague, maternal stirrings within her, and yet, if she were brutally honest, she thought that only a mother could love such a wrinkled, noisy little object.

'What will you call him?' she asked Juliana.

'Why, there's only one name for him. I shall name him after you. He shall be Thomas St Aubyn. Thomas

John St Aubyn – John being a family name. You don't
mind, Thomasina?'

'I'm flattered. I hope he grows up to be a great blessing to you. May I allow Abel's grandmother in now?'

'Of course. Was I very horrible to her?'

'Yes, and to Abel too,' Thomasina replied with complete honesty.

'I'll find some way to make it up to both of them,' said
Juliana contritely. 'Go and find them, and tell Verity
Trannack I want her to be the first to see young Thomas.
That will please her. Oh, and ask if there is any news of
the coachman. I feel dreadful about him . . .'

10

When Thomasina left the room in which Juliana was holding her new-born son, she found Verity Trannack waiting uncertainly outside. The older woman had heard the first, healthy cries of the baby, but, afraid of incurring the wrath of Sir John's mistress, had not dared enter the room to check whether all was well.

Suddenly Thomasina felt desperately tired. It had been a very eventful day. She felt now as though all the energy in her body had seeped away.

Handing over the blood-stained towels, she managed to give the other woman a weary smile. 'Juliana says she would like you to go in and see the baby.'

'Mistress Vinicombe . . . is . . . She's all right?'

'She's fine, as far as I can tell. She tells me the birth was an easy one, but it certainly frightened the wits out of me.'

'I'll put these towels in to soak, then I'll go in and see her and the babe.'

'Where's Abel? Perhaps he might like to see the baby, too?'

'He'll not want to see it,' Verity said quickly – too quickly. Recovering herself, she added, 'He went to the harbour. All the village men are taking boats out to look for poor Harry Miller, the coachman. His young wife is in some state about him. They've only been married for two months and she's expecting her first in the next month or so.'

'I'm sorry.' Thomasina was genuinely upset. She felt she should have tried harder to dissuade Juliana from insisting that they should attempt to cross the causeway, but she said nothing to the other woman of her thoughts.

'Is there any chance that Abel and the others will find him alive?'

Verity shook her head, 'Harry never learned to swim and there's a strong tide running to the east of the causeway. His wife knows he won't be coming back to her. She's started her mourning already.'

When Verity went in to see Juliana and the new-born baby, Thomasina left the small cottage and made her way slowly towards the steep path which climbed the Mount to the castle.

She had promised Juliana she would make certain the servants at the castle were fully aware of what was happening. Thomasina would then remain with the children. In the morning Juliana and baby Thomas would be carried to the castle in the ancient sedan chair used for the conveyance of elderly or infirm visitors to St Michael's Mount.

Walking along the paved quay beside the harbour,

Thomasina could see lanterns twinkling from many boats on the stretch of water separating St Michael's Mount from the mainland. They danced on the restless waves of the bay as though carried by ballet dancers on a giant, darkened stage.

The imagery belied the macabre mission of those who scoured the waters of St Michael's Bay for the body of Harry Miller.

'Hello, Miss Thomasina.'

Stepping out from the shadows at the end of the row of harbourside cottages, Abel momentarily startled her.

'Abel! What are you doing here? I thought you'd be out in a boat with the others, searching for the poor coachman.'

'If there was the slightest possibility of finding him alive, I *would* be at sea, but Harry couldn't swim. That means they're searching for a body. They don't need my help for that.'

Changing the subject, Abel said, 'As you're on your way up to the castle, I presume Juliana has had her baby?'

'Yes, it's a boy. She's naming it Thomas. I'm on my way to the castle to make certain the other children are all right and to let the servants know what's happening.'

'They'll know already. There's little that goes on in the village that they don't learn about right away. In fact, I wouldn't be surprised if they already knew the baby's name and all.'

'How do they learn things so quickly?'

By the light of the last cottage in the village she

saw him shrug. 'I don't know, but it's always been that way.'

Leaving the village behind now, they were on the path that led up the Mount to the castle. Here Abel stopped, intending to allow Thomasina to proceed on her own.

Quickly she asked, 'Will you come up to the castle with me, Abel? The only time I've ever walked along the path was when I came down to the village to take the boat with you to Falmouth. It seemed very steep in places.'

'It's downright dangerous, especially if you don't know it well. I'll take you up to the castle door.'

'Can I take hold of your arm? I think I'll feel safer if I do.'

She took his silence to be assent and linked her arm through his.

They walked on in silence for a short distance before he asked, 'Was there much belonging to you being carried in the carriage?'

'A whole lot – although Juliana had even more. Some was clothing I'd brought from Malachi's house, but most was new, bought in Falmouth only today. I suppose it's all lost now, like poor Harry Miller?'

'Not necessarily. We tied a small buoy to the carriage when we rescued you and Mistress Vinicombe. Unless we have any bad weather during the night – which I doubt – we'll be able to recover the carriage tomorrow.'

'That at least is good news! None of the clothes will ever be as they were when we bought them, but

Juliana and I will certainly be able to do something with them. Was the buoy your idea, Abel?'

She sensed, rather than saw, the nod of his head.

'That was very clever of you, but then you seem to keep your head, whatever the emergency. If you didn't, I doubt if I'd be here now.' She squeezed his arm almost unconsciously and felt him stiffen. It was an instinctive reaction, but she went on, 'I'm sorry, would you rather I let go of your arm?'

'No.'

They both realised his reply had come too quickly. Breaking the silence that followed, Abel added jocularly, 'Having saved your life once or twice, it wouldn't do for me to lose you off the edge of the path now, would it?'

She gave a light laugh, quite content to continue to hold his arm. After a while she asked, 'What brought you back to the Mount after you'd spent years travelling the world as a marine, Abel?'

She felt him shrug, 'I've always looked upon it as being home, I suppose.'

'There wasn't anyone in particular to bring you back here?'

'Only my grandmother.' After a few moments' hesitation, he corrected the brief statement. 'No, that isn't strictly true. There *was* someone I came back hoping to see, but she had got married and moved away by the time I returned. I went off to sea for a few years then, working for a time as mate on a coaster out of Bristol. I stood in as master on another ship belonging to the same company and planned to make it my life. Then I got word that my grandfather had died and my grandmother wanted me, so I came back here to be close to her, and Sir John offered me work as his head boatman for the time I was here. I never left – and here I am!'

Thomasina thought that working as head boatman for Sir John St Aubyn was a considerable come-down for a man who had once had command of a deep-sea vessel. She said as much to Abel.

Once again he shrugged. 'Perhaps it is. I've never thought about it too much, for I enjoy living on the Mount. Although that's not to say I wouldn't move on if anything special came along. My grandmother has recovered from the loss of my grandfather and could manage well enough without me now. But I'm not looking for anything. There are worse things than being a St Aubyn boatman.'

'I suppose so, even though the situation up at the castle isn't exactly a normal one.'

'It doesn't seem to worry Sir John too much – nor anyone else, come to that. He's greatly respected by everyone in Cornwall – and farther afield, too.'

'All the same . . .'

Thomasina broke off what she was saying as they both heard the sound of someone breathing heavily, labouring up the steep pathway behind them.

Afraid that something might have gone wrong with Juliana and that whoever was on the path behind them was seeking her, Thomasina pulled Abel to a halt.

'Who's that? Are you coming after me?'

'Thomasina? Thank the Lord. I was at home in Ludgvan when I heard about the accident with the

carriage. I thought something might have happened
to you.'

It was Humphrey St Aubyn.

11

'Thank God you're safe, Thomasina! I was told that the carriage carrying you and Juliana from Falmouth had been washed from the causeway and I hurried here straight away. When I saw the boats in the bay, obviously searching for something, I feared the worst. You don't know what a relief it is for me to find you here.'

'As you can see, I am perfectly safe. The boats are out searching for one of the Mount coachmen. He was washed away when our carriage went off the causeway. But I'm touched by your concern, Humphrey. Perhaps you would also like to know about Juliana and your new half-brother.'

Before Humphrey could reply, Abel coughed discreetly in the background darkness.

'Who's that?'

'It's me, Master Humphrey. Abel.'

'Abel? What are you doing here with Miss Thomasina?'

Thomasina wondered whether Humphrey's indignation was because his effusive expression of relief that she was safe had been overheard by Abel, or outrage that he had found the two of them together in the darkness.

'I asked Abel to guide me along the path to the castle. I have only walked it once, and never in the dark.'

'I would have thought you would have been out in a boat searching for the coachman, Abel.' Humphrey was not mollified by Thomasina's explanation.

'If they find anything at all, it will be a body,' said Abel. 'They don't need me for that.'

'Had it not been for Abel, they would have been searching for me and for Juliana, too,' explained Thomasina. 'He came out in a boat in the darkness and rescued us.'

'He seems to make a habit of rescuing you,' said Humphrey peevishly. 'It must be very satisfying for him.'

'What an incredible thing to say!' declared Thomasina. 'I owe my life to him. I've no doubt your father will be grateful to him for rescuing Juliana, too.'

'No doubt,' said Humphrey, almost grudgingly. 'I'm grateful too – that he was able to save both you and Juliana. The St Aubyns are fortunate to have a boatman with such skill and initiative.'

Despite the jealousy which had overwhelmed him when he discovered that Abel was with Thomasina in the darkness, Humphrey meant it. He was not a mean-minded young man.

'I'll make certain my father rewards you generously when he returns, Abel. Thank you for escorting Miss Thomasina to the castle, too, but I'm here now. You may go back to the village and see if there is anything you can do to help in the search for the coachman.'

'You can *both* escort me to the castle,' Thomasina declared. 'I shall consider myself fortunate indeed to have two such gallant men attendant upon me.'

'No,' Abel said, 'Master Humphrey is right. I should be down at the harbour, seeing if there is anything I can do to help in the search. I'll have word sent to you tomorrow, when we recover the carriage. It shouldn't be too difficult at low tide.'

Trying to hide her disappointment, Thomasina said, 'Well, all right then. I'm sure the poor coachman's widow would feel much more at peace with herself if his body could be recovered. Thank you again, Abel – although mere thanks seem totally inadequate to someone who has saved my life not once, but twice.'

'I am glad I was there on both occasions. Good night to you both.'

When Abel had left them, Thomasina resumed her walk to the castle with Humphrey. They walked with Humphrey between her and the sheer drop to the right. But although they walked close together, Thomasina did not take his arm.

'Abel is a sound and reliable man,' Thomasina said conversationally. 'He seems to have had an interesting life, too. Your family is fortunate to have him working for you.'

'Yes.'

'Life can't have been easy for him. I mean, not knowing who his father is – or was.'

'No.'

Alone in the darkness with Thomasina, the last thing Humphrey wanted to do was spend the time talking about Abel. But she was not deterred by his lack of enthusiasm.

'Does anyone have any idea who his father might be?'

They were both aware it was a sensitive question. Much to Thomasina's surprise, Humphrey did not try to side-step it.

'There have always been a great many rumours. Some say he has St Aubyn blood in his veins. I have to admit there *is* some resemblance to the family, but no one has ever come forward to make any claims about it. Besides, whatever other faults they may have, the St Aubyns have never evaded their responsibilities. Had he been a St Aubyn, I feel certain he would have been acknowledged as such. Has he ever said anything to you about the matter?'

'It's nothing we've ever discussed,' she lied. 'But I admire your open-minded attitude on the subject. I think Abel might, too.'

'To be perfectly honest, I rather admire the man,' said Humphrey. 'He's already done far more with his life than I ever will.'

'But I thought you were going into the Church? That will make you one of the most important and respected men in the parish to which you are appointed.'

'That's what my mother is always telling me,' agreed Humphrey unhappily. 'I suppose she's right. It isn't what I *really* want to do, but my brother Robert is a curate, so I suppose I'll have to become a cleric, too – because that's what my father expects of us. I sometimes wonder whether putting us all in the Church is a way of atoning for his own life.'

'If you really feel so strongly about becoming a parson, you could always go off and do something else.'

'If I did, Father would cut me off without a penny. He's said as much. No, Thomasina, I'll do as he wishes, but I'll never be anything more than a very comfortably off, but rather mediocre country parson.'

Thomasina thought there were a great many men who would be perfectly happy to settle for such a state of affairs, but she said nothing.

'Of course, things might be very different if I were to be blessed in marriage with the right woman. One who would give me her full support as the wife of a parson; who took an interest in what I was doing. Who knows, I might then go on to become a dean – or a bishop, even.'

Thomasina thought the idea of Humphrey becoming a bishop far removed from his statement of only a few minutes before. Nevertheless, she hoped he would prove to be a successful servant of the Church.

With no object in mind but to humour her companion, Thomasina said, 'There are lots of women who would be proud to be the wife of a churchman, Humphrey. I'm sure you'll find one and go on to great things.'

'I think I already have found the woman I want to help me through life, Thomasina. I haven't said anything to her about my intentions, yet. But if she will have me, I have no doubt that all you say might come about.'

His statement took Thomasina by surprise. Early marriages were by no means uncommon among the society from which she came, but the sons of gentlemen – especially *titled* gentlemen – tended to marry later in life.

'What will Sir John say about you making an early marriage? I presume he knows nothing about it yet.'

'Nobody knows – except you. That's the way it should be, really. You see, I believe *you* are exactly the wife I have always dreamed of having, Thomasina. You are courageous, determined . . . Oh, everything that a man like me could ever want. This might come as a great surprise to you, Thomasina, but I am making you an offer of marriage. Please say "yes".'

12

'You saw me for the first time only a couple of weeks ago. We've had hardly any time together since then. Why, you know nothing at all about me, Humphrey!'

Thomasina and Humphrey stood outside the main entrance to the castle on St Michael's Mount. After recovering from the initial shock of his remarkable offer of marriage, she had tried to pass it off as a bizarre joke. However, Humphrey had assured her that he was in deadly earnest. As a result, Thomasina had spent the remainder of the walk up the steep path to the castle telling him how preposterous such a proposal was.

'Time has nothing to do with one's emotions, Thomasina. Once in a lifetime someone will come along and you know immediately that he, or she, is the only one you will ever love. *Really* love, that is.'

'I don't believe that, Humphrey. You need to know

someone for a long time before you can be sure you love them. To know how they behave in different situations. Whether you can trust them. Rely upon them.'

'I don't doubt that is what parents would have us believe, Thomasina. They are more concerned with the practicalities of marriage than with the romance of two people falling in love. The poet, Byron, looks at things very differently . . .'

'Humphrey! You have just asked me to marry you! Marriage is about making a life together and accepting responsibilities. Children. Matters of substance, not . . . poetry! I've no doubt Sir John would tell you the same, if you were to tell him you wanted to marry.'

'I don't think he is in a position to tell me anything of the sort, Thomasina. He could hardly have a more unconventional lifestyle – and all in the name of "love".'

'Very well, since you consider "love" to be all-important, I don't love you, Humphrey. I have grown fond of you, in the short time we have known each other, and have great respect for you as a person. I am also deeply grateful to you for the part you played in rescuing me after the shipwreck, but that's not a strong enough basis for marriage.'

'You would grow to love me, Thomasina, I am quite certain of it. No one could love you as I do and not be loved in return.'

'Life doesn't work that way, Humphrey. Wanting something very badly doesn't mean that you will one day get it.'

'Promise me you'll at least *think* about my proposal, Thomasina. Please don't dismiss it out of hand.' Desperate at her refusal, Humphrey tried to find a vestige of hope to which he could cling.

'Of course I'll think about it.'

Aware how desperately unhappy he was at this moment, Thomasina tried to restore some of his wounded pride. 'I doubt if I will be able to think of very much else for many days. But, just for now, let's not talk of it again. I would like us to get to know each other a little better before we do – and please don't mention this to anyone else. If word of your proposal were to reach the ears of Sir John, it would be very difficult for me to remain at the Mount.'

'As long as I know you are considering my proposal, I will not say a word to another soul. It will remain our secret. But in all your deliberations please remember that I *do* truly love you, Thomasina.'

Sir John St Aubyn returned to the Mount nine days later. He had left London post-haste when news reached him of the birth of his fifteenth acknowledged child, and his sixth son by Juliana. Given sketchy details of the circumstances leading up to the birth, he was anxious to learn the full story of the accident which had occurred on the submerged causeway.

The baronet entered Thomasina's room, after no more than a cursory knock at the door, while she was working on the financial details of Malachi's legacy.

Abel had taken a boat to Falmouth the day before, carrying with him a letter from Thomasina to her solicitor. He had returned with details of the monies and assets willed to her by Malachi.

'I do hope I am not disturbing you, Thomasina,' said Sir John. 'I felt I had to take the earliest opportunity of thanking you for all you have done for Juliana and our latest son. I heartily endorse Juliana's decision to name him Thomas in your honour. Indeed, as a result of her foolishness in insisting upon crossing the causeway on a rising tide, I doubt if *either* of them would be here today had it not been for your courage and resourcefulness. We owe you a debt which can never be repaid.'

'I've already been amply repaid by the kindness I have been shown since my rescue from the French man-o'-war. If anyone is to be thanked for what happened on the causeway, it should be Abel. Without him none of us would be here. He's the true hero.'

'Yes . . . of course.' Sir John St Aubyn was not a man who was easily embarrassed, but he appeared discomfited now. 'I have arranged for him to be given a hundred pounds. No amount of money could repay anyone for saving Juliana – and yourself, of course – but it will give him an indication of my deep gratitude.'

'I'm sure it would be even more appreciated, were you to present it to him yourself, Sir John. Abel has a very high regard for you.'

Sir John seemed even more ill-at-ease than before. 'Unfortunately, I am unable to remain at the Mount for very long. This is the most fleeting of visits. There are urgent Parliamentary affairs that must be dealt with personally in London. Before that I need to visit

Helston and Penryn to discuss forthcoming elections. However, I felt my first priority was to thank you for your part in saving Juliana. She tells me you have remained on the Mount at her request. I trust you will stay for a while longer? Indeed, there will *always* be a room at the Mount for you – and at Clowance too, if the builders ever complete the work they are carrying out there. In the meantime, I hope you will regard the Mount as your home, for as long as you wish to make use of it.'

'Thank you, Sir John. I am sorry to hear you will be absent from the Mount again so soon. Juliana misses you. Humphrey and your other children do, too.'

'Humphrey? Well, he will soon have other matters to think about. He will be leaving for London tomorrow morning. I have made arrangements for him to stay with a friend, a bishop, who will take him under his wing and introduce him to a few ecclesiastical friends. Hopefully, they will prove useful to him in the future.'

Suddenly thoughtful, he looked at her speculatively. 'You are aware, of course, that Humphrey is destined for a career in the Church? That he has a number of years of study ahead of him in order to fulfil that goal?'

'Of course. He's spoken of it on many occasions. He'll make an excellent parson, one day. You must be very proud of him?'

Partly relieved, but still uncertain that Thomasina's interest in Humphrey was purely platonic, Sir John said, 'Yes . . . yes, I am indeed. I am proud of all my children. I hope young Thomas, too, will grow up to justify all you did to ensure the survival of him and his mother. You are a remarkable young woman, Thomasina. Juliana and I are eternally gratefully to you.'

When Sir John had gone, Thomasina thought of all he had said. His offer of a permanent welcome on the Mount fitted in with her own plans very well. An idea for a business venture based largely on the Mount was already forming in her mind.

Sadly for Humphrey, he was not included in her plans and the knowledge that he would be going to London so soon came as a considerable relief. He had once more broached the subject of marriage, and his absence in London would be welcome to her.

She felt her immediate future was tied up with the Mount, but there were a great many things to be done before any of her ideas could move forward and take substance.

13

It was a very unhappy Humphrey who set sail from the St Michael's Mount harbour the following morning, en route for London.

Thomasina knew that much of his misery was caused by the knowledge that he was leaving her behind and would probably not see her again for many months. She was also aware there was a much deeper reason for his unhappiness. Humphrey was not convinced that his future lay with the Church.

However, there was little she could do about this. As she had told Humphrey, it was a matter that must be settled between him and his father.

Thomasina went to see Humphrey begin his journey from the small harbour at the Mount, taking two of Juliana's children with her.

Nine-year-old Catherine and five-year-old Richard were both eager to wave their older half-brother off on his voyage and Thomasina felt that, with both children present, Humphrey was unlikely to become over-emotional.

Because of this, she even allowed Humphrey to give her a farewell kiss before he boarded the London-bound ship.

It was no more than a friendly gesture, but one she might not have been so ready to permit had she noticed Abel coming towards them along the quayside.

When she realised he must have observed the kiss, she coloured up and greeted him with unreasonable belligerence.

'Have you taken to spying on me now?'

Raising his eyebrows, Abel retorted, 'Why should I wish to do that? What you, or the gentlemen of the castle, get up to is none of my business, Miss Thomasina. I'm interested only in getting Master Humphrey's ship out of the harbour to make room for the *Celestine*. It's hove to in the bay at the moment. It will be the largest ship to enter the harbour for as long as I can remember. No doubt the children would like to stay and see it arrive.'

Her anger forgotten, Thomasina expressed her interest. 'Why should such a large ship be coming in here? What load will it be taking out?'

'Copper ore, bound for a Swansea smelting-house. There have been cartloads of ore arriving at the pens for days now. However, unless I am sadly lacking in my judgement of Sir Charles Hearle, the profit on a single cargo of ore is unlikely to keep him happy.'

Thomasina started at mention of the baronet's

name. Now she asked, 'What has Sir Charles Hearle got to do with the *Celestine*?'

'It's the ship he bought with the money left to him by his aunt. He'll no doubt get a return on his investment, but I doubt if it will be enough to satisfy his spending habits.' Aware that he might have said more than was circumspect, he asked, 'Is Sir Charles Hearle a friend of yours?'

'Far from it, and from what little I know of him I'd say you're right about his attitude towards small profits. But with the Spanish merchant fleet returning to sea in increasing numbers and eager for any cargo that's going, he's not likely to make a fortune with a ship in the short term. Even smuggling is out until the French war is over.'

'War has never stopped the smuggling trade – and it never will,' Abel replied. 'It might have stopped Cornish boats trading direct with France, but there's enough undutied spirits hidden away in the cellars of Jersey and Guernsey to satisfy demand for the next ten or fifteen years.'

'You seem to know a great deal about such things,' observed Thomasina. 'Far more than might be expected of a boatman who earns his daily bread ferrying between the Mount and Marazion.'

'I'd have to be deaf and blind not to know something of what's going on,' Abel retorted. 'Besides, I doubt if there's a clergyman, magistrate or country gentleman in the whole of Cornwall whose cellar isn't stocked with wine and brandy that wasn't even a flower on the vine when this war started.'

'Would you involve yourself in smuggling if you

were master of your own ship?' Thomasina hoped it sounded a perfectly innocent question.

'Not if men like Sir Charles Hearle were night-trading in the same area,' Abel replied. 'A successful smuggler needs a good ship, a reliable crew – and a close mouth. Sir Charles has none of these . . . But here's the *Celestine* coming in to harbour now – and carrying far too much sail.'

Almost as Abel said the words, the sails of the large sailing ship were hurriedly furled. While this was taking place seamen could be seen scurrying about the deck belatedly preparing to make things ready to berth the large vessel.

Despite Abel's misgivings, the *Celestine* came alongside the quay without mishap. Thomasina watched with considerable interest as he and the other Mount men secured the large vessel and busied themselves about it.

'Isn't she one of the most beautiful sights you have ever seen?'

Startled by the question, Thomasina swung around to find the subject of her recent conversation with Abel standing behind her. She suddenly felt as though the breath had been squeezed from her body.

She had not observed Sir Charles cross the gangway from his ship and walk to where she was standing with the two children.

She was wearing a hat known as a 'Dolly Varden', which tilted down almost to the tip of her nose, hiding much of her face and making recognition difficult – even if Sir Charles had been aware they had met before.

The hat in question was extremely popular and had been much copied by working girls. Her own hat was of the more expensive variety, purchased in Falmouth, but immersion in sea water in the St Aubyn carriage had destroyed its original pristine condition.

And her hair had been allowed to grow. Gathered behind her head, it was secured with an elaborately worked silver hairpin, a present from Juliana. It was highly unlikely that Sir Charles would recognise her – from anywhere – but she still felt uneasy in his presence.

'It's a very fine ship,' said Richard, trying to act grown-up. 'I hope my father will allow me to look over it sometime.'

'Your father?'

Richard's manner of speech and air of confidence alerted Sir Charles to his family ties. It was hardly necessary for Richard to provide confirmation.

'My father is Sir John St Aubyn. He owns this harbour, you know?'

'Indeed I do. I have brought my ship here with his express permission. But we have no need to wait until he comes visiting. Please allow me to show you and your sister over the *Celestine* right now.' Shifting his attention to Thomasina for a moment, he continued, 'You too. You'll not have an opportunity to see such a ship again.'

Thomasina realised Sir Charles had made the assumption that she was the children's nursemaid. She had personal experience of his behaviour towards female servants, but she would not allow the children to be taken on board the *Celestine* without her.

'I'd love to come, but would you mind if Sir John's senior boatman came too? He's very interested in ships and was telling us about yours when it was on the way in.'

She indicated Abel, who was standing with his back to them, looking up at the ship's tall masts. He was not close enough to have overheard the conversation.

After a brief hesitation Sir Charles said, 'Of course not. One of the crew will show him around. Shall we go, children?'

His momentary lack of enthusiasm at the thought of having Abel join them was enough to alert Thomasina. Sir Charles had not changed his ways. She suspected that his response to the children's interest in his ship had little to do with a desire to satisfy their curiosity.

Calling out to Abel, she said, 'You were telling me what a wonderful ship the *Celestine* is, Abel. Sir Charles has kindly invited you to look over it with us.'

'Do come with us, Abel,' said Richard excitedly. 'You've often told us about the ships on which you've served. Come on board and tell us what you think of this one.'

Abel had correctly guessed the reason why Thomasina had suggested he should go on board too, but he said, 'I would love to look over such a beautiful ship, but Sir John has just sent for me, Master Richard. I'll ask one of the boatmen to go with you instead.'

14

The *Celestine* was a large vessel, but it did not exude the same air of efficiency that Thomasina had come to accept on board the *Melanie Jane*.

Unfurled ropes snaked across the deck and there was an indefinable air of slackness among the crew, who either stood around talking or were going about their tasks in a lacklustre manner.

Nevertheless, Thomasina found the same thrill of excitement she had felt when she stood on the deck of the ship that she and Malachi had owned. She would have enjoyed it even more, had Abel come on board with her.

Richard was fascinated by all he saw and, as they went around, the various crew members pointed out to him the features of the ship most likely to appeal to a five-year-old.

Determined not to be completely overawed by the

sheer size of the vessel, Catherine dutifully followed her brother, Thomasina and Sir Charles around, saying very little.

When they had been on board the *Celestine* for about fifteen minutes Thomasina said, 'I think we should go now. We only came down to the harbour to see the children's half-brother off to London. Everyone at the castle will be wondering where we are.'

Sir Charles had always been an opportunist where women were concerned and he had no intention of allowing Thomasina to escape so easily. 'Nonsense, there is still a great deal of the ship to see . . .' Awkwardly scooping Richard up in his arms, he continued, 'We haven't visited the galley yet, have we, young man? We must go down and see if the cook has anything nice for you.'

When Sir Charles hurried off towards a hatch at the stern of the vessel, Thomasina's suspicions were immediately aroused. The galley on most ships of this size was situated towards the bows. But he was carrying Richard, with Catherine close on his heels. She could do nothing else but follow.

Thomasina's suspicions increased as they descended the ladders and were faced with a couple of cabin doors.

A third door was set in another bulkhead. She decided this probably gave access to a cargo hold.

'I thought you were taking the children to the galley for something to eat,' Thomasina said accusingly to Sir Charles.

'I am, but I remembered something of interest

that they might enjoy seeing first. It's here, in my cabin.'

Putting Richard to the deck and throwing open the door, he startled a seaman who was tidying the cabin. 'There, have you ever seen a more magnificent room anywhere?'

Although she remained wary of the baronet, Thomasina had to agree it was indeed a splendid cabin, far superior to the one Malachi had occupied on board the *Melanie Jane*. Panelled in fine mahogany, it was furnished in the manner of the study of Henry Vincent, at Trebene.

Sir Charles's next words explained this. 'Much of the furniture came from the home of my late uncle. I was allowed to choose a few bits and pieces from his home when he died. I picked them with just such a cabin in mind. The panelling is very special indeed. It came from the admiral's cabin on board a French ship-of-the-line. The ship was captured after a fierce battle and was too badly damaged to be commissioned into our own navy. I saw it in Plymouth when we took the *Celestine* there to have some work carried out. I bought the panelling and had it fitted there and then . . . But here you are, children, this is what I brought you to see. Have you ever seen a fish that flies? Well, now you have. This was also in the French admiral's cabin. See those long wings?'

The flying fish was in a glass case on a desk. As the children looked at it more closely, Thomasina asked the baronet, 'Do you intend using this cabin and sailing in the *Celestine* yourself?'

Flattered by her interest, Sir Charles replied, 'Occasionally. However, when the war with France is over – and I don't think that day is very far off – trade with Europe will recommence. The *Celestine* will begin trading with France. I will be able to offer a luxury cabin to anyone who wishes to travel to the Continent in comfort.'

'Do you think you will be able to find such passengers prepared to travel from St Michael's Mount harbour?'

Thomasina believed Sir Charles was being unrealistic. She felt that most prospective passengers in the area would prefer the facilities offered by ships from the nearby ports of Falmouth, Penzance or other large towns.

Impressed that Thomasina should have asked such a pertinent question, Sir Charles replied, 'Sir John St Aubyn has told me he is looking forward to the day when it is possible to travel to France once more. No doubt his many sons will want to visit that country, too – and where the St Aubyns go, others in the area will certainly follow. But enough of such talk. We can't have the children becoming bored, can we?'

Turning to the seaman who had been tidying the room when they entered, he said, 'Symonds, take the children to the galley. Have Cook make them something special.'

With a knowing smirk in Thomasina's direction, the seaman said, 'Certainly, Sir Charles. The cook has children of his own, he'll know what boys and girls enjoy.'

'I'll go with them,' Thomasina said hurriedly.

'Nonsense! They'll be delighted to escape from your authority for a few minutes. You'll enjoy a brief time away from them too, I don't doubt. While they are away you can help me make lemonade for them.'

Jerking his head at the seaman, in what he believed to be a surreptitious signal for him to depart with the children, Sir Charles continued, 'I purchased a whole bag of lemons only yesterday. They were brought to Falmouth on a ship newly returned from Spain. I also have water and sugar here. Sadly, I lack experience in catering for the young. I believe their tastes differ from my own.'

Sir Charles had placed himself between Thomasina and the others as he was speaking. It would be impossible now for Thomasina to escape from the cabin without creating a scene that might upset the children. Increasingly concerned, she was taken back to a similar situation at Trebene House, some two years before. Had he not been so drunk at the time, she felt that Sir Charles might have remembered it, too.

When the door closed behind the children and their escort, Sir Charles beamed at Thomasina in what he clearly hoped was a reassuring expression. 'Now, where did I put those lemons? I know they are here somewhere. While I try to recall their whereabouts, why don't we have a drink ourselves? What can I offer you? I have brandy, sack, whisky, gin – and some excellent port. It was brought back from Lisbon by my cousin.'

'Thank you, but it's far too early in the day for me to begin drinking.'

'It's never too early in the day to enjoy a drink, girl. Here, I'll pour two glasses.'

He poured two large glasses of port. When she declined to take one from him, he set it down on a small nearby table.

'I thought we were going to make lemonade for the children,' Thomasina reminded him.

'There's lots of time for that. They'll be kept amused in the galley by the crew. Sailors love having children on board ship.'

'I'd like to make it now, if you don't mind,' Thomasina declared stubbornly.

'Please yourself.' Sir Charles shrugged. Then, belying his earlier statement, he said, 'You'll find lemons in the cupboard over there, in the corner. Sugar too – and plenty of water in the jug on the table.'

While she crouched down, removing lemons and sugar from the floor-level cupboard, Sir Charles sipped his port and watched her, observing with increasing arousal how her dress tautened over her buttocks as she crouched in front of the cupboard.

Putting his drink down, he strode across the cabin to her. 'Here, allow me to help.'

Leaning over her, he reached out to take the sugar from her, at the same time staring down inside the front of her dress as she leaned forward to reach inside the cupboard.

'I can manage, thank you,' she said firmly.

'Don't be so damned independent, girl. You should learn to relax a little more. Life is far too short to allow a sense of dignity to stand in the way of enjoyment.'

'What you mean is that *my* dignity is standing

in the way of *your* enjoyment,' Thomasina retorted. Standing up suddenly with some of the ingredients for the lemonade in her hands, she almost knocked the lecherous baronet off balance. 'Perhaps you'll bring a couple more lemons to the table.'

Sir Charles successfully contained the anger which flared up at what he considered to be Thomasina's impertinence. She might be no more than a nursemaid, but she was a *damned* handsome woman. One who would doubtless prove worthy of a little patience. However, time would not allow his patience to be stretched too far.

Putting down his glass, he picked up three of the lemons, recovering one when his crippled arm caused it to drop to the cabin floor.

'Here you are, young lady. Now I insist that you take a glass of port with me.'

He brought the glass to her, but she ignored it, busying herself with mixing the ingredients for the lemonade.

After standing holding the glass out towards her for a while, Sir Charles frowned, set the glass down on the table beside the items with which she was working, then crossed the room to refill his own glass.

He had refilled it once more before Thomasina finished her task. Looking at him boldly, she asked, 'Shall we take it to the children, or will you send someone to fetch them back here?'

'Symonds will bring them back when they have had something to eat,' he replied. 'You haven't touched *your* drink yet.'

'I told you, it's too early for me, and I must be getting the children back to the castle. I'll go and find them now.'

She reached the door just ahead of him, but as she lifted the latch on the door, his good arm came over her shoulder and held it closed. 'Just a minute . . . please?'

She swung around to face him and he staggered back with a cry of pain. The glass he had been holding dropped to the carpet and his hand went up to his neck. When he took it away and looked at it, there was a smear of blood on his finger.'

'I'm terribly sorry, I completely forgot I had this in my hand.' She was looking down at the silver hairpin from Juliana, as though she had forgotten she had been holding it. 'I thought I had put it back in my hair.'

'You might have killed me!' Sir Charles looked at her in disbelief.

In truth there had been a brief moment when Thomasina had been sorely tempted to plunge the long pin deep into his throat.

'Yes, indeed I might have. That would have been very careless of me. Never mind, it's really only a scratch. In a day or two you'll have forgotten all about it.'

Still holding the hairpin, she smiled sardonically at him. 'I think I should go and fetch the children now, don't you?'

'You are treating the fact that you might have killed me as some kind of joke. Go and fetch the damned children, but don't bring them back here. I'll have the lemonade brought up to the main deck. I must put something on my neck to stop it bleeding.'

He hurried to a small cabinet fixed to the bulkhead of his cabin. With a fleeting smile, Thomasina left the room. Once outside, she replaced the hairpin in her hair, then went off in search of the two children.

15

Halfway up the steep pathway leading to the castle, Thomasina and the two children met up with Abel, who was returning to the harbour.

Greeting them all, he asked, 'Have you had a good time on board the *Celestine*? I think it must be the largest ship you've ever seen here.'

'I don't think there's anything special about it,' said Catherine, with a determined lack of enthusiasm.

'Sir Charles showed us a fish that had wings,' Richard told Abel animatedly. 'Sir Charles said it could fly out of the water, just like a bird.'

'That was exciting,' said Abel.

'It was,' agreed Richard.

'No, it wasn't.' Catherine contradicted him with all the superiority that came with being four years older than her brother. 'Our Uncle George, who lives in London, has one. His is much larger than the one Sir Charles showed us.'

'We had some nice lemonade,' said Richard, doggedly determined to prove that they had enjoyed themselves, '. . . and I had a piece of maggoty pie.'

Abel looked puzzled and Thomasina laughed. 'I think Richard must mean "muggety" pie. It's made from a sheep's insides. It's about as cheap a meat dish as you're likely to get anywhere.'

'Ugh!' exclaimed Catherine in a grimace that left no one in any doubt about the disgust she felt at Thomasina's explanation. 'No wonder I didn't like it.'

Abel gave the nine-year-old girl a sympathetic smile. 'It doesn't sound as though you enjoyed your visit to Sir Charles Hearle's wonderful new ship.'

'I didn't,' she agreed emphatically. 'I don't like Sir Charles very much, either.'

'Now, Catherine, that's very uncharitable of you. After all, he did invite us on board his ship.' Thomasina gently chided the young girl.

'It was *you* he really wanted to go on his ship,' Catherine said perceptively. 'As soon as we got there he wanted to get rid of Richard and me, so he could be with you.'

'Catherine! You shouldn't say things like that,' said Thomasina, but once again it was a very gentle admonition.

'Well, that's what the sailor who took us to the galley said to the cook. Anyway, you didn't like him very much either, did you?'

'Now how can you possibly know that, Catherine? You mustn't make up such stories.'

'I'm not making it up,' Catherine said indignantly. 'When the sailor said Sir Charles had sent him with us to get us out of the way, because he had you in his cabin, the cook said in that case he'd probably have us for the whole of the morning. The sailor said he wasn't so sure about that. He said you seemed like someone who wouldn't take any of Sir Charles's "old buck". What does "old buck" mean?'

'That doesn't matter. He shouldn't have been talking like that in front of you.'

Ignoring Thomasina's admonition, Catherine continued with her recital of the sailor's conversation. 'He said that if you wouldn't take any of Sir Charles's "old buck", we'd be off the ship quicker than . . .' Catherine was about to repeat the sailor's swear word, but thought better of it, '. . . quicker than you could say anything. So he told the cook he'd better hurry up and dish something up for us. Richard had only just finished eating his pie when you came for us.'

Less aggressively she added, 'I was glad you *were* so quick, though. It meant I didn't have to eat my pie – and I think "maggoty" is a better name for it than "muggety".'

'Well, *I* liked it,' declared Richard sulkily. 'I don't care if it *was* maggots.'

Abel's glance had shifted to Thomasina while Catherine was talking. Now he asked, 'Are you all right? You had no trouble from Sir Charles Hearle?'

'Nothing I couldn't handle.'

'So he *did* try something?' Abel's anger flared. 'No

woman has ever been safe anywhere near him. It's high time something was done about that man.'

'Nothing happened, Abel.' Thomasina was secretly delighted by his reaction, but she felt obliged to ensure that he did nothing foolish. 'I made it very clear I would welcome neither the drink he offered to me nor his advances. He accepted it without question.'

Thomasina was not entirely certain Abel believed her, but she gave him no opportunity to dwell upon the matter.

'He told me his ship will be carrying copper ore to Swansea, but his cabin is much too grand for an ore vessel and I doubt if he'll find many passengers wanting to go to Swansea from the Mount.'

'True. He'll not make many trips carrying ore, either. There are too many small boats, with a crew of three or four, ready to carry a cargo of ore for little more than a living wage. He'll need to look farther afield if he wants to take on profitable cargoes, but I doubt if the *Celestine* is capable of deep-sea trade without a lot of work being carried out on it. The ship's getting old and was laid up without attention for far too long. The signs are there for anyone with a seaman's eye to see. Everything above deck should be checked, and much of it needs replacing. What the ship is like below the water-line is anyone's guess. I certainly wouldn't want to take her to sea – even if the master's cabin was fitted out in pure gold.'

'Sir Charles told me the war with France will soon be over. When it is he expects to open trade with the French ports, carrying passengers in the cabin.'

Abel snorted derisively. 'Napoleon won't acknowl-edge he's beaten until Paris itself is threatened. That's not likely to happen for at least another couple of years.'

'So what will Sir Charles do if the markets he's hoping for aren't open to him? Do you think he might take to smuggling, through Guernsey?'

'It's possible. Something like that is certainly more in keeping with his character than legiti-mate trading. But to be successful he should have chosen a different ship. The *Celestine* is too large, too old and much too slow – and neither Sir Charles nor his captain are the right men for moonlight trading.'

'What sort of man is right for smuggling, Abel? Most Cornish sailors try it when times are bad.'

Abel gave her a crooked smile. 'That's quite true. Given the right boat and an owner I could trust, I would do whatever was needed to turn in a profit, too. But I'm no longer a deep-sea man. I'm Sir John St Aubyn's boatman and I'll give him my loyalty for as long as he pays my wages.'

'Can we go up to the castle now? I'm cold.' Catherine was not having a happy day. She was bored with standing waiting on the path while Thomasina and Abel talked and there was a cool breeze blowing across the slope of the Mount from the west.

'Come on then, we'll have a race to the castle door. Hopefully we'll be home before Sir John sets out for Helston.'

'He's not going today after all,' said Abel. 'After checking on the tides, he's decided to put off his journey until tomorrow, or even the day after. He too saw Sir Charles's ship enter harbour. He said he'll likely go down to pay a call on him. Probably later this morning.'

16

Thomasina and Juliana were seated on the castle terrace enjoying a pre-lunch drink when Sir John returned from his visit to the *Celestine*. Baby Thomas was sleeping in a canopied cradle nearby.

They were sheltered from the cool westerly breeze here and although rain clouds were building up on the horizon, the Mount was bathed in warm sunshine.

Unlike Thomasina, earlier in the day, Sir John had not declined Sir Charles's invitation to drink with him. As a result, he was in a jovial mood.

After peeping beneath the lace canopy at his newest son, Sir John beamed at the two women. Sitting down heavily upon an empty chair, he said, 'You know, Juliana, I really think Sir Charles Hearle has turned over a new leaf, at long last.'

'Really, dear?' Juliana recognised that Sir John had

drunk enough to feel at peace with the whole world. 'What makes you say that?'

'This ship of his. He seems to have taken on a new sense of responsibility now that he's bought it. Full of enthusiasm. Lots of plans for the future, that sort of thing. He's fitted the ship out rather well, too. We'd be proud to have a room in the castle that was furnished half as well as the cabin he occupies on board.'

'I hope he's saved enough money to spend on the rest of the ship.' Thomasina repeated what Abel had said to her without disclosing they were not her own views. 'There's a whole lot of rigging needs replacing. The masts and spars should be checked out, too. The *Celestine* was laid up for a long time without any work being carried out on it. A ship needs constant attention if it's to remain fully seaworthy.'

'I was forgetting you come from a family which has produced a number of sea captains and have yourself spent a great deal of time at sea, Thomasina. You'll have an opportunity tonight to tell Sir Charles what you think he should do with his ship. I've invited him to the castle for dinner.'

'I really can't, Juliana. I don't think I could bear to spend the whole of a meal with that man. Try as I might, I just don't like him. I couldn't wait to get away from him this morning.'

'That seems to be the feeling of every woman in the castle,' commented Juliana. 'I can't stand the man, either – and Catherine told me when she came back from the ship that *she* thinks he's sly. For someone who has the reputation of being a "lady's man", he seems to have failed miserably to impress anyone here.'

'What excuse can I possibly make?' repeated Thomasina. 'I don't want to offend Sir John, but I really don't want to share the same table as Sir Charles Hearle.'

'I'm sorry, Thomasina. In any other circumstances you would have my full support. Unfortunately, if you fail to join us for dinner, it means I will need to entertain Sir Charles without you. I doubt if I would be able to carry it off successfully. We'll go to dinner together, put on a brave front and provide support for one another. Who knows, with each of us being aware how the other feels about our unwanted guest, it might turn out to be an amusing, if *not* an interesting evening.'

Thomasina had doubts about the potential for amusement in the forthcoming evening. Furthermore, should details of any of her previous meetings with Sir Charles be recalled, it would prove disastrous.

Sir Charles was not in the best of moods when he arrived at the castle. The wind had increased from the west, bringing with it the rain that had threatened for much of the day.

The breeze had snatched at the umbrella he carried, turning it inside out, and rain had made his bicorne hat soggy, leaving his carefully curled hair wet and bedraggled. Much of his clothing had been kept dry by a waterproof coat which had a fitted cape, but the lower half of his pantaloons were wet and his shoes had lost all their shine.

He was grateful to Sir John for hurrying him off to a guest room in order to tidy and dry himself as best he could before joining the two women for pre-dinner drinks.

Despite this brief respite, it was not possible to entirely eradicate the effects of wind and rain. As a result, Sir Charles was aware that he was not at his debonair best when he was escorted to the sitting-room by a servant.

Standing in the doorway, he was welcomed by Sir John, who stood between him and the two women. 'Ah! Here you are at last, Charles! I trust you have managed to dry off. I am sorry we couldn't arrange better weather for your visit, but a glass or two of good brandy will put some cheer back in you – but is that blood I see on your neck? Have you hurt yourself, old chap?'

'No.' Sir Charles put a hand up to his throat, self-consciously. 'I nicked myself shaving, that's all. I must have set it off bleeding again when I dried myself. It's nothing.'

Sir Charles stepped inside the room, bowed to Juliana, then turned to Thomasina, who had been hidden from view by the castle's owner until this moment. He started to bow to her too – then suddenly recognised her from the morning. Jerking upright, he turned to Sir John, seeking an explanation for her presence.

Instructing a servant on the drinks he was to pour, Sir John did not observe Sir Charles's shocked expression. Juliana did and she was quick to react.

'You've met Thomasina, of course, Charles. She and the children were kindly shown over your boat this morning. You have met her before too, when she and I were shopping together in Falmouth. She is a great friend and has been a wonderful companion during my recent confinement.'

'Thomasina has been absolutely marvellous,' enthused Sir John, breaking into the conversation. 'Saved Juliana's life when their carriage was washed off the causeway, you know?'

'. . . And brought baby Thomas into the world,' Juliana added. 'In fact, we named him after her.'

She was intrigued by Sir Charles's reaction to Thomasina. She looked forward to having Thomasina on her own in order to learn what lay behind it.

'I . . . I'm sorry,' said Sir Charles, finding a voice that did not sound like his own. 'As I remember, Thomasina wore a veil when we met in Falmouth, and this morning . . .'

He faltered and Thomasina said, 'This morning Sir Charles thought I was nursemaid to Catherine and Richard. I failed to enlighten him, I'm afraid. It was very naughty of me.'

'Nursemaid, indeed!' Sir John chortled. 'There has been a sight more to Thomasina's life than looking after young children, Charles. A damned sight more! She was a prisoner on that French ship we drove ashore on the Mount. Brought ashore unconscious by my son Humphrey and one of the boatmen. They all thought it was a young lad until they went to dress a wound inflicted by one of the mainlanders.

They soon discovered their mistake! It caused quite a stir at the time. At least, it did among our people. Quite a tale to tell, has Thomasina – and I suspect we haven't heard a fraction of it yet.'

Recovering some of his composure, Sir Charles said, 'I am intrigued, Sir John. Perhaps Thomasina will tell us something of her life over dinner? I, for one, would love to hear her story.'

'I'm sure there are far more interesting things to talk about, Sir Charles. You, for instance, and how you came about the injury to your arm. A war wound, is it?'

'Well, no, not exactly . . .'

The two women exchanged brief glances that contained a hidden meaning. Without going into any details, Thomasina had told Juliana how she and Malachi had met Sir Charles on the quayside at Falmouth, when he claimed his arm had been crippled as a result of enemy action.

'Charles is being modest,' said Sir John, unaware of the women's thoughts. 'He tackled two desperate highwaymen who tried to rob the carriage in which he was travelling with his uncle and aunt. Despite being wounded, he shot both of the villains. One was later captured, convicted and hanged. The other escaped, but Charles is convinced he badly wounded him, so he probably died too. Charles was the toast of the county at the time.'

'Nevertheless, I cannot ever forgive them,' declared Sir Charles. 'The injury prevented me from fulfilling my dearest wish, that of obtaining a commission in a cavalry regiment and serving with the Duke of

Wellington on his glorious campaign in the Spanish peninsula. Instead, I have had to be content with command of a militia company.'

'You are serving King and country as best you can,' Sir John declared. 'No man can do more.'

Thomasina had gone cold at the mention of the abortive hold-up in which Jeffery had been seriously wounded. This gave way to anger at Sir John's inaccurate description of what had happened on that fateful night.

Gaining control of herself, she said, with apparent sympathy, 'Such an injury must make it very difficult to carry out a great many everyday activities, Sir Charles. It's hardly surprising you cut yourself shaving. You were fortunate it was nothing worse.'

An expression of acute embarrassment momentarily crossed Sir Charles's face. It made Juliana more determined than ever to question Thomasina at great length about what had taken place that morning on board the *Celestine* in the St Michael's Mount harbour.

The small dinner party was hardly an unqualified success. Sir John's blatant efforts to pair Thomasina off with Sir Charles failed miserably and she blocked every attempt by Sir John's guest to learn more about her background. Any details that did emerge came from Sir John and were largely inaccurate.

The only information Sir Charles Hearle was able to glean with any certainty was that Thomasina was an unexpectedly wealthy young woman.

This alone was sufficient reason for him to take more than a passing interest in her.

The evening was drawing to a close when five-year-old Richard, dressed in a night-gown, put in an unexpected appearance in the sitting-room to which the four diners had adjourned.

Sleepily the young boy complained that he had been woken by the crying of his baby brother.

'That must be where the servant girl is who should have been taking care of Richard,' said Juliana. 'I'll take him back to bed and settle him down. It should not take more than a few minutes.'

Juliana had hardly left the room before Sir John made an excuse to hurry after her. His hope was that Thomasina and Sir Charles might get on better with each other if left alone.

When the others had gone, Sir Charles said, 'May I take this opportunity to say how terribly sorry I am for my unforgivable behaviour this morning?'

Thomasina said nothing.

'I really do not know what got into me. It is not the way I would normally behave, I can assure you.'

Thomasina would have enjoyed telling him that she *knew* differently, but once more she remained silent.

'I can fully understand your attitude towards me, Thomasina – indeed, I deserve nothing less – but may I be permitted to call on you?'

'I am only a guest in this house, Sir Charles. I can't invite anyone to come calling. Nor do I have any control over who does, or does not, visit the house.'

'Of course. I am aware of your difficulty, but should I pay a call, would I be welcome?'

'As I said before, this is not my home. I would not

abuse Sir John's hospitality by being rude to anyone who is a welcome guest in his house.'

'In that case I will leave here tonight happy in the knowledge that we will certainly meet again. I hope you will allow me an opportunity to prove that your first impression of me is not an accurate one.'

Thomasina had no wish to point out the inaccuracies in Sir Charles's statement, but she *did* wish to talk with him again. However, she would prefer it to be in the company of others.

She had heard a great deal that evening about his plans for the *Celestine*, but wanted to know more. With this in mind, Thomasina would put on an act of civility towards Sir Charles. Nevertheless, inside she carried a smouldering hatred of the man. When it eventually flared into life, she hoped it would prove powerful enough to consume him.

17

Thomasina saw Sir Charles Hearle only once more before the *Celestine* sailed for the Swansea smelters with her cargo of copper ore.

The baronet did not go with his ship. Instead, he returned to his home near St Mawes, a short ferry trip away from Falmouth town.

Before he left, he paid a further courtesy call on Sir John St Aubyn, at the castle. It was a fine day and Sir John, Sir Charles, Juliana and Thomasina stood on the terrace admiring a squadron of ten ships-of-the-line.

Sheltering in the Mount's bay overnight, the ships had just weighed anchor and were tacking to westward, heading for the open waters of the Atlantic Ocean.

'That's where the *Celestine* will be heading in a few months' time,' said Sir Charles, 'out to the open sea.' As he spoke he passed to Thomasina the telescope being shared by the viewers.

'Then you must intend taking ore farther afield than Swansea,' Thomasina said.

'There's very little profit to be made in shipping ore anywhere,' replied the baronet, confirming the observation that had been made to Thomasina by Abel, some days before. 'Too many ship-owners involved in the trade are willing to carry ore for next to nothing. No, Thomasina, I have been told of a much more lucrative market.'

'Can you share this exciting news with us?' asked Thomasina, 'or are you going to keep us guessing?'

Pleased at her unexpected interest, Sir Charles said, 'I can tell this company, but it is important that it should go no further. Hubert Fox, probably the most important shipping agent in Falmouth, visited the fish cellars on the Mount yesterday. He was here to check on the quantity of pilchards caught and how many are likely to be cured. He has received word that the Italians will allow pilchards to be taken into Leghorn – but it is an unofficial concession and must not be generally made known.'

'I don't doubt it's "unofficial",' Thomasina said scornfully. 'But I'm sure Napoleon will have something to say about an English ship trading with a country he controls.'

'A "say" is probably all he will be able to have about it right at this moment,' said Sir John. 'Napoleon has over-extended himself in his Russian campaign. As a result, many of the countries he has occupied are taking advantage of his weakness. Besides, there is little chance of Charles's ship being taken by the French. They hardly dare put to sea these days.'

'That's quite right,' agreed Sir Charles. 'And Mr Fox says that in Italy a ship-owner with nerve and initiative can make at least eight times the price that pilchards are fetching anywhere else in the world. The Italians have always been particularly partial to Cornish pilchards, but they have not been available for many years. The first boat to land them there will make a killing.'

'Hubert Fox has proved himself a keen business-man in the past,' commented Sir John. 'And he has a near-monopoly on the product in question in these parts. He'll no doubt be asking a high price for them?'

'Higher than anyone would dream of paying for the home market,' admitted Sir Charles. 'But with the money they will fetch in Italy, it is well worth paying.'

'When will you send off your ship?' Sir John put the question.

'Hubert Fox says he should have a good cargo ready for me by late October, or early November.'

'I envy your crew the voyage, at least,' Sir John said. 'It is a good time of the year to get away and enjoy the Mediterranean sunshine.'

Thomasina nodded in agreement, but her thoughts were not of sunshine. She had heard Malachi speak of Hubert Fox, but she had known of him long before that. Many years ago he had fallen out with the fishermen of Mevagissey. As a result, they refused to sell their catches to him. As far as she knew, their ban on trading with him still stood. This might be the very opportunity for which she had been waiting in order to strike a momentous blow at Sir Charles Hearle.

The following day Juliana announced to Thomasina that Sir John wanted her to accompany him to London to finalise arrangements he had made for their children. The older boys would be going to Westminster School while the girls were to stay with an aunt, who would ensure they learned all the skills demanded of young women of breeding.

They would also be formally introduced to the society in which they would one day meet young men considered suitable husbands for wealthy young women.

'How long will you be away?' Thomasina asked.

'We will probably stay in London for the whole of the winter,' Juliana replied. 'We rarely spend any time in the castle during the cold months and leave only the minimum of staff here. Unfortunately it is such a cold and dreary place then. But if you wish to remain here . . .'

'I wouldn't dream of it,' replied Thomasina, 'although I would like to stay on the Mount for a while longer, if it's at all possible. I am very happy here. Do you think I might move into the new house that's been built and furnished for the steward? I understand he prefers to remain in Marazion for the time being. Perhaps I could rent it for a while?'

Aware that Thomasina owned property in Falmouth, Juliana was taken aback by her request. 'I am quite certain it will be no problem,' she said, 'but I thought you would want to move to Falmouth? You will meet far more people there.'

Thomasina shook her head. 'I don't need people – or the memories that are there. No doubt I will go to Falmouth occasionally – quite soon, in fact – but I really would prefer to live here.'

'Then Sir John and I would be very happy for you to move into the steward's house. If ever the steward decides to live on the Mount you will need to vacate it, of course, but I don't doubt we will be able to find you somewhere else. But you will need to take on some staff . . .'

'I've thought of that,' said Thomasina, delighted to be remaining on the Mount. 'I decided that, if you agreed I could live in the house, I would ask Abel's grandmother to act as my housekeeper.'

'You could do a lot worse than to take on Verity Trannack,' said Juliana thoughtfully. 'She's a well-respected woman. You would have Abel on your side, too. That would pose no problem to you, I am sure. But how do you think Sir Charles will behave when he learns you are living on your own in the steward's house? He might try to take advantage of the situation.'

Thomasina had told Juliana, in confidence, of what had occurred when she and the younger children had visited the *Celestine* on the ship's first arrival in the St Michael's Mount harbour.

'That's why I want Verity Trannack for my house-keeper. It would ensure that Abel was more likely to be around whenever Sir Charles was on the Mount.'

*   *   *

On the day that Sir John St Aubyn, Juliana and the children left the Mount, bound for London, Thomasina moved into the newly built steward's house. Situated at the foot of the Mount itself, it was on the edge of the village. Although sandwiched between two fishing cellars, it was a large and impressive building.

The house had been furnished by the St Aubyns and Thomasina's few possessions were carried down from the castle by Abel, at her request, the move being supervised by Verity Trannack, who was taking her new duties very seriously.

'You are going to be very comfortable here,' commented Abel, depositing a chest of clothes in the bedroom Thomasina had chosen for her own. It was the same chest he had once carried from Malachi's house in Falmouth to the St Aubyn boat. 'You have a fine view of the harbour, too.' Unexpectedly he added, 'Does Sir Charles Hearle know you're moving in here?'

It seemed to be a fairly innocuous question, but Thomasina felt it contained an unspoken query.

'He doesn't know yet, but he'll no doubt learn about it when he next visits the Mount. That's partly the reason why I've asked your grandmother to act as my housekeeper. One of her tasks is to ensure she's always in the house with me whenever Sir Charles is on the island – and to call you if I'm in need of help.'

A brief raising of Abel's eyebrows represented a possible expression of disbelief. 'Then it would seem the village gossips have it wrong.'

'Have what wrong?' Thomasina demanded.

'They're saying you've set your cap at Sir Charles Hearle,' replied Abel, his expression telling her nothing of his own thoughts. 'Opinion is fairly evenly divided on whether or not you'll catch him.'

'If they're taking money on it, you'll be safe betting against it – whatever the odds. I have nothing but contempt for Sir Charles Hearle. As for "catching" him . . . I'd rather catch smallpox.'

Abel smiled then, a genuine, open smile that she had rarely seen. 'I'll take you at your word and see if I can't persuade someone to take a wager on the outcome.'

Returning his smile, she said, 'You've worked hard for me today, Abel. Toiling up and down to the castle must have been warm work. I'll ask your grandma to make some tea for us – and I do appreciate your help in moving in here.'

He shrugged. 'The causeway's open and there's not much for any of the boatmen to do while Sir John and the family are away.'

'That reminds me,' Thomasina spoke as though she had only that moment thought of what she was about to say, 'do you need to take a boat to Falmouth in the near future? I have some business there.'

'I've nothing specific to go there for, but Mistress Juliana said I was to take orders from you as though you were one of the family. Tell me when you want to go and I'll sail you there.'

18

'Is there anything you need me to help you with while you're in Falmouth?'

Abel put the question to Thomasina as he took the St Aubyn boat between Pendennis Point and Black Rock. They would soon be entering Falmouth's busy harbour. There would be little opportunity for conversation while he was guiding the boat between the vessels of all sizes that always crowded the Cornish sea port.

They had made good time from St Michael's Mount. It was Thomasina's hope that she would be able to explain her business proposition to the solicitor, Zachariah Bennett, leave him with sufficient details to enable him to carry out some enquiries on her behalf, and be free to return to St Michael's Mount early in the afternoon.

'I don't want to stay in Falmouth for too long, Abel.

I should have finished my business soon after midday. Why don't you join me for a meal somewhere?'

Abel and Thomasina had come to know each other a little better since her decision to move into the unoccupied house that had been built for the St Aubyn steward. The previous evening, he, Thomasina and his grandmother had shared a meal in the kitchen of the house.

Despite this, the invitation to join her for lunch in Falmouth came as a surprise.

'I can't go to the type of inn you're used to, looking like this.' He made a gesture that took in his clothes. 'I'm dressed for work, not for dining out – and certainly not with a friend of the family who employs me.'

The two crewmen were out of hearing in the bow of the boat, sorting out mooring ropes, so Thomasina said quietly, 'I'm a friend of Juliana's because fate had me shipwrecked on St Michael's Mount. I might just as easily have been cast away on an island among cave-dwellers. When fate doesn't take a hand, I like to choose my own friends. If those friends prefer to eat at a sailors' inn so as not to feel out of place, then I'm perfectly happy with that. Besides, I shall be hungry and I don't enjoy eating alone. Where shall we eat?'

Abel was constantly being reminded that Thomasina neither thought nor behaved like any other woman he had ever known. Yet her suggestion that they should eat together in public had taken him by surprise.

'Are you quite sure . . . ?'

'Of course I'm sure! Where do you suggest we go?'

He tried to think of an inn suitable for her. He was not only concerned about the clothes he was wearing. The choice was limited by the small amount of money he carried in his pocket.

Thomasina was shrewd enough to realise that his hesitation was not entirely due to the manner in which he was dressed. 'One other thing. As it's my idea, I'll be paying the bill.'

Putting the tiller hard over in order to clear the path of an outgoing merchant vessel, which had unexpectedly altered course to catch the wind, Abel said, 'I suggest we make it the British Marine, on the harbourfront. The food is good and I served in the Marines with the landlord. He runs a respectable inn.'

'That sounds fine. I'll meet you there at one o'clock.'

Solicitor Zachariah Bennett greeted Thomasina effusively, expressing genuine delight at seeing her. Showing her to his inner office, he instructed a junior clerk to make tea and bring it to them.

When he had drawn up a chair for her, he scurried around to the far side of his huge, highly polished desk and beamed at her.

'Your visit is most timely, Miss Varcoe,' he declared. 'The insurance company has made a settlement for the loss of the *Melanie Jane* and its cargo. It is a most generous settlement, if I may say so. I have also discovered two more houses that were owned by Captain Ellis. He purchased them prior to putting his affairs into my hands. They were brought to my attention as a result of a notice I placed in a newspaper in connection with his death. It adds a substantial sum to your wealth, my dear. Would you like me to suggest some investments that I consider to be both safe and wise?'

'We can discuss that at a later date,' Thomasina replied. 'I'm here today because I have an idea of my own. I want to buy a ship, Mr Bennett. A large deep-sea ship of at least two hundred tons – and I want it to be a fast ship. Indeed, speed is essential if I am to carry out the plans I have for such a vessel.'

Zachariah looked at Thomasina sharply. 'Do you intend using the vessel for smuggling? I must warn you, Miss Varcoe, that since the navy has assumed anti-smuggling duties, it has become an extremely hazardous business.'

Thomasina smiled disarmingly at the solicitor. 'Buying a ship for smuggling is not in my plans, Mr Bennett. I want it to be speedy in order to beat other ship-owners to markets that I see opening up in countries where Napoleon's grip is weakening. I believe a great deal of money is to be made in such trade – especially for those who are among the first to take advantage of the situation.'

Relieved, but not yet fully convinced, Zachariah said, 'I don't doubt you are correct in your assessment of the trading situation, Miss Varcoe. Indeed, I can recall the late Captain Ellis sitting in that very chair and telling me that your business acumen was at least equal – if not superior – to his own. But bearing in mind your requirements, would you want a ship built to your own specifications?'

'That would take far too long. I want a ship as

soon as it can be found. Certainly within a month or so.'

'That might prove difficult,' Zachariah said dubiously. 'Even if you were able to purchase the boat you are looking for, there is still the question of a captain and crew . . .'

'I already have a captain in mind,' Thomasina said. 'He would find his own crew . . . But I have a further requirement. The purchase must be made by a third party. I don't want it known that *I* am the buyer. It is to be kept a closely guarded secret shared only by you and me. Not even the captain is to know.'

Zachariah peered at Thomasina over the top of his spectacles for some seconds. 'Is there a reason for such extraordinary secrecy, Miss Varcoe?'

'Yes, but you don't need to know what it is, Mr Bennett – at least, not right away.'

'Hm!' The elderly and somewhat staid solicitor was perplexed, and it showed in his expression. 'Are you quite certain you have nothing illegal in mind? If you have, there is my reputation to consider . . .'

'You have my solemn word, Mr Bennett. Furthermore, the man I have in mind to command the ship is as honest a man as you'll find anywhere.'

'Very well, Miss Varcoe, but if we are to keep such a transaction secret, I will need to bring in the third party. A shipbroker.'

'Do you know of one you can trust?'

Zachariah nodded, 'Yes, my brother-in-law, Claude Coumbe. I believe he was the shipbroker used by Captain Ellis on a number of occasions.'

'That's right, he was – but you must swear him to secrecy about my identity.'

'If that is your wish. He will no doubt be as full of curiosity as I am at such unprecedented secrecy, but he will accept my word that you are a bona-fide customer.'

Now that he had agreed to do as she wished, Zachariah seemed more relaxed. Leaning back in his chair, he said, 'You never fail to intrigue me, Miss Varcoe. I hope you will one day feel able to confide in me the need for such secrecy in this particular transaction?'

'I hope so too, Mr Bennett. Now, when will you be able to speak to your brother-in-law about the possibility of buying such a ship as I have in mind?'

'I have some business to attend to this morning, my dear, but I could call on him this afternoon. If you care to call in to see me later in the day, I will be able to tell you what he has said and perhaps provide you with details of any ships on offer that meet with your requirements.'

19

Abel was waiting for Thomasina outside the British Marine when she arrived at the inn. Much to her surprise, he was no longer wearing his boatman's jersey. Instead, he had on a clean, white linen shirt.

When she commented upon the change, he appeared mildly embarrassed. 'I thought about it and decided you shouldn't be seen with me in my old working clothes, so I borrowed this from Jim, the landlord here. I told him about you and said you had offered to buy me dinner, but I wasn't dressed to sit down at table with a friend of my employer. He agreed and loaned me a shirt. At my request he has also set a table for us in a private room. I hope you don't think that was presumptuous of me, but he gets a lot of seamen in here. The language they use shouldn't be overheard by a woman. I didn't think you would feel comfortable walking into a crowded inn by yourself, either. That's why I decided to wait out here for you.'

Thomasina smiled at him. She doubted whether the patrons of the British Marine would talk about anything she had not heard discussed on the *Melanie Jane*, or in any one of the many bars she had frequented when disguised as a boy. However, she was touched by Abel's consideration for her.

Taking his arm, she said, 'I appreciate your thoughtfulness, Abel, but why are we standing out here talking? I'm hungry.

Abel had apparently impressed the landlord of the British Marine with his story of Thomasina's social standing. He hurried to meet them when they entered the inn, personally escorting them to a small private room where a single table had been elaborately laid for lunch.

The first drinks came with the compliments of the landlord, then they were served with a meal that Thomasina enjoyed as much as any she could remember.

As they ate, she told Abel that her business in Falmouth town was going to take longer than she had anticipated. Because of this, she would not be returning to the Mount, as planned.

When he expressed disappointment, she suggested that he might return for her the following day.

'Unfortunately, tomorrow is probably the only day when I can't come to Falmouth,' he said apologetically. 'Polly Miller, the widow of the coachman, is moving from the Mount to Penzance. Sir John said I'm to help her. It's been arranged for tomorrow, but will probably take two days.'

'The poor woman.' Thomasina was genuinely sympathetic. 'Of course you must do all you can to help her. Is there a Falmouth boatman you could recommend to take me back to the Mount?'

'Not one,' said Abel emphatically. 'You'd be better taking the Penzance coach and leaving it at Marazion – unless you'd prefer to stay in Falmouth until I can come back for you in a couple of days' time?'

Thomasina thought about his suggestion, but dismissed it almost immediately. She did not relish the thought of spending long hours in the house that had once been Malachi's.

The only way she might go out after dark would be to disguise herself as a young man once more. Somehow, she had lost all enthusiasm for such an adventure.

She had money and was hoping to buy a ship, which would bring her a handsome profit and at the same time achieve her aim of ruining Sir Charles Hearle. That was sufficient excitement for the moment . . .

Bringing her thoughts back to the present, she said, 'I don't want to spend any more time than I need to in Falmouth town. I'll catch the coach back to Marazion as soon as I can. Either that, or I'll buy a horse and ride back. That will get me there more quickly and it might be useful to have a horse available whenever I have need of one.'

Abel looked doubtful, but he already knew better than to question a decision made by Thomasina once she had made up her mind about something.

Thomasina's meal with Abel lasted for more than two hours. At the end of this time she walked back with him to the St Aubyn boat. When they reached it she was aware, as was Abel, of the nudges given by one crewman to the other, and of the sly looks they both gave Abel when he stepped on board. The boatmen carefully avoided looking in Thomasina's direction.

She remained on the quay, watching the boat until it was well clear of the harbourside, then she made her way to the offices of Zachariah Bennett.

The solicitor had not yet returned to his office and it was another half an hour before he put in an appearance.

It was immediately apparent to Thomasina that Zachariah and his brother-in-law had enjoyed a lunch that would not have met with the approval of the town's Temperance Society, which was holding a meeting on the quay only a short distance from the solicitor's office.

However, Zachariah's animated manner was not entirely due to the amount of alcohol he had consumed. Ushering her to the inner office and carefully shutting the door behind them, he said, 'My dear, I do apologise most profusely for keeping you waiting, but when I tell you my news I am certain you will forgive me. I think I have found a vessel that meets with your every requirement. It is certainly fast – very fast indeed, I am told. It is almost new and may, hopefully, be purchased for a very reasonable sum of money.'

'If it's such a wonderful ship, why hasn't it been

snapped up already?' asked Thomasina sceptically.

'Because it's a prize. A captured American schooner, due to come up at auction next week. It was taken in a Swedish harbour by a privateer. I am told that, had the two ships met on the high seas, the American would have disappeared over the horizon before the privateer had time to make a positive identification!'

Thomasina knew that the Americans had built some very fast ships. She had seen some of them in American waters. They were capable of far greater speeds than could ever be coaxed from the ill-fated *Melanie Jane*.

A number of American sea captains had been taken by surprise by the United States's declaration of war against Britain in June of that year. The result had been that they proved easy prey for the British navy and the predatory privateers that sallied forth from many British ports.

Thomasina remembered something else about these fast American vessels.

'Don't the American schooners have a different sail conformation to most British ships?'

'I believe my brother-in-law did say something of the sort – but there are seamen in Falmouth who have sailed on such vessels. It could work very much in your favour, my dear. Cornish seamen are a conservative breed. The fact that the vessel is slightly different from those we are used to seeing here will undoubtedly affect bidding at the auction. You could possibly acquire the vessel for a bargain price.'

Thomasina thought about it for some moments, then said, 'When can I look at this ship?'

'Right away, if you wish. My brother employs a boatman who will take us all there. Should he be inclined to talk indiscreetly, we will make it clear that my brother-in-law is taking us to the American ship purely as a social exercise.'

Thomasina fell in love with the American vessel at first sight. It was anchored a short way up the Penryn River, close to the little village port of Flushing. Ironically, the port had carried out a flourishing trade with America until the present war brought such business to an end.

As they approached, Thomasina could see the name *Henry Mallory* painted on the stern. Claude Coumbe said that whoever bought the ship would need to rename and register the vessel in an English port.

A watchman was kept on board the ship. He had a strong aroma of alcohol about him and grumbled incessantly at having his afternoon nap disturbed, but he helped the trio on board before disappearing inside the crew's quarters, leaving them free to wander over the ship at will.

'It's a beautiful ship,' declared Thomasina, when the watchman had gone. 'I don't think I've ever seen better.'

'Nor will you,' replied Claude Coumbe, enthusiastically. 'I believe such ships are known as "Baltimore Clippers". The *Henry Mallory* is certainly Baltimore-built and, with this particular sail configuration, requires a smaller crew than an English ship of comparable size. As for its speed under full sail

. . . I doubt if there's a ship in the world could outpace it.'

Thomasina and the two men spent almost an hour on board, during which time she examined the *Henry Mallory* from stem to stern. Not only was it of an outstanding design and construction, but it had been lovingly and carefully maintained, in a manner of which she thought Malachi himself would have wholeheartedly approved.

It was without doubt the finest ship she had ever seen. She grew more and more enthusiastic with everything she saw and had already decided that she had to own the vessel, yet she managed to contain the excitement she felt.

'You have made no comment about the ship,' said Claude Coumbe despondently. 'No doubt you feel, as others have before you, that the ship's design is somewhat revolutionary for British waters. I can fully understand your reservations, but, I assure you, you have just inspected a very fine vessel indeed.'

'I wouldn't argue with you, Mr Coumbe. She *is* a fine ship. If I seem preocupied, it's simply that I am deciding what I will call her when she is mine – and she *will* be mine, whatever the cost.'

Turning from the astonished shipbroker to the solicitor, she said, 'Mr Bennett, I trust I can leave the financial details in your hands? If Mr Coumbe is right, we might purchase the vessel for a bargain price, but I will leave the bidding in Mr Coumbe's hands. You know how much I can afford to spend in order to purchase the ship, but do not lose it because you feel the price is going too high. I want the *Henry*

Mallory, although my name is not to be revealed. Is this fully understood?'

Both men agreed that her wishes would be respected. It was a very happy trio who returned to Falmouth town that evening.

20

In the office of Claude Coumbe the shipbroker drew up an outline contract for Thomasina to sign. It would give him the necessary authority to purchase the *Henry Mallory* on her behalf.

'I will need to register the vessel in another name,' he said. 'Would you like time to consider what you might call the ship?'

Thomasina shook her head. 'No, the ship will be called the *Edward V.*'

Jeffery had provided the money that had enabled her to become a co-ship-owner in the first place and she would have liked to have called the ship the *Jeffery and Malachi*, but that might have alerted a number of people to the new ownership of the American-built vessel.

Both men were curious about the reason why she was giving that particular name to the ship but neither put the question to her and she did not explain that it was named in honour of her father, Edward Varcoe.

'I believe you have a captain in mind?' said Claude Coumbe. 'May I be permitted to know his name?'

'Of course,' agreed Thomasina, 'but my ownership must be kept a secret from him, too. If he knew, he would probably refuse to accept command of the ship, even though he is the right man.'

'All this is most irregular.' Claude Coumbe shook his head disapprovingly. 'I wish you could tell me the reason for such unprecedented secrecy. Should there be anything involved that is in any way illegal . . .'

'I have already convinced Mr Bennett that I have nothing illegal in mind,' Thomasina declared firmly. 'I'll give you the same assurance, Mr Coumbe. I *do* have very good reasons for not revealing my ownership of the *Henry* . . . the *Edward V*, but they are of a personal nature.'

'Very well.' The shipbroker sighed, not entirely convinced. 'If that is your wish, I will honour it – but who is this captain you have in mind?'

'His name is Abel Carter – you have met him, Mr Bennett. He came to your office to give you a statement about finding poor Malachi, after the shipwreck. At the moment he is head boatman for Sir John St Aubyn, at St Michael's Mount. Before that he spent some years in the Royal Marines, seeing a great deal of action, I believe. He has also been mate on a deep-sea merchantman and has occasionally carried out duties as master. He's the man I want.'

Zachariah Bennett and Claude Coumbe exchanged

concerned glances, but it was the solicitor who spoke. 'Do you think he has sufficient experience to take command of a ship such as this, my dear? It would pose a challenge to a seaman of considerably more experience than this "boatman" appears to possess.'

'I feel fully confident that Abel will rise to any challenge,' Thomasina said. 'So confident that he is the *only* man I am prepared to take on as master of the *Edward V*. I might add that, if it were not for Abel, I would not be discussing the purchase of a ship at all. Abel is the man who pulled me from the sea when the French ship was driven on to the rocks at the Mount. He risked his own life to do so.'

The two men relaxed visibly at her words. They felt they now had a logical answer to at least one of their many doubts about her actions.

Their relief showed and Thomasina thought she would give them another crumb of comfort. 'Abel is a very proud man. If he knew the offer of captaincy of the *Edward V* came from me, he would think it had been made out of gratitude and not from recognition of his ability. As a result, he would refuse to accept it. He must *not* know and you must think of a good story to explain why he is being asked to take the ship.'

Now the two men had been given a reason for Thomasina's actions that they were able to accept, Claude Coumbe promised to do his best to persuade Abel to take the post of master of the *Edward V*.

'There is one other thing,' said Thomasina. 'Once Abel has his crew and they are thoroughly familiar with the ship, I have their first voyage planned. In order for it to be a success you will need to travel to Mevagissey, Mr Coumbe. I want you to purchase all the cured pilchards that the *Edward V* is capable of carrying. Her first voyage will be to Leghorn, in Italy. I know it's still under Napoleon's control, but my information suggests that the *Edward V* will be allowed to land her catch – and to negotiate a price that might well fetch eight times what it would in this country. But – and this is vitally important – the *Edward V* must be loaded and on its way by the end of September. Any later and it will be beaten to Leghorn. In that event the cargo's value would drop by an unacceptable amount.'

As she spoke, Claude Coumbe had been making rapid pencilled notes. Putting down his pencil, he looked up at Thomasina admiringly. 'I apologise for doubting you earlier, Miss Varcoe. You have a keen business mind – as Zachariah told me when he first spoke of you. I very much look forward to acting as your shipbroker. I feel it will prove to be highly profitable for all concerned.'

The next morning, while Thomasina was eating a late breakfast, there came a heavy knocking on the front door of the house.

It was unusual to have callers come to the house at any time. For someone to arrive at this hour of the day was unheard of. Frowning, she rose from the breakfast table and made her way to the front of the house.

On the way, she thought it might be the woman who came to the house to check that all was well. Today was not one of the days when she would normally come to the house, and she had a key, but there was only one way to find out about the mysterious caller.

Opening the door, Thomasina was astonished to see Abel standing outside.

'Abel! What are you doing here? Is something wrong at the Mount?'

'Nothing at all,' Abel assured her. 'But when I spoke to Polly Miller last night, she said she wasn't quite ready to make her move to Penzance. She asked if we could put it off for a few days. That left me free today. I knew you would prefer to return to the Mount by sea – so here I am!'

'That's very thoughtful of you, Abel, and you're quite right. Travelling by coach is a nightmare and hours spent riding side-saddle would be almost as bad. But why are we standing talking at the door? I was just having some breakfast. Come and join me.'

As he stepped inside the hall of the house, Thomasina closed the door behind him. Leading the way to the kitchen, she said, 'I'm sure you're ready for something to eat. What time did you leave the Mount in order to get here at this time of day?'

'We saw the sun-up at sea,' Abel confessed. 'I was worried that if we didn't arrive early enough, you might already be on your way back to the Mount.'

'I'd intended going out to buy a horse and tack this morning,' Thomasina confessed. 'But I wasn't looking forward to it. Now, let me pour you a cup of tea. While you drink it I'll finish my own breakfast. When I've done I'll cook something for you.'

Thomasina enjoyed cooking breakfast for Abel. As

she said to him, 'It's far better than either wasting good food or leaving it for a cleaner who may, or may not, come in to work while it's still edible.'

Abel sat down to porridge, followed by eggs, bacon, fried bread and some cold beef, left over from the joint she had bought at a cooked-meat shop the previous evening.

Cooking, eating and sitting together at the breakfast table seemed a very intimate and cosy thing to be doing. It was a feeling of which they were both very much aware.

Thomasina wished she could have told Abel about the *Edward V* and how he was to be an essential part of the plans she had for the ship, but she was convinced it would be a dreadful mistake.

Their intimacy would need to extend far beyond having breakfast together before she felt able to confide her plans to him. Besides, she was not entirely certain that she herself fully understood the reason she had decided he was the only man she wanted to become master of the American-built ship.

One thing of which she was far more sure: she was going to miss Abel when he was at sea on board the *Edward V*.

21

The wind direction had changed during Abel's absence from the Mount. When he set off it had been blowing from the south west. However, during his stay at Falmouth the wind had shifted around to the east.

It made leaving harbour difficult, but sailing became easier when the boat reached the open sea beyond the two fingers of land protecting the deep-water anchorage for which Falmouth was famous. Once they rounded the Lizard the wind would be astern of them and they would make good time to the Mount.

Shipping was always busy on the approaches to Falmouth and Thomasina found dodging among the varied craft exciting. In addition to the many boats operating from the Cornish fishing communities, there were coastal and deep-sea traders, packet ships which worked from Falmouth and a couple of warships patrolling farther offshore.

As the harbour dropped away behind them, the volume of shipping gradually decreased, but there was still much to occupy Thomasina's attention.

Soon they were steering south-eastwards, hugging the coast of the land mass known as the Lizard. Suddenly Thomasina noticed a ship that was tacking on an opposite course to the St Aubyn boat.

'That ship's finding it hard work making Falmouth.'

The vessel was steering a zigzag course between coast and open sea in a bid to make headway against the unfavourable wind.

'It's a big ship,' Abel commented. 'Far too big to be sailing so close to shore. A vessel that size needs plenty of room to turn. Whoever's in charge isn't giving himself enough sea space.'

Thomasina could see that the decks of the ship in question were crowded with women, men and children. When she pointed this out, one of the boat crew said, 'It's a troop transport on its way back from Spain, I'd say. It'll have wounded men, wives, widows and children on board.'

'Then they deserve a safe homecoming,' Abel commented. 'But if that damned fool of a master isn't careful, he'll put them on the Manacles.'

The Manacles constituted a group of half-submerged rocks off the Lizard coast, feared by every sailor who sailed the south Cornish seas. Over the years they had claimed a vast number of victims.

'Look! He's taking her around again!'

The cumbersome transport ship had appeared to

be heading for the safety of the open sea, but now the vessel slowly came about once more, wallowing with flapping canvas for a few minutes before the sails caught the wind and billowed out, taking the ship in towards the coast.

The captain appeared oblivious of the white foam that swirled around the rocks of the Manacles, between sea and shore.

'She's going to strike!' The youngest member of the St Aubyn boat's crew cried out in horror.

'They must surely have posted a look-out?' Thomasina expressed disbelief at the drama taking place in front of their eyes.

'If they have, then he's fallen asleep,' Abel said grimly. 'There's no way they can sail clear of the Manacles now. We'd better get across there. They're going to need all the help they can get.'

Glancing away from the doomed ship for a moment, Thomasina saw that other boatmen were also aware of the impending disaster. As the notorious reef prepared to claim yet another victim, boatmen and fishermen abandoned what they were doing and headed for the rocks.

When the transport struck the Manacles, it seemed to Thomasina that everything happened in slow motion. The captain made no attempt to steer clear of the hazard. Indeed, it was quite apparent that he did not realise the rocks were there, maintaining his suicidal course to the very end.

Rising with the swell, the bow of the ship hung in the air for a few long moments, before beginning to fall. Suddenly it struck the rocks and the ship came to an immediate, grinding stop, sending passengers on the upper deck sprawling in tangled heaps, screaming with alarm.

This first impact tore a great hole in the transport below the water-line. As water poured inside the doomed ship, the panic-stricken passengers fought each other for a place on the ladders leading to the upper deck.

Some failed to make it even this far. The transport was carrying wounded and sick soldiers, many too weak or too badly maimed to rise from their cots and hammocks.

Unable to escape from the reef upon which it was impaled, the vessel seemed to Thomasina to be writhing in agonising death-throes as the motion of the sea pounded the ship's hull to splinters on the relentless rocks.

A number of fishing boats were on the scene ahead of the St Aubyn boat. By this time some of the more courageous passengers were already leaping into the sea from the stern of the transport, which was still clear of the rocks. Once in the water, they struck out desperately towards their would-be rescuers.

Only the strongest of them made it to safety. Others, caught by the swell and a treacherous current, were carried back to the very rocks that had proved the undoing of the transport ship.

Despite the very real dangers posed by sea and rocks, it was evident that those still on board would soon have to follow the example of those who had already abandoned the ship. The transport was breaking up. Before long it would slide from the reef and disappear beneath the water to join many other wrecks littering the seabed around the Manacles, taking with it those who remained on board.

Terrified passengers, many of whom could not swim, sought anything that would float and support them. Wooden deck lockers, broken spars, hatch covers, even items of cabin furniture were somehow hauled up from below decks. All were utilised.

When a passenger took possession of such an item, he, or she, would throw it overboard immediately to prevent it being stolen by other fear-stricken passengers, then leap into the sea after it.

The St Aubyn boat was among the wreckage and the survivors now, and those on board began reaching over the side to drag half-drowned survivors into the vessel.

Other boats were doing the same. A Royal Navy man-o'-war, outward bound from Falmouth, had dropped anchor and lowered all its available boats to help pluck luckless men, women and children from the sea.

Despite all the efforts to save them, it seemed to Thomasina that, for every person rescued, there were two or three more screaming out for help.

Before long the St Aubyn boat had twenty-five survivors on board, far more than she could safely carry. Then Thomasina heard someone screaming just over the side from where she stood, soaking wet as a result of helping to pull others into the vessel.

Looking over the side, Thomasina was horrified to see a young woman desperately trying to keep a child of perhaps two years of age above the water. She was largely successful, although her own head was below the surface of the water more often than above it.

As the woman and child bumped against the boat, Thomasina reached down and managed to take a hold of the child's clothing. Pulling the child screaming and coughing into the boat, she dumped it unceremoniously into the arms of a uniformed soldier before turning back with the intention of pulling the child's rescuer to safety.

To Thomasina's dismay, the woman had disappeared!

Pushing aside the retching, crying survivors, Thomasina fought her way to the boat's stern, where Abel was fighting to keep the heavily overladen boat clear of the Manacles. She peered into the water, hoping to see the woman surface, but there was nothing. The woman who had succeeded in saving the young child had disappeared.

'Are you all right?' Abel called the question to a distraught Thomasina as she stood at the stern of the boat staring down into the sea, wondering what she could do next.

'No! I just pulled a young child on board. Its mother, if that's who it was, has disappeared.'

'A great many women have disappeared, Thomasina. So have their children. Men, too. We must be thankful for those we've been able to save and pray that God will take care of those we haven't.'

Thomasina made her way back to the place where she had left the child. Greatly relieved, the soldier passed the terrified and crying infant back to her.

Now she was able to see for the first time that the

child was dressed in a girl's dress and, after the terror
of her ordeal, was shaking with cold.

Hurriedly stripping off the child's wet clothing, Thomasina pulled off her own flannel petticoat,
which had remained comparatively dry beneath her
dress, and wrapped it around the sobbing child.

'We've got as many on board as we can safely take,
Abel. Probably more, in fact.' The concern of the older
of the two St Aubyn boatmen was fully justified. The
boat was packed with wet and shivering men, women
and children, many of whom were weeping. Others
were calling out to those they recognised, who were
still in the water.

'But . . . there are still so many left,' cried Thomasina.
'We can't just leave them here.'

'All those we've already rescued will be back in
the water if we try to take any more on board,' said
Abel grimly. 'But, like you, I can't bear the thought
of leaving so many of them behind . . .'

Having a sudden idea, he called to the two boatmen. 'Tie a rope to the two oars – make sure it's
secure, then throw the oars over the stern. We'll tow
them behind us and hope that some of those still in
the water will have the strength to hold on until we
reach shore.'

'Are we taking them back to Falmouth?' asked
Thomasina.

'No, we need to use the wind and make the nearest landfall. We'll put into Coverack. It will be a
smoother run there than to anywhere else.'

22

A small knot of villagers was waiting when the St Aubyn boat bumped against the quay in Coverack village. Most were women and children, with only a sprinkling of old men. The remaining men were either among the fishermen who had been at sea and gone to the aid of the troop transport, or had put to sea to help save lives – or see what might be retrieved, depending upon their particular inclination.

The boat's mooring ropes were secured by two small boys. Then a number of old men, assisted by women, pulled in the survivors who were still clinging to the rope and oars towed behind the boat.

Village women, who in other circumstances might have been as eager as the Mount's Bay villagers to profit from a wreck near at hand, were touched by the sight of the injured, bedraggled survivors.

Crowding close to the boat, they helped soldiers

and their women and children to the shore, then hurried them off to the shelter of their homes to offer dry clothes and 'a little drop of something to put life back into you, my poor soul!'

As the last of the survivors stepped from the boat, Abel turned to see Thomasina still holding the small girl she had plucked from the sea.

'What are you going to do about the poor little maid?' he asked.

'What *can* I do with her, Abel? Who is she? Who does she belong to?'

'*I* don't know – but somebody must.'

'Then let's ask among those we've just landed. We might get a name, at least. Unless we do, we can't just dump her on a stranger and say, "I think her mother has drowned. I don't want her, you have her"!'

As she spoke, Thomasina jigged the small girl up and down in her arms, in a bid to put a stop to the body-racking sobs that still escaped from her.

Abel admitted that the girl posed a problem, but added, 'What will you do if no one knows anything of her?'

Thomasina had no answer to the question. She shrugged. 'I don't know . . . I suppose I'll have to spread the word that I have her and wait until someone comes forward to lay claim to her. There's nothing else I can do for her, poor little scrap.'

Abel had deep reservations that this would provide an answer to the identity and ownership of the young survivor, but all he said was, 'Then I suppose we had better set to and see what we can find out.'

Between them, Abel and Thomasina spoke to most

of the survivors they had landed at Coverack. The result was very much what Abel had anticipated. Most had no recollection at all of the young girl before today.

A few claimed to have a vague recollection of seeing her on board, but were unable to agree about her identity. Some thought she was the child of a wounded soldier. Others that she had been in the care of a nursemaid accompanying the widow of an officer killed in the fierce battle which had caused so many of the casualties on board the transport – the battle to take the city of Salamanca.

When the last of the survivors had been questioned, Abel said to Thomasina, 'We're no further forward than we were when we started speaking to everyone. What do we do now?'

'Take her back with us to the Mount,' said Thomasina firmly. 'I've spoken to the local vicar. He'll pass on the word that if anyone has lost a small girl, I have her, at the Mount.'

The rescued child in question, exhausted by her ordeal, was now asleep in Thomasina's arms as she sat in the stern of the boat, talking to Abel.

Looking down at her, Thomasina's expression softened. 'In the meantime I'll take care of her and try to help her forget all she's been through today.'

For lack of a name to which the rescued child would respond – and Thomasina had exhausted all those she knew – she decided she would call her 'Emma'.

By the time Emma had been with Thomasina for a week, two survivors from the wrecked transport had come to the Mount in the hope that she was their missing child. On both occasions Thomasina had been forced to endure their harrowing anguish when they confirmed she was not the child in question.

When two letters were delivered to the Mount, one for her and the other for Abel, Thomasina thought, with a sinking heart, that hers would contain news from the St Keverne vicar that more desperately hopeful women would be calling on her.

She opened it with mixed feelings, not entirely due to the thought of witnessing the raw grief of mothers who had lost a child. Although she felt that Emma should be returned to her parents – if they were still alive – Thomasina had grown extremely fond of the little girl during the time she had been taking care of her. She would miss Emma greatly if she were claimed.

In fact, the letter proved to be from Zachariah Bennett. Claude Coumbe had successfully bid for the American ship at auction. The *Henry Mallory* was now hers.

As Coumbe had anticipated, the ship had not proved popular with the Cornish ship-owners. He had purchased it for even less money than had been forecast. He had already taken steps to have the ship renamed the *Edward V* and had told his brother-in-law to inform Thomasina she had obtained a wonderful bargain.

Abel's letter was from Claude Coumbe himself. It said that through his offices an American schooner, taken as a prize, had been purchased by one of his clients and that the name of Abel had been put forward as a possible master of the vessel. Coumbe said that if Abel were interested, would he please present himself at the shipbroker's Falmouth office as soon as possible. He would then have an opportunity to be taken over the ship, which was to be known as the *Edward V*. Should he agree to become the ship's master, terms of employment would be discussed. Coumbe added that he felt quite certain Abel would find his salary an extremely generous one.

Abel was utterly bewildered when he brought the letter to the steward's house to show to both his grandmother and Thomasina that same afternoon.

'I can't understand it,' he said, for at least the third time during the ten minutes he had been in the house. 'Why *me*? It's been such a long time since I was at sea in a deep-sea vessel. There must be any number of masters they could have chosen.'

'The letter says it's an American-built ship schooner,' said Thomasina. 'Didn't you once tell me about such a ship? There must be many others who are aware of your experience. Your friend, the landlord of the Falmouth inn, for instance.'

Abel nodded. 'Yes, he knows all about me – and he's a great one for gossiping with anyone with time to talk. This offer has probably come about as a result of something he's said to someone.'

'More to the point,' said Thomasina, 'do you intend taking up the offer?'

'Of course he doesn't,' snapped Verity. 'He's got a perfectly good job right here on the Mount. Why would he choose to go gallivanting off all over the world? He's already done that once.'

'There's nothing wrong with working here for Sir John,' Thomasina agreed, 'but any one of a hundred men could be a boatman and none of them will ever make a fortune doing it. On the other hand, taking over as master of a deep-sea ship, especially one such as this, Abel could become a rich man. I saw some of these schooners when I was in the Americas. They're probably the fastest ships sailing the oceans. I'd *love* to sail in one. I can't think of anything more exciting. You can't possibly turn such an offer down, Abel!'

'What about Sir John?' asked Verity, tight-lipped. 'What do you think he'd say about it, after him going over the heads of many others to make Abel his head boatman?'

'He'd say the same as me,' declared Thomasina. 'It's a wonderful offer.'

'Grandma has a point, though,' said Abel uncertainly.

He was torn between a sense of loyalty to both Sir John and his grandmother and the unexpected opportunity to return to a way of life he had loved, and had given up only because he felt Verity had needed him when his grandfather died.

She had now recovered from the grief she had felt and was well able to cope with her daily life. She would certainly be more comfortably off if he were to take the opportunity that was being offered to him. Abel would be able to give her enough money to make her fully independent.

'Sir John would urge you to take it, I know he would,' said Thomasina. 'If you like, when I next write to Juliana I'll tell her all about it and of your reluctance to leave the Mount. I'll say it was me who insisted that you take it. You saved her life, too, remember? She'll wish you well.' Thomasina shrugged. 'Of course, you might not want to go to sea again, even as the master of such a wonderful ship . . .'

'No man in his right mind would *not* want such an opportunity,' said Abel. He looked at his grandmother, who was registering stern disapproval, then looked away again, his mind made up.

Speaking to Thomasina, he said, 'You're right. Only a fool would turn down such an offer. Thank you. I'll write to Sir John myself and tell him *why* I'm leaving, but I'd be grateful if you'd write to Mistress Juliana at the same time and explain things to her, too.'

'It seems I have no say any more in what's best for my own grandson!' Chin in air, Verity added, 'I'll leave you to arrange his plans with him, Mistress Varcoe. I know my place – and I have work to do.'

With this parting shot, Verity turned and walked out of the room.

'I'll not be happy going away from the Mount if Grandma is going to be so upset,' said Abel uncertainly. 'After all, I'm the only family she has.'

'She'll be all right, believe me, Abel. She doesn't like the thought of you going away, but she'll get used to it in no time. You gave up everything for her sake once, don't do it again.'

Thomasina could not tell Abel that she herself would probably miss him quite as much as his grandmother. But at least she had Emma now. 'When you bring your ship into St Michael's Mount harbour – as I have no doubt you will – your grandmother will be the proudest woman on the island. You just wait and see.'

23

Abel left the Mount for Falmouth the day after receiving the letter from Claude Coumbe. Three days later another woman arrived at Thomasina's door, clutching a letter from the vicar of St Keverne. It stated that she was a survivor who had lost a child when the transport foundered on the Manacles.

She believed that Emma might be hers.

Thomasina took an instant and quite unreasonable dislike to the woman from the moment Verity showed her into the sitting-room. Although Verity had still not forgiven Thomasina for the part she had played in persuading Abel to leave the Mount, she did little to hide her own disapproval of the visitor.

Introducing herself as Jean Toms, the woman had a thin, pock-marked face and eyes that seemed incapable of focusing on anything, or anyone, for longer than a second or two at a time. In addition, her nose would twitch when she sniffed, which occurred every minute or two.

The woman's clothing was shabby and none too clean, but Thomasina, trying to be generous, reminded herself that the visitor had survived a shipwreck and had lost her every possession – and lost her child, too.

Waiting while Thomasina read the St Keverne vicar's note, Jean Toms said, 'The reverend gentleman told me how you'd saved Sophie from the sea and said I was to come here and fetch her.'

'That's not *exactly* what is written here,' said Thomasina, 'but suppose you begin by telling me something about the child?'

'What is there to tell?' asked the woman, her glance shifting from one place to another around the room, but not touching upon Thomasina. 'She's my little girl, my Sophie, that's all.'

'No, it's *not* all,' retorted Thomasina. 'How old is she? Where and when was she born – and what was she wearing when you lost her?'

'Like I told you, her name's Sophie,' said Jean Toms. 'Named after me late, dear husband's mother. As for when she was born . . . No one worries about dates and such things when an army's on the march, and that's where Sophie was born. On the march. It might have been Spain, or it could have been Portugal.'

When the woman fell silent, Thomasina prompted her, 'What about the colour of her eyes? What would you say they were?'

'Why . . . I can't say I've ever thought about it

too much, but they're like mine, I suppose. Sort of a greyish-brown.'

'They're bright blue,' Thomasina replied.

'Of course,' Jean Toms said hurriedly. 'The same as her father's were. To tell you the truth, I've never been able to tell one colour from another, not properly, I haven't.'

'What about the clothes she was wearing when the ship went on the rocks?'

'Now how do you expect me to remember that?' Jean Toms asked indignantly, her glance pausing just long enough to meet Thomasina's eyes for a fleeting moment. 'There were so many clothes I might have dressed her in. Fresh ones for every hour of the day, if she wanted 'em. I just dressed her that day, that's all. I didn't know the ship was going to go down and that I'd have to remember every little thing I did before it sank.'

'The future of a small girl is no "little" thing,' Thomasina said. 'And what future is she likely to have with you?'

'I'll have you know that she wants for nothing,' Jean Toms declared indignantly. 'Her poor late father's family have money. He used to tell me about the market stall they own in Petticoat Lane, up in London. He used to say that if anything happened to him, I was to take young Sophie there to find 'em and they'd look after us. Never want for anything for as long as we lived, that's what he used to say.'

Thomasina refused to believe that this shifty, untidy woman was Emma's mother, but until this moment she had been unable to think of a reason why Toms should want to claim Emma as her own. Now she thought she knew.

'So you've never actually met your late husband's family?'

'No. Me and Jed were married in Spain, when I was widowed for the first time.'

Thomasina was slightly taken aback and Jean Toms explained defensively, 'It happens when you're married to a soldier who's fighting in a war. Some of the women who follow the army have been married four, five or even six times. Mind you, I never married outside the regiment. All me husbands were Buffs. The best regiment in the army, that is.' She spoke proudly. 'Wellington himself used to come and talk to us whenever he had the chance. Spoke to *me* once, he did.'

'We're talking of a young child's future,' Thomasina said curtly. 'Not of your life with the army. I'll be perfectly honest with you, I don't believe she belongs to you.'

Again Jean Toms's glance met Thomasina's, but it contained anger now. 'How can you tell? I haven't even seen her yet.'

Instead of replying, Thomasina went to the door and called Verity. The housekeeper was so close to the door that Thomasina felt she had probably been eavesdropping on the conversation taking place inside the room.

'Verity, will you please go upstairs and fetch Emma down. I know she's awake, I heard her just a few minutes ago.'

'Are you sure that's what you want to do, Miss

Thomasina? If you ask me, I think you should send this "baggage" packing. She's no better than she ought to be. As for being Emma's mother . . . !' She made an expressive sound through her nose before adding, 'Them two are no more related to each other than a pilchard is to a chicken.'

'I'm inclined to agree with you, Verity, but we need to put it beyond any doubt. Bring her down to the room just as she is. Don't change her clothes.'

Returning to the sitting-room, Thomasina spoke briefly to Jean Toms. 'She'll be down in a few minutes.'

'I can't wait to see her again,' the other woman gushed. 'I'll know her right away, you'll see.'

Thomasina said nothing.

When Verity entered the room, Emma was in her arms and half-asleep. She had been laid in her bed wearing her daytime clothes. Only her shoes had been removed.

As she entered the room, Jean Toms said immediately, 'It *is* my Sophie, I'd know her anywhere. Come to Mummy, my lovely.'

Emma looked at her just once, uncertainty on her face, then hurriedly turned away. As she did so she caught sight of Thomasina. Her arms went out to her immediately.

Taking her from Verity, Thomasina said, 'I think Emma has given us the answer we were all looking for. She doesn't know you.'

'Of course she does,' Jean Toms said. 'She's been through such a bad time that she's confused, that's all. Why, I even recognise the clothes she's wearing. I bought them myself, in Badajoz. Spent a whole week of her father's pay on them, I did.'

Thomasina and Verity exchanged triumphant glances. 'I think you've just settled the matter once and for all, Mrs Toms – if that's your real name. The clothes Emma is wearing today were bought for the children of Sir John St Aubyn. They were borrowed from the castle when Emma came here, because she had only the clothes she was wearing.'

Aware that she had been caught out, Jean Toms began to bluster that after all she had suffered it was easy to make a mistake, but Thomasina cut her protestations short.

Handing Emma back to the housekeeper, she said, 'Take Emma to the kitchen, Verity. Give her whatever she wants. Mrs Toms and I have some things to talk about.'

Kissing Emma, she passed her over to the housekeeper once more.

When they had left the room, Thomasina rounded upon the woman who had claimed Emma for her own. 'You have some explaining to do and I want the truth from you. Either you tell me what this is all about, or you can explain it to a magistrate.'

'I *did* have a daughter. One just like Emma, but now she's gone. Dead . . .' She began to cry noisily, but Thomasina was convinced it had more to do with the likelihood that she might meet up with a magistrate than with any bereavement she might have suffered.

Following her instinct, Thomasina said, 'You may

very well have lost a child – but it had nothing to do with the shipwreck, did it?'

Jean Toms looked up at Thomasina and for a moment it seemed she would challenge her statement. Then she dropped her glance to the floor. 'No, my Sophie died soon after I lost Corporal Willis, my third husband. Not that we were properly married. You see, Sophie wasn't his daughter, either. Like I said, Sergeant Toms, my second and proper husband – and the best of 'em all – was her father. Almost a gentleman, he was.'

When Thomasina felt she had a grasp of Jean Toms's tangled matrimonial affairs, she believed she knew why the woman had tried to claim Emma for her own.

'This Sergeant Toms . . . is it his family who has the stall in Petticoat Lane?'

Jean Toms nodded.

'. . . And they know about him having a daughter, but don't know she's dead. Am I right?'

Once again the woman nodded without speaking.

'So in order to deceive them you would have claimed Emma as your own, even though you would always know she wasn't. It wouldn't matter to you that she would might never know who her real parents were?'

'I'd have taken good care of her,' Jean Toms replied defensively. 'I'd have treated her as though she *was* my own – and she'd have had Jed Toms's family to love her. If they were the same as him, she'd have wanted for nothing.'

She began crying once more. This time Thomasina believed the tears were genuine.

'I *would* have looked after her well, just as I did Sophie. When we were retreating from the French, some of us got parted from the main army. That's when Sophie died. There was rain and mud and we had practically no food. When men and women fell – and they were doing it all the time – they just got trampled into the mud. I had nothing to eat for nigh on five days – but I made sure Sophie never wanted for anything. If there was no shelter when we lay down at night, I stayed awake to cover her up with myself, best I could. Then she caught the fever that had already carried off half the children. In twenty-four hours she was dead. I couldn't believe it at first and carried her with me for another day and night before the sergeant-major had her buried. If I could have died in her place I would have done, believe me.'

The sobbing became noisier and Thomasina said sharply, 'That's enough of that.'

'I . . . I'm sorry.' Giving Thomasina another of her rare direct looks, she said, 'Can I go now? I won't trouble you again, honest.'

Moved, despite herself, by the woman's story of the ordeal she had undergone, Thomasina nodded. Then, as Jean Toms turned to leave the room, she called, 'Just a minute.'

Going to a small bureau standing beneath a window, she opened a drawer. Taking a small box from it, she picked out a number of gold coins and held them out to the woman.

'Here, these will help you on the way to wherever it is you're going.'

For a few moments the woman looked down at the ten guineas she held in the palm of her hands. Then, reaching down the front of her dress, she pulled out a small bag attached to a cord worn around her neck. Pulling open the drawstring, she poured the coins inside.

Instead of saying 'Thank you', as Thomasina was expecting, she asked, 'Do you have the clothes the girl was wearing when she was taken from the sea?'

It was such an unexpected question that Thomasina replied, 'Yes . . . why?'

'I was a dressmaker before I married a soldier and went off to follow the drum. I'm not good at remembering faces, but I've an eye for clothes. If I was to see those she was wearing, I might be able to tell you something about the child.'

Thomasina looked at the woman uncertainly, then, satisfied she was telling the truth, hurried to the door. Opening it, she called, 'Verity, will you bring the clothes Emma was wearing when she was pulled from the sea?'

A few minutes later Verity entered the room with the clothes over her arm.

Jean Toms pounced upon the dress immediately. 'This is one I've seen before. I'd know it anywhere. I saw it on board more than once. It must have been worn by the child you've got.'

'You know her? Who is she?' Thomasina's heart was thumping, 'Can you give me a name?'

Jean Toms shook her head. 'No – but I can tell you

about her parents. Both of them were on board. He
was an officer who'd been wounded in the leg. A
Guards officer – Foot Guards. The only one of his
regiment on board. His wife was pregnant and they
had a nursemaid. I spoke to her once, a Spanish girl
she was, name of Mary. Spoke good English, too. Yes
. . . I remember now, she told me she was going with
the family to their home, just outside Newhaven. I'm
sure about that, because that's where the battalion
sailed from when I was married to me first husband.
A something "Hall", it was. Very proud about it,
was the young Spanish girl. Thought she was going
to live the life of a lady there, she did.' Handing
back the small dress, Jean Toms said, 'That's all I
can tell you.'

Going to the bureau once more, Thomasina gave
the delighted woman another five guineas.

Once Jean Toms had left the house, Thomasina sat
down to gather her thoughts. Although she now had
a lead which could take her to Emma's family, she
was suddenly not certain it was what she wanted.

She had come to love Emma as though she were
her own.

24

Thomasina had not made up her mind what she should do to follow up Jean Toms's story, when the *Edward V* sailed into St Michael's Mount harbour, three days later.

As word went around that this was Abel Carter's ship, the Mount villagers turned out to watch it berth. In the village school, lessons were suspended in order that the children might witness the arrival of the American-built clipper ship.

Standing beside Verity, with Emma in her arms, Thomasina could almost feel the pride emanating from Abel's grandmother, despite her opposition to his decision to leave the Mount.

When the ship was safely berthed, Abel, smiling happily, threw the vessel open for the inspection and approval of his former neighbours.

When Thomasina, Verity and Emma went on

board, Abel greeted them warmly. 'Let me show you around,' he said enthusiastically. 'She's the best ship I've ever set foot on – and to think I'm the master! I wake up every morning convinced it must all be a dream!'

'It's certainly a lovely ship,' Thomasina agreed, adding, 'You've had no problem finding a crew?'

'None at all. I was amazed at how many seamen in Falmouth had sailed on ships such as this – and they're as keen to sail on board her as I am. The mate I've taken on gave up a good berth on a packet ship to join the *Edward V*. He's a first-class man, too, quite capable of having his own command, if that was what he wanted.'

'What are you doing in St Michael's Mount harbour?' asked Verity.

'The shipbroker has given me a fortnight to get myself and the crew familiar with the ship. This is our first trip and our first experience of entering harbour. I don't think I need fear doing it again. The ship handles beautifully, and the crew know exactly what they're doing. I'm a very lucky man.'

Thomasina wished she could tell Abel how pleased she was to have made the right decision about appointing him as captain of *her* ship, but the time was not yet right.

'What do you think, Grandma?' he asked Verity. 'Is the *Edward V* a good ship, or is it not?'

Determined not to sound too enthusiastic, Verity replied, 'A ship's just a ship to me. It's no better, nor no worse, than any other that's come in here – but I doubt whether you'll have a job for life, as you would have had if you'd stayed with Sir John. Who's the owner of this wonderful ship of yours, by the way?'

Abel frowned. 'I can't tell you – not because I don't want to, but because I don't know. The shipbroker says he doesn't want his name known. It's not unusual. The *Edward V* was taken as a prize. If the person who bought it has other ships and this stupid war with America comes to an end, he might find all his ships boycotted in America. Better to keep his name quiet and stay in the background.'

'That's all very well, if you ask me . . .' said Verity, '. . . but then, no one *is* asking me, so I can only wish you luck. You certainly won't accept anything else from me.'

Abel met Thomasina's glance and they both smiled.

'It's a beautiful ship, Able. I envy you sailing in her. Where will you go when you leave the Mount?'

'I thought I'd sail eastwards, along the Channel. There should be enough British men-o'-war to frighten off the French. If we do meet up with a privateer, we have the speed to lose them.'

Thomasina was thoughtful for some time, then she said, 'Would you consider taking on board a couple of passengers and putting into Newhaven, Abel?'

'It depends very much on who the passengers are,' replied Abel cautiously.

'I'm thinking of me and Emma.'

When Abel expressed his surprise, Thomasina gave him brief details of the visit of Jean Toms and told him of all she had said.

'Do you believe her?' Abel asked.

'She had no reason to lie to me, Abel. At least, not by then.'

'You haven't got a great deal to go on when you get there,' said Abel doubtfully.

'Don't try to stop me going, Abel,' said Thomasina. 'I wouldn't need a lot of persuading to forget all about trying to find any family Emma might have, and keeping her for myself. But it wouldn't be fair to her, to me or . . .' Thomasina made a gesture that indicated resignation. 'It just wouldn't be fair to anyone.'

Making a determined effort not to appear too emotional, she added, 'Anyway, if we don't find her family then, it will still be a wonderful experience to sail with you in the *Edward V*. She's a truly beautiful ship, Abel.'

Fully aware of how much Emma had come to mean to Thomasina, Abel thought that Thomasina's decision to make such a determined effort to locate the child's family did her great credit, but he said nothing of his thoughts. Instead, he said, 'I keep forgetting that you're almost as experienced a sailor as I am. You'll enjoy the voyage, at least, I can promise you that. Would first thing tomorrow suit you?'

'That will be be perfect. Now I must take Emma home and let her have a few hours' sleep. Come to the house for dinner tonight, Abel. Verity will be delighted to cook for you. Over our meal we'll discuss what else we're going to do.'

Dinner that evening was a happy affair, with Verity apparently having forgiven her grandson for leaving the Mount, and Thomasina doing her best not to think that Emma might be taken from her in the next few days.

Instead, she got Able to tell her all about the *Edward V*. Verity understood very little about ships and was more interested in speculation on the identity of the mysterous ship-owner – and the reason for keeping his identity such a close secret.

Thomasina tried to keep the conversation away from the subject, but it was Abel who gave Verity an explanation that she accepted – albeit reluctantly.

'You see, it's not entirely uncommon for a ship-owner to be in competition with friends. Rather than lose their friendship, he keeps his identity secret. He might put them out of business, but he doesn't want to lose their friendship!'

'That's immoral,' Verity exclaimed indignantly.

'And so it might be,' agreed Abel. 'It's also business. Now, if we're all to make an early start in the morning I suggest you and I go home, Grandma. Miss Thomasina will need to get some sleep and the hour is getting late.'

'I have some clearing up to do before I've finished for the night,' said Verity.

'Leave it until tomorrow morning,' Thomasina suggested. 'Abel is right, I must get some sleep. Emma will be awake at the crack of dawn. If you're working it will only keep me awake.'

As Verity and Abel walked to his grandmother's home, Abel said, 'I don't know whether to hope we find Emma's family or that we don't. Thomasina will be very unhappy if she has to part with the little girl.'

'How she feels is none of your business,' Verity said sharply, 'and you'd do well not to forget it. She's neither fish nor fowl, that one. She may be living on the Mount, as a guest of Sir John, and have that Sir Charles Hearle dancing attendance on her, but she's not one of *them* and never will be. She's not one of us, neither. She's got money – more than any of us will ever see in our lifetime – but no one's heard the truth of how she came by it. Nor shall we, if I'm any judge of character.'

'That's hardly fair, Grandma. I don't think she's being particularly secretive. She's just keeping herself to herself, that's all. Some of the money came from the insurance on her father's boat, when he was lost. The rest was left to her by the uncle who died on board the ship I helped to sink.'

'So she says,' said Verity uncharitably. 'But has anyone been able to check on her father – or this uncle? There's no doubting that she's Cornish, but where exactly does she come from? That's what I'd like to know.'

'Well, when I first took her to Falmouth, I made a statement to a solicitor there about the death of her uncle, so I know that's the truth, at any rate. Anyway, what are you doing working for her if you dislike her so much?'

'I haven't said I dislike her,' said his grandmother. 'She's got more spirit than most of the girls around here. But she's doing neither herself nor Emma any good by lavishing all the love she does on the child.

She doesn't belong to her and, sooner or later, someone will claim her.'

'Well, you should soon have your mind put at rest,
Grandma. If we find her family at Newhaven, we'll
be coming back to the Mount without Emma.'

'I've grown fond of the child, too, so I hope you do.
Emma needs her own family – and so does Mistress
Thomasina. The sooner she finds a husband and
raises a family, the better it will be for her. She's
likely to do well for herself, too. They're saying up
at the castle that Sir John's son Humphrey is besotted
with her. There's also a very strong rumour that
Sir Charles Hearle would give up his bachelorhood
– if not his bachelor ways – and make her *Lady*
Thomasina. That's not bad for a girl who came to
the Mount out of nowhere.'

Abel said nothing. He too had day-dreamed about
a future with Thomasina – with more hope than
before, now that he had achieved a certain status. But
he had nothing to offer her that could compete with
either Humphrey St Aubyn or Sir Charles Hearle.

He decided he would need to lavish his affections
upon his new ship, the *Edward V*.

25

Early the following morning, Thomasina arrived at the harbour with a still-sleepy Emma in her arms. A number of crewmen spoke to the young child, but she would not respond, turning away and hiding her face in Thomasina's shoulder.

As a result, she was declared to be 'a shy little maid'.

The *Edward V* set sail from the Mount at eight o'clock that morning. Abel estimated that, with a lightish south-westerly wind, their sailing time to Newhaven would probably be in the region of thirty-six hours. It would be the longest voyage undertaken by him and his crew since taking over the ship.

Abel had given his cabin to Thomasina and Emma. He would be sharing a much smaller cabin with the mate.

As the ship left the harbour behind, more sail was

crowded on and the schooner began slicing through the water, at the same time rising and falling with the powerful motion of the sea's swell. It was a motion that brought back many happy memories for Thomasina and she began to enjoy it immediately.

Not so Emma. Whether it was because she had less happy memories of the sea, or because she was in unfamiliar surroundings, she clung to Thomasina even more than usual.

Eventually, having prepared the cabin for their brief time on board the *Edward V*, Thomasina carried the small girl to the upper deck. Here, aware of Emma's recent tragic experience, the sailors tried to put her at ease by offering to let her hold the wheel and 'steer the ship'.

When this failed to work, they drew her attention to the large flag, billowing from the mast in the breeze, but Emma refused to allow herself to be seduced from the shelter of her shyness.

Standing beside the helmsman, feet wide apart on the deck to maintain his balance against the movement of the ship, Abel smiled at Thomasina.

'What do you think of the *Edward V*? How does it compare with the ship you sailed in with your Captain Malachi?'

Mention of Malachi's name gave Thomasina a brief moment of pain. When it passed, she said, 'If you can command the same loyalty from your crew as Malachi had, then the *Edward V* will be the happiest ship afloat. I believe that it's probably already the speediest.'

'You're witnessing the birth of a legend.' The

helmsman unexpectedly broke into their conversation. 'Once in a lifetime, if a sailor's very lucky, he'll find himself crewing on a ship like no other he's known before, or will ever know again. I believe the *Edward V* is just such a ship. The rest of the crew feel the same, too. We're all excited about being on board her.'

Addressing Thomasina, he said, 'I knew your Captain Malachi Ellis and actually sailed with him for one voyage, many years ago. It's my opinion that he'd feel the same about the *Edward V* as we do.'

Moved by the man's words, Thomasina observed, 'If that's what you truly feel, then Abel is a very lucky man.'

Aware of the depth of Thomasina's feelings about Malachi, Abel said, 'I *am* a very lucky man – and I have you to thank for it, Miss Thomasina.'

Startled, Thomasina looked at him in alarm, wondering whether he had discovered the truth about his appointment as captain of *her* ship. His next words reassured her.

'If you hadn't been so persuasive, I might never have had the courage to accept the offer to become master of the *Edward V*. Had I turned it down, I would have missed the greatest experience of my life.'

They made good time that day. When Thomasina sat down in her cabin for a meal, they had passed Start Point and would be out of sight of land for the whole of the night hours. Abel said that they should be passing south of the Isle of Wight at about eight o'clock the next morning, with perhaps another twelve hours of sailing before they arrived at their destination.

With Emma asleep in a hanging cot in the cabin, Thomasina sat down at the table with Abel and the mate. Jamie Stocking was a young but experienced sailor who was proud of the fact that his home was Burnham Thorpe, in Norfolk, birthplace of Admiral Lord Nelson. As a small child, Jamie had met that most famous admiral on more than one occasion.

A great deal of the conversation at the table was about Nelson, until they turned to the reason for their voyage to Newhaven. Jamie asked if they had any definite plan in mind to find the family of the couple who might, or might not, have been the parents of Emma.

When Thomasina confessed that she had been unable to come up with anything that guaranteed success, Jamie offered an idea of his own.

It was one that Abel wryly suggested would no doubt have great appeal for those crew members chosen to take part.

It had already been decided that the ship should be anchored offshore. Jamie's suggestion was that half the crew, including Abel, should remain on board. That would leave enough crewmen to take the ship to sea should an emergency arise.

The remainder of the men, led by himself, would go ashore. Once there they would disperse and seek out the inns and taverns of Newhaven. In each establishment they would make enquiries about an officer in the Foot Guards who lived locally and was known to have taken his wife to the war in the Spanish peninsula.

It was possible that news that he was a casualty would have reached England long before he took passage in the ill-fated transport.

By the time the two men left the cabin, it had been agreed Jamie's plan should be given a trial. Indeed, it was the only one they had.

Checking on the small child before she herself went to bed in the captain's bunk, Thomasina gazed at Emma for a very long time. She secretly hoped the plan would not succeed.

If the search to find the girl's family was unsuccessful, Thomasina felt she would be able one day to tell Emma in all honesty that she had done all she could to locate them and learn her true identity.

26

Thomasina found sleep elusive that night. She was still awake when the sailors who had been onshore returned to the *Edward V*.

She wondered whether they had learned anything and did not have to wait too long in order to find out. Minutes after their return there was a light tap on the door of her cabin.

Swinging herself out of the bunk, she put on a robe and answered the door. One of the crew stood outside and said, 'Sorry to disturb you, ma'am, but Captain Carter thought you might like to come up on deck. The mate has some information for you.'

When Thomasina climbed the ladder to the upper deck, she found Abel and Jamie waiting there for her.

'I hope we didn't wake you, Miss Thomasina,' said Abel, 'but Jamie has found out something about the family we were seeking . . . But I'll let Jamie tell you himself.'

Trying hard to conceal his excitement, Jamie said, 'We all went around the town and one of the men and I went to the Paris Inn. I spoke to the landlord and explained why we were there. He called for silence, told everyone of our quest and asked if anyone knew anything that might help us. We struck lucky. One of the men in there said that Lord Pardoe has a son who is in the army. He was recently returning home after being wounded in Spain and his ship was wrecked on the coast somewhere off Cornwall. The man wasn't sure, but he thought he'd lost a child, too.'

'Where does this Lord Pardoe live?' asked Thomasina, not at all certain she wanted to know.

'In Walkden Hall, in a village of the same name. It's about five miles from Newhaven.'

Thomasina thanked him for his information, but was by no means sure now that she wanted to follow up the information he had obtained.

When Jamie had gone below, Thomasina remained on deck, thinking about all she had been told. If the information was accurate, she might lose Emma the next day.

'Miss Thomasina . . . ?'

Abel broke into her thoughts and Thomasina said irritably, 'I do wish you wouldn't call me *Miss* Thomasina, Abel. I *hate* it. It smacks too much of master and servant. I am just plain "Thomasina". Will you call me that, please?'

'Thank you,' said Abel understandingly. 'Look, I

know you're unhappy about this. If you like, we can forget all about this family, which may, or may not, belong to Emma. We can go back to the Mount and carry on as before.'

'No, Abel, I can't do that. I would wonder every time I looked at Emma just how much better off she might have been had we found her own family – especially if they're titled.'

Abel was not entirely convinced, but he agreed to accompany Thomasina the next morning when she called at Walkden Hall.

The following morning, Thomasina, Abel and Emma went ashore and Thomasina hired a carriage in which they would travel to Walkden. She also persuaded the daughter of the carriage owner to come, too. Thomasina had decided she would not take Emma into the house immediately, but would assess the situation first, while Emma remained in the carriage in the care of the young girl.

By the time they entered the drive of Walkden Hall and came within sight of the house, Thomasina was trembling. She was so nervous that Abel reached out and took her hand to comfort her.

Walkden Hall was a very grand house indeed. It had extensive lawns, formal flower-gardens and a great many gardeners in evidence. From the rear of the garden, grooms were taking a number of pedigree horses out for exercise. It was apparent to both Thomasina and Abel that this was the home of a very rich man.

Thomasina suddenly felt uncertain of what she was

doing. What if Emma was nothing to do with the Pardoe family and they thought she was trying to make money from a family tragedy?

'It's all right, Thomasina,' Abel tried to reassure her. 'Either Emma belongs to this family, or she doesn't. If she belongs to them, you've made everyone happy. If she doesn't . . . Well, you've tried your best for her – and she's still yours.'

Giving him a wan smile, Thomasina turned to Emma. 'Stay with the lady for a few minutes, darling. I'll be back directly.'

Emma started to protest, but the carriage owner's daughter had a great deal of experience with children, having several brothers and sisters of her own. Producing a peg doll, which had a brightly painted face and was dressed in cleverly home-made clothing, she began to hold a conversation with it, telling the doll about Emma.

Satisfied she was leaving the small girl in good hands, Thomasina left the carriage and set off for the front entrance of Walkden Hall, with Abel at her side.

The entrance was as impressive as the great house itself. Overawed by the grandeur of the building, Thomasina thought that if this was indeed where Emma belonged, she had nothing to offer the young girl that could take its place.

Reaching the door, Thomasina hesitated for a moment before tugging at the bell-pull. In that brief time the door was opened by the imposing figure of a uniformed butler.

'May I help you?' he asked, politely enough.

'Yes,' Thomasina said. 'We'd like to speak to Captain Pardoe.'

'I am afraid that is not possible, Miss. The captain is in London. At the War Office, I believe.'

'Oh!' The word expressed both Thomasina's disappointment and relief. She found it difficult to forget she had once been a servant in a house considerably less grand than this one.

'Do you know when he'll be back?'

'I do not, Miss. I am not kept informed of such matters.'

Aware that the butler had begun to talk down to her, Thomasina said sharply, 'Then perhaps I should speak to someone who *does* know.'

The butler was uncertain how he should deal with this young woman and her companion. Her manner of speech betrayed her country origins, yet she was expensively dressed and displayed a disturbing air of confidence.

'May I ask your name, Miss?'

'It's Thomasina Varcoe – and this is Captain Carter, master of the schooner, the *Edward V*, moored off Newhaven. Neither name would mean anything to Captain Pardoe, but I am here on a matter of some importance.'

Slightly reassured now that he knew one of the two callers was a sea captain, but still uncertain of Thomasina, the butler said, 'I am quite certain Mrs Pardoe is aware of the captain's plans, but the staff have been given strict instructions she is not to be disturbed. She recently suffered the loss of a child . . .'

Startled, Thomasina looked at Abel excitedly, then

asked, 'This Mrs Pardoe . . . she survived the wreck of the transport?'

'Yes, both she and Captain Pardoe, but . . .'

'Then it's more important than ever that I see and speak to her. Very important indeed.'

Convinced at last by the urgency in her voice, the butler said, 'If you care to come into the hall and take a seat, I will speak to Lady Pardoe, Captain Pardoe's mother.'

The hallway was in itself as large as most houses – and considerably loftier. From it, a magnificent staircase curved away to the upper storeys of the grand building.

Seated in two padded chairs beside the staircase, neither Thomasina nor Abel spoke. Both were over-awed by their surroundings, although Thomasina's excitement almost overrode such a consideration.

It was a few minutes before the butler returned, walking a few paces behind Lady Pardoe.

Thomasina had expected the mistress of such a grand house to be tall, elegant – and perhaps some-what formidable. In fact, Lady Pardoe was short, plump and had a kindly manner.

Before the butler could introduce the visitors, Lady Pardoe said, 'Good morning . . . Miss Varcoe and Captain Carter, is it? I understand you have expressed the wish to speak with my daughter-in-law, Lavinia. I am afraid she is far too ill to receive visitors. Perhaps *I* may be able to help you?'

'Yes. Yes, you probably can.' Thomasina decided she would explain her mission to this woman. 'It's about the child she's lost. Her little girl . . .'

'Little *girl*. No, I am afraid there must be some mistake, my dear. The child she lost was a son. It would have been my first grandson.'

'Oh, I'm sorry!' Thomasina was devastated. 'We've been wasting your time. I thought . . .'

She was interrupted by Abel, who said, 'We *are* talking of a child who was lost when the transport bringing them back from Spain was wrecked off the Cornish coast?'

Startled, Lady Pardoe said, 'No, but the baby she was carrying was lost as a result of the shipwreck . . .'

Belatedly she realised the implication of Abel's words and her eyes widened in an expression of dismay, 'You don't mean . . . you must be talking of Maria, the daughter born to Lavinia and my son in Spain. Oh dear! Has the . . . Have you recovered the child's body? Oh, dear, dear! This will be too much for poor Lavinia. I cannot tell her. I cannot . . . Although the body of the child's nursemaid was identified by my son, Lavinia has always hoped . . .'

Interrupting the increasingly distraught viscountess, Thomasina produced a child's dress that had been tucked inside her coat. 'Lady Pardoe, would you please show this to your daughter-in-law? It's very important.'

When the other woman hesitated, Abel said, 'Please do as Thomasina asks, Lady Pardoe. If we are given the answer we are hoping for, I promise you your daughter-in-law will not be upset.'

After looking at both their faces for some moments, Lady Pardoe took the dress and hurried away up the curving staircase without saying another word.

She was away for some minutes, then both Thomasina and Abel heard the sound of running feet. A moment later a young, pale-faced woman appeared at the top of the stairs. In her hand she held the dress Thomasina had given to Lady Pardoe.

Hurrying down the stairs, she held out the dress to Thomasina and cried, 'This dress, it's Maria's. I bought it for her in Madrid. She was wearing it when the ship struck the rocks. You . . . you've found her body.'

Lavinia Pardoe was trembling and Thomasina reached out and clasped both her hands in her own. 'No . . . no, there is no body. We have Maria. We've brought her here with us. Abel . . .'

She did not need to explain. Abel was already hurrying from the house. Minutes later he returned with the child Thomasina had called 'Emma'.

There was no need to ask whether she belonged here. Her mother screamed Maria's name and, after only a moment's hesitation, the small girl cried out 'Momma' and there was a reunion that no one who witnessed it would ever forget.

'Emma' had been reunited with her mother and the family she might never have known, had it not been for Thomasina's tenacity and selflessness.

27

The *Edward V* weighed anchor later that same after-noon, but Thomasina did not leave her cabin until the sun had disappeared beyond the western hori-zon of the English Channel.

She had broken down and wept in the carriage on the return journey to Newhaven. Abel had done his best to comfort her, but she did not regain full control of herself until the carriage reached the first houses in the port.

Now, in the darkness, Thomasina made her way to the upper deck, where a number of seamen were still working to ensure that the ship sailed safely through the night hours.

Abel was standing beside the helmsman, but in the light of a quarter-moon he saw her emerge from the hatchway that led to the cabins and came to meet her.

Solicitously he asked, 'Are you feeling better now? Would you like me to send someone for something to eat? Cook told me you'd eaten nothing. He is worried about you. In fact, the whole crew are.'

'I'm sorry I've caused you all concern. I'm all right now, but don't feel like eating. Thank you for asking, though. Thank you for everything. I'm glad I had you with me. Very glad. Without you I couldn't have got through the day.'

Aware of her conflicting emotions about parting with the girl she had learned to love as 'Emma', he said, 'It's probably no consolation, but you did the right thing, you know? Not only for Emma . . . sorry, I mean Maria. She's now where she should be. With a mother who was breaking her heart over the loss of two children, and with a family who can give her everything she'll ever want.'

'I'd have given her everything, too,' declared Thomasina unhappily. 'She'd have wanted for nothing.'

'Except her own family and rightful name,' Abel pointed out. 'One day her father will take *his* father's title and she will become "The Honourable Maria Pardoe".'

'She'll be no happier for that,' Thomasina said fiercely. She apologised immediately. 'I'm sorry, Abel. It's just . . . I didn't realise I would miss her quite as much as I do.'

She was gripping the rail which ran around the stern section of the ship. Abel put his hand over hers and squeezed it sympathetically. For a moment she leaned against him, then the ship bounced on a wave and they were both obliged to move in order to maintain their balance.

'When do you expect to reach the Mount?' Thomasina asked. The question was as much to fill the silence that had fallen upon them after a moment in which each had been acutely aware of the closeness of the other.

'The day after tomorrow,' Abel replied. 'But I have a cargo of pilchards to take on board from Mevagissey some time soon. I thought of calling in there to see if they are ready yet.'

The thought of putting in to Mevagissey, where she would undoubtedly be recognised, alarmed Thomasina, but she succeeded in sounding calm as she said, 'If it's all right with you, I would prefer to go straight back to the Mount. There are a number of things I want to do that were put off while Emma – "Maria" – was with me.'

'Fine, then we'll go straight to the Mount. I can come back to Mevagissey later in the week. There's no urgency.'

Abel's statement about the lack of urgency involved in his proposed visit to Mevagissey had to be revised when the *Edward V* reached St Michael's Mount harbour.

Sir Charles Hearle's ship, the *Celestine*, was there loading a cargo of pilchards.

The sight of the other ship taking on its cargo troubled Abel almost as much as it alarmed Thomasina. If the *Celestine* reached Leghorn before the *Edward V*, then all her plans would come to nothing. But she could not allow her feelings to show.

'I wonder where the *Celestine* is finding a market for pilchards?' mused Abel. 'I doubt if it will be a home port.'

'I can give you the answer to that,' replied Thomasina. 'Sir Charles Hearle told me he intends sending the cargo to the Mediterranean – to Leghorn, I believe. He's had information that any ship bringing in pilchards would be welcome there, even though Napoleon has banned English ships from trading.'

'My first cargo will also be pilchards and is destined for the same area. It's quite probable that Claude Coumbe has the same information as Hearle. But only the first ship to reach Leghorn will be able to command a high price for its cargo.'

Making up his mind, Abel said, 'I'm afraid this calls for a change of plan, Thomasina. I'll call to one of the Mount's boats and send you ashore before I turn the *Edward V* around. I need to go to Falmouth and tell Claude Coumbe what I've seen here. It will probably lead to me being given new orders.'

'You have no alternative,' agreed Thomasina, 'but can you give me a few minutes? I'd like to pen a quick letter to Zachariah Bennett. Perhaps you would have it delivered for me. It won't take a few minutes.'

Below deck in her cabin, Thomasina wrote to her solicitor confirming all that Abel would report to the shipbroker. She stressed the importance of ensuring that Abel loaded his cargo as quickly as possible and reached Leghorn ahead of the *Celestine*. Zachariah was to inform his brother-in-law immediately.

Sealing the letter carefully, she gave it to Abel.

Then, before climbing down the ladder to the waiting boat, she surprised and delighted Abel by giving him an affectionate kiss, thanking him once more for his kindness on what had been a very difficult mission for her.

She waved to Abel from the boat and had her gesture acknowledged, but by the time the St Aubyn boat bumped against the stone steps set into the harbour wall, the *Edward V* had cast loose the pilot boat and was shaking out sail in preparation for a fast run to Falmouth.

28

Thomasina was not pleased to find Sir Charles Hearle waiting for her at the top of the harbour steps. He too was unhappy.

Handing her up the final, high stone step, he said, 'I presume that the ship you have just left is the one under the command of Sir John's late boatman?'

'That's right, he took me to Newhaven.'

'Had you asked me, I would willingly have put the *Celestine* at your disposal. It would have assured you of a passage in a reliable ship, with an experienced captain.'

'I have no complaints,' Thomasina replied. 'The *Edward V* is an exciting ship and Abel as fine a captain as you're likely to find anywhere.'

Sir Charles scowled. 'It was foolhardy of you to put your reputation at risk by spending nights at sea with an ex-employee of Sir John. Especially one who might have felt you owed him something more than gratitude because he had saved your life not once, but on two occasions.'

Thomasina was extremely angry at Sir Charles's unwarranted insinuations, but she kept a firm rein on her temper. 'I suggest that my reputation was far safer on the *Edward V* than it would have been had I taken a voyage in *your* ship,' she said. 'Anyway, my reputation is none of your business. Now, if you'll excuse me, I wish to go to my home.'

Turning away from him, she called down to the men in the St Aubyn boat, who were making no attempt to hide their delight at the conversation they had just overheard. Sir Charles's reputation with women was well known to all of them.

'Bring my trunk to the steward's house, please.'

Falling in beside her as though no harsh words had passed between them, Sir Charles said, 'I am glad to have caught you before the *Celestine* sails, Thomasina. I shall be away from England for some time.'

Taken by surprise by his words, and her anger with him temporarily forgotten, Thomasina said, 'You're going with the ship? I thought you were an army man, not a sailor.'

'You are quite right, I am a landsman,' agreed Sir Charles. 'But a great deal of money will be changing hands on this voyage. I trust Captain Carberry, of course, but in order to ensure there are no misunderstandings with the authorities, I feel it might be better if I were to carry out the negotiations in Leghorn. I speak fluent French, you know?'

Sir Charles Hearle was the last person with whom

Thomasina would have chosen to hold a conversation, but the movements of the _Celestine_ were important to her. 'When do you sail?'

'It was to have been tomorrow,' replied Sir Charles, flattered that Thomasina should be showing an interest in his activities, 'but we have been unable to find a full cargo here. We will need to take on more from Newlyn.'

Newlyn was a very busy fishing port on the western shores of Mount's Bay.

'Does that mean you'll be around for a few days yet?'

'Probably, but we must not leave it too long. We have good reason to believe we will be welcome in Leghorn at the moment, but things in Europe can change overnight.'

'Of course,' Thomasina agreed. By now they had reached the steward's house and she said, 'Thank you for walking me home, Sir Charles. I trust you will have an enjoyable voyage to Leghorn.'

'Thank you, Thomasina – but won't you at least invite me in for a drink?'

'No, Sir Charles,' said Thomasina firmly. 'I am very tired after my own voyage and have much to discuss with my housekeeper. Good night, sir.'

Thomasina let herself into the house. Resting with her back against the door, she breathed a sigh of relief when she heard the sound of the baronet's footsteps as he returned to the harbour. Verity would not have known when to expect her return and was not in the house, but Thomasina had not wanted Sir Charles to know that she was there alone.

Thomasina did not remain alone for very long. News travelled amazingly fast on the island. By the time the St Aubyn boatmen were carrying her trunk upstairs to her bedroom, Verity had learned of her return and hurried to the steward's house.

Her first words were of 'Emma'. Thomasina was obliged to tell the housekeeper the outcome of the voyage and the girl's true identity.

'Well, I never!' Verity said for the third time. 'Fancy that! Her poor mother must have been overjoyed to have her back again, after believing her drowned.'

'She was,' agreed Thomasina, 'but this house is going to feel empty without her.'

'You'll soon find plenty to occupy yourself, my dear. Maisy, housekeeper up at the castle, tells me Sir John and Mistress Vinicombe will be returning to the castle sometime next week. It's to do with an election for Parliament, I do believe. Takes such matters very seriously, does Sir John. There'll be a whole lot of partying and coming-and-going until it's all settled, I dare say – but why hasn't Abel come back with you? I didn't see it myself, but my neighbour said his ship hardly put its nose inside the harbour before it turned around and went back out again.'

'That's right, Verity. He had to go and call upon the shipbroker in Falmouth. Abel is the captain of a ship and a very important man now, and he takes his duties very seriously. Mind you, when Sir Charles Hearle met me at the harbour and walked me home, I wished that Abel *had* returned to the Mount. Sir Charles was at the very bottom of my list of those I wanted to talk to.'

Verity had been expecting Thomasina home throughout much of that day and a kettle had been gently steaming on the hob. Using the water to make a pot of tea, she asked, 'Where does Master Humphrey come on your list?'

'Higher, certainly, than Sir Charles – but he's gone off to be a parson. Why do you mention him?'

'Because he's not a parson yet – and he's back here, in Cornwall. He arrived the day you went off in the *Edward V*. He's called here at least twice every day since then.'

'Where is he now? At the castle?' Thomasina wondered what was wrong. She had understood that Humphrey was to take on a curacy somewhere in the London area.

Verity made a scornful sound in the back of her throat. 'Her up at the castle hardly tolerates any of Sir John's first mistress's children when their father is at home. They rarely go there when he's not – and never when the family is away. No, Master Humphrey is over at Ludgvan, with his mother, poor woman.'

Curious, Thomasina asked, 'Did you know her, Verity?'

'I knew her well. Worked for Martha Nicholls when Sir John first took her to his house at Clowance, then up to the castle. She was no more than seventeen or eighteen in those days and as pretty a little thing as you'd find anywhere hereabouts. At least, she was before she bore five children to Sir John. She was never built to carry children, that one.'

'Why did Sir John leave her?' Thomasina asked. It

was the first time she had ever met anyone willing to talk about Sir John's first mistress.

'Because he had fallen for Mistress Vinicombe. He'd had his eye on her since she was a young girl, even paid for her to go to one of the best schools in the country. Soon after young Master Humphrey was born, it was off with the old and on with the new. He moved poor Martha out to Ludgvan and brought Mistress Juliana to the castle in her place. Mind you, I believe he still has a soft spot for Martha. There's many a night when he's home you can see a lamp placed in one of the upper windows of the castle. They say it's a signal to Martha, over at Ludgvan, that he's not entirely forgotten her.'

'It must be very difficult for Martha Nicholls's children, especially if they're discouraged from coming to the castle.'

'It hasn't been too bad for the older ones, I suppose. Sir John has made good marriages for the girls, and James knows he'll be the one to inherit from his father. It's Humphrey I feel sorry for. He's never really known his father and has had to watch Sir John's affection being lavished on his half-brothers and -sisters. He must feel he's been left out of his father's life, for all that he seems fond enough of Mistress Juliana's children.'

'Thank you, Verity, I think I understand the family up at the castle a whole lot better now – but I'm still very fond of Juliana.'

Verity sniffed. 'Well, you know her and I don't. I'm sure she has her good points as well as bad, the same as the rest of us. Now, can I be cooking something for you? I don't suppose you had anything worth eating when you were on that ship.'

In fact, the cook on the *Edward V* had produced some very good meals, but Thomasina did not want to dispute another of Verity's prejudices. 'I won't have anything to eat, Verity. This cup of tea is what I have been looking forward to while I've been away. I'll finish it and go to bed. I didn't sleep well on the *Edward V*, especially on the voyage back. You can go home whenever you feel like it. There's just one favour I'd like to ask of you.'

'If it's something I can do, I will,' declared Verity.

'It's just that . . . if Sir Charles Hearle is seen heading in this direction, you'll hurry here as quickly as you can – no matter what time of day or night it might be.'

'I'd do that without you having to ask,' Verity assured her. 'I heard on the way here that you'd told him off in no uncertain terms. You've posed him a challenge, and from what I've heard that's something he enjoys. At least, it is when it's posed by a woman. I don't think he has the same courage if a man's involved.'

29

Humphrey St Aubyn arrived at the steward's house as Thomasina was having breakfast the morning after her return to the Mount.

She was not dressed to receive visitors, especially *male* visitors. Verity's expression left Thomasina in no doubt of the housekeeper's disapproval when she told her to show Humphrey into the breakfast-room.

He entered the room in a state of considerable agitation and blurted out, 'Thomasina! Thank heaven you are home safe and sound!'

Puzzled, Thomasina asked, 'Is there any reason why I shouldn't be?'

'I was out of my mind with worry when I came looking for you and heard you had gone off somewhere in a ship with Abel Carter – without a chaperon.'

'You're beginning to sound like Sir Charles Hearle, Humphrey, and I'm no happier with what you're saying than I was when *he* said it. You are aware of the reason I made the voyage to Newhaven, I presume?'

'Yes, but . . .'

'There is no "but", Humphrey. I reunited a small child with her mother. The child is the granddaughter of Viscount Pardoe – if that means anything to you. It wasn't easy for me to go at all. I had grown to love her and would have liked to keep her for my own.'

Thomasina had control of herself, but only just. Fortunately, Humphrey possessed the sensitivity to recognise this and apologised immediately.

'I'm sorry, Thomasina. I did not mean to cause you any distress.'

'Then we'll say no more about it – but you haven't explained what you're doing here. I thought you'd gone to London to enter the Church?'

An expression of anguish crossed Humphrey's face. He avoided her eyes as he said, 'After thinking long and hard about it, I have reached the conclusion that I don't have the right temperament to become a priest.'

Giving him a quizzical look, Thomasina asked, 'What sort of temperament do you think a priest *should* have? I must confess I don't have a great deal of experience of parsons and the like, but I wouldn't be at all surprised to learn that they're very much the same as the rest of us. You know, good ones and bad ones; lazy and hard-working ones; clever and dull ones . . . Don't you think you could fit in there somewhere?'

'That isn't what I mean,' said Humphrey uncomfortably. 'To be a priest you need to possess a deep and unswerving faith. I'm not at all certain I have that.'

'What an absurd thing to say!' Thomasina declared, in her best no-nonsense voice. 'My father used to say that only fools have blind, unswerving faith – and you're no fool, Humphrey. Why, even Jesus Christ had doubts at times. You'll make a very good parson. You're gentle, kind and thoughtful. All the things a parson ought to be.'

'It's very kind of you to say so, Thomasina, but a good parson also needs an equally good wife to support him in his work.'

'Of course – and I have no doubt you'll have no difficulty in finding one. Someone from a similar background to yourself, who'll have the respect of everyone, from the pauper to the squire.'

'You could be such a woman, Thomasina,' Humphrey said hopefully.

Thomasina shook her head. 'No, I couldn't. You know absolutely nothing about me, Humphrey. I'm certainly not the sort of woman who'd make a parson's wife.'

'That settles it then. I'll not be a parson. Marry me, Thomasina, and we'll do something else – just so long as we do it together.'

'What do you think Sir John would have to say about that? He would certainly cut off your allowance. What would we live on?'

Once more Humphrey would not look at her. 'I'd find something to do.'

'And until then? Would we need to live on my money, Humphrey?'

When he failed to reply, Thomasina said, 'It's not much of a proposition to put to a woman, is it? No, Humphrey. Go back to London, do what you have to do there, then work as a curate somewhere for a while. After that I'm sure you'll find a parish of your own when the time is right, perhaps here in Cornwall.'

Humphrey felt uncomfortable. Thomasina was echoing the words of his mother when he had told her he did not want to take up a career in the Church.

'I would do that if you promised to wait for me until I returned to Cornwall.'

Thomasina shook her head. 'I will make no promise to any man, Humphrey, and would be very unhappy if I felt you had given up the chance to become a parson because of me. Very unhappy indeed. You are a very dear friend and I hope you will write to me from London.'

'I haven't said I will go back there,' Humphrey said sulkily.

'No, you haven't,' she agreed, 'but I think you should, certainly by the time your father arrives here.'

Startled, Humphrey said, 'He is coming back to Cornwall? When?'

'Next week. He and Juliana – the children too, I expect. It's something to do with an election. I don't know how long they'll be staying.'

'It will be for at least a month, possibly two.' Despite his earlier bravado, Humphrey sounded concerned.

'You *will* return to London before he arrives, Humphrey? I don't want to be the cause of a disagreement between you and your father.'

'I suppose that if I'm not welcome here, there's no reason for me to stay.'

'That's a silly thing to say.' Thomasina was speaking to him as she would to a naughty child. 'You'll always be welcome in my house. Anyway, the Mount is more your home than it is mine. All I want is what will be best for you – and I'm convinced that is a career in the Church.'

'There's no one else in your life, Thomasina? You *would* tell me if there was? You mentioned Sir Charles earlier – there is nothing between you and him?'

'I think you had better leave before you insult me any more, Humphrey. There would be nothing between Sir Charles and myself if we were the only two people left on earth.'

'I'm sorry, I really didn't mean to insult you.'

Thomasina smiled at him. 'I know you didn't, Humphrey. You're a dear, and I really am very fond of you. But, please, don't do anything silly on my account. Go back to London, enter the Church and make me proud of you.'

'All right, if that's what you really want, but I haven't given up hope that you'll marry me one day.'

'I am extremely flattered, Humphrey. Now, you really must go. I haven't finished my breakfast yet and I need to dress for the day. You too will have a busy day making the necessary arrangements to return to London.'

At the door he hesitated and said, 'I believe the last time we said goodbye you kissed me.'

'And I intend doing so again.' She was making good her promise when Verity entered the room with the second course of breakfast. Thomasina could see by the housekeeper's expression that she was shocked by what she saw.

She was not surprised when Verity returned to the room after she had shown Humphrey out and broached the subject immediately.

'You might tell me it's none of my business, Miss Thomasina, but I'm a woman who is used to speaking her mind, and I can tell you I won't stay working in a house where there are any "goings-on".'

'I am very pleased to hear it, Verity. There will be no "goings-on" in this house. That's why I asked you to make certain you put in an appearance if ever Sir Charles Hearle is seen coming here. What you saw – or thought you saw – just now was not "goings-on". It's not every woman who needs to turn down a man's proposal of marriage before she's even eaten her breakfast. I was merely trying to make my refusal as kindly as possible.'

Thomasina had not intended mentioning Humphrey St Aubyn's proposal to anyone, but Verity's objection to 'goings-on' had left her with no alternative. She was the mother of Abel, and Thomasina did not want her character blackened to him.

The knowledge that this mattered came as a surprise to her and she thought about it for much of the day.

30

The *Edward V* unexpectedly returned to the Mount three days after Humphrey's proposal and departure for London.

The ship's arrival was so unexpected that Thomasina sent Verity to greet Abel when he came ashore, fearing that something had gone wrong.

She was particularly concerned because the *Celestine* had sailed from Newlyn bound for Leghorn the day before. It already had a full twenty-four hours head start on the *Edward V*.

The sailing had been witnessed by many of the Mount fishermen, the news being relayed to Thomasina by Verity, who included it in her daily résumé of Mount gossip.

It turned out that Abel had called at the Mount in order to collect some clothes he felt he would need on the voyage. He also took the opportunity to offload a hogshead of cured pilchards for Verity and Thomasina, which he accompanied to the steward's house.

There were some three thousand fish in the over-sized barrel and he said, 'You won't want to use them all. Share them out with anyone you feel might benefit from them. It's one of five barrels the Mevagissey fisherman gave me as a present for taking the whole of the stock he had in his cellar. I got the cargo for a reasonable price. It should make a good profit when I reach Leghorn.'

'Only if you can beat Sir Charles and his ship there,' Thomasina pointed out. 'He set out a day ahead of you.'

'True,' Abel grinned at her obvious concern, 'but he's sailing in a ship that should have been beached and scrapped before ever putting to sea. I have the fastest ship that's ever been seen in these waters. I could give the *Celestine* four days' start and still be in Leghorn a full twenty-four hours before she called for a pilot to enter the harbour there. I'll be offloaded and out of Leghorn before the *Celestine* arrives.'

'What about a return cargo?' Thomasina queried. 'Will you be taking it on board in Italy?'

Abel shook his head, 'No, it would be too risky. I'll offload, collect my money and get out of Leghorn as quickly as I possibly can. Napoleon would make life very difficult if he were to learn that an English ship had landed a cargo in a port he controls. I'll sail to a Spanish port and pick up a cargo there. Marble, fruit and some wine, perhaps. All in all, I think this should prove highly profitable for everyone connected with the *Edward V*.'

'The owner will be very happy about that,' said Thomasina, speaking with less authority than she felt. 'I wish you a very successful voyage.'

'Thank you.' Peering at her more closely, he asked, 'Are you feeling more settled now about giving up Maria?'

'Yes. You were quite right, Abel. There was no other course I could have taken. It was the best thing for Maria.'

'I never doubted it,' said Abel. 'I admired you for what you did then, and still do. It wasn't easy for you to part from someone of whom you were so fond. It never is.'

Thomasina sensed a deeper meaning behind his statement – and it had nothing to do with Maria. She believed he had come closer than ever before to declaring that he cared for *her*.

In an attempt to lighten the moment, Thomasina said, 'Who am I going to be able to turn to when things go wrong while you're away, Abel – as I've no doubt you will be for a great deal of the time in the future?'

'Humphrey St Aubyn, perhaps? Ma told me he called on you. She also said he proposed marriage to you.'

'That's right, but I persuaded him to return to London and follow Sir John's wishes that he take up a career in the Church. He left the same day.'

'He'll be back. Humphrey isn't right for the Church. He's a romantic who is constantly dreaming up ideas for novels and thinking of himself as one of the characters in them. Still, he's a nice enough young man for all that.'

'Yes, he is, but he's not a man I would choose for a husband.'

Once more the glance that passed between them said more than the words, and once more the awkward silence that followed was broken by Thomasina.

'I envy you the voyage you're making, Abel, but take care and return safely.'

'I fully intend to. I shall also be happy in the knowledge that Sir Charles Hearle is on his way to Italy, so won't be around to pester you. Take care of yourself, Thomasina. With luck I will be back within the month – and with some fine wine for a present.'

'We'll share it over a celebratory meal. I would like that.'

When Abel had gone, Thomasina felt happier than she could remember feeling for a very long time. They had only *half*-said so many things, but she believed even this had taken them an important step closer to one another.

A week after Abel had set sail from the Mount, Verity was dusting the sitting-room in the steward's house while Thomasina sat at a desk checking tradesmen's bills.

As was usual when the two women were in the same room, Verity was bringing Thomasina up-to-date with the latest Mount gossip.

'I expect young Agnes Collins will be getting married very soon. At least, she will if she doesn't want to stand before the altar with William John's baby in her arms instead of in her belly. She needs to hurry up about it. William's been putting the wedding off for so long that people are beginning to talk. They're saying he's spending all the hours God's given him out there fishing, in the hope that the press-gang will take him up before poor Agnes does.'

Thomasina smiled. 'He wants to be careful it's not a French man-o'-war or a privateer that takes him up, instead of the press-gang.'

'If he was really unlucky he would be picked up by the French, have his boat taken away – then be rescued by the English navy and brought back in time for a wedding. Mind you, he wouldn't enjoy it very much if he wasn't rescued and was held prisoner for as long as them Mevagissey men that Abel heard about.'

Thomasina looked up at Verity in surprise. 'What Mevagissey men, Verity?'

'Didn't Abel tell you? I expect he had other things on his mind. I wonder where he is now? Do you think he's arrived at the place he was heading for?'

'Leghorn? No, it'll probably take him another day or two yet – but you were telling me about the Mevagissey men . . .'

'So I was. Abel said it was a wonder the women in the cellars there were able to get the pilchards packed in time. It seems one of our men-o'-war took a French ship, somewhere off the French coast, and found it full of British sailors. Some had been held by the French for years and none had been able to let their families know they were safe. They'd been in some small prison way up in the mountains close to the Spanish border. Wellington's army was getting close,

so the French were moving them by boat to another
prison, close to Paris. Seven or eight of 'em were
Mevagissey men, so the man-o'-war that got them
back dropped them off there. Abel said there should
have been more, but things were so bad in prison that
two had killed themselves and one of those brought
back was completely out of his mind. Sad the way
some men treat others, isn't it? None of them from
Mevagissey were fighting men, either. Most were just
ordinary seamen; others were fishermen.'

As Verity was talking, Thomasina became very
excited, so much so that she had difficulty containing
it. When she had left the house of her Aunt Mary,
more than two years ago, there had been no more
than five Mevagissey men who had vanished at sea
– and her father had been one of them. True, there
would undoubtedly have been more since then, but
Verity had said some of the released men had been
prisoners for years.

She wished Abel had mentioned the incident to her
when he returned to the Mount. She would have been
able to question him more closely. As it was . . .

Suddenly and unexpectedly, she made up her
mind. She had thought of her Aunt Mary and Dolly
often of late. She would go to see them again, if only
just the one time.

Abel's news gave her the excuse she needed. She
would pay her aunt a visit. It was possible her father
might be one of the released prisoners . . .

Thomasina did not allow herself to think of what
she might do if he were, or of the risk she would be
taking.

31

When Thomasina boarded the Penzance to Falmouth coach the following morning it was crowded with West Cornwall clerics. They were on their way to meet the Bishop of Exeter, who was paying a rare visit to this outpost of his extensive diocese.

Listening to them talking among themselves, it seemed to Thomasina that they were almost equally divided into two separate groups, each with a different view of their anticipated meeting with the bishop.

The first group comprised relatively simple men of God, who were greatly excited at the thought of meeting a man who held such an authoritative position in the hierarchy of their Church. For others it offered a rare opportunity to impress the exalted pastor, in the hope that he might one day help them to enjoy similar eminence.

Remembering Humphrey, Thomasina had a momentary feeling that a career in the Church might *not* after all be a suitable career for a man like him.

But she had other matters to think about during the hours before the coach reached the bone-juddering cobblestones of Falmouth and brought sustained thought to an end.

Excited though she was at the possibility of her father being alive, it posed many problems for her and her present lifestyle.

Her father would want to know details of her life during his absence. She would need to think of a very plausible story to explain the wealth she had acquired. Thomasina felt that Malachi would provide an answer. A rich, lonely old man with no close relatives, who had befriended her and become a father figure . . .

But that could wait for now. First, she had to find her father.

Once in Falmouth, Thomasina put her small trunk in the care of a young, barefooted boy with a handmade wheelbarrow. They walked together to the house she had once shared with Malachi.

Along the way the boy chatted happily about the ships in the harbour, but told Thomasina he intended becoming a soldier when he was old enough.

When they reached the house the boy carried her trunk upstairs to her bedroom and she rewarded him with double the sixpence he asked for his services. Overjoyed, the boy blessed Thomasina with a fervour that would have put to shame most of the clerics with whom she had so recently parted company.

It was still early afternoon, so Thomasina decided to call on her solicitor before going shopping in the town.

It would be inappropriate to visit her Aunt Mary dressed as befitted a lady. She would need to purchase the sort of clothes a housemaid might choose for her best walking-out attire.

Thomasina felt a thrill of excitement whenever she thought that her father might be at her aunt's cottage at this very moment. It had been almost eight years since he had set sail, never to return. She was concerned that he might not recognise her after all this time, but he too must have changed . . .

She brought herself down to earth with the reminder that it was by no means certain her father had been among those prisoners taken off the French ship.

In order to take her mind off the disappointment she would feel deeply if this were so, she began to think about Aunt Mary, and her cousin Dolly. The young girl would be about sixteen now and Aunt Mary would have her working.

The bitterness Thomasina had once felt at being forced to take employment at Trebene House had faded somewhat, but she doubted whether her aunt had changed her belief that girls should be put out to work as early as possible.

That afternoon, when Thomasina was shown into Zachariah Bennett's office, the solicitor immediately sent for his brother-in-law.

Claude Coumbe was able to give Thomasina full details of the purchase of the *Edward V*. He also confirmed that Abel had taken a cargo of five hundred hogshead of pilchards from Mevagissey, paying for them the sum of seven hundred pounds.

'I had no hesitation in taking the money from your account, my dear,' put in Zachariah. 'It really was a very, very good transaction. Your captain bought at the lowest possible price.'

'Are there any rumours of what Sir Charles Hearle paid for his cargo?' Thomasina asked.

'I can tell you exactly,' said Claude Coumbe smugly. 'His ship has a larger cargo capacity than yours and he purchased eight hundred hogshead at thirty-five shillings each. A grand total, if my arithmetic is accurate, of one thousand, four hundred pounds. Exactly twice the sum you paid – and for only three-eighths of a cargo more.'

Beaming at her, Coumbe added, 'But then, Sir Charles was not aware that the man from whom he bought the bulk of his cargo is the uncle of his ship's captain. Had he employed me – or any other shipbroker – he would have been informed of the fact.'

'He didn't employ a broker? I'm surprised, especially when he has so little knowledge of the shipping business.'

'I am not,' said Zachariah. 'Sir Charles Hearle was bequeathed money in the will of his aunt. Soundly invested, it should have kept him fairly comfortably off for the whole of his life. Unfortunately, very little that Sir Charles does comes under the heading of "sensible". After paying off his gambling debts – and running up more – he chose to invest his remaining money in a ship no one else wanted, and a cargo that will give him a good return only if he can deliver it thousands of miles away before anyone else beats him to it. I might add that I am breaking no confidences by telling you this. It is common gossip, not only in the taverns of Falmouth, but throughout Cornwall. The same rumours suggest that Sir Charles has left himself so short of money that neither the *Celestine* nor its cargo is insured.'

Thomasina gasped in disbelief and Zachariah Bennett said, 'That is utter madness in such uncertain times.'

'I fear all times are uncertain for Sir Charles Hearle,' commented Coumbe. 'And I have a feeling they are going to get worse for him, rather than better. Sadly, I find it difficult to sympathise with him. Now, changing the subject, Miss Varcoe, do you have any ideas about future cargoes for the *Edward V*?'

32

Thomasina departed on a very early coach the next morning, leaving Falmouth at seven-thirty. Carrying mail from a packet ship which had arrived late the previous night, it reached Truro in time for Thomasina to transfer to a Plymouth-bound coach, which dropped her in St Austell, the nearest town to Mevagissey, at eleven-thirty that same morning. Here she booked accommodation at the White Hart Inn.

Too excited to contemplate a midday meal, Thomasina had her small trunk taken to her room, then set off to walk to the small cottage she had left two and a half years before in order to take work as a lowly housemaid.

Walking along the valley road which would take her to her destination evoked many memories for her.

She passed within a short distance of the great

house she had always admired so much as a small child, when her father would bring her to St Austell for the Summer Fair.

Then, at the hamlet of London Apprentice, she saw the blacksmith at work in the smithy where she had watched with her father while a horse was shod.

Farther on were the tin-stream workings, now only a shadow of former years.

Just past Pentewan village a wide break in the cliffs offered a fine view of St Austell Bay. From here, on a clear day, it was possible to see the coastline all the way to Rame Head and watch ships of the King's navy working their way in to the port of Plymouth.

It was here, too, among the grass-covered sand dunes of the 'Winnick' that Jeffery had first made love to her.

The thought of Jeffery and the fate he had met caused tears to spring to her eyes. Brushing them away, she began the long climb to the top of the hill where Aunt Mary's cottage was situated.

Once in sight of the small thatched cottage, which also held many memories, albeit mostly unhappy ones, Thomasina for the first time entertained doubts about the wisdom of what she was doing.

It would all be fully justified if her father was one of the Mevagissey men rescued by the Royal Navy, of course, but if not . . . ?

Despite such misgivings, Thomasina continued on her way. There could be no turning back now.

At the cottage gate she paused. The front flower garden was neat and tidy – neater than she remembered it being before she left. What could be seen of the vegetable garden was well tended, too, and stocked with a wide variety of vegetables.

As she took stock of the garden, a woman appeared in the doorway. Seeing Thomasina, her expression registered disbelief. It was her aunt.

'Hello, Aunt Mary.' Thomasina spoke first.

'You! What are *you* doing here?'

Her aunt made no attempt to leave the cottage doorway and come forward to greet the niece she had not seen for more than two years.

'I've come to see you. To ask if you have any news of my pa.'

Opening the gate, Thomasina walked up the path to the house. Still her aunt did not move, and now her presence barred Thomasina from entering the cottage.

Stopping uncertainly, Thomasina said, 'Well, now I'm here, can I come in?'

Without moving, Mary said, 'I'll have no thief in my house!'

'Thief . . . !' Thomasina was taken aback for a moment.

'That's what I said. I heard all about your dismissal from Trebene. You were lucky not to be taken before the magistrate, so I was told.'

'You were told wrong,' said Thomasina angrily. 'I never took a thing from Trebene House.' Even as she made the declaration, she knew it would have no effect. She had been dismissed from the house of 'gentry'. It had to be *her* who was in the wrong.

'That isn't what I was told – and if you've come here expecting to be taken in, then you're out of luck. I'm not a widow-woman any more. I'm married to Harry Mitchell, gardener up at Heligan. It's a good job and I'll not have it put at risk by word getting about that he's related in any way to you.'

Thomasina remembered Harry Mitchell as a stern, unbending Methodist who had been married to a very sick wife. It seemed she must have died.

'I have no intention of staying. The only reason I'm here at all is because I heard that some Mevagissey men who were prisoners of the French had been rescued. I wondered – I was hoping . . .'

Now the moment had arrived, Thomasina found it difficult to put the question to this cold, unfriendly woman who showed no sign of affection towards her.

'If you're asking whether your father was one of them, the answer is . . . yes, he was.'

'Pa's alive?! He's come home? I can't believe it!' All Thomasina's resentment of her aunt's attitude towards her dropped away in an instant. 'Where is he, Aunt Mary? Has he tried to find me? What . . . ?'

'He's in St Austell, in the workhouse – and if you have any sense you'll leave him there and forget he ever came home.'

Mary's callous reply brought Thomasina up short. 'In the workhouse? But . . . why? How could you let him go there? Even if he's lost his boat, he can work. He's a good sailor.'

'Not any more. I don't know what they did to him while he was a prisoner, but whatever it was has turned his brain. He's insane.'

Horrified, Thomasina cried, 'But . . . he'll get better

now he's back home with us, Aunt Mary. How could you allow him to be taken to the workhouse? He was the husband of your only sister. What would she have thought?'

'I've told you, girl, I'm married again now and need to put my husband first. I couldn't expect him to put up with having a lunatic in the cottage. It might have been different, had Dolly still been here, but since she upped and married Billy Kivell we've got used to having the place to ourselves.'

Open-mouthed, Thomasina asked, 'You let Dolly marry Billy Kivell? Why, she's barely sixteen and he must be getting on for fifty!'

She remembered the occasions when she and Dolly had joked about marrying Billy in order to inherit his father's farm. She looked at her aunt in disbelief. Had she always been so callous and uncaring? Thomasina thought she probably had.

'Billy Kivell may not be much of a catch as a man,' retorted Mary, 'but the farm goes with him – and that's a lot more than you'll ever have, I'll be bound.'

Thomasina wished for just a moment that she could tell her aunt of her present lifestyle, but that would lead to too many questions being asked. Instead, she said, 'I'm not so poor that I haven't been able to send you twelve guineas a year for the last couple of years – or did you believe the money was a heaven-sent gift?'

Thomasina had been sending the money each Christmas without disclosing that it came from her.

'As you're married and don't need it any more, I'll

spend it on my pa instead,' Thomasina said bitterly. 'And just in case you were thinking of paying him a visit in the workhouse, don't bother. He won't be there. I'll go there now and take him out. Goodbye, Aunt Mary. I'm sorry not to have seen Dolly, but I wish her well. You needn't worry about your new husband and his work – I won't be coming back here again.'

Thomasina turned about and walked away from her aunt and the cottage that had once been her home.

She did not look back.

33

Thomasina returned along the road to St Austell a great deal faster than she had walked the other way. At times, when she thought about her father, she felt she wanted to run.

She had very confused feelings about him. First and foremost was incredible joy that he was alive, but she was concerned about his mental state. She nursed a desperate hope that his reason would return when he saw her, but she did not know what to expect.

The workhouse was a large and grim, grey-stone building, occupying a prominent position on a hill overlooking the small town of St Austell. Thomasina had seen it many times, but had never taken a great deal of notice of it before today.

She shuddered at what she saw now. It had more the appearance of a prison than of a building intended to succour the poor and needy.

The woman who answered the door to Thomasina informed her that the occupants were busy going about their various chores, as well as carrying out work intended to bring money in to the workhouse. Visitors were not allowed at such a time. Indeed, unless they had a special reason for calling, visitors were discouraged at all other times, too. She added that the inmates found it disturbing to have callers from the outside world.

When Thomasina told the woman she was there not to visit, but to remove one of the inmates, the woman became less officious. 'You'd better come in and wait in the office while I find Mr Skinner. He's the master here. What's the name of the person you wish to take out?'

'Henry Varcoe. He's only been here a short while.'

At the mention of the name, the woman gave her a look which Thomasina found difficult to inter- pret. 'I see . . . well, I'd better go and find Mr Skinner.'

She was away for about ten minutes. When she returned she was accompanied by a man Thomasina would not immediately have associated with the post of workhouse master. Small, plump and jolly, he held out his hand to her and shook it warmly.

'Good afternoon, Miss. I understand you wish to relieve us of Mr Varcoe? I am pleased. Very pleased indeed. You are a relative, I presume?'

'Yes, his daughter.'

'Splendid! It is always gratifying when respon- sibility for one of our inmates is taken over by a close relative. We do our best for them in here, of course, but it is never the same for them as enjoying personal care. When do you wish to remove him?'

'As soon as I can . . . but may I please see him first? I only learned yesterday of his return to the country. For years I had thought him dead.'

'You mean . . . you have not seen him since his return?'

'No, I no longer live in the area.'

Skinner and the woman employee exchanged concerned glances before the workhouse master spoke to Thomasina again.

'Are you aware of your father's mental condition? He is certainly not the man you would have known when he went away.'

'My aunt told me that something had happened while he was in a French prison to turn his brain. I'm hoping that when he sees me it might help his recovery.'

The workhouse master shook his head sadly. 'Oh dear. Oh dear! I feared that was what you might be thinking. I am afraid that is not so, my dear. We are fortunate enough to have the services of a great many local physicians, given free to those in our care. One worked in Bedlam, in London, for twenty years. He has seen your father and pronounced him incurable.'

'May I see him, please?' Thomasina was trying hard to hide the dismay she felt at the master's words.

'Of course – but it will be necessary for me to accompany you. We have had no trouble with your father yet, but the physician says that violent conduct cannot be ruled out in his particular condition.'

The more that was said, the worse it became, but Thomasina still nursed a hope that he would be proven wrong. That when her father came face-to-face with the daughter he had adored, at least a degree of normality might return.

'I'd like to see him now, if you please.'

'Come with me.'

Thomasina followed the master through the building, walking through large rooms where women knitted or crocheted busily and passing a room where other women were washing clothes.

Inmates were busily engaged everywhere they went, but the thing that Thomasina found utterly uncanny was the silence in each of the rooms. It was only later that she learned that speaking was banned while the inmates worked. It was felt that talk would affect their work.

Eventually, the master came to a door fitted with a stout lock. Choosing a large key from a ring attached to his belt, he inserted it in the lock, turned it with some difficulty and opened the door.

The first thing that assailed Thomasina was the stench. The second was the noise. Quiet as the rest of the workhouse had been, it made the noise in here all the more startling.

It was gloomy inside, the only light entering the room from small barred windows set high in a stark, whitewashed wall. On the other side of the long, almost bare room were eight or nine men, all chained to stout rings set in the wall.

'Keep close to the wall when you walk through here, then they won't be able to reach you.'

The need for Skinner's warning became apparent when they were no more than a quarter of the way along the length of the long room. With frightening suddenness, one of the chained men leaped at Thomasina.

Terrified, she flattened herself against the white-washed wall, but the precaution was unnecessary. When the frenzied man reached the end of his chain, it jerked him off his feet. He crashed to the floor two arms' lengths away from her and lay there screaming in pain and frustration.

Thomasina was still trembling when the master reached back and took her hand. 'It's all right, none of them will be able to reach you – as long as you stay close to the wall.'

Appalled, Thomasina wondered whether this was how her father would be. As though reading her thoughts, Skinner said, 'These are the worst of them. Your father is at the far end.'

Thomasina saw him long before they reached him, but for some moments failed to recognise him. He appeared to have shrunk and his hair was far longer and greyer than she remembered.

Then he turned listless eyes in her direction and she saw it was him.

'Pa! Pa . . . it's me, Thomasina!'

Releasing her grip on the master's arm, she ran to her father, oblivious of Skinner's warning to stay close to the wall.

Reaching him, she flung her arms about him, aware momentarily of how thin he was. Indeed, there seemed to be little flesh on his body.

For a moment there was no reaction. Then she felt him begin to tremble – and the screams began.

Startled, Thomasina released him. He promptly turned upon her, striking out and shrieking obscenities. She was rescued by the master, who pulled her to the safety of the whitewashed wall as her father fought against the restraint of the chain to get at her once more.

Crouching against the wall in the arms of the master, Thomasina was aware that it was not only her father who was shrieking now. It seemed that his attack had aroused every other man in the room to a frenzy. She found their cries terrifying.

'That's what I was afraid might happen. Come, we must go quickly, before some of them injure themselves.'

'But, my father . . . ?'

'We'll talk about it in my office, but we must get out of here now!'

It seemed to Thomasina that the screams and shouts of the men in the lunatic wing of the workhouse followed them even when the door to the room had been locked behind them and they were far away.

Suddenly and unexpectedly, Thomasina began to cry. She sobbed uncontrollably for a long time. It was the way she had cried the day she was told her father's ship was overdue and he had disappeared without trace.

The difference was that then she had been left with hope, albeit seemingly in vain as time went on. Now there was none. The man she had just seen was her father in name and body – but nothing else. It was as though she had been wiped from his mind.

'I am very, very sorry, my dear,' said the kindly master. 'I feared that might happen, but desperately hoped it would not. So often, when the mind goes in a certain way, the object of their violence is those they once loved the most.'

When Thomasina felt there was no more anguish left in her and her sobbing had subsided, she said, 'Will it always be like that? Will he ever get better?'

'I wish I could give you the answer you want, my dear – but I cannot. I doubt if your father will ever regain his sanity, and his reaction to you is always likely to be one of extreme violence.'

Sadly the master added, 'Now you have seen him, I presume you will want him to remain with us here?'

'No . . . Oh no, I don't want that. I can't leave him here, chained up like a rabid animal. I will take him away. Take him somewhere where he has all the comforts of a good home, at least. It's just . . . I will need a few days to arrange things. In the meantime, may I give you some money to ensure he enjoys a few luxuries? Whatever you can get for him?'

'It will be gratefully received and used as you wish.' The workhouse master looked pityingly at her. 'I am so sorry, Miss Varcoe. I wish things might have been otherwise, but at least your father has someone who cares enough to bring some comfort into his life. Most of the others here have no one – and I can do only very little.'

'Thank you for your kindness, Mr Skinner. I don't know how long it will take me to make the necessary arrangements for someone to care for my father. It should not take more than a few days.'

'We will look after him – but on no account should you try to care for him on your own. You are the one most at risk because, as I said before, you are the one he loved most of all. Take what comfort you might from that.'

34

Travelling between St Austell and Falmouth, Thomasina fought hard to come to terms with all that the past few days had brought into her life.

After so many years of believing her father dead, she had found him again – only to discover that he was insane and have him attack her.

It was a nightmarish situation to which there seemed no solution. Only one thing was certain. She would take him away from the horror of the insane ward of the St Austell workhouse as soon as was humanly possible.

She shuddered violently at the thought of what she had seen, causing the nervous, gaunt spinster seated beside her to edge an inch or two along the seat away from her. The extremely plain woman was rewarded with a lewd smile of misunderstanding from a middle-aged purveyor of patent 'cure-all' medicines, seated on her other side.

By the time Thomasina arrived at Falmouth she had formulated the outline of a plan. First, she needed to speak to Edith Hocking, the woman who had cleaned Malachi's home for so many years and whose husband tended the garden.

Thomasina was aware that Edith had a married daughter living with her. The daughter's husband was a seaman on an East India Company ship and was rarely home. Nevertheless, Edith complained that even such infrequent visits came around too often, because some nine months after each homecoming her daughter would give birth to another child.

The Hockings now shared their house with this particular daughter and six grandchildren.

Thomasina felt she had a solution that might suit the whole family. If the two Hockings agreed, Thomasina would have her father brought to her own house. The two older Hockings could then move in and give him the constant supervision he would need for the remainder of his sad, twilight life.

As it was a day when both Hockings were working at the house, Thomasina was able to put her proposition to them, giving them as much of the background story as she felt they needed to know.

Edith's first thought was for Thomasina. 'You poor soul! To find your father alive after all these years, only to learn he's lost his reason. It's enough turn your own mind.'

Arthur Hocking was more practical. 'What form does this madness take? Is he violent with it?'

'The workhouse master told me he isn't – although

he did try to attack me . . .' She choked on the words, but recovered quickly. 'I was told that sometimes happens, even with the most docile of them. They'll attack the one they love most.'

'That's perfectly true, dear,' said Edith knowledgeably. 'You remember your Florence, Arthur?'

To Thomasina, she said, 'Arthur's sister was married to a man who went mad. He gave her a very hard time before he had a fit and died. The doctor treating him said it was because he couldn't cope with all the love that filled his poor, scrambled brain whenever he saw her.'

'We'd want to meet your father before we made up our minds,' said Arthur cautiously. 'And we'll have to talk it over with our daughter.'

'Of course,' agreed Thomasina. 'I would, of course, pay you both well – and I'd like you to come to a decision as quickly as possible. I can't bear the thought of him staying in that terrible place for a minute longer than is absolutely necessary.'

Once more her voice broke as she recalled the scene in the long room filled with chained lunatics.

'Don't you upset yourself, dear,' said Edith kindly. 'We'll speak to our Sybil this evening and let you know in the morning what we've decided.'

'Thank you, Edith – you too, Arthur. I'll write to the workhouse master this evening and let him know what's happening. I'll make certain, if you go to St Austell to see him, that he's brought down to the office for the meeting. I wouldn't want you to go up to the room where I saw him.'

*   *   *

Edith returned to the house later that same evening, as Thomasina was preparing for bed.

She explained her intrusion by saying, 'I thought I'd come round right away to put your mind at rest, dear. My Sybil is delighted with the thought of having the house to herself for a while. The longer the better, she says. So, if Arthur and I feel we can cope when we meet up with your pa, we'll take on the task of looking after him, here in your own house. That'll be much better for him and will put your mind at rest.'

'Bless you, Edith. Bless you both. When do you think you'll be able to go and see him and, hopefully, bring him back here?'

'Well, if we carry a few of the more essential things to the house tomorrow, we could go to St Austell the day after. How would that suit you?'

It was more than Thomasina had hoped for, and she said so, adding that she would stay on in Falmouth and accompany them on their journey to St Austell.

'That's all right then,' declared Edith, pleasurably embarrassed by Thomasina's gratitude. 'We haven't said we *will* take him on, but if he's not likely to be violent, then I can't see there being any problem.'

As Arthur Hocking must have weighed at least fifteen stone, and her father less than ten, Thomasina thought there would be no problem, even were her father to prove a little difficult on occasions.

It should be a most satisfactory arrangement. Her father would be living in a caring and comfortable environment and she would continue living at the Mount, close enough to enable her to pay regular visits to him.

Hopefully, as time passed, he would become less aggressive towards her and be able to appreciate the love she felt for him.

35

Thomasina travelled with Edith and Arthur Hocking on the regular mail coach as far as Truro. Here she hired a carriage and driver. Her motive in changing the mode of transport, and not employing anyone from either the Falmouth or St Austell area, was to make it more difficult for her aunt – or anyone else who might be interested – to trace her.

The interview between the Hockings and her father took place in the workhouse master's office in Thomasina's absence and proved satisfactory to all concerned.

Outside, Edith told Thomasina that she and her husband had no qualms about taking on the task of caring for the tragic figure who had been mentally destroyed by his years of internment.

It was agreed that they would return to Falmouth with him immediately, the couple riding inside the carriage with Edward Varcoe, Thomasina riding on the seat beside the driver.

On the return journey they travelled by a more direct route, taking a ferry from the Roseland peninsula direct to Falmouth. Thomasina remained in the background on the ferry when the Hockings allowed her father to alight from the carriage. She gained a great deal of pleasure from his obvious delight at being allowed to stand on the deck of the vessel with the wind and sun on his face.

It also increased the sadness she felt that she could not be included in such a simple pleasure. Edward Varcoe had looked in her direction once or twice during the short voyage, but gave no sign of recognition. Thomasina took comfort from the fact that he did not automatically become aggressive towards her.

She hoped his earlier outburst might have been brought on by his surroundings and not by her presence.

It was with great relief that Thomasina returned to the steward's house on St Michael's Mount, after an absence of seven days.

It had been a period of great stress, not least because of the need to keep her earlier life separate from the one she was now leading.

Thomasina believed, rightly or wrongly, that if her relationship with Abel was to progress beyond its present tentative state, then the less he knew, the more chance she would stand with him – and she now admitted to herself that this mattered to her. One day she would tell him as much as she felt he needed to know.

Verity seemed as relieved to see her as Thomasina was to be home.

'Mistress Vinicombe has been asking after you,' she said. 'All I could tell her was that you had gone to Falmouth and I had no idea when you would be back.'

'That's all right, Verity, she'll understand. Has she brought the children to the Mount with her?'

'Only the baby – and it has a nursemaid now. She's left the other children in London. With an election in the offing there'll be a great deal of partying up at the castle. They won't want children getting under their feet.' Verity shook her head perplexedly, 'I don't know what it is that makes Sir John and all them others so keen to get a seat up there in Parliament. It costs them a fortune to get the votes to put 'em there, that's certain.'

Juliana came from the castle to visit Thomasina that same evening. She looked fit and well and gave Thomasina a warm hug by way of greeting.

'I heard you'd returned to the Mount and thought I'd come down and satisfy myself you were well. Verity was concerned about you being away for so long. Is everything all right?'

'There were some things I needed to attend to, that's all.'

When Thomasina made no attempt to amplify her brief explanation, Juliana asked, 'Is there a man involved?'

The question bordered on rudeness, but Thomasina did not take offence. 'Yes, but not in the way you're thinking.'

'Now I'm thoroughly intrigued,' declared Juliana. 'But I'll ask no more questions – for now. One thing I *do* know: it has nothing to do with Sir Charles Hearle, for I've heard that he's sailed with his boat. Abel's at sea, too – and I was beginning to think for a while there might be something between you two. It can't be Humphrey, because he's in London, learning how to be a deacon, or a curate, I'm not quite sure which. If there's a man involved, it must be someone I know nothing about.'

'I *hope* Humphrey is in London,' said Thomasina, refusing to rise to Juliana's probing. 'He was here a little over a week ago and proposed marriage once more.'

Thomasina was not being disloyal to Humphrey. She was telling Juliana nothing she did not already know, or would not learn in the next day or two. Humphrey's visit to the Mount – and to Thomasina – was common knowledge in the village and she had already confided in Juliana about Humphrey's offer of marriage, passing it off as an infatuation on Humphrey's part.

'You refused him once more, I presume?'

'Yes.'

'Thomasina, if you *did* decide you wished to marry him, I could guarantee Sir John's approval . . . eventually.'

Thomasina smiled. 'I don't need anyone's approval, Juliana, because I have no intention of marrying Humphrey. I don't love him and have no need of his money.'

'In that case I am afraid the poor boy has nothing

else to offer,' said Juliana. 'Well, now that is settled, let me tell you the plans Sir John and I have for entertaining at the castle. I am relying upon you to help me receive the guests.'

Startled, Thomasina said, 'I can't do that, Juliana. I wouldn't know what to do. I'm all right with you, but I couldn't mix with the sort of people you'll be entertaining at the castle, really I couldn't.'

'Thomasina, you could charm the Prince Regent if you put your mind to it, and you really need not worry about being out of your depth. The men invited to the Mount during an election campaign are, in the main, those who have a vote to cast. Not all of them are "gentlemen", I am afraid. Even the few who are will be so intoxicated after an hour or so they won't know whether they are beggars or dukes – and nothing about their behaviour is likely to enlighten you.'

Thomasina smiled once more. 'All right, I'll help you out as often as I can, but I'll need to go into Falmouth at least once a week.'

'Thank you, Thomasina. I'll have a boat put at your disposal. It's a quicker way to travel and I know you don't mind going on the water. Mind you . . .' she cast a sly look at Thomasina, 'this time there's no handsome head boatman to take you.'

'True,' agreed Thomasina, 'but if my calculations are correct, Abel is likely to return from the Mediterranean during the next few days.'

'You and he get along well, don't you?'

'Yes, we do,' agreed Thomasina, unwilling to commit herself to any greater degree.

'Hm! Well, he's a go-ahead man. Handsome, too, but you could do a lot better for yourself, Thomasina.'

'As I'm not looking for a husband, it doesn't really matter.' With this statement Thomasina changed the subject. 'How are the children?'

Juliana gave an amused laugh. 'I gather I am intended to take that as a very firm "Mind your own business" – and you are quite right, of course. But come up to the castle tomorrow morning. We'll take tea and have a good chat about all that's going on – everything, that is, except the men in your life.'

When Juliana had left, Thomasina wondered what she would have thought had she known the truth about the 'men in her life'.

She felt that Juliana might have understood about her father and sympathised with her, but Thomasina believed that unpicking just one single thread of her tangled life might very easily lead to the unravelling of the whole of the respectable new image she had built up around herself.

36

The first party to take place at the castle on St Michael's Mount was a great success. It was held for vote-holding traders in Sir John's constituency. The invited guests were somewhat overawed by their surroundings and on their best behaviour. They were also forced to leave at a reasonable hour, in order not to be caught on the island by the tide.

When the last of them had gone, Sir John thanked Thomasina for her contribution to the party, adding that she had done much to ensure its success and, hopefully, his re-election to Parliament.

He was chatting to her for so long that eventually Juliana crossed the room to them. Linking her arm with that of the baronet, she declared that she was becoming jealous but added, 'You were no doubt telling Thomasina of your meeting with Major the Honourable Hugh Pardoe?'

'Good Lord, no! I forgot all about it,' said Sir John. 'This election business is driving all other thoughts from my mind.'

Admonishing him, Juliana explained to Thomasina, 'Sir John met Hugh Pardoe at the War Office in London when he went there to enquire about one of his sons-in-law, who has been wounded in Spain. Pardoe had been newly promoted and called to the War Office to discuss a new posting. When he learned that Sir John had a home here, in Cornwall, he told of how you and Abel had rescued his daughter and taken her to Walkden Hall. He was absolutely delighted when he discovered not only that Sir John knows you, but that we are all friends. He thinks you are absolutely marvellous, Thomasina. What is more, he will be coming to Falmouth to board a ship when a fleet has been assembled. He has been appointed Lieutenant Governor of the convict colony at Botany Bay, in Australia.'

'That's right,' said Sir John. 'It is unforgiveable of me not to have mentioned it before. I have invited Major Pardoe to spend a few days at the Mount while he is waiting for the fleet to assemble. We must have a little celebration when they arrive.'

Thomasina was delighted and said so, adding, 'I still miss Maria – or "Emma", as I called her then. I sometimes wake in the morning and think I can hear her stirring in her room.'

'That is because you have no children of your own,' declared Juliana. 'When you have, you will wake in the morning and pretend you do *not* hear the sound of your youngest, craving attention. Now, everybody has finally gone, but there is still a quantity of champagne left. Shall we sit on the terrace and enjoy it? It is a surprisingly mild evening – and the moon is absolutely magnificent. It is an evening to sit and dwell upon the magic of the Mount.'

Twenty-four days after Abel had set sail from the Mount, bound for Leghorn, he brought the *Edward V* back to the St Michael's Mount harbour.

Sun-tanned and jubilant, he called at the steward's house, scarcely able to contain the pride he felt in what had been achieved with the *Edward V*.

He brought presents, too. For Verity there was a fine collection of Spanish lace. It included a bedspread, tablecloths of various sizes and cushion covers.

While she marvelled at the workmanship of them, he handed Thomasina a black velvet box. Opening it, she gasped in disbelief. It contained a necklace of gold filigree, set with a collection of cut green stones resembling emeralds. Abel told her they came from a group of Spanish islands, known as the 'Fortunate Islands', off north-west Africa.

Taken aback by his gift, Thomasina said, 'Abel! I can't accept this. It's far too generous.'

'I didn't have to pay full price for it,' Abel lied. 'I struck a good deal with a Spanish trader for a cargo and he let me have it cheap. I thought it was just right for you.'

Hoping to make her forget the value of the necklace, he said, 'You'll never believe the price I got for the pilchards in Leghorn. Nine pounds a hogshead – and they paid me in gold coin! That's a profit of seven pounds and twelve shillings on each hogshead – and I was carrying a cargo of five hundred! Imagine, a profit on one voyage of more than three thousand, five hundred pounds! Then I sailed to Spain and took on a cargo of marble, lace and wine. By the time it's sold, I'm confident I will have made a profit of more than five thousand pounds on a single voyage.'

'That's absolutely marvellous!' said a delighted Thomasina. She meant it. A ship's captain received a share of the trading profits and it was more than most could expect to make in a full year's trading. 'And this necklace really is a wonderful present, Abel. I've never been given anything like it before. Thank you.'

The kiss she gave Abel was meant to express no more than her gratitude for his gift, but it caused Verity's eyebrows to rise to unprecedented heights. For some minutes Abel's grandmother forgot all about her own gift.

Aware that she had shocked Verity, and confused by her own emotions, Thomasina said, 'Did you see anything of Sir Charles Hearle's ship on your voyage?'

'There was not a sign of it, but I hope it wasn't too far behind us. Although we were allowed to land our cargo without trouble, the authorities in Leghorn weren't too happy at having us there. They were contemplating taking action against us. We got in and out with no problem, but the next ship probably won't be so lucky.'

If the Italian authorities arrested Sir Charles Hearle,

Thomasina would be delighted, but she said nothing and, instead, returned her attention to the gift Abel had brought home for her.

Later that day Sir John St Aubyn displayed his approval of his ex-head boatman's new venture when he came down from the castle to the harbour and had Abel show him over the *Edward V*.

Suitably impressed, he delighted Abel by purchasing half the ship's marble to use in the building work being carried out on the family home of Clowance.

Thomasina felt that the visit from Sir John, and his unstinting approval of Abel's new status, pleased the *Edward V*'s master quite as much as the success of his maiden trading voyage.

He sailed for Falmouth that evening a very happy man.

Abel and his ship had been gone from the Mount for five days when the *Celestine* entered the small harbour.

It was the evening of another of Sir John's electioneering parties, this time for a more affluent group of voters than on the previous occasion.

Present at the gathering were the High Sheriff, the Lord Lieutenant and a number of Deputy Lieutenants. Many would be staying overnight at the castle.

Thomasina had promised Juliana she would be present to help out, although, had she been given time to think seriously about it, nerves might have got the better of her.

She had been to see her father the previous day and found him in an unexpectedly violent mood towards her. This had upset her a great deal and occupied her thoughts for much of time.

Fortunately, most of Sir John's personal friends were charming. He and Juliana never tired of recounting the circumstances of Thomasina's arrival on the Mount and her subsequent adventures, when she helped to rescue first Juliana and then Maria. As a result, Thomasina found herself at the centre of a great deal of unexpected attention.

This was quite flattering, until she discovered that one of the most attentive of those about her was none other than Francis Vincent, son of the late Henry and Harriet Vincent.

Francis had inherited Trebene House and its extensive estates. When he issued an invitation to her to pay a visit there, Thomasina wondered wryly what he would have thought had he known that she had once been a servant in the house – and the circumstances leading to her dismissal.

There was to be another link with Trebene House later that evening. As night fell, Juliana came to Thomasina and informed her that Sir Charles Hearle's ship had just berthed in the Mount's harbour.

Remembering Abel's words about the authorities in Italy, Thomasina said, 'I wonder if he managed to offload his cargo in Leghorn?'

'I think he must have,' said Juliana. 'The servant who brought the information said his ship was riding high in the water.'

'Then he's either carrying a very light return cargo

or he's come back empty,' mused Thomasina. 'That's not very good trading practice.'

'Well, you should be able to ask him about it very soon. Sir John has sent down an invitation for Sir Charles to join us here.'

37

The thought of meeting Sir Charles once again gave Thomasina no pleasure, yet she was unprepared for the appearance of the baronet when he entered the Chevy Chase Room, where the party was being held, and Thomasina was not the only one to be shocked.

Sir Charles's clothes were creased and untidy and looked as though they were in need of a wash.

Many of those present were associated with ships and the sea. They were aware that it was well nigh impossible to keep clothes in pristine condition when a ship was at sea for weeks at a time, but one look at his face was sufficient to make the observer immediately forget the state of his clothing.

Sir Charles seemed to have aged by twenty years in the few weeks he had been away.

His cousin, Francis Vincent, saw it and was one of the first to greet him, intercepting him when he had taken only a few paces into the room.

'Charles! Is everything all right? Have you had a difficult voyage?'

'No, everything is *not* all right, cousin. Everything is all *wrong*. It's been a bloody awful voyage – and I stand before you a ruined man. Ruined . . .'

It was apparent from Sir Charles's speech that he had been drinking before coming to the castle – and drinking heavily.

Francis Vincent looked around in some embarrassment and Thomasina came to his rescue. Crossing to him swiftly, she said, 'Bring Sir Charles with you. I'll take you to Juliana's study. He can tell his troubles to you there.'

She led the way from the room and, with an arm about the shoulders of his cousin, Francis Vincent followed her.

When they arrived at the small room used by Juliana to write her letters and balance the castle accounts, Thomasina showed the two men inside. To Francis Vincent she said, 'Is there anything I can bring for you?'

It was Sir Charles who replied, 'You can bring me a drink. A large one. A *very* large one.'

'I think you have had more than enough to drink, Charles. It would have been better had you declined Sir John's invitation and sought me out tomorrow. In this state you are an embarrassment to him – and to me.'

'I've always been an embarrassment to everyone, Francis, you know that. Isn't that why Grandfather left everything to the Vincents and not to the Hearles?

He couldn't prevent me inheriting his title, but he made damned certain I got nothing more.'

When Francis Vincent tried to say something, Sir Charles drunkenly waved him to silence, 'Oh, I know your mother took pity on me and remembered me in her will. I'm grateful to her, don't think I'm not. Not only that, but I'd have made a handsome profit, had everything not gone against me – thanks to a rogue who is a friend of yours, Thomasina. I'm talking of that damned boatman who was given command of a fancy ship. You know what he did? Do you know?'

Without waiting for a reply, he proceeded to tell Thomasina and his cousin.

'He took on a load of pilchards for Leghorn – the port for which I was heading with the *Celestine*, carrying a similar cargo. Not only did he get there before me and flood the market, but he stirred up a hornets' nest among the Italian officials. No sooner had we unloaded than we were warned that soldiers were on their way to arrest us all and confiscate the ship. They actually reached the harbour as we were leaving. We had to brave a whole fusillade of musket shots on our way out. Two of our seamen were wounded, one so badly that he died soon afterwards. I lost the whole cargo, Francis – and with it every penny I'd sunk into the venture.'

'Are you saying you unloaded a full cargo in what was basically a hostile country, before you'd seen the colour of anyone's money?' asked Thomasina. 'What sort of a captain do you have who would allow you to do such a thing?'

'A damned fine captain,' declared Sir Charles defen-

sively. 'One of the best. We had planned a return
cargo, too. However, thanks to that boatman, we had
no money to pay for it and had to return home empty
– to ruination. Where's that drink you were getting
for me, Thomasina? I am in urgent need of one.'

'What you need is to sober up and start thinking
of ways in which you might recoup your losses,' said
Francis Vincent firmly.

'No I don't . . . I know what I want – and so does
Thomasina.'

'I am sorry you had to witness this, Thomasina. Will
you please give my apologies to Sir John and promise
him my fullest support in his campaign. I will take
my cousin back to his ship and proceed on my way
from there.'

Taking a firm grip on a loudly protesting Sir
Charles, Francis propelled him outside the study.
Thomasina preceded them, opening doors, and the
two very different cousins made their way from
the castle.

Later that night Thomasina was telling Sir John and
Juliana what Sir Charles had said. Neither had seen
Sir Charles enter the Chevy Chase Room. Sir John
thanked Thomasina for her part in ensuring that the
drunken baronet left the reception before he caused a
disturbance.

'It was Sir Charles's cousin who took him from
the room so promptly,' Thomasina said. 'He sent
his apologies to you, but said that I was to tell you
he would give you his full support in your election
campaign.'

'Francis Vincent and Sir Charles could hardly be more different, for all they are cousins,' Sir John commented. 'How much truth do you think there is in what Sir Charles said about Abel beating him to Leghorn and stirring up the authorities there?'

'Abel certainly arrived there before Sir Charles,' Thomasina replied. 'Even though the *Celestine* sailed from Cornwall a full twenty-four hours before the *Edward V*. As for the rest . . . I'd say Sir Charles has only himself to blame for what went wrong. He put every penny he owned into buying a ship that had been laid up for so long that prospective buyers had stopped looking at it. Then he took on a captain no one else would hire and spent more than he could afford on a cargo that was only likely to make a worthwhile profit if he got there before anyone else. The man's a fool! Aware that the port was in a country controlled by Napoleon, he should have insisted that money was put into his hands for the cargo before offloading a single item. Even if the military hadn't turned up, the cargo could have been whisked away without payment being made. There would have been nothing he could do about it.'

'You're more than just a pretty face, young lady,' Juliana commented. 'It's a pity Sir Charles didn't consult you when he was looking for an investment for the money his aunt left to him.'

'Sir Charles would have had no help from me,' Thomasina declared. 'I don't like to see serious trouble coming to anyone – but if it's going to, then I can think of no one I would rather see it happen to than Sir Charles Hearle.'

38

The morning after the party at the castle, Thomasina had only just awakened when she heard Verity let herself into the house.

Calling out, she said, 'Verity, it's highly likely Sir Charles Hearle will come calling some time today. If he does, I want you to stay near at hand – *very* near. You understand?'

'I think I do. But I don't think you need worry too much about him. Not today, anyway. His ship sailed early this morning, and him with it. I don't know what went on at Sir John's party, and it's none of my business anyway, but the men on the harbour are saying that Sir Charles was put on board roaring drunk last night and orders to sail at first light this morning were given to the captain by Sir Charles's cousin.'

'Good! Where have they sailed to, Verity? From

what Sir Charles was saying last night, I wouldn't imagine he had any money to spare for harbour dues.'

'That I don't know, but he's not on the Mount, so you don't need to worry about him. If it's all the same to you, I'll cross to Marazion and pick up one or two things we're going to need before very long.'

Thomasina thought the *Celestine* had probably sailed for Falmouth. Once there the ship would no doubt anchor in the Carrick Roads, in order to avoid harbour dues.

But the *Celestine* would not be able to remain there for long. Sir Charles would need to pay his captain and crew – an impossibility if he really had no money. The only way quick money might be made by a ship-owner was by smuggling. It was a precarious means of earning a livelihood at the best of times. Right now it was doubly so.

The Revenue Service was making a determined effort to stamp out the illegal but profitable trade. In addition, a smuggler had to run a gauntlet of British and French men-o'-war – not to mention predatory privateers operating from ports and harbours in both countries.

If Thomasina thought smuggling was the only option open to Sir Charles, then she would soon learn this was not so. The alternative the baronet had in mind was something that would never have occurred to her.

The timing of his visit also took her by surprise. She and Verity had both been looking to the *Celestine* to give them a warning of his presence.

When Sir Charles crossed the causeway on horse-back a few evenings later, they were both caught off guard.

Thomasina was preparing for bed where there came a knock at the front door. Frowning, she wondered who would be calling at this time of the evening? She decided it must be Verity, prob-ably returning to the house for something she had forgotten earlier.

Opening the door, Thomasina was taken aback to see Sir Charles Hearle standing outside. Her hand went immediately to the low neck of her dressing-gown.

'What do you want? I'm about to go to bed.'

'I would like to speak with you on an important matter, Thomasina, but first may I apologise for any embarrassment I might have caused you the other evening? I had spent days trying unsuccessfully to come to terms with financial ruin and . . . and I wasn't myself.'

'The only person likely to find the answer to his financial problems in a brandy glass is the man who makes the brandy, Sir Charles – and it isn't me to whom you should be apologising. It was Sir John's party, held for those who are important to him in the election. He's the one you should be calling upon now, not me.'

'I shall be calling on him when I leave here.'

Sir Charles spoke far more sharply than he had intended. He was angry at being lectured on his manners by a young woman – especially one from an inferior social background.

He curbed his anger very quickly. Right now her
pedigree was of little consequence. He was in serious
financial trouble. She could provide him with a solution to his problems.

'Look, we can't talk out here. May I come in?'

Although more than a little curious about his
motives for calling on her at this time of night,
Thomasina had no intention of asking him into her
home without someone else being present.

'I'm sorry, Sir Charles. I am alone here at the
moment. I have no intention of putting my reputation
at risk by inviting you in.' Beginning to enjoy the
conversation, she added, 'You will recall that I have
experience of your behaviour when no one else is
around.'

Although she was referring to the occasion when
she and the children had paid a visit to the *Celestine*,
she also recalled another time and place. One that Sir
Charles did not remember.

She had not forgotten – could not forget – but she
would never remind him of what she had suffered at
his hands.

Sir Charles looked pained. 'That was an unfortunate misunderstanding . . . most regrettable. I can
assure you my intentions this evening are entirely
honourable.'

At that moment Verity came hurrying towards the
house. A neighbour had called at her cottage to tell
her that Sir Charles had crossed the causeway and
gone straight to the steward's house, where she knew
Thomasina was home alone.

With her employer's strict instructions in mind,

Verity hurried off to the steward's house. She was relieved to find that Thomasina had kept the baronet talking on the doorstep.

'Hello, Miss Thomasina. I heard you had company and thought you might have need of me.'

'That is very kind of you, Verity. Sir Charles says he has some business to discuss with me. I wouldn't allow him in, because I was alone in the house, but now you're here . . . Perhaps you could make tea for us. I believe Sir Charles has had a long ride. He must be thirsty.'

Thomasina was well aware that something stronger than tea would have been more to the baronet's taste, but the drink she had in the house had been given to her by Abel. She had no intention of wasting any of it upon her uninvited visitor.

Once in the sitting-room, Thomasina seated herself before motioning Sir Charles to another armchair.

'Thank you.' He inclined his head to acknowledge her gesture. 'If it is all the same to you, I would rather stand.'

Thomasina shrugged her shoulders. Seated or standing, it made little difference to her. However, when Sir Charles began pacing the room she wished she had insisted that he sat down.

As he paced, the baronet started talking. At first, what he had to say made little sense to her.

'As I have already told you, Thomasina, I have recently had a bad run of luck. However, such luck does not last for ever and I already have plans to overcome my problems.'

Thomasina failed to see what his plans had to do with her, and she said so.

'Ah! But you are a very important element in my plans, Thomasina. Together we can not only come through this, but go on to achieve great success.'

'Together? What have *I* to do with any plans you've made?'

'That is what I have come here to discuss with you, Thomasina. I am convinced that together we could have a very successful business.'

'A *business*? Doing what?' Thomasina was puzzled.

'Why, trading, of course. Carrying merchandise to all parts of the world and returning with exotic – and profitable – cargoes.'

'But . . . I thought you were a ruined man? Had lost all your money?'

'That is so – for the moment. But I still have a ship, Thomasina. A very good ship.'

'I see. You want me to put up the money to buy cargoes and pay the crew of the *Celestine*, is that so?'

'Yes, Thomasina. I can assure you that time will prove it to be an excellent investment.'

'I'm sorry, Sir Charles. Quite apart from any other consideration, *you* are not a good risk. I can invest my money elsewhere and get a guaranteed return.'

Sir Charles was silent for a few minutes, then he said hesitantly, 'I am prepared to offer you something you will not be able to obtain from any other investment, Thomasina.'

'Oh! And what might that be.'

'I have already told you of the esteem in which I hold you. To prove it, I am asking you to marry me, Thomasina. In return for your investment in me, I will marry you and make you Lady Thomasina Hearle.'

When Verity entered the sitting-room a few minutes later she was carrying a tray upon which lay two cups and other items for tea. She appeared confused.

'I thought . . . ? I just passed Sir Charles in the hallway. He almost knocked me over – and I won't tell you what his reply was when I said I had brought his tea! It certainly wasn't what I'd expect from a gentleman.'

'Sir Charles may lay claim to a number of titles, Verity – but "gentleman" isn't one of them.'

'Why did he leave so suddenly – and in such a foul mood?'

'He asked me to marry him, Verity. Said he wanted to make me Lady Hearle.'

Verity succeeded in straightening the tray before everything fell from it to the floor. Hastily placing it on the table, she asked, 'What did you say to him?'

'Nothing, Verity. I just laughed. I was still laughing when he stalked out of the room.'

'Well! Well, I never! I certainly don't blame you for refusing him, Miss Thomasina, not for a single moment, but Sir Charles is not a man to cross. He can be very, very spiteful.'

'There's little you can tell me about Sir Charles that I don't already know, Verity, but I must admit his proposal took me by surprise – even though I am aware he was only after my money. But it's the second proposal I've had since coming to the Mount. They say things happen in threes. I wonder who will be the third man to propose . . . ?'

39

When Abel left the London docks after delivering his cargo, it was late in the day and the *Edward V* was obliged to anchor for the night in the River Thames, off Deptford.

As it was the mate's birthday, Abel took him ashore to an inn for a celebratory meal and a few drinks. The inn he chose was the Admiral's Arms, not far from the Royal Navy victualling yard. Here, he met up with a couple of Royal Marine officers with whom he had served many years before.

Both, like Abel, had left the service and were now employed by the transport service – both on victualling duties.

As well as becoming an extremely convivial evening, it was also to prove a profitable one. Many of the ex-marine officers' friends joined them for a drink or two. One such man was responsible for provisioning the fleet being assembled to carry convicts to Australia.

When Abel mentioned Major Pardoe, and the part he and Thomasina had played in rescuing and returning the major's daughter from the sea off the Lizard, it was deemed an additional cause for celebration.

By the time Abel took the mate back to the *Edward V*, he had struck a deal to deliver a full cargo of cured pilchards to Deptford, as food for the convicts during their long voyage to the convict colony. The price would not equal that obtained by Abel on his voyage to Leghorn, but it was sufficient to ensure that he would make a handsome profit on the deal.

In order to secure the cargo of pilchards, Abel put the *Edward V* in to Mevagissey harbour on his return journey to Falmouth. It had been a good season for the pilchard fishermen and he had no difficulty in purchasing all the cured fish he required.

While the cargo was being loaded, Abel sent the mate off to Falmouth in a hastily hired fishing boat. He would inform the shipbroker of his movements and obtain the money with which to pay the Mevagissey fish-cellar owner.

During the loading Abel would occasionally stop to have a conversation with the Mevagissey man and it was during one such conversation that he asked him about the sailors who had returned to the village after having been prisoners of the French for so many years.

'Have they all settled back to normal life?' he asked.

'For most of 'em it's as though they've never been

away,' said the man. 'Almost all of 'em are back at sea right now.'

Chuckling, he added, 'Mind you, it wasn't such a fine homecoming for Harry Avers, or his wife. She'd been wanting to be rid of him long before he went, and when he'd been gone for three years without a word, she gave him up for dead and married again. He come back to her to find another man in his place and three young maids that he hadn't fathered. At the moment they're all living in the same house – his house. The vicar spends more time there trying to sort it all out than he does in his own church, but then, so he should. He's the one who married 'em. She was a Wesleyan till she wanted to marry again. The minister wouldn't marry her, so she turned to the vicar. He was happy enough to do it for 'em then, thinking he'd put one over on the minister. I don't think he's so happy now!'

Abel gave the other man a wry smile and agreed that it was a very tricky situation. Then he asked after the seaman who had lost his sanity during his imprisonment in France.

'Edward Varcoe?' The fish-cellar owner shook his head, not noticing the start that Abel gave at the mention of the insane fisherman's name. 'His is a sad case. He'll never go back to sea again, that's certain. He's right off his head, so much so that his sister-in-law had him put away in the workhouse, in St Austell. Mind you, I hear his daughter has turned up and taken him out now.'

'I know a Varcoe,' said Abel cautiously, 'but I'm not sure whether or not she came from this part of

Cornwall. What is the daughter's name?'

'Thomasina. Edward wanted a son, and was convinced his wife was going to have one. Had even chosen a name for him. Thomas. Unfortunately, the good Lord decided to give him a daughter instead, so Edward called her Thomasina. Bit of a wild one too, she was. Used to spend a lot of time at sea with her pa and, from what I've heard, she could handle a boat as well as any man. But that didn't stand her in any good stead once he'd gone. She could hardly go to sea as crew, could she? The result was that she couldn't settle down to anything after Edward went missing. Eventually her aunt put her into service over at Trebene, with the Vincents, but there was some scandal there and she was thrown out. No one heard of her then for a couple of years. In fact, not until she turned up to take her pa out of the workhouse. Then it seems she disappeared with him, just as mysteriously as she arrived. Mind you, there's nothing unusual in that, not for Thomasina. She wasn't one for staying in one place for long and I don't suppose she's changed. She can't be all that far away though, or she'd never have heard so quickly about her father coming back home.'

The fish-cellar owner prattled on for some time about Thomasina, her family and the other men who had returned to the village, but Abel was not listening. He was remembering that he had told his grandmother of the return of the Mevagissey men after being freed from captivity.

He believed he had the answers to many of the fish-cellar owner's queries. There was little doubt in his mind that the Thomasina Varcoe he had rescued from the sea at St Michael's Mount and the Thomasina of whom the Mevagissey man was talking were one and the same person.

Her employment and mysterious dismissal from Trebene could also explain her apparent intense dislike of Sir Charles Hearle. Abel was well aware that Sir Charles was a nephew of the late owners of Trebene House.

But why should she have remained so secretive about her past life? He thought of an answer to his unspoken question almost immediately.

Thomasina had come into money – probably a great deal of money. She was also now a companion to Juliana Vinicombe and accepted as such by Sir John St Aubyn and his friends. She would hardly want it known that she had once been a servant in the house of Sir Charles Hearle's aunt and uncle.

But each answer he found only served to pose yet another question. If she knew Sir Charles at Trebene, why had he failed to recognise her when he first met her on the Mount? Or had he . . . ?

There were a great many things Abel wanted to know. Finding the answers to his questions would not be easy, but he would need to try. Since Thomasina had come into his life he had found it increasingly difficult to get her out of his mind. He had felt recently that she was beginning to feel something for him, too.

While she was a friend of Sir John and Juliana, and he a St Aubyn boatman, their relationship could never move forward. But if she was indeed the Thomasina Varcoe of whom the cellar owner had spoken – and there was little doubt in Abel's mind – then things might be very different now that he was master of a ship.

First, he would need to find some way of having *her* tell him the truth about her past – and Abel suspected that was not going to be a simple matter.

40

When Thomasina paid the next visit to her father, she was shocked at the change she found in him.

On days when he was quiet he was allowed to roam around the house, all the outside doors being locked, but the housekeeping couple told her that he had suffered violent mood swings in recent days. As a result they were keeping him confined to a locked bedroom, the window of which had earlier been fitted with slim iron bars.

Thomasina looked in on him twice during her visit to the house, but on both occasions he rushed at her as though intent on attacking her. Fortunately, perhaps, Edward Varcoe had also grown increasingly fragile and Arthur Hocking had been able to hold him off until Thomasina left the room.

Distressed, she asked the couple whether anything had happened that might have triggered off this change in him.

Arthur shook his head. 'We followed your instructions and called in a doctor. He told us that, in his experience, such behaviour wasn't at all unusual. Unfortunately, he fears that your father is going to get worse and not better, Miss Varcoe.'

As if this news was not bad enough, the housekeeper who had cared for Malachi and his house for so many years informed Thomasina that, if Edward Varcoe's condition deteriorated any further, she would be unable to continue to care for him. She had reached an age when most women were allowing others to look after *them*. Caring for a violently insane man was more than she felt able to cope with.

Thomasina had all this on her mind when she returned to the busy harbour to board the St Aubyn boat for the return journey to the Mount.

There was still half an hour to go before the time she had told the boatmen she would want to depart. She decided to call in to the office of Claude Coumbe and enquire about the movements of the *Edward V*. The ship had not called at the Mount for some weeks and Verity had heard nothing from Abel.

Coumbe gave her a warm welcome and was delighted to produce the file he held on Thomasina's ship and to lay out account sheets showing an impressive profit on the ship's voyages.

Leaning back in his chair, the papers spread out on the desk between them, the shipbroker beamed at Thomasina. 'It is a very satisfactory state of affairs, my dear, and much of the credit is due to Abel Carter. You made a very wise choice when you put him in command of the *Edward V* – and that is more than I can say for a certain ship-owner who is known to both of us.'

'Are you referring to Sir Charles Hearle?' Thomasina asked.

Coumbe smiled. 'I will mention no names – but we both know to whom I am referring. Word is going around that his ship is being used to land certain commodities upon which duty is not being paid.'

'You mean he's involved in smuggling?' said Thomasina.

'Exactly, and if word has reached *me*, then I have no doubt at all that the Revenue men are aware of his activities – or, rather, the activities of the master of his ship, who has been given a free hand to do whatever he wishes, providing it turns in a profit at the end of the day.'

'Sir Charles Hearle may escape prosecution,' Thomasina said, 'but that won't prevent his boat from being seized – and it's his sole remaining asset.'

'The man is a fool,' declared Coumbe. 'But that need not trouble either of us. You have one of the finest ships this port has seen – and a captain worthy of the vessel.'

The man being praised so highly by Claude Coumbe was at that moment being landed farther along the sea front from one of the *Edward V*'s boats. The ship had returned from Deptford empty, and Abel had anchored in the Carrick Roads, in order to avoid paying harbour dues.

As he walked along the quayside, Abel saw the

St Aubyn boat tied up alongside the quay wall with men he knew seated in it, quietly smoking their pipes.

Greeting them, Abel asked what they were doing in Falmouth. 'We brought that maid in that you pulled from the sea dressed as a boy,' said the coxwain. 'She had some business here, I believe.'

'Thomasina's here? Do you know where?' Abel thought this might be an opportunity to speak to her without his grandmother, or anyone else, likely to interrupt them.

'None of my business,' replied the dour St Aubyn coxwain, 'but it's almost time for her to come back to the boat and for us to return to the Mount.'

'I'll wait for her,' said Abel. 'I'd like to speak with her.'

'I don't know as she's likely to want to talk to the likes of you now, Abel,' the coxwain said. 'She's come up in the world since you were last at the Mount.'

Abel frowned. 'In what way?'

'It looks as though we might all have to call her "M'Lady" before very long. It seems Sir Charles Hearle called at the steward's house specially to ask the Varcoe maid to marry him.'

'Sir Charles Hearle and Thomasina . . . ?' Abel looked at the boatman in disbelief. 'You must be mistaken, surely?'

'It's as true as I'm standing here,' said the coxwain. 'I got it direct from your grandma – and she should know, working in the house as she does. That young girl's a deep one, and no mistake, but it's my guess that she'll be Lady Hearle before she's many months older.'

*   *   *

Abel was stunned by the news given to him by the St Aubyn boatman and was at first inclined to dismiss it as no more than Mount gossip, but the man would not have lied about his grandmother passing on the news.

He was still trying to digest this when he came within sight of the shipbroker's office of Claude Coumbe. To to his amazement he saw Thomasina leaving.

Suddenly everything fell into place – and his world tumbled about him. Ducking back behind a jumble of rigging and spars piled on the jetty, he made certain she did not see him.

When she had passed by he hurried to the shipbroker's office. Ignoring the protests of the clerk in the outer room, he flung open the door to Coumbe's inner office. He had not thought of the questions he would ask the shipbroker, but questions proved unnecessary.

The answers were spread out on the desk in front of the shipbroker: accounts made out by himself; various manifests describing the cargoes carried by his ship; and, completing the story, the file on which in thick black letters was the name *Edward V*.

He was employed by Thomasina.

Abel left the office as hurriedly as he had entered it. Rushing back along the quayside, away from the St Aubyn boat, he tried to reject the obvious – but he could not. Everything made far too much sense.

Something must have occurred between Sir Charles and Thomasina when she worked at Trebene House and she had been stung by his refusal to acknowledge her when they met up again.

Whatever lay between them must have been serious because, having come into money, she had bought the *Edward V* with the sole intention of putting Sir Charles out of business and bringing him to the brink of bankruptcy. It explained to Abel why he had been instructed that he had to beat the *Celestine* to Leghorn at all costs.

Ruined financially, Sir Charles would be more inclined to heal his rift with Thomasina. Whatever she had once been, she now possessed a great deal of money – and Sir Charles was desperate enough to offer marriage to her in exchange for her fortune.

The more Abel thought about it, the more sense it made. He was both distraught and appalled by what he had learned about her and the manner in which she had used him in her schemes.

He had thought a great deal about Thomasina since speaking to the Mevagissey fish-cellar owner. Much of the mystery that surrounded her had been made clearer as a result of their conversation, but there had still been some puzzling gaps in his knowledge of her. He wished he might have been able to leave it that way.

Abel was deeply hurt. In recent weeks he had allowed himself actually to contemplate marriage to her. What a fool he had been! It was quite obvious now that Thomasina Varcoe had her sights set on someone far more illustrious than a boatman she had promoted to master of a ship merely to achieve her own ends.

41

Unaware that the cocoon of secrecy in which she had hidden for the past two years had finally been peeled away, Thomasina returned to the Mount with a great deal on her mind.

The good news was that the *Edward V*, under the command of Abel, was proving far more profitable than she had ever thought possible. It showed what Sir Charles Hearle *might* have achieved, had he commenced deep-sea trading in a workmanlike fashion, with a suitable ship and a first-class captain.

However, uppermost in her mind at the moment was the problem of her father. She was honest enough to admit to herself that she still nursed a forlorn hope that one day he would wake and find that his sanity had miraculously returned.

Such a hope would linger for her just as long as he lived, but she was forced to concede that his condition was worsening. She was also faced with the additional problem of finding someone to look after him. Someone she could trust.

Thomasina was still pondering the problem when the boat arrived at the St Michael's Mount harbour.

Entering the steward's house, Thomasina found Verity in a state of happy excitement. 'You'll never guess who I've just had in the house,' she said, hardly giving Thomasina time to step inside the door before hurrying forward to impart her news.

Without waiting for a reply, she said, 'It was little Emma – or Maria, as I suppose I must learn to call her. She's staying up at the castle with her mother and father. They came here looking for you. I said I'd send you up there just as soon as you arrived home from Falmouth.'

'Thank you, Verity,' Thomasina said resignedly. 'I'll get cleaned up, change my clothes and go off to the castle to see them.'

As she took off the clothing she had worn in the boat, Verity chatted through the doorway of the bedroom to her about Maria, her 'lovely mother' and the 'fine-looking gentleman' who was her father.

In truth, Thomasina would have preferred to have a quiet evening at home, thinking over the problem of her father – but she did look forward to seeing Maria once more.

The reunion with Maria was as warm as Thomasina might have wished. Contrary to her expectations, the little girl recognised her as soon as she entered the castle room where the family were seated with the St Aubyns.

She ran to Thomasina and, when she was picked up, flung her arms about Thomasina's neck and gave her a warm hug.

'Well!' exclaimed Thomasina happily, 'that's the most loving greeting I have ever received from *anyone!*'

As she set the small girl down upon the ground once more, Juliana said, 'Thomasina is being modest. She has received two proposals of marriage since she came to the Mount – the latest from a baronet.'

'I am hardly surprised,' said Maria's mother. 'What a remarkable story you have to tell! It would also seem that the sea captain who brought you and Maria to Walkden Hall had a part in rescuing *you*, too. Is he around, by the way?'

'No, but he could be home any day now.'

'Splendid!' Major the Honourable Hugh Pardoe, a tall, good-looking man, limped across the room to shake Thomasina's hand. 'We haven't met before, but I am truly delighted to make your acquaintance. May I call you Thomasina? My wife and I owe you a great deal and we are very, very grateful.'

'Maria's grandmother, Lady Pardoe, is very grateful too,' said Lavinia Pardoe. 'In fact, she has sent a present for you. Give it to Thomasina, Maria.'

The small girl took a small jewellery box from her mother. Carrying it with exaggerated care, she took it across the room to Thomasina.

Thanking her, Thomasina opened the box and expressed delight. Inside was a cameo brooch of finely worked gold filigree.

She looked up at Lavinia Pardoe in search of an explanation, but it was Major Pardoe who spoke. 'It's a family heirloom and would eventually have gone to Maria, but my mother wanted you to have it. She said, quite rightly, that had it not been for you, Maria would not be here today to inherit anything. As a reward for that it is a very small "thank you".'

'But – it rightfully belongs to Maria. I can't possibly accept such an expensive gift.'

'Maria will receive a very substantial inheritance,' said Lavinia. 'However much it is, it cannot compare with what you have given to her. The gift of life itself. The debt we all owe you can never be repaid.'

Moved by the gift and the thought behind it, Thomasina gave Maria a warm kiss and was rewarded with another hug.

Thomasina spent a pleasant few hours at the castle. Lavinia Pardoe was a gentle, quiet woman, who adored her husband and daughter, and Thomasina decided she liked her very much.

It was late evening when she left. Major Pardoe and his family were to depart from the Mount on Sunday. Embarking on their ship at Falmouth, they would sail with the convoy carrying convicts to the penal colonies of Australia.

Juliana accompanied Thomasina halfway down the path to the village. On the way she told her that Sir John proposed a small farewell gathering at the castle for the departing officer and his family.

'You will be invited, of course,' Juliana said. 'But I thought I should warn you that Sir Charles will also be there. He is at the moment staying nearby on the mainland, at the home of a distant relative. Sir John met him early this morning, when he went out riding.'

'I really don't know what Sir John and Sir Charles have in common,' said Thomasina. 'Except, of course, that they are both baronets.'

'There's rather more to it than that,' Juliana explained. 'Sir John and Sir Charles are both Freemasons. So too is Major Pardoe. It is possible one or two more senior Freemasons will be at the castle, too. But if they do come I will insist that they bring wives and daughters to the party.'

Thomasina did not relish the thought of meeting up with the wives and daughters of Sir John's Free-masonry friends, but then she thought of Juliana's own difficult situation in the company of such women . . .

'Don't worry, I'll be there,' she promised.

42

It had been dark for a few hours by the time Thomasina reached her home, but Verity was still in the house.

'There was a letter came for you this evening,' she said immediately. 'Delivered by a special messenger who'd ridden all the way from Falmouth with it. I'd have brought it up to the castle, but it's a long climb up there for my old bones and I was expecting you to be home earlier than this.'

Thomasina's first thought was that the letter contained news of her father. She tore it open in a state of near panic.

It was not about her father, but after scanning the contents she paled and sat down heavily on a chair before reading the letter in more detail.

'Is something wrong, dear? Bad news?'

Thomasina nodded. 'Yes . . . but it's nothing to worry about. It's business, that's all.'

Thomasina was lying. The news contained in the letter *was* something to worry about, for both of them. It had come from Claude Coumbe. He told her of Abel's unexpected and abrupt arrival in his office only minutes after Thomasina had left. The ex-St Aubyn boatman had seen all the papers spread out on his desk and must also have seen Thomasina leaving the shipbroker's office.

The ownership of the *Edward V* was a secret from the ship's captain no longer.

Coumbe said that Abel had left the office without a word after viewing the evidence. The shipbroker had been unable to give him any explanation.

Thomasina bit her lip as she read his words. It had become increasingly apparent to her in recent days that she would not be able to keep secret her ownership of the *Edward V* for ever. She would have to tell Abel the truth very soon, but had hoped to be able to choose her moment.

There was worse to come. An hour after he had left the office, Abel had returned. In the outer office he handed in a letter in which he declared he would no longer be used by Thomasina in her schemes, adding that since she had already succeeded in her aim she would need neither him nor the *Edward V* again. He had therefore resigned his command of the ship, which was currently anchored in Carrick Roads.

Although Thomasina did not know what Abel meant by a great deal of what he had written, there was no doubt that she had a disaster on her hands, and it was one she could not solve from

St Michael's Mount while Abel and the *Edward V* were at Falmouth.

Sir John had told her when she first came to the island that she might have use of the St Aubyn boat and its crew without reference to him. It was time to take advantage of his offer yet again.

'Verity, on your way home, will you tell the boatmen I would like to go to Falmouth again, at first light tomorrow? I have some very urgent business to attend to there.'

Upon her arrival in Falmouth, Thomasina hurried off to the shipbroker's office, but Claude Coumbe was unable to throw any additional light upon the letter handed in by Abel.

'Do you have any idea where Abel is now?' she asked.

'None,' replied Coumbe, 'but one of my clerks thought he saw him at the King's Volunteer, on the sea front, last night. However, I don't think you should go there. It's not the place for a woman. At least, not a *respectable* woman.'

'Then I'll try not to stay there long enough to lose my reputation,' Thomasina said. 'Thank you for your information, Mr Coumbe.'

Thomasina was halfway to the inn when one of the shipbroker's clerks caught up with her. Breathless from hurrying, he said, 'Begging your pardon, Miss Varcoe, but Mr Coumbe sent me after you. He says I am to go inside the King's Volunteer to see if Captain Carter is there, while you wait outside.'

'That's very kind of Mr Coumbe,' said Thomasina

gratefully. She would not have thought twice about going inside the inn during the days when she was masquerading as a young man, but the tavern was frequented by foreign seamen. A woman inside such an inn would be there for only one purpose.

The clerk went inside while Thomasina waited on the quay, looking out over the busy harbour.

She was watching a particular ship when the shipbroker's clerk came out of the tavern.

'I'm sorry, Miss Varcoe. Captain Carter was there last night, but he isn't there now and the landlord was unable to help.'

'Were you the clerk who saw him in there?'

'Yes, Miss.'

'Was he drunk or sober?' The clerk seemed reluctant to reply to her question, but Thomasina insisted, 'Surely you know? What state was he in?'

'I'm no expert on such matters, Miss Varcoe,' the clerk said diplomatically, 'but I would say he might have been drinking elsewhere before coming to the King's Volunteer.'

'Thank you.' The reply was what Thomasina had been expecting. She felt that Abel was hurt and unhappy because she had not trusted him sufficiently to tell him *she* was the owner of the *Edward V*. But she had her reasons and she would try to convince him they were valid ones – once she found him.

However, something else had captured her immediate attention.

'How good is your eyesight?' she asked the clerk. 'Can you read the name of that ship coming in – over there?'

She pointed to a ship making slow progress towards the quay. It had attracted her attention earlier.

'I don't need to see its name, Miss Varcoe. I recognise the ship. It's the *Celestine*, Sir Charles Hearle's ship.'

'That's what I thought, but aren't the men on board wearing some kind of uniform?'

The clerk peered at the ship, which was being pursued by a grey curtain of drizzle, before saying excitedly, 'They're Revenue men, Miss Varcoe. There have been rumours going around for a few days of what the *Celestine* was up to. It looks as though the Revenue men heard them too and have caught up with Captain Carberry – at last.'

Thomasina did not miss the meaning in the clerk's words. She wondered whether Sir Charles would be involved in any prosecution that might follow the arrest of Captain Carberry and the detention of the *Celestine*.

She decided she would speculate on Sir Charles Hearle's problems later. Mention of Captain Carberry and his employer had given her an idea of where Abel might be found.

Taking a shilling from her purse, she handed it to the young clerk. 'I am most grateful to you for saving me from possible embarrassment. Please thank Mr Coumbe for his kindness. Tell him I will be speaking to him about the future of the *Edward V* as soon as I have settled one or two matters.'

Thomasina had recalled the inn, the British Marine, where she and Abel had lunched together. The landlord was a friend of his and an ex-marine colleague.

If he was still in Falmouth, Abel would most likely be there.

It was not yet lunchtime and the inn was fairly quiet. When Thomasina entered, the landlord recognised her immediately – and guessed the reason for her visit.

'Hello, Miss Varcoe. I'm pleased to see you again. I'll be even more pleased if you tell me you've come in search of Abel.'

'He *is* here, then?'

'That's right. I'm not in the habit of telling tales about my customers, but seeing you're a particular friend of his . . . He had something on his mind last night and went on a jag that would have put lesser men on their backs in half the time. I've known Abel for a great many years, but I've never known him do anything like this before.'

'Where is he? Will you take me to him?'

'Of course.' The landlord unfastened his leather apron, folded it and set it down upon a keg standing in a corner of the room. 'Come with me.'

Thomasina followed him from the public room and along a dark passageway that led to a steep, narrow staircase. At the top of the stairs was another passageway, but this one had a number of doors leading off it at regular intervals.

'He's in number three.' The landlord stopped at the numbered door and tapped on it. When there was no reply he tapped again, with no more effect.

'He doesn't seem to be answering,' said the landlord. 'But he won't have gone out or I would have seen him.'

'Can you open the door?'

The landlord detached a large ring of keys from his belt and, after peering at them, selected one. Inserting it in the door, he tried to turn it and then swung the door open, saying, 'It's not locked.'

The blinds were drawn, but in the light that filtered around them Thomasina could see the figure lying on the bed under the bedclothes. There was a strong smell of stale alcohol in the room.

'Would you leave us alone for a while?' she asked the landlord. 'When I've woken him we are going to have a long chat. He might feel like something to eat afterwards. Although, if he was as drunk as you say, he might not be able to face food for a while.'

'I'll go off and mix up something that will make him feel a little better,' promised the landlord. 'But I have a feeling you're the only one who can *really* help him. I wish you luck, Miss, I really do. Abel is a good man, one of the very best. I didn't enjoy seeing him the way he was last night.'

43

When the landlord left and closed the door behind him, Thomasina crossed the room and drew back the curtains. Then she opened the window, allowing the stale air to escape, at the same time letting in sounds from the busy street outside.

As she turned her attention to the bed, Abel changed his position, disturbed by the noises entering the room. Thomasina could see now that he had gone to bed fully clothed except for his soft, buckled shoes. She stumbled over one in the middle of the floor; the other was lying at the foot of his bed.

Shaking Abel by the shoulder, she said, 'Wake up. Wake up, Abel. I want to talk to you.'

It was a full minute before she had a reaction from him, then it was a purely automatic one. He sought to shrug off her hand, at the same time mumbling unintelligibly.

'You might just as well wake up and speak to me, Abel. I'm not going to go away.'

Eventually it was her voice rather than her actions that got through to him. Turning his head, his eyelids flickered open to reveal bloodshot eyes. Wincing at the brightness of the light from the window, he closed them again. Then, struggling clumsily to sit up, he winced once more. This time the source of his discomfort was the pounding inside his head.

Trying to marshal an array of disjointed thoughts, not the least of which was wondering exactly where he was, and how he had got here, Abel said, 'What . . . ? What are you doing here? What time is it?'

'I doubt if you even know what day it is, Abel. As for my being here . . . I had an urgent message from Claude Coumbe. He informed me that you intended resigning as captain of the *Edward V.*'

Abel's thoughts began to assume some sort of order and he remembered. Leaning back on his pillows, he closed his eyes once more. 'Claude got it wrong. There was no *intention* about it. I resigned when I delivered my letter to his office.'

'Why, Abel? Why didn't you come and see me and talk about the things that were troubling you?'

'Why didn't *you* tell me you were the owner of the *Edward V*?'

'I had my reasons.'

'I don't doubt it. I have a very good idea what they were.'

'I don't think you do, Abel. You might *think* you know, but whatever ideas you have are probably very wrong.'

'I doubt it.' Abel wished his head was clearer and his brain not quite so determined to batter itself into painful insensibility against his skull. 'You see . . . I picked up another cargo from Mevagissey. While we were loading I got talking to the owner of the fish-cellar. He told me of a certain Edward Varcoe, captain of a small ship, who'd been captured by the French many years ago and returned to Mevagissey only recently. Sadly, he is incurably insane . . . But you'd know all about it because my grandmother would have told you.'

Abel suffered a bout of throaty coughing, the action aggravating the pain in his head. When it passed, he continued.

'This Edward Varcoe has a daughter named – yes, you've guessed it – Thomasina. Thomasina Varcoe. She was the apple of her father's eye, it seems, and would often go to sea with him. She knew as much about sailing a ship as any man, so I am told. Of course, when her father went missing it wasn't possible for her to go to sea as a deckhand, but she couldn't settle to anything else. She became "a bit of a wild one", according to the cellar owner. Then she was put to work at Trebene House, home of Sir Charles Hearle's aunt and uncle, to whom he was very close.'

When Abel turned bloodshot eyes upon Thomasina, his expression hurt her.

'This is where I need to bring my imagination into play a little, I'm afraid. The way I see it, while this Thomasina was working at Trebene, she got to know Sir Charles Hearle – a man well known to have an eye for a pretty girl. It's certain that something happened between them, but I won't speculate on what it might have been. Whatever it was must have been pretty serious – at least, I think it was for *her*. When Thomasina was dismissed from Trebene in mysterious circumstances, she left bearing a huge grudge against Sir Charles. Some time later, when she's been left a lot of money by an uncle, she meets up with him again. When he doesn't even acknowledge her, she gets very angry. So much so that, when he stupidly sinks all his money into a venture involving a ship, she thinks of a plan to *make* him take notice of her – and it's a very elaborate plan. She buys a fast ship, employs a gullible captain and gets him to do her dirty work for her. Mind you, it's worked, hasn't it, Thomasina Varcoe? Worked very well indeed. Sir Charles Hearle has come to heel, just the way you planned it. He's come running to you begging for forgiveness. More, he's asked you to marry him. You've probably got far more than you ever believed you would. A title. Lady Thomasina Hearle. Not bad for a girl who was in service in the house of her future husband's aunt. I have to admire you, Thomasina, I really do.'

Abel's voice was choked and Thomasina realised he was terribly hurt. Almost as hurt as she was by what he had said about *her* – but Abel had not finished talking.

'Now you've got what you want, you won't need a captain for the *Edward V* – and I certainly wouldn't work for Sir Charles Hearle. Besides, he has his own captain. If he has any sense now, he'll sell the *Celestine* at the earliest opportunity and use the *Edward V* to carry his cargoes. I wish you both well. Who knows, if I'm lucky Sir John St Aubyn might even take me back as a boatman. We might see each other occasionally then, you and I, when you and your husband visit the Mount. If we do, I promise I'll remember my place and be sure to call you M'Lady.'

The bitterness in Abel's voice cut into Thomasina like a sharp knife, hurting her far more than it should. Speaking very quietly, she hit back at him.

'Do you really believe all those things of me, Abel? That I'd use you in such a manner?'

'Are you denying that all the things I've said are true? That you haven't used me to get at Sir Charles Hearle?'

'No, I'm not denying that – but I haven't done it in the way you think, nor for the reasons you believe. In fact, were I to have told you the real reason why I wanted to bring him down, you would have helped me willingly, of that I'm certain.'

'Then why *didn't* you tell me? Didn't you trust me?'

'I trusted no one with the story of my life – the true story, that is – nor will I. Anyway, you've already been told enough to know what I've been and where I come from. Something *did* happen at Trebene involving Sir Charles Hearle and me – but certainly not in the way you think. What's more, his lies about me not only had me dismissed, but might well have had me hanged! Yes, I set out to ruin him. I've succeeded too, and I'm not sorry.'

Abel looked at her scornfully. 'If all that's true, then why are you going to marry him?'

'Who told you that story? I wouldn't marry Sir Charles Hearle if he brought the crown of England with him as a wedding gift. Yes, he asked me to marry him. Not because we'd ever meant anything to each other, but because he thought I'd jump at the chance to become Lady Thomasina. Then he would have used my money to get himself out of trouble. I didn't even bother to give him an answer. I laughed at him, Abel. If you don't believe me, I suggest you speak to your grandma about it. She was in the house at the time. But I don't think Sir Charles Hearle is likely to trouble anyone again for a long time. I've just seen his ship being brought in by a Revenue crew. It seems the *Celestine* has been caught free-trading.'

This news was sufficient to penetrate the fog in which Abel's brain was operating.

'Is all this true, Thomasina?'

'The *Celestine* is probably moored at the Customs quay right now.'

'I don't doubt *that*. We all knew what Carberry was up to, even though the *Celestine* is too sluggish for such a trade . . . But that isn't what I meant. I was asking about all the other things you've said. Are *they* true?'

'Would you believe me if I said they were, Abel? It's quite obvious from what you've accused me of today that you have a very low opinion of me, but I haven't lied to you.'

Thomasina was aware she had not told Abel the *full* truth, but her statement was accurate, as far as it went.

'If that's so, why didn't you tell me in the first place that you were the owner of the *Edward V*? Why keep it a secret?'

Just for a moment Thomasina thought of making up a story to explain her actions, but she had been honest with Abel thus far, she would keep it so.

'There were three reasons, Abel. The first was that, had I told you I was determined to bring Sir Charles Hearle to his knees, you would have wanted to know why – and it's a story I've never felt like telling to anyone.'

Abel digested this for a few minutes before saying, 'The other two reasons?'

'One doesn't really matter, now that you've made it so clear what you think of me – but I'll tell you anyway. I thought that if you knew I was the *Edward V*'s owner, you'd have thought twice about becoming its master. You'd have believed you were being offered the captaincy, not because I was convinced you were the right man to take it on, but out of gratitude for saving my life. You see, during my time on the Mount I've got to know you a little, Abel. I've come to realise that you're a very proud man.'

Abel nodded, apparently satisfied with this explanation, at least. 'Perhaps you should tell me the third reason?'

'That's rather more personal. You see, as well as getting to know you, I've come to respect you, too. I liked the way things were between us. I was afraid that if we became employer and employee, things would change. I didn't want that.'

Thomasina decided she had already said more than she had intended. 'Now you've been told all you need to know about me. It's far more than anyone else knows, so I'll leave you in peace. If you decide you still want to be captain of the *Edward V* . . . well, the ship is where you left it. If not, then tell Claude Coumbe and I'll have the ship put up for sale.'

The unexpected strain of unburdening herself to Abel had left Thomasina with a feeling that she had been drained of energy, both mentally and physically. She wanted only to get away from the inn and be alone for a while.

Hurrying from the room, she was on the stairs when she heard Abel call to her. She did not pause and, by the time she passed through the public room where the startled landlord was serving a customer, she was running.

Moments later she was outside, lost in a mist that had swirled in off the sea.

44

After wandering aimlessly about the quayside for almost an hour, Thomasina sat down in the lee of a small dockside store to gather her thoughts.

She had been stupid to overreact in the way she had to the situation back at the inn. She now felt both foolish and apprehensive. Abel knew far more about her than she had wanted *anyone* to know, but running from the room had served no sensible purpose.

She had set the record straight with Abel, only to hand him back the initiative by allowing emotion to override all other considerations.

Then Thomasina became angry with herself for entertaining such a thought. It was as though she regarded Abel as an antagonist. Someone from whom points were to be won, or lost.

A gust of wind invaded the lee of the building where she sheltered, bringing cold rain with it. Wet and windy weather had replaced the mist and drizzle she had experienced earlier. She began to shiver.

Thomasina's thoughts went to the St Aubyn boat. She had sent it straight back to the Mount in anticipation of deteriorating weather, intending to return to the Mount herself by coach. The boat was not very large, and she hoped it would reach its destination in safety.

She shivered once more. If she remained here for very much longer she would become chilled through and through. Fortunately, she had put on a hooded cloak to keep her warm on the boat trip. It proved to be very practical.

There was only one place she could go now and that was to the house she still thought of as 'Malachi's', where Edith and Arthur Hocking were caring for her father.

Thomasina made her slow way to the house. Climbing the steep hill from the harbour, she used one of the many alleyways leading from the main street of the port.

Had she chosen a different one she might have met up with Abel, hurrying back down the hill, having been to the house hoping to find her there.

Unaware of how close she had come to meeting him again, Thomasina tried to shift her thoughts away from him by thinking of what awaited her at the house.

She hoped her father would be in a less aggressive mood than when they had last met. She was not optimistic. It had been a horribly upsetting day so far. She had a premonition that it was not going to improve.

She realised her misgivings were justified the moment she reached the house. It was unnaturally quiet and the curtains were three-quarters pulled at the downstairs windows.

Puzzled, Thomasina opened the door and went inside. The silence was even more in evidence here. Convinced that something was very wrong, she felt the hairs on the back of her neck begin to rise.

'Edith . . . ? Arthur . . . ? Is anyone there?'

There was no reply. She wondered if perhaps they were resting, then immediately dismissed the thought. It was lunchtime, not an hour when anyone would be taking a rest. Besides, there should have been someone about to listen out for her father.

Her father! Thomasina ran through the house to the room where he was kept.

The bolt on the door was not pushed home. Lifting the latch, she cautiously opened the door and peered inside. The room was empty. Not only empty, but it had been thoroughly cleaned and tidied.

Extremely disturbed now, Thomasina considered the possibility that she had entered the wrong house by mistake. She pulled herself up quickly. She knew it could not be. Her key had unlocked the front door and everything in the house was as she remembered it.

Then another thought came to her. Perhaps Edith and Arthur had moved her father to another room and for some reason had not heard her call. It was unlikely, but she was prepared to clutch at any possibility now, however remote it might seem.

She searched the house from top to bottom, peering inside every room. The result of her search was what, in her heart, she had known it would be. The house was empty. Her father had gone. So too had Edith and Arthur Hocking.

Thomasina sat down in the kitchen and tried to think of what she could do now. She realised there was only one solution. The Hockings had to be found.

She could not remember the actual address of their house, but it should not be difficult to find. She had gone there on a number of occasions in the past, to let Edith know when she and Malachi returned from a voyage.

She decided she would go there now.

At first, it seemed Thomasina would be no more successful at the Hockings' home than at the house she had just left. Then, when she had almost despaired of receiving a reply to her persistent knocking, the door opened and a harassed-looking woman stood before her. From somewhere at the rear of the house Thomasina could hear the cries of a young child.

'Yes, what do you want?' the woman asked Thomasina. Then, in the next breath, she called over her shoulder, 'Be quiet, Simon. I'll be with you in a minute.'

'I'm looking for Edith and Arthur Hocking,' said Thomasina. 'I'm Thomasina Varcoe.'

'Oh! I'm sorry. I'm Sybil, their daughter. Mum and

Dad aren't here right now . . . but you'd better come inside.'

Thomasina stepped in through the doorway, then followed Sybil to the kitchen. Here an infant of about fifteen months sat in a puddle of his own making, proclaiming his unhappiness to the world.

Picking him up and bouncing him in her arms with teeth-rattling zeal, Sybil asked uncertainly, 'Would you like a cup of tea?'

'What I would like are the answers to some questions. First of all, where is my father?'

An expression of utter dismay appeared on Sybil's face. 'You mean . . . ? You don't know? Oh, my God! I know Mum said she had lost your address, but I thought she must have found it and got someone to read it for her. Neither she nor Pa can read, you see, and I can do little more than write my own name . . .'

'Sybil!' Thomasina's patience ran out and she brought the other woman's nervous chatter to a halt. *'Where is my father?* I want to know.'

'I'm sorry, Miss Varcoe. Very, very sorry. He's dead.'

'Dead?' Suddenly the room seemed to swing about her and Thomasina looked at Sybil in horror. 'When . . . ? Where . . . ? How?'

'Sit down. I'll tell you while I make that cup of tea – but first I'll put my little one to bed. He's over-tired and should have been asleep an hour ago.'

Thomasina felt like screaming, but she had realised that Sybil was a very simple girl. She managed to curb her frustration while the child was put to bed.

When Sybil returned to the room, both women tried to ignore the child's intermittent crying, but, as Sybil began to put out the teacups, Thomasina's patience broke.

'Sybil! I'm waiting for you to tell me what's happened.'

Flustered now, Sybil said, 'It should have been Mum or Dad telling you this, but they were so upset by the whole business that Dad has taken Mum to her sister's, up by Padstow, until she's got over it . . .'

'Sybil, if you don't tell me what happened, I'll throttle it out of you, I swear I will.'

'Well, it happened when they took your pa out for a walk . . .'

'For a *walk*?'

Thomasina echoed the words in disbelief. 'They took a man in his state for a *walk*?'

'Yes, but they had a long chain padlocked around his waist . . . It was only a light one, you understand,' Sybil explained hastily, 'with Pa holding the other end.'

Trying hard to shake off the image of her father being led through the streets of Falmouth on the end of a chain like some wild animal, Thomasina said, 'Go on.'

'Well, as it was a nice day last Tuesday, Mum and Dad thought your father would enjoy going out. They took him along the cliff path towards Maenporth. He seemed to be enjoying it, too – then this dog came along the path towards them. Suddenly your father jumped at it, shouting, and the animal went berserk. When my dad tried to drive it away, it turned on him, causing him to drop his end of the chain. The dog bit my dad three times on the legs and Mum once on her hand, before someone came along and drove it off. By then your father had disappeared. They searched for him until it got dark, then went back the next morning with a whole lot of people from round about. That's when they found him – but by then he was dead.'

'How did he die?' Thomasina felt numb with shock, but it was a question she had to ask.

'One end of the chain – the loop Pa used to hold – was caught on the branch of a tree that grew out of the cliffside, but part of the chain was looped around your father's neck. At first everyone thought he'd committed suicide, but at the inquest the coroner decided he'd slipped over the cliff and that the chain had got caught up as he fell. He said it was an accidental death.'

Sybil looked at Thomasina sympathetically. 'Your father was buried in the churchyard down by the docks, the day before yesterday. All of us went to the church. So did some of those who'd helped search for him. It was a lovely service.'

Strangely, now that she had been told the circumstances of her father's death, Thomasina felt no urge to cry. She just thought it terribly sad that her father should have died in such a tragic fashion after all he had suffered at the hands of the French.

'Do you think you could show me his grave?' she asked Sybil.

'I'd like to,' said the other woman apologetically, 'but it sounds as though Simon's just dropped off to sleep. I can't wake him up and take him out in this weather.'

'No. No, of course not,' agreed Thomasina, dull-voiced.

'You won't have any trouble finding him,' said Sybil. 'There hasn't been another new grave there for more than a year, so the gravedigger said.'

'All right,' said Thomasina. 'Thank you, Sybil. I'll go down there now.'

'But . . . aren't you going to stop for a cup of tea? I'm just about to make it.'

'I really don't think I could drink one. I'll leave you now.'

Thomasina bought some flowers close to the church and placed them on the grave, which was as easy to find as Sybil had predicted.

Then, head bowed against the blustery wind, she murmured a prayer that was as brief as it was meaningless.

She did not feel that the grave held her father, even though the tombstone she would arrange to have erected on the site would say that it did.

Her father had been lost at sea, all those years before. Lying in the ground here, in the Falmouth churchyard, was a stranger. A man who had not been capable of recognising his daughter and who could recollect no links with his past life.

Even his own name had not been familiar to him. Yet the name would be carved on a tablet of stone, for the living to see, in order that others might know – better than he – that the body lying here was that of Captain Edward Varcoe.

45

When Thomasina returned to the Mount she had forgotten the farewell dinner due to be held that evening for Hugh and Lavinia Pardoe.

She was reminded when Juliana came to the house late that same afternoon. When Thomasina told her she did not feel she could cope with such an event, Juliana protested vehemently.

'You *must* come, Thomasina. Lavinia will be so disappointed if you are not there – and so will I. You and Lavinia will be the only interesting people there. Sir John has invited a couple of generals and admirals who fought battles that everyone has long forgotten, together with wives who resent the fact that their husbands were not raised to the peerage for deeds-that-never-were.'

'I know how you feel, Juliana, but I really don't think I can face them – Sir Charles in particular. Not today . . .'

'You won't have to put up with Sir Charles,' replied Juliana triumphantly. 'He won't be there. You won't have heard, but his ship was boarded by Revenue officers and found to be loaded with undutied goods. The ship's captain is to be put on trial, together with those of his men who haven't opted to serve in the Royal Navy. The ship, of course, has been impounded by the Revenue Service and will be sold. There's no doubt that if they find Sir Charles, he will be put on trial too – but they won't find him.'

Despite the many other matters she had on her mind, Thomasina was curious. 'Why are you so certain he won't be caught?'

Enjoying the opportunity to impart some really exclusive gossip, Juliana lowered her voice conspiratorially. 'Because tomorrow he'll be on his way to Australia with the convicts.'

Thomasina was confused. 'But you said he hadn't been caught – and wouldn't be.'

'That's right, my dear. You see, he is not going there as a convict, but as an administrator. Hugh Pardoe says Sir Charles will be allowed to use his militia rank there and will probably be placed in charge of one of the smaller convict settlements.'

'Heaven help the convicts!' Thomasina exclaimed. 'Sir Charles certainly won't. I hope for their sakes no women are among them. But why should Major Pardoe do this for Sir Charles, for he knows next-to-nothing about him?'

'He doesn't need to, Thomasina. They are both Freemasons, as is Sir John. When one of them is in trouble, the others will do all they can to help.

Besides, this is Cornwall. Getting the better of Revenue men is one of life's little pleasures.'

Thomasina thought that having Sir Charles go to Australia was the finest possible result she could have gained from her campaign against him. There had been many times when she had wished him dead, but his death might have weighed on her conscience.

This way, he would be banished almost as effectively as if he had been convicted and transported. It was the first piece of good news she had received after suffering a couple of days of anguish and misery.

'So, you see, you won't *have* to be nice to Sir Charles. Besides, you've come back from Falmouth looking absolutely ghastly. I don't know what you have been up to there, but a soirée is just the thing to put some sparkle back into your life. It is always possible that some of the fogeys will bring a son or two along with them. That reminds me, Sir John received a letter from Humphrey today. It would seem the dear boy has finally accepted the Church as his vocation. He has taken a post in a London parish. Judging by the tone of his letter, he could even be contemplating taking an oath of celibacy, but I believe that is not uncommon among sensitive young men who have been spurned by the object of their affections.'

Thomasina succeeded in producing a wan smile. 'Poor Humphrey, but I would be wholly unsuitable for him and his career. One day he'll thank me for turning him down.'

'Perhaps – but promise you'll join us this evening, then I'll go away and allow you to relax for a couple of hours.'

'All right, I'll come.'

'Splendid! I knew you wouldn't let me down, Thomasina.'

Thomasina hoped Juliana might feel the same when the evening was over. She had reached a decision of which the other woman might not approve.

The gathering was a very dressy affair and for the first time since she had been attending Juliana's 'evenings' Thomasina felt very much an outsider. She wore the necklace given to her by Abel and felt it attracted far more attention than she did herself.

This, and Juliana's obvious affection for her, meant that Thomasina was not ostracised altogether, but it was made obvious that she would never be considered a suitable guest in the houses of those present.

Lavinia was aware of Thomasina's feeling of isolation and sought her company whenever she could. She tried her best to draw her into general conversation with others, but the events of the past few days had left Thomasina feeling disinclined to exchange small talk with anyone.

When the party had been under way for a couple of hours, Thomasina felt the need to escape. Believing her absence would not be noticed, she slipped quietly from the room, making her way outside to the small South Court, to escape the monotonous buzz of conversation.

But her departure had not gone unobserved. A few minutes later she was joined on the terrace by Lavinia.

'Aren't you cold out here, Thomasina?'

The night air was decidedly cool, but Thomasina said, 'No, I was finding it a bit hot and stuffy inside.'

'You're quite right. I felt it, too.'

Moving to stand alongside Thomasina, Lavinia looked out to sea, to where a storm was passing eastwards along the English Channel. Flickering lightning would occasionally illuminate the horizon, with a dull rumble of thunder following in its wake.

'Mind you,' said Lavinia, 'I would rather be here than out there in such a storm.'

'A storm at sea can be very exciting,' said Thomasina. 'You feel part of it and that somehow makes it seem less frightening.'

'You must have had a great many interesting experiences during the years you spent at sea with your uncle,' Lavinia said. 'Juliana has told me a great deal about you while I have been on the Mount. She is very fond of you.'

'Juliana has been very kind and took good care of me after Abel rescued me.'

'Ah yes, your handsome sea captain. I was hoping to see him while I was here. Maria has a small gift for him. If he doesn't put in an appearance, Juliana suggested I should give it to you to keep for him.'

'I'm afraid I don't know where he is – or whether

I'll ever see him again.' Thomasina's voice revealed far more than she realised.

'What a pity. He has such an honest, open face and gentle manners. He appeared to be very fond of you, too.' When Thomasina made no reply, Lavinia asked gently, 'Have you and he quarrelled?'

'No!' It came out too vehemently and Thomasina felt obliged to add, 'We've had a misunderstanding, that's all.'

Lavinia put out a hand and rested it on Thomasina's arm. 'Misunderstandings are far easier to right than are quarrels. I will give you the present and a letter for him. I feel quite certain you will be able to deliver them for me.'

Lightning lit up the sky over the sea once more and Lavinia continued, 'I hope the storm will have passed on by the time we board our ship tomorrow. I am not looking forward to the long voyage, but it is wonderful to know I will have Maria for company, thanks to you. When I think of what happened . . . !'

She shivered and said, 'I fear it is too cold for me out here. I grew too used to the sunshine of Spain. Will you come in with me, or do you prefer to remain here?'

'I'll come in with you,' Thomasina said. 'I just needed to be somewhere quiet for a while, to put my thoughts in some sort of order. I believe I've done all the thinking that's necessary now.'

46

Thomasina made the result of her thinking known to Juliana early the next morning when they and Lavinia were all taking breakfast together.

Her opportunity came when Juliana said, 'You're looking very serious this morning, Thomasina. Are you still feeling the effects of last night's soirée?'

'No, it has nothing to do with the party, although I must admit that in many ways it helped me to reach a decision about my future.'

Juliana paused, a piece of toast held halfway between plate and mouth. 'What is there to decide? You have a home here, can come and go as you wish – not to mention suitors who call in regularly to propose marriage! What more could any woman want?'

'I've been very happy here, Juliana, and couldn't have wished for a kinder, or more thoughtful, friend, but I feel it's time I moved on and did something else with my life.'

'What has brought you to this decision?'

Thomasina shrugged. 'A number of things, not least of which has been watching Lavinia and Maria prepare for their new life in Australia.'

'Are you quite certain, Thomasina? Nothing has happened to upset you?'

'No, it's just a feeling that my life is going nowhere at the moment.'

'But what will you do?' Juliana was genuinely upset at Thomasina's announcement.

Thomasina shrugged once more. 'I'm not quite certain. I'll first move to my house in Falmouth and make arrangements to sell the property. Then I might have a look at one or two other countries before I finally make up my mind. I've always wanted to visit Canada. I'd like to spend a little time in America, too, now that it seems the trouble between our countries will soon be over.'

'You could always accompany Maria and me to Australia,' Lavinia suggested hopefully. 'We would both love to have you with us.'

'I don't think Australia will be one of the countries on Thomasina's list,' Juliana declared. 'Sir Charles Hearle will be there with you. He is one of her most unwanted suitors. I will be very, very sorry to lose your company, Thomasina, but I must respect your wishes, of course. Sir John and I will be returning to London any day now. Do you have any idea when you might leave?'

'Yes. Now I've made my decision I'll leave as

quickly as possible, in case I'm persuaded to change my mind. I would like to accompany Lavinia and Major Pardoe to Falmouth, this morning. I've left Verity packing my things at the steward's house.'

Juliana was taken aback. 'So soon? My dear, I will hardly have time to say "goodbye" properly!'

'It's better this way, Juliana. You and Sir John have been very good to me, and you are the best friend I've ever had. Leaving you and the Mount will be a wrench. I don't want to make it any harder.'

'Of course. I *do* understand.'

Juliana was an emotional woman. There were tears in her eyes as she stood up. 'For the same reason I'll say goodbye to you here and not come down to the harbour. I don't want to make a fool of myself in front of the villagers. Goodbye, Thomasina. I am going to miss you very much indeed.'

When Thomasina also rose to her feet, Juliana gave her a warm, uninhibited hug, then without another word turned and hurried from the room, leaving Thomasina fighting back her own tears and Lavinia looking on sympathetically.

Once clear of St Michael's Mount harbour, the boat carrying Thomasina and the Pardoe family steered eastwards, riding easily over the submerged causeway.

From the ramparts of the castle, a number of figures could be seen waving wildly to send them on their way. It was impossible to make out any particular figure, but Thomasina knew Juliana would be one of them.

Before long they were so far from the Mount that waving became futile and Thomasina looked shorewards from the boat, seeing very little.

'Any regrets about what you are doing?' Lavinia put the question from her seat, close to Thomasina.

'Doubts, yes. Regrets . . . ? I'm not certain. They might well come later.'

'It's still not too late for you to decide to come with us to Australia.'

'Thank you, but that really isn't on my list of options . . .'

At that moment Maria complained that the movement of the boat was making her feel sick, and Lavinia and Thomasina both turned their attention to the small girl.

The dour boatman who had once before conveyed Thomasina to Falmouth was in charge of the boat, but he had allowed the youngest member of the crew to take the tiller.

Suddenly the older man said to the helmsman, 'Put her over to starboard and keep well clear of the ship that's coming towards us. She's travelling fast, so give her a wide berth.'

At his words Thomasina glanced up briefly – then looked once more. The ship was a schooner, an American-rigged 'clipper'. A vessel she would have recognised anywhere.

It was the *Edward V*!

Excitedly she watched as the schooner altered course to give them a wider berth. On the upper deck she could make out a number of men, one of whom was studying them through a telescope, the polished brass of which reflected the rays of the weak sun.

The *Edward V* sailed past the St Aubyn boat before turning in a tight, leaning arc until it was steering the same course and closing on them. It was sailing to windward and soon its greater bulk took the wind from the smaller boat, leaving its sails flapping untidily.

As the *Edward V* edged still closer, Thomasina saw that Abel was on deck. He must have decided to remain in command of her boat.

It was he who now hailed his successor as the St Aubyn head boatman.

'Cyrus, where are you bound?'

'Falmouth,' was the shouted reply. 'I've passengers for the convict fleet, bound for Australia.'

There were a few moments of silence before Abel's reply came back to them. 'Come alongside and transfer your passengers to me. I'll have them there in half the time and in far more comfort. There's an easterly blowing and the sea's rough on the far side of the Lizard.'

The dour boatman seemed in doubt about what he should do, but Thomasina said sharply, 'Do as Abel says.'

Her tone of voice brooked no argument and the head boatman moved to comply.

From the thwart where she sat with Maria held close to her, Lavinia asked with a smile, 'Can I presume from this that the "misunderstanding" between you and Captain Abel is over?'

'Not yet,' Thomasina replied. 'But with any luck

we'll have sorted things out by the time we reach Falmouth.'

She was feeling happier than she had for many days. She had not yet spoken to Abel, but the fact that he was once more in command of the *Edward V* was sufficient reason in itself for jubilation. It meant he had accepted her explanation of events.

The transfer of passengers and luggage took twenty minutes, then the *Edward V* surged through the choppy waters to the west of the Lizard peninsula, quickly leaving the St Aubyn boat far behind.

On board, Major Pardoe would have engaged Abel in conversation. However, Lavinia gently, but firmly, insisted that he take her and Maria to the mate's cabin, put at their disposal for the short voyage, leaving Thomasina and Abel together on the upper deck.

When they had gone below, Abel said, 'Why, Thomasina?'

'Why what?' Thomasina replied innocently.

'Why are you going off to Australia?'

'Is there any reason why I shouldn't?' she countered.

'I can think of a great many reasons. One is that you have persuaded me to stay on as captain of your ship, yet you are now going to the farthermost corner of the earth and leaving us behind. What's going to happen to your ship – and to me?'

'I've thought about that,' Thomasina said seriously. 'You're an excellent captain, Abel. You deserve your own ship. I've decided to instruct my solicitor to make the *Edward V* over to you . . . No, I don't want to hear any protest. You've already provided me with more profit than I spent to buy the ship. She'll be yours as soon as we reach Falmouth. What's more, if you have problems paying for your first cargo, I'll have him pay for it on my behalf. When the voyage is over you can repay my money and put the profit towards your next cargo. Perhaps that will atone for the way you think I've used you in the past.'

'I can't take the *Edward V*, Thomasina – and what *was* I to think . . . ?'

'Only you can answer that, Abel. You're the one who made the allegations about my motives in buying the *Edward V* and putting you in command of it. I'm merely trying to show you that your allegations were unfounded. Anyway, what are you protesting about? You have nothing at all to lose.'

There was a long, thoughtful silence before Abel said quietly, 'I have a great deal to lose, Thomasina. The only reason I returned to the *Edward V* was because of what you said to me. Because I believed you wanted me as *your* captain. If that isn't what you meant, then I want no part of the *Edward V*.'

Thomasina looked at him in astonishment. 'I've offered you a ship – the finest you'll find anywhere – and guaranteed you a profit on your next voyage. What else do you want, Abel?'

'Something that means more to me than money or a ship, Thomasina. I've been asked to take a cargo of mine-engines from Hayle to Mexico. It will be a long voyage, one that will need to have the approval of both owner and shipbroker.'

'So? I've told you I'll transfer the *Edward V* to you.

That will make *you* the owner, and I've no doubt Claude Coumbe will give you his blessing.'

'I'm quite happy to make the voyage, Thomasina, but before I do, I would like a blessing from a much higher authority first.'

'You're talking in riddles now, Abel. What do you mean?'

'The blessing I want is from the Church, Thomasina – on you and me. I know you've had two offers of marriage since I pulled you from the sea. Well, I'm making it three and hoping it will be third time lucky. Think about it, Thomasina. You love the sea and I've learned, albeit belatedly, that I love you. We could make the trip to Mexico our honeymoon. Once the cargo is delivered, we could sail anywhere you wish – and for as long as you want. I promise you'll enjoy it far more than a voyage to Australia on a convict transport. What do you say?'

Suddenly, in the course of little more than half an hour, Thomasina's life had gone from acceptance of defeat to the prospect of a new and happy future, but she would not allow her guard to drop immediately.

'Your offer is the best I've had to date, Abel, but I suggest we go down to your cabin. If my estimate of the *Edward V*'s sailing qualities are correct, that should give you an hour and a half to convince me that it's an offer I can't refuse . . .'

Author's Note

Thomasina was neither the first nor the last woman to pass herself off successfully as a man in an exclusively male environment.

It is on record that a highway*man* was taken, convicted of highway robbery and sentenced to transportation. Her sex was not discovered until she had been on a prison hulk for many months.

Similarly, a young woman named Christian Davies enlisted in an infantry regiment, was wounded and taken prisoner, exchanged and then returned to active duty. Her sex was only discovered when she was seriously wounded once more. Three times married, she was buried among the Chelsea pensioners.

Another woman, Phoebe Hessell, enlisted as a private in the Fifth Regiment of Foot and was discovered to be a woman only when she was wounded at the battle of Fontenoy. She went on to live to the age of a hundred and eight.

There are many more such examples on record.

In 1812, during the Napoleonic Wars, the guns of the Mount successfully took on a French man-o'-war, driving it ashore in the bay.

Of Sir John St Aubyn's fifteen children, all illegitimate, a number entered the Church – with mixed success. (John) Humphrey St Aubyn was forced to resign the living of Crowan, being cited as corespondent when Sir John Tyrrell divorced his wife, Elizabeth.

Sir John St Aubyn eventually married Juliana Vinicombe in 1822, when most of their children were adult, and St Michael's Mount was inherited by their son, Edward, who became a baronet in his own right and was the father of John, First Baron St Levan.

John St Aubyn, Fourth Baron St Levan, and his wife Lady Susan are the present occupants of St Michael's Mount, continuing a family occupancy which goes back for almost three hundred and fifty years.

The Mount itself is now in the ownership of the National Trust. During its very long history it has been a church, priory, castle and private home – but the full story of the tidal island that is St Michael's Mount is lost in the mists of time.

It is believed that traders from the Mediterranean came here centuries before the birth of Christ. Indeed, one of the island's many legends has it that a young Jesus himself set foot here, on a trading voyage with his uncle.

St Michael's Mount is a magical place for all whose heart is in this south-western corner of the land, where the winds of fortune still blow.

SOMEWHERE A BIRD IS SINGING

E. V. Thompson

Sally is an orphan living in Plymouth's Barbican, a late 19th century dockside slum, where a vile trade flourishes in young girls, duped and shipped off to the brothels of Europe. Her sister, Ruth, is driven to prostitution in order to support them, until she becomes too ill to work.

Now, with her sick sister to take care of in their single room home, Sally finds employment delivering wares for a local shop, meeting fisherman Ethan and, through him, Eva, a captain in the local Salvation Army. Eva has dedicated her life to rescuing the endangered girls and bringing their procurers to justice.

When Ruth is brutally murdered, Sally finds the father she has never known, but he is to bring only trouble and unhappiness into her life. When Ethan, his father and brothers are reported missing at sea on a fishing trip, Sally volunteers to help Eva's crusade – with near-disastrous results.

The loves and tragedies of a young woman fighting to escape from her environment are vividly captured in *Somewhere a Bird is Singing*.

Other bestselling Warner titles available by mail: